Dreaming of…
COLLECTION

April 2018

May 2018

June 2018

July 2018

August 2018

September 2018

Dreaming of... Italy

SUSAN MEIER

LUCY GORDON

ALISON ROBERTS

MILLS & BOON

Published in Great Britain 2018
by Mills & Boon, an imprint of HarperCollins*Publishers*
1 London Bridge Street, London, SE1 9GF

Dreaming of... Italy © 2018 Harlequin Books S.A.

Daring to Trust the Boss © 2014 Linda Susan Meier
Reunited with Her Italian Ex © 2015 Lucy Gordon
The Forbidden Prince © 2016 Alison Roberts

ISBN: 978-0-263-26665-8

09-0718

MIX
Paper from
responsible sources
FSC® C007454

This book is produced from independently certified FSC™ paper to ensure responsible forest management.

For more information visit: www.harpercollins.co.uk/green

Printed and bound in Spain
by CPI, Barcelona

DARING TO TRUST THE BOSS

SUSAN MEIER

CHAPTER ONE

"I'M OLIVIA PRENTISS, here for my first day in Accounting."

The gray-haired Human Resources director glanced up with a smile. "Good morning, Olivia. Welcome to Inferno." She happily flipped through the files in a box on her desk, but when she found the one with "Olivia Prentiss" written on the tab, she winced. "I'm afraid there's been a change of plans."

Vivi's stomach dropped to the floor. "I'm not hired?"

"No. No. Nothing like that. You've been reassigned temporarily."

"I don't understand."

"Tucker Engle's assistant was in an accident last week."

"Oh. I'm sorry." She knew Tucker Engle was the CEO and chairman of the board of Inferno. Before she'd interviewed for this job, she'd researched the company and his name had popped up. But the company's annual statements had said little about the reclusive billionaire. When she'd searched the internet, she'd only found an interview with the *Wall Street Journal* and a Facebook rant by a former employee who had called him the Grim Reaper because the only time he came out of his ivory tower was to fire someone. Still, none of that information gave her any clue what his assistant's accident had to do with her.

"As the newest employee in the company, it falls to you to stand in for Betsy."

Her already-fallen stomach soured. *She* had to work directly with a guy called the Grim Reaper by his staff?

She gulped. "An accountant stands in for a personal assistant?"

"You won't be a *personal* assistant."

Following the sound of the deep male voice, Vivi swung around. A tall, dark-haired man leaned against the door frame. Her gaze crawled from his shiny black loafers up his black trousers and suit jacket, past his white shirt and sky-blue tie to a pair of emerald-green eyes.

Wow.

"Or even an administrative assistant. You'll be an assistant." He pushed away from the door frame and walked over to her. "The assistant to the chairman of the board. The assistant who must be able to read financial reports and change things I need to have changed. An assistant who has to be able to keep up." His lush mouth thinned. "Do you have a problem with that?"

Intimidation froze her limbs, her tongue, and she could only stare.

"Good." Obviously taking her silence for acceptance, he headed for the door. "Spend the twenty minutes you need with Mrs. Martin to get your ID badge and fill out your paperwork then report to my office."

He strode out and she stared at the empty space he left in his wake.

"He's a whirlwind."

Obviously, Mrs. Martin was paid to say nice things because Vivi wouldn't call him a whirlwind. He was more like a bully. A really good-looking bully, but still a bully.

Bile rose to her throat, but she shoved it down again. She'd dealt with bullies before. "I take it that's Tucker Engle."

"In the gorgeous flesh."

"He demoted me even before I started."

Mrs. Martin shook her head. "It's not a demotion. That's what he was telling you. The assistant job is a lot more than you think it is."

"But I need to start my real job now. I have to keep my skills sharp to take the CPA exam. I don't want to fall behind."

"You'll be working with *the* Tucker Engle. The man who leads Inferno. You'll see everything he does—learn everything he knows."

That didn't mesh with the picture painted in the Facebook rant, but it sounded promising. Like something she could cling to to force herself to be able to work with him. "So he'll teach me things?"

"I don't know about *teaching,* per se." Mrs. Martin motioned for her to sit in the chair in front of her desk. She pointed to a little camera attached to her computer monitor. "Take a seat so I can get your employee picture."

Vivi sat.

"Anyway, I don't know about him teaching you, but you'll learn a lot working with him. He built this company—"

"With help."

"Help?" Mrs. Martin laughed. "You think he had help? Everybody who works here supports *him.* He's the idea man. No one else."

That *did* mesh with what she'd read. In the interview he'd given the *Wall Street Journal,* he'd bragged that he used only accountants, lawyers, PR people—support staff. He didn't want, or need, an equal.

"Fantastic."

Mrs. Martin smiled sympathetically. "I understand you're disappointed. You see this as a setback. And I probably can't talk you out of that." She paused and sucked in a resigned breath. "So, I'm going to stop the sugarcoating and be totally honest with you. Tucker Engle is a suspicious prima donna. He gives assignments piecemeal so that no one can figure out what he's working on. He's so demanding that none of our employees would volunteer to replace Betsy—even for a few weeks."

Her heart stuttered. "And you think *I* can?"

"I didn't pick you. We gave Mr. Engle the files of the accountants starting today and he chose you. Like it or not, you're stuck. But Betsy won't be out forever. Eight weeks—"

Her eyes bulged. "Eight weeks?"

Mrs. Martin grimaced. "Twelve tops."

"Oh, my God!"

"But you still get your accountant's salary. And your time with Mr. Engle counts in your seniority with the company. It's not as if you'll be starting over when Betsy returns."

"No, thanks. I'll just keep my job in Accounting."

Mrs. Martin sighed. "How good do you think it's going to look on your employee records if you refuse your first assignment?"

"It's not the position I was hired for."

"Nonetheless, it's your first assignment and if you don't take it, he may tell us to fire you."

She was really, really sorry she'd found that Facebook rant because she couldn't even argue that. "Of course he will."

Mrs. Martin's face fell into sympathetic lines. "The other option is to quit."

"The other option is to quit."

Vivi muttered those words under her breath as she made her way through the maze of red-, orange- and yellow-walled corridors, looking for the private elevator to the executive office. She finally reached it and inserted the magic key card that would start the plush car, giving her access to the inner sanctum of Inferno. Which, she was beginning to think, had been named appropriately since this company really might be the pits of hell.

The doors swished closed and she shut her eyes. She was the toughest person she knew. She had survived an attack at university that had nearly ended in her being raped and the bullying that had resulted when she'd tried to prosecute the boy involved—the son of Starlight, Kentucky's leading family. One grouchy, narcissistic CEO would not stop her from reaching her dream of being somebody. Somebody so important that the people back in Starlight would see that despite all their attempts to break her, she had succeeded.

They had failed.

And Tucker Engle wouldn't break her either.

The elevator bell pinged. The doors opened again. Like Dorothy entering Oz, she stepped out, glancing around in awe. Contrasting the slick, ultramodern red, orange and yellow "fire" theme of the public areas, this space was superconservative. Ceiling-high cherrywood bookcases lined the walls. The antique desk and chair could have been in a museum. Oriental rugs sat on luxurious hardwood floors.

"Don't just stand there! Come in!"

She pivoted around, following the sound of Tucker Engle's voice. He stood in a huge office behind the one she had entered. A cherrywood conference table sat on one side, a comfy brown leather sofa and recliner grouping filled the other. A desk and chair fronted a wall of windows at the back of the room. The view of the New York skyline took her breath away.

She walked to the desk she suspected was hers, removed her jacket and dropped it and her backpack to the chair. Then she gingerly made her way to the grand office.

Standing behind the carved desk, Tucker Engle removed his black suit coat and carried it to a hidden closet. His back to her, he slid it onto a hanger, and her gaze fell to his butt.

Perfect butt. His trousers were cut with such precision that they all but caressed him. His simple white shirt outlined a swimmer's back. She could virtually see the ripple of his muscles through the silky fabric. If he didn't do laps in a pool every day, he did something.

She swallowed just as he turned.

"What?"

She swallowed again. Add what appeared to be a perfect body to his dark hair and chiseled features, and he had to be one of the most handsome men on the planet. And he'd just caught her staring at him.

"Nothing."

"Good. Because we have lots to do." He sat and motioned her to one of the two captain's chairs in front of his desk. "Anything you hear in this office is confidential."

She bit her tongue to stop the *duh* that wanted to escape. Not only was that immature, but she had to work with this guy. For weeks...maybe months!

"I'll need more than a dumbfounded look, Miss Prentiss. I'll need a verbal yes."

"Yes. I know about confidentiality. I took ethics classes."

He leaned back. His shirt stretched across his muscular chest. "Lots of people take ethics classes. Not everybody has ethics."

Her eyes narrowed. After two years of being called a liar—a girl who "claimed" she was attacked, most likely in the hope of extorting money—she hated having her integrity questioned. Fury surged through her, but she stopped it. Anger had never gotten her anywhere. A cool head and resolve had.

"I have ethics and I'll keep your secrets."

"Great. Then let's start by filling you in on my latest project. It's the reason I couldn't muddle through the next few weeks with the help of only secretarial support staff."

"Mrs. Martin said you wouldn't tell me your project.

That you'd give me assignments piecemeal so I wouldn't be able to guess what you were doing."

"Mrs. Martin is ill informed."

"Maybe you should correct that impression."

His eyebrows rose. "Maybe you should remember with whom you're speaking. You don't get to tell me what to do. Or even make suggestions. Your only job is to perform the tasks I give you."

Embarrassment flooded her. Damn her defense mechanisms for clicking in. She might be proud of the confidence and courage she'd developed to deal with the bullies who'd pushed her around after Cord Dawson attacked her, but Tucker Engle wasn't pushing her around. He was her boss. He was supposed to give her orders.

"Are we clear?"

She didn't hesitate. "Yes."

"Good." He rose, came around to the front of the desk and rifled through some files sitting in the corner. "Constanzo Bartulocci is looking to retire. Do you know who he is?"

"No." The spicy scent of his aftershave drifted to her and her gaze ambled along his torso, down the neat crease of his obviously expensive trousers to his shiny, shiny shoes. If this guy hadn't grown up with money, somebody, somewhere had taught him how to dress. "I don't know who Constanzo Bartulocci is."

"Of course you don't. The über-rich have ways of keeping themselves out of the limelight."

Well, that explained why she hadn't found much about Tucker Engle on the internet.

He located the file he was looking for and returned to his chair. "He never married and he has no children. But he has two nephews and a niece, all three of whom claim to speak for him. Our first job is to weed through the baloney and see who really does know his plans. Our second is to get that person to give us the inside scoop so I know exactly what to offer him for his entire operation."

"You're going to buy a whole conglomerate?"

"Not your place to question, remember?"

"Yes. Sorry." She drew in a breath. How was she going to deal with this guy? Rich, successful and good-looking were bad enough. But she wasn't accustomed to corralling her tongue. Sometimes she even prided herself on being sassy—never letting anybody push her around, condescend to her, make her feel less than.

It would be a long eight weeks if she didn't soon figure out how to keep her place. That is, if he didn't fire her for insubordination.

He handed a file across the desk to her. "Your first assignment is to check the financial reports and records of all of our Bartuloccis."

She glanced up into his bright green eyes and her stomach fluttered. The assignment was pretty much what she'd expected to be doing in the accounting department. So part of the flutter was relief. But the other half came from those striking emerald eyes. He really was one gorgeous guy.

One gorgeous, *difficult* guy, she quickly reminded herself. The difficult canceled out the handsome. And even if it didn't, she'd gone this route before. Cord Dawson had been rich and smart. And in the end, he'd attacked her, nearly raped her. No matter how gorgeous, she wanted nothing to do with another rich guy. She wasn't in their league. Didn't know how to play in their world. It was a lesson she'd never forget.

Taking the file, she rose. "Okay."

He returned his attention to the papers on his desk. "Shut the door on your way out."

She gladly left his office. Closing the door behind her,

she squeezed her eyes shut in misery. Even if she learned to hold her tongue, it would be a long eight weeks.

Tucker Engle picked up the employment application, college transcripts, private investigator's report and reference letters HR had sent on Olivia Prentiss. He'd reviewed it all before he'd chosen her, of course, but after meeting her, he needed to be reminded why she'd been his choice to stand in for Betsy.

Excellent grades.

Reference letters that sang her praises as if she were the next Queen of England.

A Facebook profile without pictures of cats—always a plus.

A Twitter account that barely got used. So she wasn't a talker, someone who might inadvertently spill secrets.

Private investigator's report that showed only one incident that had happened her second year at university. A kid from Starlight had sued her for slander. But he'd later dropped the suit. Tucker suspected it was one of those young-love, he-said–she-said things.

Otherwise, she came from a normal blue-collar family in Middle America. Which, he grudgingly admitted, explained why she didn't understand that working directly with him was a coup, not a punishment. God knows, he would have loved someone to give him this kind of opportunity when he'd been through school and starting out in the work world. But after years of moving from home to home as a foster child, he knew it wasn't wise to get close to people he could lose. So, there had been no one to so much as offer him a word of advice when he'd finally started his career. Still, he'd been okay. He'd worked his way to the top—the same way the professors who'd written Olivia's reference letters said she wanted to. Actually, she was a lot like him. Bright. Ambitious.

Unfortunately, she was a little prettier than he'd expected with her long strawberry blonde hair and her big blue eyes. But he would never get involved with a coworker. Plus, he didn't get involved with women just because they were pretty. He liked his dates to have some class, some charisma and a lot of knowledge. Etiquette and protocol could be taught. And there might be charisma lurking behind Olivia Prentiss's quirkiness. But knowledge? The ability to chat with his peers at a cocktail party or gallery opening? She wouldn't come by that for years. Thus, she did not appeal to him.

Luckily, he hadn't chosen her to be a date. He'd chosen her to write reports, change reports, analyze reports. Her high marks in her accounting classes indicated she could probably do anything he needed to have done.

Satisfied, he made two conference calls. Just as he disconnected the second, his door opened.

"I'm sorry—"

Temper rumbled through him. It was one thing to be clueless about the etiquette of an executive office, to need some experience. It was another to be rude and open a door without knocking. "What are you doing?"

"I don't know how to operate the space shuttle's worth of computer equipment you refer to as a phone, and a call—"

He sighed. "You're supposed to screen calls. I don't talk to just anybody who phones. Go find out who it is. Take their number. I'll decide if I'm calling back."

Her mouth thinned. Her pretty blue eyes filled with storm clouds.

Fine. He didn't like wimps. But he also didn't like interruptions. And there was no better way for an assistant to learn that than by having to go back to her desk and apologize to a caller.

"It isn't a caller. At least not a call for you. The security guard in the lobby is on the line. You have a guest."

"Same instructions. I don't see people who just drop in. Call the lobby, tell them to get the person's name and if I want to I will call him back and schedule an appointment."

"Okay. I guess that means you don't want to see Maria Bartulocci."

His head snapped up. "What?"

"Maria Bartulocci is here. She wants to know if you have time for her. I guess the über-rich don't just know how to keep themselves out of the limelight. They also drop in unexpectedly."

He replaced the receiver of his phone. "Tell them to send her up. Then get a notebook. I want you to sit in and take notes."

She nodded and raced back to her desk.

Missing experienced, polite, sophisticated Betsy, Tucker ran his fingers through his hair. Two minutes later the elevator bell rang. He listened as Olivia greeted Maria and sighed with relief when she was nothing but polite and efficient.

Thick cloying perfume reached him long before dark-haired, dark-eyed Maria did. Tall and regal, educated at Harvard, and well-versed in art and music, Maria was exactly the kind of woman Tucker liked to be seen with. Arm candy with a brain.

"Tucker, how sweet of you to make time for me."

Vivi almost gagged. Holy cow on the cologne, but calling Tucker Engle sweet? This woman obviously wanted something.

"I'm sorry for the wait." He glanced at Olivia, then smiled at Maria. "A little miscommunication with my assistant."

Vivi shook off the insult of that. He hadn't told her any of his preferences, especially not about calls. But he probably assumed she knew those kinds of things, which meant she'd have another assignment that night. Not only did she have to figure out how to stifle her tongue, but she'd have to call her mom, a lifelong administrative assistant, to learn a bit about working for the top banana of a company.

"I'm thrilled you decided to drop in on us." Tucker seated Maria with him on the sofa and motioned for Vivi to sit on the chair beside it.

She opened her notebook.

Maria smiled at her. "No need to record our conversation, darling."

"Miss Prentiss isn't going to record our conversation, just the salient points."

Laughing, she patted Tucker's knee. "Is your memory that bad, Tucker?"

He slid his arm across the sofa, and nearly around Maria. "There are three of you. I'm going to talk with all of you and compare stories."

Her lips turned down into a pretty pout. "Really? You don't trust me?"

He chuckled. "A man doesn't get to where I am without having fail-safe mechanisms in place. Miss Prentiss is one of them."

Maria's gaze crawled over to her.

She took in Vivi's khaki trousers and simple white blouse. Then the long strawberry blonde hair Vivi had put into a ponytail that hung over her shoulder.

"I see."

A flush crept up Vivi's neck to her cheeks. As if the condescending appraisal wasn't bad enough, Maria Bartulocci's tone dripped with disapproval.

Memories of walking down the street, being pointed at, whispered about and called names rushed through her. It had been a long time since she'd remembered that, but it had also been a while since she'd been with someone who so clearly disliked her.

Still, those bullies had nothing to do with her job, so she ignored the feelings, the memories. She'd learned lots of coping skills in the three years that had passed, and it would take more than a crappy look from a snotty socialite to drag her down.

Tucker said, "Rumor has it your uncle is considering retiring."

"That's not a rumor. It's true."

"Has he set a date?"

"More like a time frame. Next spring." Maria rose. "Take me to lunch and I'll tell you about your competition."

Tucker followed suit, rising to stand beside her. "I know my competition."

"Such a smart man," Maria purred, stepping up to him and running her hand down his tie. "Let's leave the little one behind and get ourselves a drink." She flicked her gaze at Vivi with a laugh. "Really, Tucker, where did you find this one? And why don't you pay her enough to buy decent clothes?"

Vivi's mouth fell open. Seriously? A stinky debutante who was throwing herself at a man had the audacity to criticize *her* clothes?

Tucker caught Maria's hand and led her to the elevator, leaving Vivi behind without a backward glance or even a nod toward telling her how long he'd be gone or how he could be reached in an emergency.

"I don't care what my employees look like. They only have to be able to do their jobs."

The elevator door opened. "I know, but seriously. Did you get a look at her?"

She heard Tucker's voice, but couldn't make out what he said or Maria's reply. The door closed on his laugh.

Vivi glanced down at herself. These were her best trousers, her best blouse. And even she knew she looked like a street waif.

She might have coping mechanisms, but she couldn't argue the truth. She didn't belong here.

CHAPTER TWO

HUMILIATION AND DISAPPOINTMENT followed Vivi out of the city and up the stairs to the two-bedroom apartment she shared with her university friends Laura Beth Matthews and Eloise Vaughn. Because she and the Grim Reaper had worked late, she knew her roommates would have already eaten supper. The scent of spaghetti permeated the darkly paneled walls of the hall to their third-floor walkup. But she didn't care. She was too tired to eat.

Short, sweet, brunette Laura Beth gasped as Vivi entered the apartment. "You look like hell."

"Thanks." She walked to the refrigerator, which was only ten feet away from the sofa in their tiny, open-floor-plan living space, and pulled out a bottle of water.

Eloise, a tall blonde beauty whose wealthy parents had spoiled her rotten, laughed. "First day of accounting not fun?"

"I'm not in Accounting."

Laura Beth patted the couch cushion beside her and motioned for Vivi to sit. "What happened?"

"Tucker Engle's assistant was in an accident and no one else will work with him. So I have to be his assistant for about eight weeks. But that's all I can tell you because "the" Tucker Engle might share secrets with me, so I'm not allowed to talk to anyone about anything that goes on in his office. Otherwise, I think it's an ethics violation."

Eloise and Laura Beth just stared at her.

Vivi squeezed her eyes shut in misery. "I'm sorry for babbling. I'm tired."

"You're freaking out," Eloise corrected.

"You would be, too, if you spent twelve hours working with a guy you didn't like, who has visitors who are obnoxious."

"You didn't punch anybody did you?"

Vivi took a long drink of water. "No, but I was tempted."

"Are you going to tell us details or are you going to make us guess?"

"I already told you I can't reveal anything that goes on in that office. Confidentiality and all that. But I will say this—I haven't been treated so rudely in three years."

Eloise and Laura Beth exchanged a look. "Bad things happened to you three years ago."

"Exactly."

Laura Beth caught her hand. "Maybe you shouldn't have taken the assignment."

"I didn't have a choice."

"So you have to work with a guy who reminds you of the worst time in your life?" Eloise sucked in a breath. "At least tell me he doesn't look like Cord."

"No and he doesn't act like him either." Cord had always been the life of everybody's party. Grouchy Tucker Engle barely smiled. "But his one visitor today was exactly like Cord's mom...Cordelia Dawson. The woman who thinks her son does no wrong."

"You mean the woman who defended the kid who got you drunk and then attacked you. He would have raped you if you hadn't gotten away."

Vivi froze. They'd talked about this before, but never had Eloise been so blunt, so casual. Laura Beth shot her a warning look.

"Well, I'm sorry, but I think it's better for her to talk

about it than to let it fester." She patted Vivi's hand. "Right?"

"Actually, yes." Before that morning, she hadn't thought about being attacked in at least a year. All because she had friends who believed her. Talking, finding people who didn't merely believe her but who'd hurt with her until the hurt was gone, had made her whole.

But she was in the big city now, not in Starlight, Kentucky, at their tiny university. She had to make this job work. "I can tolerate Tucker Engle and his obnoxious guests for eight or so weeks. In fact, I'll do more than tolerate them. I'll be the best damned assistant he's ever had. Then when his real assistant returns I'll go to Accounting where I belong."

Eloise said, "That's the spirit."

Laura Beth patted her hand. "How about if I reheat the leftover spaghetti?"

"No thanks." Vivi rose from the sofa. "I'm exhausted. I think I'll just go to bed."

"Are you sure you're okay?"

"I'm fine. My past is behind me." She forced a smile. "Plus, if tomorrow's anything like today, I'll need all the rest I can get."

After washing her face and changing into pajamas, she crawled into her twin bed beside Laura Beth's, pulled out her cell phone and hit speed dial.

"Hey, Mom."

"Vivi? What time is it?"

"It's around ten. Did I wake you?"

"No, but if I don't get out of bed, I'll wake your father." There was a quiet pause and the click of the closing of her mom's bedroom door. "So what's up? How was your first day at Inferno?"

"Awful. I'm not working in Accounting. I'm the assistant to the CEO."

"Oh! That's exciting!"

Unexpected relief unknotted the tight muscles of her shoulders. If her mom thought this was exciting, then maybe it was. "Really? I should be happy?"

"You're working with the guy at the top. You should be taking advantage of the opportunity to make a good impression."

"He's kind of a grouch."

"Most older men are."

"Actually, he's not older."

"He isn't?"

"He's kind of young."

Worry filled her mom's voice. "How young?"

"Thirty-ish."

"Thirty-ish? And he's a CEO?"

"He's the *owner* of the company. Which is why he's so bossy. I read online that some of his employees call him the Grim Reaper."

There was a silence. Then her mom said, "I don't like this."

Drat. She should have realized her overprotective mother would be suspicious of any man under fifty. Since her episode with Cord, her parents distrusted every man who looked at her twice. Which was part of the reason she'd moved to New York. She needed some space.

"I'm fine. I'm working for him, not dating him. Plus, his assistant will be back in a few weeks."

"A lot can happen in a few weeks."

"Including that I could prove myself to him like you said I should."

"I don't know, Vivi. I suddenly got really bad vibes about this guy."

"They're the wrong kind of vibes. Mr. Engle has zero interest in me. And all I want is to be able to do this job."

Her mom grudgingly mumbled, "You should be fine. Your grades were great."

"I know I can handle the work. I just need to know some of the etiquette."

Loraina filled her in on a few tips for answering the phone and not speaking unless asked a direct question, but she finished her remarks with, "You be careful with this guy."

As that warning came out of her mother's mouth she winced, realizing what was coming next.

"Your dad and I didn't want you moving to the city. If you could be attacked in a small town by someone you'd known since high school…how the devil can you trust yourself to eight million strangers?"

"I'll be fine, Mom."

"It's just that we worry."

"I know. But trust me. This guy isn't even slightly attracted to me."

Her mother huffed out a breath. "You think. But you're a pretty blonde—"

"Who doesn't have the right clothes or makeup or manners to attract a guy like him." She laughed, remembering the way he liked stinky Maria purring up to him. "Seriously, Mom. I'm perfectly safe with him."

They ended the call, and she settled down on her pillow. Exhausted, she immediately fell asleep and didn't stir until her alarm woke her the next morning.

She showered, headed for her closet and stared at her clothes. She had three pairs of taupe, tan or beige trousers, one pair of dark brown, one pair of gray and one pair of black, as well as seven or eight mix-and-match tops and two summer sundresses that she saved for "good."

Her gaze rolled to her bedroom door. Across the hall was the queen of clothes. Eloise had everything from business suits to ball gowns. They were the same size. She could

borrow a nice dress or a fancy blouse and probably fit better into Tucker Engle's world—

No, damn it. She refused to let some condescending socialite bully her into trying to be somebody she wasn't. She
was a simple girl. Someone who wanted to prove herself
based on her skills and abilities, not her looks. And after
her mother's reminder that she should take advantage of this
time to prove herself, she'd decided that's how she'd endure
these eight weeks. She'd prove herself with her work. Not
dress like somebody she wasn't.

When the elevator door outside Tucker's office door opened,
he glanced up and saw Olivia Prentiss entering. Today she
wore gray trousers with a gray blazer and some kind of
clunky sandals. He stifled a laugh. After the way Maria
had treated her, he'd wondered if she'd change the way she
dressed. He gave her credit for not buckling under to Maria's insults. In fact, he gave her points for that. He hadn't
hired her to be pretty or fashionable. They had work to do.

He hung up his phone and walked to the outer office.
"Good morning, Miss Prentiss."

She slid her worn backpack to her chair. "Good morning."

Her soft voice told him she didn't want to be here. If
she stayed this unhappy, it was going to be a long eight
weeks.

He headed for his desk. "We have a busy day today."

She followed him. "Should I get a notebook?"

"No." He paused for a second then made up his mind.
Working for him had its boring elements. But he also did
some fun things. Maybe if he took her to his signing that
morning, she'd see the value of being his assistant. "I need
you to study certain files before we go to a meeting."

"We're going out?"

He fell to his chair. "Yes. I'm signing papers this morning to buy a controlling interest in a startup."

Her eyes lit. "Really?"

A zing of pleasure ricocheted through him. He wasn't the kind of guy who needed his employees to be daft with joy all the time. But he did love enthusiasm. And he had made her smile. Which was probably the reason for the zing. Her whole beautiful face lit when she smiled.

"I don't want any snags. So, just in case, I want you and Betsy's laptop with me."

"What am I supposed to do?"

"If there's a question or a problem and I need information, you must be able to find the document and the information in the document."

"From the laptop?"

"Yes." He leaned back in his chair. "I don't keep my files in the company network. It's all in that laptop or my personal internet storage. Betsy had a very simple filing system. You should be able to figure it out quickly. Everything is in a folder called Jason. There will be subfolders under that with names like Legal Documents, Agreement, Financials, Personal. Peruse everything. Get familiar enough that you can find what I need when I need it."

"Sounds simple enough."

"As I said, I don't think there will be a problem. The agreements are already written and preliminarily approved. But just in case."

She nodded and left the room. He stared after her. Her pretty pink top outlined a slim torso. The gray trousers hugged a shapely bottom. Today her long hair cascaded down her back, a shiny strawberry blonde waterfall.

Even dressed like an office worker, she was a knockout. But something was definitely off about this woman. He understood that with her blue-collar background she wasn't quite as classy as most of the women he knew. But that wasn't it. There was something more. She was too cautious.

Shaking his head, he went back to his call list. As long as she did her work, whatever was wrong with her wasn't any of his business.

Vivi spent the next hour skimming files, agreements, financial reports.

A little after ten, Tucker came out of his office, carrying a briefcase. "My car is waiting."

Anticipation stole through her. She probably should have been embarrassed to be so thrilled, but Tucker Engle made superstars out of upstarts, and she would be at one of his agreement signings. She would see what he said, how he behaved. If nothing else, she would see a sharp, savvy guy in action.

They rode down in the private elevator in silence. With the strap of the laptop case over her shoulder and standing straight as an arrow in her gray pants and blazer, she felt like an executive.

The elevator door opened and she followed Tucker Engle to the revolving door and the waiting black limo. He motioned her in first and she slid across the plush leather seat. He sat beside her.

Her blood virtually hummed with joy, but a knot of fear shadowed it. She'd found the files, familiarized herself with the agreements, the background financials and the sub-agreements over things like whose name would be where as well as the side perks given to the two founders of Jason Jones, a search engine that did simple background checks for real people. She was as ready as she'd ever be.

"Jason Jones is an interesting concept."

Vivi couldn't believe she'd actually spoken, but her excitement had gotten the better of her. And now Tucker Engle would reprimand her.

But he surprised her by chuckling. "When I heard about it, I couldn't believe I hadn't thought of it myself."

"You think you should have come up with it?"

He shrugged. "I would have liked to have thought of it." He peeked at her. "But the best inventions come from ordinary people."

"Really?"

"Yes. People with problems get frustrated looking for answers and sometimes invent or create something with universal appeal."

She nodded.

"Take our startup for instance. Jason Jones is the code name for a private investigator who followed the ex-girl-friend of one of the founders, watching her until he found sufficient evidence to have her convicted of stalking."

She gasped. "One of the founders was stalked?"

"The woman nearly ruined Ricky's life until he realized he had to be proactive and hire a private investigator. The fees were exorbitant. Ricky knew he could have avoided the whole mess if he'd been able to search her on the inter-net *before* he asked her out."

"But he could have done that."

"No. He could have done a search but not necessarily gotten access to the information that would have saved him. He investigated the systems and Elias Greene wrote the programs. Now innocent men and women everywhere will be able to know a prospective date's *complete* history for fifty bucks and the click of a few keys."

"Amazing."

"Which is exactly why with my help the company will eventually be worth about a hundred million dollars."

The limo rolled to a stop in front of a shiny glass-and-chrome building. They rode to the penthouse in another private elevator, which opened onto a living room. Elec-tric-blue chairs angled beside a black leather-and-chrome sofa, which sat on a modern print rug. A wet bar took up the entire left wall. Huge windows at the back of the room let in the June sunshine as they displayed another fantastic view of the New York City skyline.

Olivia's breath stuttered. She couldn't believe she was here. Not just in a fantastic city, but part of a huge financial deal. Maybe working with Tucker Engle wouldn't be so bad after all?

Two men bounced off the sofa and raced to greet Tucker.

"Hey, Tuck." The first one—a guy who was a lot older than she'd expected, extended his hand. "Big day for us."

"A big day for all of us," Tucker agreed. He motioned to Vivi. "My assistant, Miss Prentiss."

He shook her hand. "I'm Rick Langley." With black hair and silky brown eyes, he was gorgeous. She could understand how he'd meet a woman who wouldn't want to let him go. "The guy with the good fortune to be stalked."

She laughed.

"And I'm Elias Greene."

Vivi shook his hand, surprised when he gave an extra squeeze before releasing her.

Rick bounded to the bar. "Do you want a drink while we wait for our perpetually late lawyers?"

"Miss Prentiss and I are good." He turned to Vivi. "Unless you'd like a water?"

She smiled her appreciation. In one easy sentence, he'd gotten her out of a potentially uncomfortable situation. He really, really wasn't so bad.

She faced Ricky. "Water would be great, thanks. I'd also love a place to set up the laptop."

Elias raced over and took the laptop from her hands. "We're using the dining table as our conference table."

"Sounds great."

Tucker directed her to follow Elias to the table. When she reached it, he pulled out her chair. Ricky handed her a bottle of water as Elias sat beside her.

"So where are you from?"

She cleared her throat. "Kentucky."

"No kidding?" Elias smiled broadly. "Are you a farm girl or something?"

She laughed. "No. I grew up in a small town."

"I'd love to hear about small-town life, if you'd like to have dinner.... Maybe tonight?"

She stared at him. He was serious? Asking her out in front of her boss? But, worse, he was a stranger. And he was asking her out—

She hadn't been out with anyone since Cord.

Heat filled her. She wasn't freakishly afraid of men or dating. After the attack, she'd simply focused on getting her degree. She'd also become selective—too selective to go out with a guy she didn't know.

She drew in a slow breath. "I'm sorry but I don't date people I don't know."

Ricky laughed. "You could always run him through Jason Jones."

She laughed, too, though Elias's proximity suddenly shot shivers of fear through her. Giving him the benefit of the doubt, she chalked his enthusiasm up to excitement over the big, big deal represented by the agreement he was about to sign. But that didn't make his nearness any less overwhelming.

She rose. "Could you direct me to the powder room?"

Elias popped off his chair. "Sure. It's right back along this hall."

Her nerves went on red alert as they walked down a long dark corridor. A memory flashed. *Cord leading her down a dark hall. Her giggling. Him forcing her into a room. Her fighting to get away and eventually freeing herself. But she'd lost a shoe and her blouse was torn—*

Oh, God. This was bad. She'd put all this behind her. Why was it coming back to her now?

In the half bath, she took a few slow breaths. In the quiet, she realized Elias reminded her of Cord. Not looks-wise, but personality-wise. A little too pushy. A little too sure of himself.

That's why she wasn't going back out there until the lawyers arrived.

She washed her hands, combed her fingers through her hair and realized she wouldn't hear the attorneys arriving. Nice as he was being on this trip, even Tucker Engle would have his limits. He would be angry with her if she wasn't around when they came.

With a deep breath, she left the bathroom and returned to the main room as the elevator door opened and three gray-suited men stepped out.

Relief stole through her and she quickly made her way to her chair and her laptop.

Laptop! She'd left the laptop containing all of Tucker Engle's business information—information he wouldn't even put on his own company network—unattended.

He was going to kill her.

Tucker watched Olivia with something akin to pride as she not only got herself away from Elias, but also stayed as silent as a church mouse through the entire signing. No smart remarks. No unwanted questions. Just a nice, quiet assistant.

When the papers were signed and after they'd toasted with champagne, which he noticed Olivia refused, they headed for the limo.

As the car wove into traffic, he couldn't stop the compliment that rose up in him. "You did very well in there, Miss Prentiss."

"I did nothing."

"That was your job. You were there in case we needed you. Since we didn't, remaining silent was your only job."

She rubbed her hand down her thigh. "I...um...left the laptop unattended."

"If I remember correctly, you needed to get away from Elias." The memory of Elias ogling her sent a wave of dislike through him, but she'd handled him, and in such a way that there had been no scene and no resultant bad feelings. "And I was in the room. No harm done."

"Really?"

The anxiety in her voice again struck that nerve that told him something about this woman was off or wrong. For a second he toyed with asking her. After all, if she were someone he wanted to do business with he wouldn't hesitate. He always needed to know everything about his partners. But this wasn't a potential business partner. Olivia Prentiss was a temporary assistant. A young, single woman. Did he really want to risk hearing about her bad weekend or latest breakup?

No.

He picked pretend lint off his black trousers. "As I said, you did very well in there."

"Thanks."

She hazarded a glance at him and gave him a shy smile. His instincts hopped again. Trapped by her pretty blue eyes, he sat frozen as the urge to smile back plucked at the corners of his mouth and an unexpected desire to flirt with her rose up in him.

Fortunately, that brought him to his senses. She was a pretty girl and like any normal man, he was attracted to her. But she was an employee. A struggling working girl who shouldn't have to worry about her boss hitting on her.

This "attraction" he felt was purely sexual. The normal reaction of a man to a very pretty woman. Not a big deal. And certainly not something he'd pursue.

The limo pulled up outside the office building. Tucker exited first and offered his hand to Olivia to help her out.

She took it instinctively, then was sorry she had. Little sparks of electricity spiked up her arm.

Confusion rattled through her. She had been pleased that he'd treated her normally during the limo ride to the signing and again as they drove back to the office. But what she felt right now wasn't boss-employee goodwill. These sparks were attraction.

Really? After Elias had just scared the snot out of her? Three years since she'd even been on a date, she picked today to be attracted to someone? Her boss?

But she hadn't really "picked" anything. This feeling was natural, an instinct. And Tucker Engle wasn't anything like Elias. He wasn't sleazy or overly complimentary or all over her the way Elias had been, the way Cord had been the night he'd attacked her. Tucker was mature, savvy, handsome—sophisticated.

Sheesh, no wonder she was attracted to him. Personality-wise he was Cord's polar opposite.

Fortunately, she didn't think he liked her.

So her being attracted to him was irrelevant.

Thank God.

She slid out of the limo and stopped in front of him on the sidewalk. Their gazes caught and held. Her breath slid in then stuttered out as he just stared at her. His smoldering emerald eyes held her captive. Tingles danced along her hand where their palms touched.

Their palms touched!

Good grief! She still had his hand! No wonder he was staring at her.

She dropped it like a hot potato. "Um. Thanks for taking me with you."

He stepped back. "You're welcome." He took another step away. "I have a lunch meeting. Don't expect me back until two."

"Right." Without waiting for him to get into the limo, she turned and scrambled to the revolving door.

She would not be attracted to her boss.

She would not be attracted to her boss.

She would not be attracted to her boss.

That would be about as stupid as the poorest girl in town dating the son of the local rich family.

And she'd never be that stupid again.

CHAPTER THREE

AT NOON THE next day, Olivia called out "I'm going to lunch," grabbed her backpack and hit the button for the elevator. But before the door opened, the phone on her desk rang.

Not wanting to further disturb Tucker, who'd come back from his business meeting the day before quiet and sullen and hadn't spoken two words to her today, she raced to the phone and answered it. "Tucker Engle's office."

"This is Stewart, the lobby security guard. There's a man and woman here who say they're your parents."

Heat flooded her face and her chest tightened. *Her parents?* Oh, Lord! Their overprotectiveness had now reached its legal limit. It was one thing to check up on her. Checking out Tucker Engle was quite another. How could they embarrass her like this?

"Mr. Engle doesn't allow us to send anybody up to his private offices without prior approval and they aren't on the list."

She thanked her lucky stars for that rule. "No. Of course not. I'll be right down."

"Right down where?"

Hearing Tucker immediately behind her, she pressed her hand to her chest to still her thumping heart, hung up the phone and spun to face him.

"Lunch. I'm going downstairs to lunch, remember I told you that?"

"I did hear you say something. But that was before the phone rang." He caught her gaze. "Who was on the phone?"

Manipulating the timing hadn't worked. And she didn't lie, so this was a moment of truth. Literally. "It was Stewart."

Tucker frowned. "Is he sending someone up?"

Heat blossomed on her cheeks. "No. The people in the lobby didn't have prior approval. So I'm going down."

He turned to his office. "Get him back on the phone. I have time today. I can see whoever is down there."

She stood frozen.

When she didn't answer, he stopped and faced her again.

The warmth in her face intensified. "There's no need to call Stewart. He told me who was in the lobby."

His eyebrows rose.

She sucked in a breath. "It's my parents."

"Oh."

Though it pained her, she knew she might as well go the whole way with this. "I have a sneaking feeling they're here to meet you."

"Sneaking feeling?"

"You know. A feeling that just sort of creeps up on you when you don't want it to."

"Ah." He waited a second then said, "You don't want me to meet your parents?"

"No! No!" What else could she say? "That's not it."

"Then have Stewart send them up. If they're here to see the city, I'll give them my driver for the afternoon and they can go to all the sites."

Though that was nice of him, risking one meeting was bad enough. Risking a second when they returned the limo was insanity. They'd ask questions about his background. Want to know his intentions. Read between the lines of everything he said, making sure he wasn't a closet pervert bent on hurting their little girl. Embarrassment and humiliation collided and turned her stomach. She could not let that happen.

"That's way too kind."

He brushed her concern off with a wave of her hand and headed back into his office. "Call Stewart. Send them up."

With no choice but to obey, Olivia did as she was told.

Fortifying herself for the worst, she stood in front of her desk waiting for the elevator ping. As the doors opened, she didn't see just her mom and dad. Her brother, Billy, and her sister, Cindy, stood beside them. Even before she was off the elevator, her mother reached out for a hug.

As her mother's arms wrapped around her, she closed her eyes. It was really hard to be mad at somebody who loved you so much.

"Hey, guys."

Her mother squeezed her even more tightly.

"I'm fine, Mom."

As her mother released her, her dad caught her up in a bigger hug. "It's just so good to see you."

She laughed. "I've only been gone a month."

As she said the words, Tucker Engle came out of his office. Her brother and sister froze. Her mom spun to face him. Her dad blatantly gave him a once-over.

Tucker smiled. He had this. If there was one thing he was good at, it was people. Let her dad narrow his eyes. He would still win him over.

Tucker held out his hand to shake her dad's. "I'm Tucker Engle. Olivia's boss."

Tall and bald, Olivia's dad looked like a man who labored for a living. His calloused hand confirmed that.

"Mr. Engle, these are my parents, Loraina and Jim Prentiss and my sister, Cindy, and brother, Billy."

Billy also shook his hand. A boy of about sixteen, who appeared to be trying to be a man, he wore jeans and a T-shirt like his dad.

Her sister Cindy looked a year or so younger than Olivia and was nearly as pretty. Both Prentiss daughters had their mom's strawberry blonde hair and blue eyes. Cindy shyly said, "It's nice to meet you."

But her mom didn't say anything. She caught his gaze and held it as if trying to see into his soul.

He'd never had anyone look at him that way before.

Her pretty blue eyes narrowed, her mouth thinned.

Okay. So her mother didn't like him. He could fix that, too. "I've called my limo driver and instructed him to take you anywhere you want to go this afternoon. It'll be much easier to see everything with a driver who knows the city."

Cindy gasped and Billy said, "All right!"

Jim said, "That's very nice of you." He produced some bags with the logo of a popular Chinese restaurant on them. "But we were just about to have lunch. We brought enough for an army and we'd love to have you join us."

Tucker smiled. "Thank you, but I was planning to work through lunch today. I have a meeting across the street at one. I thought I'd pick up something when that's over."

Loraina surprised him by hooking her arm through his. "Oh, now, you can't skip lunch. And we can't eat in front of you! Besides, if you really are giving us your limo for the afternoon, we owe you."

He sought Olivia's gaze and she shrugged, though her red face was the picture of apology.

He'd never had a family, so he could only imagine how embarrassing this was for her. Especially since her mother was already on the way into his office.

"This is perfect." She pointed at the sofa grouping. "We can sit around the coffee table."

It wouldn't be the first time he'd eaten Chinese food at

that coffee table. He did some of his best business deals in that quiet, comfortable atmosphere. He'd never, however, eaten breakfast, lunch or dinner with the family of an employee.

Unfortunately, he couldn't figure out a way to refuse them without sounding like he was kicking them out of his office.

Her dad put the Chinese food on the coffee table. Her brother and sister sat on the sofa and began opening the bags, looking for chopsticks.

Olivia caught his arm and pulled him back, away from her family. "I'm sorry. They're just very comfortable people. They think everybody is a new friend."

He drew in a breath. "That's actually a nice philosophy."

"I swear. In twenty minutes they'll be gone."

Okay. He could deal with that. Hell, he could deal with anything for twenty minutes. "No need to be so embarrassed or so hard on them. I love the food from the restaurant they chose and as your mom said, everybody needs to eat."

She visibly relaxed and nodded, and his instincts jumped again. All along he'd thought there was something about her. Her family reminded him she was new to the city. Maybe even here alone. And if he got comfortable with her family, maybe she would become more comfortable with him?

He took the big chair at the head of things, reached for a carton of sweet-and-sour pork and dished some onto one of the throw-away plates Olivia's mom had handed out.

"So what do you do for a living, Jim?"

"I'm in construction."

"That's wonderful."

Loraina beamed. "He paid for Olivia's schooling by flipping houses."

"Wow." That took hard work and brains, the ability to

find a good house and spend only enough on remodeling that you could still make a profit when you sold it. He could see where Olivia got her talent with numbers.

"He'll do the same for Cindy now."

Cindy faced Olivia. "Are we going to get to see your apartment?"

"I don't know. How long are you guys staying?"

Billy said, "Two days. We have to fly back tomorrow night."

Tucker said, "That's a short stay for such a long trip."

All five Prentisses grew quiet. Olivia's face reddened again. And again the sense that there was something he was missing nagged at him.

But Loraina brightened. "Hotels are expensive in this city. We're just happy for the time we get."

Olivia suddenly said, "Who wants an egg roll?"

Her dad and brother immediately shoved their plates at her, but Tucker suspected she'd craftily changed the subject.

When she faced Cindy, and asked, "Are you ready for school?" he was certain of it.

"I may never be totally ready." Cindy grabbed a different carton of the food and dished herself a serving. "Billy made the football team."

Olivia spun to face him. "Oh, my gosh! Shouldn't you be at practice?"

Billy scowled.

Loraina said, "You can miss a practice or two. It's not every day you get to see New York City."

Ignoring Billy's plight, Cindy said, "I was sort of hoping you'd take me shopping."

Olivia laughed gaily. "Me? I can just barely dress myself. If you want expert advice, you need to take Eloise with you."

Jim said, "I don't think there's time for shopping."

Billy said, "You can shop at home."

Loraina agreed. "You get better bargains there anyway. I saw designers on TV the other day showing how to make clothes from your local store look like big-city fashions."

"I don't want them to *look* like big-city fashions. I want them to *be* big-city fashions. Can't we stay another day?"

Billy exploded. "No! I'm missing two practices already! I'm not missing three!"

"You and your precious football."

"You and your precious *clothes!* At least some day football might get me a scholarship. What are clothes going to get you?"

"A boyfriend?"

"You don't need a boyfriend!"

Both parents said that at once and might have made Tucker laugh, except Cindy's next whine started a discussion that had all five Prentisses talking at once. Tucker had been in boardrooms where five people talked at once. He'd been in boardrooms where five people yelled at once. But this discussion—sort of stupid, but very important to the people talking—whipped around him like a tornado. He had absolutely no idea of what to say.

Worse, he didn't think they cared or wanted him to say anything.

A feeling of alienation stole over him, which didn't surprise him. In foster homes, you didn't comment on another kid's life or problems. You weren't really family; you were boarders. He remembered falling asleep trying to imagine himself in a family like this and never quite being able to put himself into the picture. He couldn't put himself in this picture either. Even though he was actually, physically here.

Olivia's laugh penetrated his discomfort and he glanced from the arguing teens to Jim to Loraina who groaned and said things like "Settle down" and "If you don't stop fighting nobody's getting anything."

He peeked at Olivia again. Her pretty face relaxed in her laughter.

Now she was happy and he was the one who felt like an outsider.

Olivia had never been so glad to see an elevator door open and take people away as she was to see her parents and siblings leave Tucker Engle's office. He made good on his promise of his limo for their use that afternoon, but he'd been quiet through their lunch.

"Do you want me to go back to reviewing Bartulocci financials this afternoon?"

"Yes."

He said the word while staring at the elevator that had just taken away her family and his limo driver.

A minute ticked off the clock. Then another. Then another. He just kept staring at that elevator.

"Are you okay?"

"I'm fine."

But Olivia didn't think he was. Normally, he was a tad brisk. Formal. Even with Elias and Ricky from the start-up, two guys who considered him a friend, he'd been formal. She didn't like this sullen side of him. "I want to apologize again for my family."

"Your family is very nice."

She winced. "My brother and sister fight all the time."

He turned away from the elevator and headed to his office. "I've heard that's normal for brothers and sisters."

She scrambled after him. If this mood was the fault of her family, she had to help him get rid of it. "Heard?"

"I don't have any brothers and sisters."

He strode to his desk and bent down to retrieve a briefcase from the floor. He stopped so quickly, bent so quickly and rose so quickly, that Olivia didn't have time to get out of his way. When he stood again, they were mere inches apart.

She caught his gaze. She could smell the vague scent of his aftershave, feel the raw maleness that drifted off him. After being attacked, she hadn't often let herself get close to a man. Especially not someone as far out of her league as the town rich kid had been—as Tucker Engle *was*.

But he was so handsome and she couldn't seem to step away, or break contact with his beautiful emerald eyes.

When she spoke. her voice was a mere whisper. "You're an only child?"

"You could say that."

Though they were talking about something totally innocent, electricity crackled between them. "You don't know if you're an only child?"

"No." He took a long breath. "I'm a foster child."

"Oh."

He stepped away. "Don't feel sorry for me. I'm fine."

"Yes, of course."

He walked around her and strode to the door. "This meeting shouldn't last more than an hour."

With that he was gone and Olivia let out her breath in a grand whoosh. A foster child? Her heart ripped in two. Not because he wanted her to feel sorry for him, but because he didn't.

CHAPTER FOUR

WHAT THE HELL was that?

Tucker walked through the building lobby, pushed open the revolving door and stepped onto the sidewalk, his heart beating out a weird rhythm and his mouth dry. He'd told Olivia he was a foster child because it would have been odd to keep a secret that was a matter of public record. He'd said it as if it were no big deal, but having her parents in his office, seeing physical proof of how much they loved her, he knew it was. Eating with them brought back memories filled with scars that had felt like open wounds. Then he'd turned and there she'd been, right at his fingertips, close enough to touch, and damned if he hadn't been tempted.

He combed his fingers through his hair and stopped to wait for the traffic light to cross the street. He could still feel the rush of heat that whipped through him, the swell of sharp, sweet desire. He couldn't remember ever being this attracted to a woman—especially one he barely knew. But standing so close had all but made him dizzy, and holding her gaze had sent molten lava careening through him.

The light turned and he hustled across the street and down the sidewalk. He had a meeting with a few bankers who had a sudden case of nerves about the terms of a deal he'd offered to purchase a struggling manufacturing plant. They needed to be coddled. He couldn't be distracted by an attraction that was out of line.

Ridiculous.

So far off base it shouldn't even be acknowledged.

All he wanted from Olivia Prentiss was for her to do her job.

And he needed to do his.

Heading for the building lobby, he went over the terms of the agreement for Echo Manufacturing in his head. He'd crafted this deal with the precision of an artist. He wouldn't change anything. He had to make the bankers see things his way.

After a two-hour meeting spent attempting to alleviate the concerns of stubborn autocrats with no vision, he was crossing the street again. As persuasive and charming as he'd been, they'd ordered him to totally redraw the offer.

Though that made him forget everything that had happened that morning, it did not make him happy. In fact, if fury were a living thing, his temper would be Godzilla.

His head filled with facts and figures, he entered the elevator to his office suite. He was so immersed in his work that when the doors opened he probably would have walked straight through Olivia's office without even a greeting. But as the doors slid apart, the word *gin!* blasted him.

He stopped. There at Olivia's desk, an empty Chinese food carton on his right, a cup of coffee on his left and a deck of cards between him and Olivia, was Constanzo Bartulocci.

Short and round in the tummy, but dressed elegantly in a tailored gray suit, Constanzo grinned at him. "Good afternoon, Tucker."

"Constanzo?" His head spun. First her parents had arrived and reminded him of everything he hadn't had as a child. Then she'd bowled him over with a little close proximity and eye contact. Then bankers had turned him down. And now the owner of the company he wanted to buy was playing gin—with his assistant?

He wasn't sure he could handle any more surprises today.

The Italian jumped off his chair. "*Sì!* It's good to see you!"

As Constanzo enveloped Tucker in a bear hug, Tucker caught Olivia's gaze.

Her face reddened and she mouthed the words, "He was hungry."

Constanzo released him. "Seven hours on a plane. Two hours in traffic to get here. Starvation and boredom were killing me." He gestured to Olivia. "I hope you don't mind that I begged your assistant to share her food with me."

She grimaced. "We did have leftovers."

His assistant had fed one of the richest men in the world cold Chinese food. Where the hell had his office dignity gone? Where was decorum?

"Yes. I see." He smiled at Constanzo. "I'm glad she had time for you."

Constanzo laughed. "I'm sure she had work, but your Vivi, she is generous."

One of Tucker's eyebrows quirked. *Vivi?*

Constanzo waved his arm in the direction of Tucker's office. "Come. Let's talk about these rumors I'm hearing that you want to buy me out."

Excitement obliterated his anger over the Echo deal and the emotions left over from Vivi's parents' visit. If Constanzo was here at his office, eager to talk about his company, it could only be because he'd made the short list of potential buyers. He motioned for Constanzo to walk before him. "Lead the way."

They headed for the door but Constanzo stopped suddenly. "Vivi, you come, too."

Olivia squirmed on her chair. "Oh, I don't think you need me in there."

"Of course, we do." He inclined his head toward the door. "Come."

Tucker's eyes narrowed. He had no idea why Constanzo wanted her in the room, but one didn't argue with a billionaire who wanted to deal. "Sure, *Vivi,* come."

Olivia smiled sheepishly and rose to follow them. Constanzo barreled ahead, but Tucker waited. Before Olivia reached the door, he caught her arm and stopped her just short of hearing distance for Constanzo. *"Vivi?"*

She shrugged. "It's my nickname. If you'd asked, I'd have let you use it, too."

With a roll of his eyes, he walked into his office, slid out of his jacket and sat on the sofa beside Constanzo. Vivi took the chair across from them.

Attempting to return the room to its usual dignity and decorum, Tucker said, "I'm thrilled to have you in town."

"I like New York."

"You should keep a home here."

Constanzo laughed. "I intend to enjoy not traveling when I retire."

Tucker smiled. *This* was the kind of conversation he expected to have with a billionaire legend. Not a discussion about leftover Chinese food. A feeling of normalcy returned, including the urge to pounce.

Still, he wouldn't jump the gun. He'd continue the small talk until Constanzo brought up the subject of his conglomerate again.

"You might try something like staying in Italy for six months and living in New York six months."

He waved a hand and blew out a "pfft" sound. "Retirement is supposed to be about no plans." He stopped, smiled at Olivia, then turned his attention to Tucker. "Maria tells me you want my company."

"Yes, I do."

"I have something I want, too. If you get it for me, I will negotiate exclusively with you for my conglomerate."

Dumbfounded, Tucker fought a wave of shock. "So there wouldn't be a short list? There would just be me?"

"For a year." Constanzo laughed. "Even you have to admit if we can't come to terms in a year, then there is no deal. But we will negotiate fairly because I want to retire next year. You will find me amicable."

Fighting a feeling that this was too good to be true, or that there had to be a big, ugly catch, Tucker asked, "What do you want me to get for you?"

"You and three others expressed interest in my company."

Tucker had figured as much, so he inclined his head.

"I checked all of your financials, then hired a private investigator."

Not surprised by the review of his financials, but a bit put off by the P.I., Tucker said, "To see who could come up with the financing?"

"No. To see who can bring my son home to me."

Tucker narrowed his eyes. This wasn't a catch. It was a trick. "You don't have a son. You never married. You have no children."

Constanzo laughed. "I see you did your homework too."

"We're both smart businessmen. There's no sense pretending we aren't."

Constanzo slapped Tucker's knee. "That's why I like you. You're on top of things."

"Yet somehow or another I missed the fact that you have a child. Either that, or you're trying to trick me."

"No trick. No one knows I have a child. Thirty years ago on a very busy, very hectic day, a girlfriend approached me saying she was pregnant. Believing she only wanted money, I had her removed from my office. She never tried to contact me again."

Tucker sat forward. "And now suddenly you believe this woman's claim, and you want me to find this child you're not even sure exits?"

"Oh, he exists." He glanced over at Olivia. "I've found him. I only need you to bring him home to me."

"Constanzo, I—"

"—Don't usually get involved in personal family problems to do a business deal?" He laughed. "Is that why you took Maria to lunch on Monday and promised to do something about her annoying cousin?"

"That was part of prying for information."

"That was her undercutting her cousins."

Tucker couldn't argue that so he didn't even try.

"Antonio's mother—the girlfriend I spoke of—died when Antonio was a baby." He reached into his pocket, pulled out an envelope and handed it to Tucker. "He's in Italy now, but he grew up in foster care in the U.S."

Tucker's nerve endings puffed out. *Foster care.* The son of one of the richest men in the world had been raised by strangers. Had gone to sleep lonely. And probably grew up resenting the dad who'd abandoned him.

Which was why Constanzo wanted Tucker to be the one to talk to him. Without even knowing Constanzo's son, he understood him.

"Your investigation went a lot further than I would have expected."

"Yes, and you should be glad because until I went back as far as I did, other candidates to buy my company looked more promising."

Tucker said nothing.

Constanzo sighed. "You're the only one of the candidates who will know how to tell my son he has a father."

"You're saying he doesn't know who you are?"

"No. He does not."

"And you don't want me to just drop in and say, hey, it's your lucky day, your biological father is a billionaire."

He rose. "I don't care what you say. I leave that entirely to your discretion. With the stakes as high as they are I'm sure you won't make a mistake." He turned to Olivia. "Vivi, a pleasure to meet you. I think you will enjoy Italy."

About to rise, Tucker stopped. "You want me to bring Miss Prentiss to Italy?"

He glanced at Tucker. "Why not?"

"Because she's temporary, only standing in for Betsy, and she doesn't know anything."

"This trip has nothing to do with what she knows. You're buying *my* company. Even you don't know the things I'll share if you win the chance to buy my enterprise."

"Even so, she should stay here so that she has access to things I'll need."

"We have the internet in Italy, Tucker." He laughed. "Besides, I now owe her for her hospitality. I pay her back at my home." He grinned at Olivia. "My cook prepares a lasagna that will make you weep."

She laughed.

He faced Tucker again. "I'm hoping to see you at my villa in the next day or two. Particulars are in the envelope. Good luck."

He left the room and though Vivi popped out of her seat, Tucker watched the realization come to her face that it was too late. Constanzo had already reached the elevator. He pressed the button and the door swished open. There was no point in racing out to escort him.

As the elevator door closed behind Constanzo, Tucker ran his hands down his face. Suddenly the Echo deal falling apart meant nothing. He had an opportunity to get Constanzo Bartulocci's entire enterprise. But, to get the chance for exclusive negotiations, he had to integrate Constanzo's son into his life. And he had to take Olivia Prentiss with him. *Had to*. A wealthy man like Constanzo Bartulocci didn't do anything without reason. He might be trying to make it look casual that he'd invited Olivia along, but after a few seconds to let it all sink in, Tucker knew better. There was a reason.

"I'm not exactly sure why Constanzo wants you on this job, but from the fact that he so clearly handpicked me, I'm guessing there's a reason he's insisting I take you." He motioned her back to her chair. "Sit down. Let's see what's going on here." He ripped open the envelope.

"You're doing it? You're going to Italy to explain to an orphan that he has a dad?"

"There was never a doubt." He glanced at her. "He's offering me exclusive negotiations on a multi-billion-dollar conglomerate."

"Because you were a foster child?"

The words rankled. He should have been pleased that for once his status had gotten him something. Instead, he thought of Olivia's mom and dad. Her arguing sister and brother. He wondered what it might be like to grow up surrounded by people who loved you enough that they traveled thousands of miles to see you simply because they missed you.

And got angry with himself. He'd forgotten all this, let it go. One episode with a quirky family shouldn't make him long for things that couldn't be. No one could change the past.

His gaze fell to the documents in the envelope. Pictures of a young man with Constanzo Bartulocci's eyes. A birth certificate that named the baby's father as unknown. But a DNA test that proved Constanzo was the father.

"Well, I'm not sure who his P.I. was but he's thorough."

Vivi rose from her chair and sat beside him so she could see the papers. "Why do you say that?"

He turned to hand the DNA test to her but their gazes

caught and those weird feelings swept through him again. The pinpricks of awareness. The warmth of excitement. The swirl of desire. Except this time they came with the knowledge that he was taking her to Italy. They'd spend seven hours alone on a plane, eat every meal together—

But Tucker dismissed those concerns simply by looking away. He might be attracted but he wouldn't pursue it. She was his employee but more than that, she wasn't his type. He liked sexy sophisticates. She was a family girl. Too sweet for him. Or maybe he was just a little too rough for her.

"To get DNA for the test, Constanzo's investigator probably trailed the poor kid until he could get his used cup at a coffee shop or something."

Vivi laughed. "Really? You think that's what he did?"

"He certainly couldn't ask for a lock of his hair."

"Not unless he wanted to get arrested. Or alert Constanzo's son that someone was investigating him. I'm guessing Mr. B. doesn't want his name even mentioned until the road is clear for a congenial meeting."

Tucker sat back on the sofa. She'd brought the situation down to its real bottom line, and quickly enough that Tucker wondered if that was why Constanzo wanted her to go to Italy. She'd probably said something while they were playing cards to make him think she was smart, intuitive, good with people.

And maybe she was. Tucker might understand being a foster child, but she understood being poor. She also knew about family.

"Are you sure you don't mind me going to Italy?"

"Constanzo Bartulocci is one of the richest men in the world. You don't get rich by being stupid or by not understanding people. He sees something in you. Something he thinks I might need. Wouldn't I be a little foolish to refuse his backhanded advice?"

"I guess."

He slid the papers back into the envelope. "Pack tonight. We'll leave tomorrow after work."

She rose. "Okay."

He walked to his desk, dismissing her, but stopped suddenly. "And Miss Prentiss make sure your parents are on board with this trip."

There was no way he'd take her anywhere if big Jim and narrow-eyed Loraina didn't want him to.

CHAPTER FIVE

Vivi called her parents and made arrangements to meet them at a pizza place by their hotel for dinner. When she dropped the bomb about Italy, her dad went ballistic. Her mom absolutely forbade her from going.

"I'm twenty-two. You can't stop me. Besides, you met him. He's a wealthy man who can have his pick of women. Trust me. He doesn't want the local street waif." Even as she said the words, she knew they were something of a lie. Not a total lie, but kind of close. She didn't know what had happened when Tucker Engle had bent to pick up his brief-case and suddenly they'd been two inches away from each other. But her attraction to him had turned her voice to a whisper and she'd seen the spark of something in his eyes.

Still, he'd ignored it. Pretended it wasn't there. He might find her attractive but he didn't want to. Which meant he wouldn't act on the weird feelings hopping between them, and, technically, that was all her parents were interested in.

"You're a very beautiful woman. You don't think it's odd that you go to work for him one day and three days later he decides to take you across the Atlantic?"

She brightened. "That's just it. He doesn't want me to go. He wants to buy the company of a man named Constanzo Bartulocci. Mr. Bartulocci dropped in today unannounced and gave Mr. Engle the chance to be the sole bidder on his company. But to get the chance to bid, he has to go to Constanzo's estate in Italy."

"With you?"

"Only because Mr. Bartulocci wants me to go, too."

"Why?"

"Because I'm part of Tucker Engle's team. With his regular assistant gone. I'm his go-to girl."

When her parents still looked unconvinced, she sighed. "I am twenty-two years old. I had something really bad happen to me three years ago. I got beyond it. And do you know why? Because if I didn't, if Cord had made me too scared to live, then he didn't just steal my reputation from me. He also stole my life and, frankly, that's something I refuse to give to him."

Her dad tossed his napkin to the table. "You have a point."

Her mother shook her head. "It's just that Tucker Engle is so young."

"Yes, he is young, but he's a very smart guy. Before you found out how old he was even you told me I could learn from him."

She reached across the worn table of the pizza place and caught her mother's hand. "Don't trust him, Mom. Trust *me*. I need to get out in the world to prove I've recovered."

Twenty minutes later, she was walking home to pack.

The next day she brought her single piece of luggage and a toiletries case to work. Tucker had meetings out of the office all day in preparation for being away, so he had left the limo for her and told her he would meet her at the airstrip.

Traffic kept her on the road until almost seven, filling her with panic. But when she saw the long, sleek jet that stood at the ready, she forgot all about being late and gaped at it in awe. Tucker Engle *owned* that glossy little jet. For all she knew he also owned the airstrip.

He was a former foster kid who at thirty or so now owned a plane. Maybe an airstrip. It was phenomenal.

And she suddenly understood why she was so drawn to him. He'd done what she wanted to do. He hadn't let his past hinder him. He'd gotten beyond it.

Technically, she might not be attracted to him as much as she admired him.

She thanked the driver who assured her he would see to her luggage, and casually headed for the plane.

A tall, blue-eyed pilot greeted her as she entered. "Good evening, Miss Prentiss."

She smiled. "Good evening."

"The flight is approximately seven hours. Accounting for the time difference, we'll be arriving at Mr. Bartulocci's private airstrip around 7:00 a.m. local time."

"So, you're basically telling me to sleep on the flight?"

"Yes, ma'am." He motioned her toward the roomy six-seat cabin.

Tucker Engle sat at a compact workstation at the very back of the plane. Paperwork had been spread out on the table in front of his seat. Though he said good evening, he barely looked up from his work, confirming that he might be attracted to her but he wasn't interested in her. Her parents had nothing to worry about.

She slid into one of the six butterscotch leather seats and buckled in. The pilots taxied to the runway and the plane took off smoothly.

She reclined her seat, preparing to fall asleep. But soft as it was, without a pillow or a blanket, she couldn't quite get comfortable.

"There are blankets in a cupboard back there."

She sat up and faced him. He angled his thumb toward the back of the plane. "And pillows."

She unbuckled her seat belt and rose. "Thanks."

She walked to the cupboard, but she didn't open it. Her hand hovered over the door knob. "Would you like one?"

"No. I'm working."

She nodded and returned to her seat with a pillow and a blanket. She turned off the light above her, reclined her seat and nestled into her covers.

She closed her eyes and took three long, calming breaths, but they didn't help. She couldn't imagine how someone went from being a foster kid to being a billionaire. She had had help from her parents, but still couldn't live in New York City on her meager salary without roommates. Starting at the bottom, she had absolutely no idea how to climb the ladder from where she was now to where he was now.

And that's what she wanted. To be somebody. So that when she went back to Starlight everybody would see she hadn't needed to fake an attack to extort money from Cord Dawson. She had always had the talent and drive to be successful on her own.

She sat up, swiveled to face him. "So how does somebody go from being a foster child to owning all this?"

He didn't even look up. "Perseverance."

"There's got to be more to it than that."

"There isn't."

"It's not like I wouldn't understand. I'm pretty smart and I really want this. Plus, it's not like anything you'd say would shock me. I had a friend who was a foster child. And I also had some really crappy things happen to me at university."

He knew she had. He remembered she'd been sued for slander. Even though the kid had dropped the suit, she'd probably been terrified.

He twirled his pencil between his fingers. He shouldn't talk. He should keep everything between them strictly professional, but she'd opened the door and curiosity about that "something" about her wouldn't allow him to let the opportunity to ask her a few questions pass. If she wanted to know his secrets, first she'd share hers. "I know about the lawsuit filed against you three years ago."

Her eyes widened. "You do?"

"Like Constanzo, I go the extra mile with people who are going to know my business."

She said nothing, but her face had gone pasty white.

"I understand the kid dropped the suit, but it would still be very difficult to be nineteen and have somebody sue you."

She nodded.

"So what happened?"

"Happened?"

"No twenty-year-old boy files a slander law suit without good reason. So whatever you said, it had to have been a doozy."

Her chin lifted. "I told the truth."

"Then it couldn't have been slander."

"I couldn't prove what I said."

"Oh." He caught Olivia's gaze. "But it was true?"

She nodded.

"Which was probably why he dropped the suit. He didn't want to risk that you'd find a way to prove it."

"Oh, he knew I couldn't."

Curiosity spiked again, and he nearly kept going, so intrigued about her that the work in front of him had lost its appeal. But he suddenly realized he was comfortable, talking about personal things—the kind of things he never talked about with anybody, especially not an employee.

He'd already decided he didn't want to be attracted to her, so what was he doing getting to know her?

"Why don't you try to sleep while I do some work? This trip to Italy is going to cost me a hundred other things if I don't get my ducks in a row now. So no more talking."

"Okay."

She turned around and he forced his attention back to work. Work had made him who he was today. He didn't need conversation. He didn't need family. He needed only to be the best he could be.

Tucker Engle's plane landed at Constanzo Bartulocci's private airstrip in the Italian countryside. A driver waited by a white limo and they headed for Constanzo's villa.

Vivi stared out the window in awe. A sea of green grass flowed to mountains. The sky was the bluest blue she'd ever seen, hovering over the grassy slopes like a benevolent blue god. "This is gorgeous."

Pulling a document from his briefcase, Tucker said, "Italy's a beautiful country."

She almost asked if he always worked but she knew the answer to that. Of course, he did. Now that he'd told her he'd been a foster child, so many things about him made sense. Just as she saw success as a way to vindicate herself, he probably saw it as a way to prove his value to a world that hadn't wanted him. It was why he'd flown to Italy in a black suit, white dress shirt and black-and-silver striped tie, while she'd worn plain trousers and a yellow shirt. He never stopped. Never relaxed. Everything was work to him.

And she supposed she had her answer for how he'd climbed his way from foster child to billionaire. He worked all the time.

They arrived at Constanzo's country villa and Vivi nearly broke her neck looking around, trying to see everything at once. Trees and shrubbery provided privacy. Lush green grass bordered stone walks that took them to the front door of a stone house that could have been hundreds of years old but had been updated.

"Welcome! Welcome!" Wearing dress pants and a short-sleeved shirt, open at the neck, Constanzo greeted them in the foyer. A colorful tile stairway with a black iron railing led to the second floor. Antique tables along the walls held vases of fresh flowers. Though the house was big, it wasn't the stuffy mansion Vivi had expected a billionaire to live in. Beautiful and colorful, it was also homey.

Constanzo hugged Vivi then Tucker. "My staff is putting your things in your rooms. Would you like time to freshen up?"

Vivi yawned. "Actually, I'd like a nap. I couldn't sleep on the plane." Her brain had been so jumpy she hadn't been able to relax. So she'd pulled her book out of her purse and read for most of the flight.

Constanzo laughed. "Vivi, Vivi. The best way to get accustomed to a new time zone is to pretend your body is already on our time."

"I've been up twenty-four hours! I'll never make it."

Constanzo put his arm around her shoulder. "Of course, you will. It'll be bedtime here before you know it." He led her up the winding staircase. "Take a shower, put on fresh clothes. Something comfortable like jeans and I'll show you around. We'll go to a little café in town for lunch, then come back here for supper."

"Or she could take a nap by the pool while you and I discuss business."

In her tired state, she'd actually forgotten that Tucker was behind them. But she wasn't surprised he wanted to talk details of their deal. He was here to work.

Constanzo laughed. "Before we discuss business, you have a mission."

"Yes, but there are plenty of details we could—"

Constanzo made the "pfft" noise again. "We'll get to the details after I show Vivi around."

For the first time since she'd become Tucker's right-hand girl, she got a tug of assistant responsibility. Now that she understood a little about him and his work ethic, she knew what she had to do. "Actually, I'd rather see the town on a day when I'm rested." She smiled at her host. "Besides I have a feeling I could spend the day exploring your villa and the grounds."

Constanzo waved his hand dramatically. "Then that's what you'll do."

She laughed. Constanzo showed her to a little room decorated lavishly in shades of lavender and white. A June breeze fluttered the sheer white curtains, bringing with it the scent of fresh grass and wild flowers.

"This room is beautiful. Like art."

"Life is art. It's to be enjoyed." Constanzo opened the door on a stunning bathroom with white marble tiles and showed her a closet where her clothes already hung.

"Your staff is fast!"

"They like their jobs and want to keep them."

"So, Tucker and I will leave you to explore. If you need a swimsuit, dial five-one on the phone and explain what you want. We have plenty for guests. And my staff speaks English."

She smiled her thanks and he and Tucker left.

She breathed in the scent of fresh air, something she hadn't smelled since her last visit to Kentucky, and twirled around. She was in Italy! On the estate of a billionaire! She fought the urge to pinch herself and, instead, slipped out of her sandals.

The bed called to her but she agreed with Constanzo that the best way to adjust to her current time zone would be to eat, drink and sleep at the appropriate times. Which meant she had to entertain herself for the next few hours.

After a quick call to the staff, a maid brought her a raspberry-colored one-piece swimsuit in the size she requested. The tags had been trimmed, but she could tell the suit was new.

She showered, shimmied into the tight spandex suit,

slid into the cover-up and big straw sunhat the staff had also provided, and grabbed her book before she made her way downstairs. To the right were closed double doors. A formal dining room, complete with crystal chandelier, sat on the left. A slim hall ran down the middle. She followed the corridor to a huge great room. Floral sofas flanked by crystal lamps dominated the room. Huge double doors provided a view of the pool, its blue water sparkling in the sun.

She walked through the double doors onto a gray stone patio to a row of canvas chaise lounges. Kicking off her shoes, she tossed her book to the chair so she could remove the white lace cover-up.

When she finally had herself settled on the chaise, the June sun warmed her and giddy peace filled her. She was in Italy. *Italy.* She'd ridden a private jet across the Atlantic, driven in a limo, been brought to a villa where maids unpacked her meager belongings and now she lounged by a pool.

After leaving Olivia in her room, Constanzo had shown Tucker to the lavish suite he would be using. He'd suggested Tucker might want a nap or maybe a few minutes to freshen up. But Tucker insisted they use the time to hash out some of the details of the conglomerate acquisition. So Constanzo had led him to a den at the back of the first floor.

A pool table sat in the center of the room. Four big-screen TVs, one for each wall, hung in strategic spots. A bar that looked like an old English pub took up the back corner.

Constanzo immediately strode to the bar. "So what's your pleasure?"

"Details. You're offering me a billion-dollar conglomerate. I'd think the first order of business would be to stipulate how we'll determine market value."

"No! No!" Constanzo laughed. "I meant your drink. You like American bottled beer or what I have on tap?"

Tucker held back a sigh of impatience and politely said, "I'll try what you have on tap."

Constanzo drew two drafts and handed one to Tucker.

"Thanks. So how are we going to determine market value?"

Constanzo pushed a button and a dartboard appeared. "We could use the numbers in my annual statement."

"And disregard what's happened since it was released? How do I know your companies haven't gone down in value?"

He opened a carved box filled with darts that lined both the bottom of the box and its lid, and offered them to Tucker. "Because you've been watching me. You know exactly what I'm worth."

Tucker chuckled. He took a dart, aimed at the board and made a bull's-eye.

"Ah. A real challenge for me today!"

Tucker sighed. "You're not going to talk business, are you?"

"No. You're tired from your trip. It wouldn't be fair."

"Right. Don't try to kid somebody who makes his living knowing when people are lying to him."

"All right. You want to be blunt. We will be blunt. If you can't deliver my son to me, totally understanding my position—that his mother contacted me once, on a busy day, when I was so overwhelmed I barely registered what she said, let alone had brain power to believe it—then you don't get my company."

"So there's no point in talking specifics?"

"Exactly." As he spoke, Constanzo opened the drapes of the den, revealing his shimmering pool. The gray stone outdoor space had furniture groupings that ran the gamut from formal seating areas to casual placement of chaise lounges around the pool.

And on one of the chaise lounges lay a pale woman in

a one-piece, pinkish-purple bathing suit. A lock of strawberry blonde hair blew in the slight breeze.

Olivia. *Vivi*. Casual, happy, like-me-as-I-am Vivi. The woman who'd actually drawn him into a personal conversation the night before.

"I worry she'll fall asleep in the sun."

Tucker took a swig of beer. "If she does, she'd better have sunblock."

"She is pale."

She was pale. Trusting. And he'd finally realized that was the thing that drew him about her, even as it annoyed the hell out of him. She wanted to understand, asked a million questions, because she wanted to trust life.

Trust life. As if one could.

He took in her smooth shoulders, her trim tummy. Even being exactly the opposite of what he liked in a woman, she tempted him.

Which was ridiculous. He liked sleek, sophisticates. Not hometown girls.

She shifted on the chaise, onto her side. The hat slid over her face, but the position pushed her breasts precariously high in the brightly colored suit. Her long legs stretched out, bared to him on sand-colored canvas. All right. She was sexy. She might not be sleek or sophisticated, but she was definitely sexy.

"Vivi…she is more than your assistant?"

Tucker swung around. Good God. Now the woman had him staring. "No." He walked over to the bar and grabbed three darts. "I told you, she's really not even my assistant. Betsy, the accountant who generally works with me was in an accident. Vivi—" Oh, Lord. Had he just used her nickname? "Is a temp."

He laughed. "I see."

"She probably won't be with me the next time we meet. But you'll like Betsy. She's incredibly competent."

And he was counting the days until she finished rehab and returned to the office. He didn't want a sexy assistant. He didn't want to wonder about the slander suit filed against her. He wanted Betsy back so his life could return to normal.

Still, every time Constanzo took his turn at the dart board, Tucker's gaze drifted out to the pool.

"Drink, Miss?"

The white-coated butler scared Vivi awake and she jumped. She shouldn't be surprised that she'd drifted off to sleep since she hadn't even had so much as a nap on the plane. But she didn't want to sleep. She wanted to adjust to her new time zone.

"Sorry for jumping."

He smiled benignly. "It's quite all right."

She wasn't in the mood for a drink, but a little caffeine might give her some energy. "Do you have iced tea?"

"Yes, ma'am."

He left as quickly and quietly as he'd arrived, brought her drink and disappeared again. She sipped her tea, then flipped over so she didn't get too burned.

But even before she settled on the chaise, she had the strangest feeling. Like someone was watching her.

She sat up and glanced at the house. The entire back of the first floor of the renovated house looked to be a wall of windows. Because of the framing, she guessed some of the 'windows' were actually double doors. But the angle of the sun made the glass dark. She couldn't see inside.

She adjusted the strap on her suit, smoothed her hands down her legs, unable to shake the feeling of being exposed.

She frowned. Of course, she was exposed. She was outside. Lounging on the patio of a house that had at least one maid, a butler and a driver. There was probably a cook and a gardener, too. Four people could be gawking at her if they wanted to be. But why would they want to?

It was stupid to be paranoid. A better explanation for what she was feeling was guilt that Tucker and Constanzo were working and she wasn't. She hadn't come to Italy to lie about. As it was, Tucker Engle didn't like having her along. Even if the trip had been grueling and she was tired, she had to get to work. Plus, she'd had a nice little nap. She had her brain back.

After gathering her cover-up, she padded to her room, put on her plain trousers and yellow shirt and headed downstairs again.

The house was a maze of corridors and beautifully decorated rooms. She could have stopped in every parlor to examine the furnishings and art she was sure was real, but needing to find Tucker and Constanzo, she kept looking until she found the pair in a den.

Playing darts. Drinking beer.

She shook her head. "You know, I was out by the pool, feeling bad because I wasn't working, and here's where I find you guys? Playing darts."

Tucker faced her. His suit coat lay across the back of an overstuffed recliner. His white shirt sleeves had been rolled up to his elbows, his black-and-silver striped tie loosened. He looked so casually gorgeous, she swallowed hard.

Her foolish attraction was growing, but at least now she understood why. He'd grown up poor, but he was successful now. Just as she wanted to be. They had common ground. He wasn't just a good-looking guy. He was somebody she wanted to know.

"Vivi, come in! Do you throw?"

Glad for the distraction of Constanzo, she settled herself on the arm of an overstuffed chair beside the pool table. The room wasn't dripping with diamonds or gold the way one might expect a billionaire's house might be. Instead it seemed to exist for Constanzo's comfort. Which, she supposed, was the way a billionaire should live.

"No, I don't throw."

"Your boss is beating me."

She laughed. But Tucker kept his attention focused on the dart game. She hoped he wasn't angry with her. He was the one who had suggested she sit by the pool while he and Constanzo talked. So he *couldn't* be angry with her.

She let her gaze drift around the room but she stopped suddenly when she saw the chaise lounge with the empty iced-tea glass sitting on the table beside it.

Her gazed jerked to Tucker's. This time he didn't look away. His perfect emerald eyes heated. Her breath leached out in a slow hiss. Pinpricks of awareness skittered down her spine. He'd seen her in the bathing suit.

She tried to be Zen about it, because, really, it was a one-piece suit. So what if he'd seen her legs? It meant nothing.

But he didn't let go of her gaze and she couldn't let go of his.

Okay. So it meant something.

He picked up a dart and tossed it toward the board. It landed with a thud that mirrored the thudding of her heart. She didn't want to like another guy who was so far out of her stratosphere...but how did she stop this? Her feelings for him were unexpected. So natural she didn't have any warning they were going to pop up until they did. And his?

She had no idea.

CHAPTER SIX

PLEADING A NEED to get some work done, Tucker left the den shortly after Olivia arrived and she didn't see him again until he entered the dining room for dinner that evening.

As Tucker walked in one door, Constanzo entered from the other side. Concern wrinkled his forehead and turned his mouth into a frown. "I'm so sorry. There's a problem at one of my companies. We are video conferencing in ten minutes. I would tell you that I'll return shortly and join you for dinner, but the problem is significant."

Vivi's heart stuttered. She and Tucker Engle had to eat alone?

Tucker said, "I understand."

She just barely kept herself from groaning. It absolutely looked as if they were eating alone.

"Excellent. You and Vivi enjoy dinner."

He scurried out of the dining room and Tucker faced her.

As always, he wore a dark suit that looked to have been made for him, white silk shirt and silver tie. She wore a light-weight floral dress with thin straps, something she'd bought at the end of the season the year before and paid less than half price for. Her hair hung straight—freshly washed, but just straight. His shiny dark hair had been combed to perfection.

If that wasn't a reminder that they lived in two different worlds she didn't know what was. He'd never make a pass at her and, if he did, she'd never flirt back because they did not belong together. They were too different.

But even before she finished that thought, he loosened his tie and pulled it off then undid the top two buttons of his shirt.

"Good evening, Miss Prentiss."

Oh, Lord. He was dressing down for her. And casually, so he wouldn't embarrass her. It was the sweetest thing, but she reminded herself they weren't a good match. He might be the first guy she was attracted to since Cord, but he wasn't interested in her. He was only being polite. A man who was interested wouldn't call her Miss Prentiss.

"Good evening, Mr. Engle."

He motioned toward a chair and she walked over. He pulled it out and she sat.

Ambling to the seat across the table from hers, he asked, "Do you know what Constanzo's cook prepared?"

"This afternoon he told me she was making a lasagna as lasagna is supposed to be made."

He laughed. "Leave it to him to be melodramatic."

"If it tastes as good as it smells, I think he's allowed a little melodrama."

As servants filled their glasses with water, Olivia struggled to think of something to say. Thick with the protocol of servants and a long row of silverware, the scene reminded her yet again that she and Tucker Engle had nothing in common.

When the servants left, she took a quiet breath and said, "Constanzo beat me in four games of pool this afternoon."

"It was kind of you to entertain him."

"He says it's boring for an old man to sit around his house with nothing to do. He says he should have grandkids and be teaching a little girl how to swim and a little boy how to hustle pretty girls in pool."

He laughed.

Her chest loosened a bit. This wouldn't be so bad. All she had to do was keep talking. "I think he was just distracting me with chitchat so I wouldn't notice how badly he was beating me."

Servants arrived with salad and bread and they dug in. For the next few minutes conversation revolved around how delicious the crusty bread was, then the table grew quiet.

She scoured her brain to think of something to say and couldn't come up with anything. Seconds ticking off the clock felt like hours, reminding her yet again that she shouldn't be attracted to a man with whom she had nothing in common.

The main course came. At the first bite they groaned in ecstasy and complimented the lasagna, but the conversation stopped again. The longer they were quiet, the more obvious it was that they had nothing to say to each other and that any attraction she felt for him was foolish.

When she finished her dessert, she looked at her watch. Not even nine o'clock.

Across the table, Tucker surreptitiously looked at his watch, too.

For two people with palpable chemistry, they were certainly eager to get away from each other.

Tucker rose from his seat, tossing his napkin to his empty dessert plate. "So how about if you and I play a few games of pool?"

Her head snapped up. "Really?"

"If we go to bed now, we'll be up at four o'clock. Do you want to sit around with nothing to do for hours and hours?"

"I was kind of thinking if we went to bed now I'd sleep for hours and hours."

He laughed. "Are you ready to retire for the night?"

She shrugged. "I don't know. I think your idea of staying up a few more hours might be better."

"Great."

They walked to the den in silence. As she chose her pool stick, Tucker racked the balls. With a nod toward the table, he let her break. She dropped one of the striped balls into the pocket but missed her second shot and Tucker took over. The den filled with the crack of his stick against the balls and the plop, plop, plop of ball after ball falling into a pocket.

In the face of the beating she was taking, she forgot all about the quiet. Why was it she could beat any group of guys in a bar, but not whip the butts of two billionaires?

"Okay. I wasn't quite ready to play. Rack the balls again. This time I won't be so easy."

He laughed. "We'll see."

"Ah, smug, this time around?"

Tucker arranged the balls on the table. "Not smug. I just watched how you play. My technique is better."

"Right."

He motioned to the table as he walked behind the bar to pour himself a draft. "Go ahead. I'll give you the advantage. Break again."

She strolled up to the table, aimed her stick and broke with a resounding crack that echoed around them. Two solid balls dropped. She faced him with a grin. "I have you now."

He leaned against the bar. "What? You think solid is going to be lucky for you?"

"Yes." She walked around the table considering her next shot. When she found it, she bent across the table to take aim.

But Tucker shook his head. "Your form is all wrong."

"My form is fine."

"No. Look at your stick. It wobbles." He walked behind her and leaned down with her so he could adjust her arm. "See? Isn't that better?"

The feeling of his chest along her back sent waves of awareness flowing from her back to her toes. He stepped away, as if totally oblivious and, shell shocked, she took the shot.

Miraculously, the ball she aimed for fell. She jumped up with a whoop of joy. "I did it!"

He motioned at the table. "Keep going."

She picked a shot and leaned over the table, but again he shook his head.

"Your stick still wobbles." Positioning himself over her, he leaned down and straightened her arm. Then he froze.

The room grew quiet.

Warmth radiated from him into her and would have sent a shudder through her if she hadn't ruthlessly stopped it. She turned her head slightly to catch his gaze. His green eyes smoldered.

Oh, boy. This wasn't good.

Tucker stayed frozen. The woman was the softest thing he'd ever touched. Every hormone in his body awakened at the feel of her skin sliding against his. His hand itched to leave her pool stick and cruise along the curve of her waist, to turn her around, so he could kiss her.

The instinct was so strong, so natural that it shook him to his core and brought him back to planet earth. She was an *employee. Smart executives did not kiss employees.*

He stepped away and ambled back to the bar, pretending nothing had happened, confused that he couldn't seem to get himself under control around her.

As he picked up his beer from the bar, Constanzo walked in.

"Great! I see I'm just in time! I'll play the winner."

Olivia took her next shot but missed this time. Without looking at him, she said, "Your shot."

He licked his suddenly dry lips. Okay. That thing between them? He now had confirmation she felt it, too. But he could handle this. *They* could handle this. They'd just pretend it hadn't happened.

He set down his beer, picked up his pool cue and walked to the table. He got two balls in then missed, surprising Olivia who quietly walked up to the table again. She hit the remainder of her balls into the pockets, beating him soundly.

"Looks like you and me, Vivi," Constanzo said, happily rubbing his hands together.

But Olivia yawned. "You and Mr. Engle play. I think it's time for me to go to bed."

He didn't know if she really was tired or trying to get away from him, but he breathed a sigh of relief.

Until Constanzo said, "Tucker will walk you to your room."

The blood froze in his veins. He couldn't walk her to her room! He was unstable around her. Confused. He wanted to be away from her, not walking down a dark corridor with her.

Olivia shook her head. "I'm fine. I know the way."

But Constanzo said, "Vivi, you will not go upstairs alone. Walking a lady to her room is what a gentleman does."

It *was* what a gentleman did and that reminder corralled Tucker's hormones and got him back to reality. He was a gentleman and she was an employee. Worry that he couldn't keep himself in line was ridiculous.

He set his beer glass on the bar. "Nonsense. You're asleep on your feet. I'll walk you to your room."

They said goodnight to Constanzo who racked the balls again. Walking out of the den, Tucker heard the sound of silence left in their wake. Constanzo had put on the soccer game, and there was noise when he broke the balls on the pool table, but just beneath the surface of those sounds was a quiet nothing. And he suddenly understood why Constanzo wanted his son. When he retired, *this* would be his life. Entertaining an occasional visitor or two would fill the void, but mostly he would be alone. He wanted that "nothing" filled with the sound of his child, and maybe, someday, grandchildren.

"Why do you call me Miss Prentiss?"

They'd reached the end of the hall and were heading for the stairway in the front foyer. Focused on Constanzo, he hadn't noticed how far they'd come. He'd also forgotten about his attraction. But the minute she spoke, his body reacted.

Still, she was an employee and he was a gentleman. He motioned for her to precede him up the stairs. "I call you Miss Prentiss because it's your name."

"So is Olivia. Or Vivi." She stopped and peered back at him. "And I have to admit, sometimes it feels a bit weird having to call you Mr. Engle when everybody else is calling you Tucker."

Just what he and his hormones needed, for another of the barriers between them to come tumbling down. "I'm always on a first name basis with people I do business with. You are an employee."

"An employee who has to call you something different from what everybody else calls you."

He should have been annoyed with her impertinence. Instead, he understood. They were two incredibly attracted people who, in any other circumstance, would be getting to know each other, probably pursuing this attraction. But she was an employee. And he was a gentleman.

He repeated it like a mantra in his head as they walked down the hall. When they reached her door, she stopped and faced him.

"Good night, *Tucker*."

Damn it. He almost laughed. She could be such a smart-ass. Worse, he'd liked the sound of his name on her lips. He liked that she was so bold.

"You're a brat."

"No. I just don't appreciate anyone trying to make me feel less than."

Confused, he stepped closer. "You think that's what I'm doing? Trying to make you feel less than me?"

She shrugged. "Isn't it?"

"No!" All this time he was fighting an attraction to her and she thought he didn't like her? "I'm just trying to keep a sense of dignity for my office. Decorum."

"I don't think it works."

This time he did laugh. "Not with you."

When she didn't reply, the corridor grew quiet. But this quiet was different from what he'd felt as he left Constanzo in the den. This quiet hummed with electricity.

He liked her. He didn't want to like her but he did. And he wanted to kiss her.

He took another step closer. She looked up at him, her blue eyes wide and unsure. Temptation whispered through him. Once, just once, be with somebody who might truly understand. Be honest. Be yourself.

Her eyebrows rose.

Was she asking him to kiss her?

His gaze dropped to her mouth then returned to her eyes. He could imagine the smoothness of her succulent lips, see every move he'd make in his mind's eye. He wouldn't be gentle. She wasn't gentle. She was open, frank, honest. He would kiss her that way.

A second ticked off the clock. Two. Three. He couldn't quite get himself to bend and touch his lips to hers. Not because he didn't want to. But because he so desperately did. An aching need filled his gut, tightened his chest. No one had ever caused feelings like these in him. No one had ever made him want so badly he could see a kiss before it happened.

She whispered, "Good night, Tucker," and turned to grab the doorknob, her fingers trembling.

When she disappeared into her room, a rush of relief swooshed through him. They were wrong for each other. Too different. Nothing would come of them kissing. Especially not a relationship. And without a relationship, a kiss was—unwelcome? Unwarranted? A smart executive wouldn't open himself to the trouble kissing an employee would bring.

Early the next morning, they climbed into one of Constanzo's cars and headed even farther into the hills. Tucker set the GPS on his phone to Italian and Vivi's mouth dropped.

"You speak Italian?"

He risked a sidelong glance. This morning she wore scruffy jeans that caressed her perfect behind and a pink casual top that brought out the best in her skin tones. After the near-miss with kissing her the night before, his body reacted as if he had a right to be interested, attracted, aroused by her innocent, girl-next-door sexiness.

He told his body to settle down. Yes, she was attractive and, yes, he was interested in her, but only sexually. In every other way they didn't mesh. She had to be off-limits. "You *don't* speak Italian?"

"No."

Yet another thing added to the pile of reasons his attraction to her was ridiculous. "Well, don't worry. Constanzo said his son was raised in the U.S., remember?"

Wind blew in through her open window and tossed strands of her hair across her face. Pulling them away, she asked, "Have you figured out what you're going to say to him?"

"I'm going to flat out tell him who he is."

She gaped at him. "I think that's a mistake!"

And here was the real reason he wouldn't kiss her, knew they'd never have a relationship, knew the taste of her lips that he longed for would only get him into trouble. If he wanted one route, she always wanted another. If that wasn't proof his attraction to her was pointless, he didn't know what was.

"I don't think it's a mistake. If my father had found me, that's how I would want to be told. Up front and honest. I might be angry at first, but eventually I would mellow."

"That just sounds wrong to me."

"Of course it does."

"What if Constanzo's son's not like you? What if he's shy? Or quiet? Artistic types, as Constanzo's file says his son is, aren't like businessmen."

"Oh, and you know a lot about this?"

She shrugged. "I know some. Everybody knows artists aren't like businessmen. Otherwise, they'd be businessmen. They wouldn't be artists."

"Well, if he's a shy starving artist who wears his heart on his sleeve, kick my shin and take over the conversation."

"Me?"

"Hey, Constanzo wanted you here. Maybe this is why." Which was the reason he couldn't put her on his plane and send her back to the accounting department in the Inferno corporate offices in New York. Constanzo might pretend to be an easygoing, open book, but like any clever businessman he had his secrets, his ways of reading people. He'd seen something in Olivia that made him want her here. Tucker wouldn't argue that. He'd use it.

She sighed and eased herself back to her seat. "I agree about kicking your shin, but if I do, you should just shift gears."

"Let me assure you, Miss Prentiss—" he paused and

sighed "—*Vivi*, if you kick my shin, you had better have a plan."

The rest of the drive passed in silence until an isolated farmhouse came into view. Not renovated as Constanzo's had been, Antonio's run-down house had seen better days. The manicured grounds of Constanzo's estate were replaced by fields teaming with tall grass and wildflowers.

"Obviously, the guy doesn't own a lawn mower."

"Or he likes nature."

Tucker sniffed a laugh.

"What would you rather paint? A mowed lawn or a field of wildflowers against a blue, blue sky."

Cutting the engine, Tucker rolled his eyes and shoved open his door. Vivi quickly followed suit. Behind Tucker, she picked her way up the loose stone walk. When they reached the door, he knocked three times in rapid succession.

Inhaling a big breath of fresh air, he glanced around. It really was quiet, peaceful, beautiful. He supposed he could understand why an artist would choose to live here. Especially if he'd come to Italy to get to know his mother's country, to meet his extended family, and still have privacy.

The wooden door swung open. A man about as tall as Constanzo, wearing jeans and no shirt stood before them. "Yeah?"

"I'm Tucker Engle and this is my assistant, Olivia Prentiss."

Vivi reached forward and extended her hand. "It's nice to meet you. You can call me Vivi."

The man cautiously took her hand, his dark eyes narrowing.

"Are you Antonio Signorelli?"

"Yes. Who are you?"

Tucker said, "Can we come in a minute?"

He started closing the door. "Actually, I'm very busy. And I don't have time for sales people."

Wedging his shoe between the door and its frame, Tucker laughed. "We're not sales people. We're here representing—"

Olivia kicked him in the shin. He yelped and jumped back.

She smiled sweetly at Antonio. "We're representing a private collector who's interested in sponsoring a showing of the artwork of someone new and fresh."

Antonio visibly relaxed. "Really?"

"Look how he's dressed?" She angled her thumb at Tucker and he glanced down at his suit coat and green tie. Sure he was a bit overdressed for the country. But he was a businessman not a hippie.

"I'm okay." She rolled her eyes dramatically. "But he's obviously not a tourist and his clothes are too expensive for him to be a salesman. As I said, we represent a private collector."

"And you want to show *my* work?"

Vivi stepped forward. "Well, we haven't seen your work. Our client is an art patron, but he's not a sap. Your work would have to meet certain standards." She smiled. "We'd love to see it."

As they waited for Antonio to take Vivi's hint and let them in, Tucker scowled. She'd made fun of *his* clothes? Antonio had no shirt. Bare feet. Jeans that hung low on his hips. Sheesh. With his black curly hair tousled, the guy was a walking cologne ad. At least Tucker was fully covered.

Finally, Antonio opened the door wide enough for them to enter. "The place is a mess."

Vivi put her hand on his forearm. "We're not here to see the place. We're here to see your work." She glanced around. "I understand your primary venue is painting."

"Yes."

They entered a house desperately in need of updating. Lines in the plaster and a cracked window were the high-lights of the room Antonio led them to. A half-finished painting sat on an easel. But many canvases leaned against the back wall.

The paintings lured Tucker into the room. Vivid colors and stark images dominated. He turned his head slightly and caught Antonio's gaze.

"You have a unique way of looking at the world."

Antonio laughed. "I had a unique upbringing."

Tucker swung his gaze to Olivia. If ever there was an opening to tell him about his father, this was it. But she quickly shook her head.

He sucked back a sigh. She had better know what she was doing.

She turned to Antonio with a smile. "What was unique about your upbringing?"

He shrugged, walked to the stack of paintings where Tucker stood and flipped the first away from the second. "My mom died when I was young." He took painting one and slid it aside so Tucker could more clearly see painting two. "I was raised in foster care."

"So was I." This time he didn't look to Olivia for con-sent. This was Business Conversation 101. Identify with your client and have them identify with you. "Someone left me in a church." He focused attention on the painting Antonio had bared for him. It was the proverbial field of wildflowers Vivi had talked about. Antonio had painted his backyard and it was stunning. He could almost feel the warmth of the sun, smell the flowers.

Antonio removed painting two, displaying painting three.

Olivia said, "So tell us more about yourself."

"As I said, my mom died." He slid it aside and stood beside Tucker again, patient, as if he'd had others view his work before and knew the drill. "I don't know who my father is. But my mom was from around here. When I got old enough and had saved a few bucks, I came here to meet my relatives." He laughed lightly. "And with landscapes like this to paint, you can see why I never left."

Tucker reverently said, "I can."

Olivia hung back. She didn't have an artist's eye, but she knew the paintings were good. Tucker, on the other hand, clearly thought they were magnificent. But it didn't matter. Her brain had stalled on his quiet statement that he'd been left at a church, didn't know his parents. Her heart broke a little bit picturing a tiny baby, wrapped in a blue blanket, alone for God knows how long in an empty church that had probably echoed with his cries.

But she forced herself to think about business. They'd opened a door for discussions about his parentage and one for displaying his work in a showing. She didn't want to push too hard, too fast. It was time to go.

She stepped forward. "Mr. Engle will give you his cell phone number." She smiled at Antonio, then Tucker. "And you can give us yours." Antonio quickly tore a sheet from a drawing pad and scribbled his number before he handed it to Tucker. He tore off another sheet and offered it to Tucker to write his number too.

Instead Vivi's boss pulled a business card from his jacket pocket.

"You'll be hearing from us."

Antonio beamed. "Great."

The second they were in the car, Tucker turned on her. "What the hell was that all about? We could have stayed there for hours, asked a million questions. He loved us. He'd have done anything we wanted."

"We're supposed to be scouting, not hiring him on the spot. I wanted this to look real."

"There were at least three chances for us to have 'the' real conversation. I could have easily told him who he was."

"And he could have easily turned on us. He's proud of his work. You seemed to agree with his assessment that it's very good. We'll go back to Constanzo's, tell him my plan, see if he likes it. If he does, we ease into Antonio's life over the next few days and ease Constanzo into the art show plan. When the moment is right, we'll tell him."

"Do you know how many ways that could go wrong?"

"Yes. But I also know that if we do it my way, give them a little time together before we drop the bomb, even if he freaks and heads for the hills, he'll still know his dad and when he calms down he could come back."

Tucker started the car. "You'd better be right."

"I may not be."

He gaped at her.

"But I think my plan is better than just dropping him in a pot of boiling water." She peeked over at him. "You know the rule about cooking a live frog don't you?"

His eyes narrowed.

"You put him in warm water, water he's comfortable with and turn up the heat so gradually he doesn't even realize the water is boiling until it's too late."

He shook his head, but didn't argue.

Vivi relaxed. "So, how did you learn about art? Anything looks good to me. I mean, it was clear Antonio's work was good, but I couldn't tell you if it was exceptional. Yet you knew it was."

"It's in the eye of the beholder. If the technique is good, you just check your gut…did it touch you, say something?"

"And what did his work say to you?"

Tucker turned onto the country road again, heading back to Constanzo's. Seconds ticked off the clock. Then a minute. Vivi wondered if he was going to reply to her question.

Just as she was about to ask again, he sighed. "His work tells me that he sees beauty even in an ugly world."

"He thinks the world is ugly?"

"He *knows* the world is ugly. He was raised as a foster kid, remember? Even the foster parents who loved him probably gave him up from time to time, depending upon their own conditions. A foster dad can need heart surgery or a knee replacement. Sometimes they just can't keep you. When he turned eighteen, government help ended. And it's possible he might have suddenly found himself out on the street."

He spoke with such confidence, such surety, that her heart melted a bit. She pictured the baby in the blue blanket, crying in the church again. "I'm guessing some of that happened to you."

He sighed. "I'm not special and I'm not crazily depressed. Things like that happen to a lot of kids. Growing up as a foster kid isn't easy."

"But you made something of yourself."

"Yes, I did."

"And you still think the world is ugly?"

"I think the world is hard, not a sweet soft place like you do."

She gasped. "Are you calling me a Pollyanna? I'm not a Pollyanna!"

He sniffed a laugh. "Right."

"There are things in my past, too."

"Uh-huh. The law suit."

Her chin lifted. "It was humiliating."

"And I'm sure it probably scared you. But I also know the kid dropped his suit. And I'm pretty sure your two parents cuddled you the whole way through it."

"Well, you snob!"

His mouth fell open. "Snob?"

"Do you think everybody with parents had it easy?"

"Certainly easier than those of us who didn't have parents."

"Parents can't fix everything."

"And what happened to poor Miss Vivi that couldn't be fixed? Boyfriend break your heart?"

"My boyfriend turned out to be nothing like everybody thought he was."

"So you called him evil names, his parents sued and you ended up the bad girl."

"Leave it alone."

He sucked in a breath, suddenly so curious he couldn't stop himself. All along he'd recognized there was something about her, something different, something important. And he *knew* it had something to do with that lawsuit. Yet she wouldn't tell him. She pushed and pushed and pushed to hear everything about his life. And he'd coughed up one fact after another. Yet here she was refusing to tell him something he could probably find for himself.

"I could look it up."

She blanched. "Don't. This is painful for me, as painful as your past is to you."

He pulled the car to the side of the road and cut the engine. "Seriously? You have some kind of teenage Romeo and Juliet thing happen to you and think you can compare it to being left in a church? Abandoned? Raised by people who only took care of you because the state gave them money?"

She licked her lips.

"Come on. You started this. You ask me questions all the time. Now I'm pushing you. What the hell did this kid do that was so bad you had to try to ruin his reputation and force his parents to sue you?"

She glanced down at her hands. "He attacked me. He would have raped me if I hadn't been able to get away."

Tucker froze for three seconds before regret poured

through him like hot maple syrup. "Oh, my God. He attacked you?"

"And the thing I did that was so bad that his parents sued? I tried to have him prosecuted."

He'd never felt this combination of remorse and fury before, and had no idea how to deal with it. For every bit as much as he wished he could take back his angry words, he also wanted to punch the kid who'd hurt her. "I'm so sorry."

"We were dating. Everybody assumed we were doing it. After all, he was the star quarterback on the local college football team. Handsome. Wealthy. Every girl in town wanted to date him and he picked me."

"You don't have to go on."

She pulled herself together. Right before his eyes she went from being weak and vulnerable, to being Vivi. His sassy assistant. "Oh, why not? After all, you can look it up."

Regret slithered through him. "I didn't mean it. I'm sorry that I pushed."

"You wanted to know. Now you know."

And he suddenly got it. Her impertinence, her sassiness was a defense mechanism. She'd rather be bossy, pushy, than weak.

Right now, to make up for his stupidity, all he had to do was give her that. Deal with her bossiness, her sassiness rather than her pain.

"Whatever." It physically hurt to downplay her experience, but he knew that's what she wanted. She'd rather be sassy than weak. "You'd just better be sure you're right about Antonio."

"I'm right."

"And you're the one explaining this to Constanzo."

She straightened her shoulders. "I have no problem with that."

"Fine."

"Fine."

The determination in her voice should have heartened him, but he kept picturing her at nineteen, innocent, trusting…and some kid, some smart-assed small-town bully with parents who thought he could do no wrong… accosting her.

It was everything he could do not to beat his hand against his steering wheel.

Especially since he was the one who'd brought up those memories for her.

CHAPTER SEVEN

CONSTANZO MET THEM at the door of his lavish home. "So?"

"So, we met your son."

After their conversation in the car, Vivi was abundantly glad Tucker was a workaholic who thought of nothing but his business. Any day of the week, she'd rather think about work than her past. He didn't care that he'd ripped open old wounds. He didn't care that her nerves were shattered, her brain was numb. He'd pushed for answers and he'd gotten them. Then he'd moved on, leaving her to deal with the repercussions.

Yet another reason to ignore the attraction that hummed between them.

Constanzo motioned for them to follow him back down the hall. "You met my son and—?"

"And he's a gifted artist. Your friend *Vivi* made up a story about you wanting to do a showing for a promising artist and he was one of the people we were checking out. He ate it up like candy on a spoon."

As they reached a living room with soft white sofas, modern-print area rugs, a stunning stone fireplace and a wall of windows that displayed the pool, Constanzo faced her. "Is this so?"

She winced. As if it wasn't bad enough she'd just told the guy she had feelings for about the most horrific thing ever to happen to her, and he hadn't shown her one ounce of compassion, now he'd fed her to the lions.

"I just felt he would need time to get to know you before we dropped the bomb that you're his dad. We can bring him here every day to look at your house and figure out how he'd like to show his paintings here—"

Constanzo shook his head. "No. No. If we do this, we do it right. We rent a gallery with a curator who will do a real showing." He glanced at Tucker. "His work is good enough for this?"

"His work is amazing."

When a gleam of happiness came to Constanzo's eyes, Vivi's heart stopped. She forgot all about her discussion with Tucker in the car. She forgot her worries that she'd handled everything badly. She just saw that gleam.

"You, Vivi, are every bit as bright as I believed you were."

Tucker snorted a laugh as Constanzo walked to the bar. "You disagree with her plan?"

He shrugged. "I'm cautiously optimistic because I want this to work. But I would have just told him."

Constanzo reached for a bottle of Scotch. "I like Vivi's way better." He pulled out three glasses and poured. "So when do I meet him?"

Filled with euphoria that felt a lot like walking on air, she happily said, "Whenever you want."

Handing a glass to Vivi and then Tucker, he said, "I think I would like tomorrow."

Tucker said, "Whoa, Constanzo. We have a lot of work to do first."

"Such as?"

"Getting the gallery for one," Vivi reminded him.

"I have friends and money. I'll have a place for you tomorrow."

Vivi smiled. "Then as soon as the curator is ready for a

trip to Antonio's that's when we'll go. But, remember, you can't tell him you're his dad."

"Not even if things are going well?"

"He needs to get to know you." She pulled her lower lip between her teeth. "And, honestly, Mr. B., I think you need to get to know him, too. You're a wealthy man and he's very poor. What if he's a hustler?"

Constanzo's lips turned down. "You think my own son would cheat me." He waved his hands. "Of course, he might. We don't really know who he is."

"Exactly. That's why I figured it was best to keep who you are a secret until you know each other better."

Constanzo pulled out his cell phone. "We will start tomorrow."

Twenty minutes later Constanzo had a gallery booked and the owner coming to his house the following morning. They toasted with Scotch, which Vivi hated, had lunch, then played pool until it was time to dress for dinner.

Vivi had never seen anyone as happy or animated as Constanzo was that day. But after an afternoon of sipping Scotch, he drank a little too much wine at dinner and left the table early.

Alone with Tucker in the silent dining room, their discussion in the car came tumbling back to her. But a funny thing happened. Before those thoughts could take root— thoughts of Cord and the shame and humiliation of being attacked then sued and bullied when she'd done nothing wrong—she remembered the happiness in Constanzo's eyes. And she felt strong again. Yes, she was disappointed in Tucker pushing her then behaving as if her pain was inconsequential, but that just pointed out what she'd always realized. They weren't good for each other.

As if confirming that, she and Tucker ate their dessert in near silence. She was abundantly glad when her last bite of cobbler was finished and she could excuse herself.

She headed toward the stairs and her bedroom, but she wasn't tired.

She didn't really know what she was. Part of her was excited about Antonio and her plan. The other part was really disappointed in Tucker. But her mind no longer automatically jumped to Cord. What he would think. How he would feel about her success. It was like all of that no longer mattered. And that confused her even more.

Maybe she just needed some fresh air?

She turned from the stairs and walked toward the big formal living room with access to the pool. A few lights broke up the darkness and created sporadic twinkles on the blue water, but the area itself wasn't lit. Using her memory of the patio, she found her way to the nearest chaise, sat and stretched out.

"Nice night to just sit outside and look at the stars."

She almost jumped out of her skin. "Tucker! For the love of God! You couldn't have given me a warning you were already out here?"

"That was the purpose of my comment."

She could barely make out his long legs on the chaise, though his shiny black shoes picked up a bit of the light from the well-spaced fixtures around the patio. His white shirt was a lot easier to see. When her gaze reached his face, he smiled.

"You did a good job today."

She sniffed in disdain. "I thought you didn't like my idea."

"I don't. I'd rather bulldoze this thing and get it done. But Constanzo likes your plan and he's the client, the one we have to please." He toasted her with a drink he must have brought from their dinner table. "And you pleased him."

Syrupy warmth filled her and she relaxed a bit on the chaise. It was really difficult to stay disappointed in a guy who seemed genuinely pleased with her work that day. And maybe how she felt about him didn't matter? It wasn't like they were friends. They were boss and employee.

Plus, bright white stars twinkled overhead. A breeze chilled the night air. She didn't want to go inside yet.

"My only concern is that he's too happy. You do know how easily this plan could backfire."

She frowned. "I can think of about three ways. First, Antonio could dislike Constanzo."

"Constanzo could dislike Antonio."

"Or Constanzo could adore his son—"

"Who might be furious when he learns Constanzo is the father who abandoned him."

She studied the stars. "But he didn't really abandon him. If you listen to the story, Antonio's mother gave up after one measly attempt to contact him."

Tucker chuckled. "Miss Prentiss, I don't think I need to remind you of a little thing called pride."

Her face scrunched in confusion as she considered that. Finally, she said, "So you're saying Antonio's mother got her feelings hurt so she kept Constanzo's son from him?"

"Exactly."

"Sounds petty."

"Really?" He rolled onto his side. "What if you, poor as you are right now, got pregnant by a man with billions of dollars? A man so far out of your stratosphere that even if he believed your baby was his, he'd question your motives. He'd make you feel cheap and like a gold digger who'd deliberately gotten pregnant for money."

Her face heated. He could be describing the two of them. He was rich. She was poor. And the implications of what he said brought her to her senses very quickly. Forget about his pushing her in the car that day. *This* was why she'd stay away from him, why she should have stayed away from Cord. He hadn't needed to be insensitive with her that morning. Women with no money, no social status, always got burned when they got involved with wealthy men. She'd learned that lesson the hard way and she wouldn't forget it.

"I don't have to worry about that."

"Really?"

"Come on, *Tucker*," she said, deliberately using his first name because, as with the conversation in the car, he was pushing her buttons again. "I know my place. Billionaires can have their pick of women. They don't go for the dirt-poor, average-looking waifs. They go after the beauties."

He laughed. "Really? You're gonna toss that at me?"

"Toss what?"

"An underestimation of your self-worth."

She blew out a laugh. "I know who I am and what I look like."

"You seriously don't think you're beautiful?"

"Beautiful?" She laughed. "I'll give you pretty. But only when I wear makeup. Which I don't."

"You don't need it."

She laughed gaily at the stupidity of this conversation. Though they were talking about her, it was much better than worry over Constanzo and Antonio or speculating about Antonio's mom. "According to Maria Bartulocci I do."

"Maria was very clearly angling that day. She wanted my attention and she wanted a commission for getting me close to Constanzo. If she put you down, it was to make sure she didn't have competition."

"Competition?" She snorted. "Maria knows she's a beautiful woman."

"You think?"

"You don't?"

He shook his head.

Her eyes widened. "You seriously don't think she's beautiful?"

He snorted. "How would I know? Underneath all that makeup she could have the face of a howler monkey."

"Howler monkey?" Vivi gaped at him. "That was mean!"

"No. That was honest."

She heard the sound of him shuffling on his seat and turned to see he'd sat up and was facing her.

"What I did to you this morning…pushing you to talk when you didn't want to…that was mean."

She was glad for the darkness so he couldn't see the pleasure that came to her face at his apology. Just as at the Jason Jones signing, his behavior proved he wasn't such a bad guy after all. "You didn't know."

"No. I didn't, but I should have suspected something serious had happened from the law suit. You wouldn't have just called somebody a name on the street or harassed someone. You're not a flippant girl, Olivia."

Her heart stuttered, filled with warmth. Not only did he believe her, but no one ever called her Olivia. No one. The way her name came off his lips was sensual, mesmerizing.

"You try to be flippant. You use your sassing as a way to make people think you're in control. Then you turn around and ask a million questions, proving you're not."

Good Lord. No wonder he was rich. He saw right through a strategy that had worked for years. She wasn't sure if she was pleased or frightened.

"There's nothing wrong with asking questions. It's a good idea to try to get a handle on what's going on when you're confused. But you really should ditch the sassing."

She laughed, but kept her gaze averted.

He caught her chin and forced her to look at him. "I am sorry about this morning."

The smoothness of his fingers against her skin nearly made her shiver. And his eyes—those striking green eyes that saw everything—held her prisoner. Her heart trembled with longing. She hadn't even kissed a guy in years and she desperately wanted him to kiss her. A short, sweet, simple kiss...or a kiss filled with passion and honesty. She didn't care. She just wanted a kiss.

But that was wrong. As she'd begun recovering from Cord, she'd promised herself that she'd never again put herself in the position of being with a man so far beyond her socially. And she'd meant it.

So it was best to let him off the hook about pushing her and return them to their normal relationship. "It's okay."

He sighed and rose from his chaise. "No. It's not."

"Yeah. It is." She rose. too. "You see, when we got back to Constanzo's and we started talking about his son, all those emotions you had dredged up were eclipsed by the feeling of pride I had over doing a good job with Antonio."

He stopped a few feet short of the pool and faced her. "So you're okay?"

She shrugged. "I've been okay for a while. But it felt different—better—that I could totally forget it once we started talking about work."

"So demanding answers from you was a good thing?"

She laughed. "Don't push your luck."

Somehow they'd ended up standing face-to-face again. Under the luxurious blanket of stars, next to the twinkling blue water, the only sound the slight hum of the filter for the pool.

He reached out and cupped the side of her face. "You are a brave, funny woman, Miss Prentiss."

Though she knew it was dangerous to get too personal with him, especially since his nearness already had her heart thrumming and her knees weak, she was only human. And even if it was a teeny tiny inconsequential thing, she didn't want to give up the one innocent pleasure she was allowed to get from him.

She caught his gaze. "Olivia."

"Excuse me?"

"I like it when you call me Olivia."

He took a step closer. "Really?"

She shrugged, trying to make light of her request. "Everybody calls me Vivi. Sometimes it makes me feel six again. Being called Olivia makes me feel like an adult."

"Or a woman."

The way he said *woman* sent heat rushing through her. Once again, he'd seen right through her ploy and might even realize she was attracted to him—

Oh, who was she kidding? He *knew* she was attracted to him. After the episode playing pool the night before, neither one of them could be coy anymore.

Even as yearning nudged her to be bold, reality intruded. The guy she finally, finally wanted to trust was rich, sophisticated and so far out of her league she was lucky to be working for him. She knew better than to get romantically involved with someone like him.

She stepped back. "I wouldn't go that far."

He caught her hand and tugged her to him. "I would." He kissed her so quickly that her knees nearly buckled and her brain reeled. She could have panicked. Could have told him to go slow because she hadn't done this in a while, or even stop because this was wrong. But nobody, no kiss, had ever made her feel the warm, wonderful, scary sensations saturating her entire being right now. Not just her body, but her soul.

His lips moved over hers smoothly, expertly, shooting fire and ice down her spine. Her breath froze in her chest. Then he opened his mouth over hers and her lips automatically parted.

The fire and ice shooting down her spine exploded in her middle, reminding her of where this would go if she didn't stop him. Now. Just as Antonio's mom had been, she was poor. Very far out of Tucker's league. It was foolish to even consider kissing him.

She jerked away, stepped back. His glistening green

eyes had narrowed with confusion. He didn't understand why she'd stopped him.

Longing warred with truth. If he could pretend their stations in life didn't matter, she could pretend, too. Couldn't she?

No!

She'd done this before. She was a small-town girl and he was a man of wealth and power. She might be nothing more to him than a conquest. She was too wounded, too cautious to take the risk that someone like him could be serious about someone like her.

She took another step back. "Well, okay then. I guess I'll see you at breakfast."

It was the stupidest, most inane thing she could have said but she took pride in having any voice at all as she turned and raced to her room. She closed the door and leaned against it. She hadn't even kissed a man in years, but in another thirty seconds, she would have willingly let him take her. A man she barely knew. A man with whom she had nothing in common. A man who might only want sex from her. Hell, she wasn't even sure he liked her. Yes, he was attracted to her, but it never really seemed that he liked her.

And her feelings for him? Well, they were getting out of control and she had no idea how to stop them.

CHAPTER EIGHT

THE NEXT MORNING, the full idiocy of what she had said—
and done, she couldn't forget she'd run from the patio—hit
her, and when she went downstairs for breakfast she had to
steady herself outside the dining room door.

She ran her damp palms down the skirt of her second
sundress, grateful to have her favorite dress to wear for
confidence. But that didn't help much now that she was two
seconds away from seeing the man she'd kissed last night,
the man she was growing to like, even though it was wrong.

She didn't know how to stop any of this. Her fears after
being attacked had robbed her of the normal dating experi-
ences most women had. Though those fears were subsiding
and Tucker was making her long for things most women
took for granted, she knew—absolutely knew—she was
going to get hurt.

Still, she had to go in. If she didn't, it would only make
things worse. With a deep breath, she held her head high
and stepped into the dining room to find Constanzo and
Tucker reading the paper.

Constanzo rose. "Sweet Vivi, good morning."

He pulled out her chair and helped her sit. When he returned to his seat, Tucker looked up from the newspaper.

"Good morning...*Olivia*."

Her blood rushed hot through her veins again, but she
refused to be embarrassed or even think through what it

might mean. Had he taken her request to heart that she liked to be called by her first name? Or was he taunting her? Reminding her of a kiss that had warmed her blood and made her feel like a woman just as he'd suggested the night before.

Constanzo's maid brought a woman who looked to be about thirty into the dining room. Wearing a suit that had to be handmade and carrying a Gucci bag, she could have given Maria Bartulocci a run for her money.

Constanzo jumped up again. "Patrice!" He caught her hands and kissed both of her cheeks. "Tucker, Vivi, this is Patrice Russo."

After shaking both their hands, she said something to Constanzo in Italian. Constanzo smiled. "Tucker speaks Italian. Vivi, no."

"Then we speak English."

Constanzo pulled out a chair for Patrice. "Would you like breakfast?"

"Just coffee." She smiled at Vivi. "So you are my contact."

"Actually, Mr. Engle is in charge of the project." She glanced at him briefly, long enough to see his eyes narrow as she spoke. Embarrassment flared. Why couldn't she have thought of something suave, something sophisticated to say before she'd ran from him and his earth-shattering kiss? Why couldn't she have sashayed into the house as if the kiss had meant nothing?

Taking his seat, Constanzo laughed. "She is modest, our Vivi. This is her plan."

Vivi's gaze shot to Tucker again. He turned his attention to his breakfast. "It is her plan. And Antonio seems to respond to her. She *should* be your contact."

A serving girl poured coffee for Patrice, and Vivi explained her idea. Patrice very quickly outlined the process of bringing an artist's work to a gallery for a showing.

"The very least amount of time we'd need would be two weeks. But I'd suggest a month. We'll spend the first week ironing out the details of our agreement and then I'll take three weeks to choose paintings and get things set up."

"Sounds great."

After finishing breakfast, they wasted no time. Constanzo called for a limo to be brought out front. Vivi and Patrice entered first. Constanzo slid in and sat beside Patrice. Tucker automatically sat beside Vivi. No hesitation. No comment. No complaint.

Knowing it would look childish to slide as far away from him as she could, she stayed where she was, but it was torture. The vague scent of him brought back memories of that kiss. Worse, she had no idea what he was thinking. Had he even liked kissing her? Did he think she was an idiot?

Probably.

When Antonio answered the door, Patrice took over, stepping forward and shaking his hand. "Antonio! It's wonderful to meet you. Mr. Engle and his assistant, Miss Prentiss, raved about your work and we knew we had our artist for the showing Mr. Bartulocci wants to do." She stopped talking, turned to Constanzo and brought him forward. "This is Constanzo Bartulocci. He is your benefactor for the show we'd like to put together."

Tears filled Constanzo's eyes and Vivi blinked back a few of her own. He was meeting his child, his *son,* the person who should be heir to everything he owned. The person who should be filling his quiet life with noise and love and laughter.

Antonio held out his hand. "It's a pleasure to meet you."

Composing himself, Constanzo shook his hand. "It's good to meet you, too." He pulled in a quick breath and smiled. "So where are these remarkable paintings?"

Antonio laughed. "I don't know about remarkable."

Tucker said, "Antonio, this is no time for modesty. Hundreds of people will come to your showing expecting a man confident about what he's done. Confident that he's made a statement. You need to be that guy."

Antonio laughed again and Vivi, Tucker, Constanzo and Patrice followed him into the room he referred to as his painting room.

Patrice looked at the pictures then glanced at Tucker. "You're right. They're splendid."

Relief wove through her voice, but Vivi's nerve endings crackled anyway. Maria Bartulocci definitely wasn't Tucker's type but pretty, stylish, educated blonde and beautiful Patrice? Tucker belonged with somebody like her.

She drew in a quiet breath and told herself not to care as she walked over to Antonio. Tucker and Patrice lost themselves in discussions about his paintings and Antonio looked a bit like he was going to throw up.

"First time having anybody see your work?"

"No. I had a lot of interest in New York, but nothing ever panned out."

Constanzo put his hand on Antonio's shoulder. "This will pan out. We'll do the showing. People will love your paintings. This time next month, you could be famous."

"I don't want to be famous. I want to paint...and eat." He laughed nervously.

Constanzo frowned. "Don't you want people to enjoy what you've done?"

"Yes."

Like a father, Constanzo softly said, "Then this is all good."

Vivi said, "You'll be fine. You'll simply have to figure out how to strike a balance between fame and a private life. Lots of people do it."

"Thanks."

They spent another hour looking at the paintings and talking with Antonio. Before they left, Patrice gave him

her card and told him to be at her office the following day
to sign papers. Constanzo explained that because he was
footing the bill for the showing, Antonio would get every
cent paid for any of his paintings, minus the commission
for Patrice's gallery. But there was still a need for a formal agreement.

As a precaution, Tucker had Patrice email the agreements for him to peruse that night. They arrived in his
in-box right at dinnertime, but Tucker told Constanzo he
wasn't hungry anyway. He stayed in his room all night, and
Vivi was sure he thought her so much of a ninny he didn't
even want to be in the same room if possible.

But he came to breakfast the next morning and seated
himself. "You've given your son quite a good deal."

Constanzo laughed. "Of course, I have."

Vivi relaxed. "So, we're paving the way for you to tell
your son who you are."

"I don't think we're quite ready for that yet."

Her gaze shot up and over to Tucker. But Constanzo
laughed. "You've switched sides." He pointed at Vivi. "First
you wanted to hold back and he wanted to tell." He faced
Tucker. "Now you want to hold back and she wants to tell."

"Whatever Olivia wants is fine."

She quickly looked away. "Since we started off slowly
maybe we should continue to move slowly." But when she
risked a peek at Tucker a few minutes later, he was still
watching her, studying her.

After breakfast they took the limo to retrieve Antonio
then drove along twisting country roads to Bordighera.
Cobblestone streets and walkways took them to Patrice's
villa gallery. As they drove, Constanzo pointed out the
villa of a British royal, the sites Monet had painted and the
homes of two novelists.

When they stepped out of the limo, the June sun washed

them in warmth. The sound of the surf caused Vivi to turn and see the ocean.

"It's beautiful."

Antonio said, "Now you can see why I decided to stay."

She laughed and nodded, as Patrice opened the front door of her villa and welcomed them inside.

Vivi glanced around in awe. Rich red Oriental rugs accented the white marble beneath them. White drapes billowed to the floor. Chandeliers were everywhere. Eight or ten paintings hung on each wall. Antique tables held small sculptures and blown glass.

"I can't imagine living here."

"I don't," Patrice said, leading them to a stairway and her office. "Well, technically, I do since I have an apartment on the third floor. But I always thought this villa too beautiful to keep to myself." She smiled at Vivi. "I made it a gallery so I can share it."

They signed the agreements in Patrice's office—a warm, welcoming space, different than the formal rooms of the gallery. Right from the beginning, working for Tucker Engle had been eye-opening, and coming to Italy would probably top her list of favorite things she had done in her lifetime. But standing in a gallery, surrounded by paintings and sculptures, blown glass and jewelry so perfect it had to be displayed as art, was surreal.

Oddly, she felt she belonged here. As if she had come home.

Antonio, Constanzo and Patrice shook hands. Patrice made arrangements to go to Antonio's house the next day to begin selecting paintings. Constanzo suggested dinner at his home to celebrate and though Patrice declined, Antonio happily accepted.

They played pool. Ate dinner outside. Drank Scotch.

And the whole time Tucker watched her.

It made an otherwise enjoyable evening nerve-rack-ing. As early as politely possible, she excused herself and headed for her room. She showered and almost slid into her pajamas but it was still too early to sleep. Knowing the men would spend hours playing games in the den, she put on jeans and a T-shirt and headed for the pool.

This time she saw Tucker standing by the sparkling water before she turned the doorknob to go outside. Boldness surged through her. He'd badgered her until she'd told him about Cord. He'd held her feet to the fire, forcing her to take charge of the Antonio project since they were using her idea. And he'd kissed her.

Then today he'd stared at her all day as if she were some sort of bug under a microscope.

Half of her wanted to go out and brag. Her idea might not have seemed like a good one to him, but he had trusted her with it and it was working. *Her* idea was working. She was not going to fail.

The other half wanted to go out and…well, brag too. But in a sharing way. She wanted to say, "Look what we're doing! Look what we're accomplishing! We're bringing together a lonely dad and his son. Even though we don't seem like we belong together, we are a good team."

But that was actually the point. If she went out there and they celebrated their success, weren't they tempting fate?

He might like her but he didn't want to. Hell, he wasn't even really sure he wanted her as an assistant. Forget about anything else. And she knew the dangers of getting too close to someone so far out of her league.

She took one last longing look at him, standing by the pool, looking as if he might be waiting for her—

She turned and went back to her room.

CHAPTER NINE

THE NEXT DAY they returned to Antonio's with Patrice. As he had the day before, Tucker watched Vivi happily help Antonio as he worked with Patrice, an odd feeling in his gut. When he looked at her and Antonio, he saw a couple. When he thought of himself and Olivia together, he saw a disaster.

So why—two days later—did the memory of her breathy request to call her Olivia still fill him with a yearning so primal, so hot, that he wanted to do more than kiss her?

He had no idea. But sharp need pressed in on him. Something about her appealed to him on an elemental level he'd never experienced before. And maybe it was time he stopped denying it?

Patrice began examining paintings, setting two side by side, and a minute later sending one to a group on the right and the other to a group on the left. A process that Tucker would have thought would take days seemed to be taking minutes.

Finally, she sighed. "Here's the deal. I like them all. I can put almost half of these in the downstairs of my gallery, but if I open the second floor I could double that number."

Though Tucker thought that was wonderful news, anxiety flitted through Antonio's eyes.

Constanzo apparently didn't notice. His face beamed with pride. "And we will invite everybody. I have ordered my personal assistant to begin a list. I'll have a thousand people at that showing."

This time Antonio looked like he would faint. Olivia caught his arm. "Hey, this is your showing. If you don't want a thousand people, just tell us what you do want."

Tucker frowned. Interesting that she wasn't nervous around Antonio. Only around him. No. Strike that. She wasn't nervous around him either. Except when they were close. Or getting personal. Then she got antsy.

He knew the feeling. Once he'd gotten through puberty no woman had made him nervous or confused. Yet with her everything was weird. Different. Confusing.

Antonio took a breath. "I'd like the doors to be opened and people to come in off the street." He glanced at Vivi. "Because they want to come in. Not because they're invited."

Patrice smiled patiently. "But you also need to advertise. Send out invitations at least for the opening night."

Olivia said, "How about this? We'll send out invitations for the opening. That will let Mr. Bartulocci's friends know he's sponsoring a showing. We'll get RSVPs for the actual opening night and invite the rest to stop by while your pieces are on display."

Pride stirred within Tucker. Once again she saw what everybody else seemed to miss. While Patrice thought about making money and Constanzo had found a way to introduce his son to the world, Olivia watched the star and knew he was falling.

Antonio sucked in a breath. "That sounds a little more doable."

"The goal of your show is to sell your paintings," Patrice reminded him.

"And our goal," Constanzo quietly countered, finally seeing what Vivi had noticed all along, "wasn't to make money but to introduce a wonderful new talent. That's why I'm paying for everything. There's no chance of a loss for you."

Patrice smiled woodenly. "Of course."

Antonio hugged Vivi. "Thanks."

Her face reddened, but her eyes danced with pleasure. Still, she didn't get the look—the look she'd gotten when she'd asked him to call her Olivia. The look that still filled his blood with lust every time he thought of it.

She might like Antonio but she wasn't interested in him. Not the way she was interested in Tucker.

Constanzo chatted through the entire limo ride. But when they got to his house, his maid approached him with a message. He read it then excused himself to make a call. Olivia went to her room. Tucker ambled back to the den, poured himself a draft and threw a few darts before Constanzo joined him.

"I'm afraid I have some bad news."

Tucker turned from the dart board. "Bad news?"

"The call I had to return was to Maria." He winced. "She's managed to get herself into a bit of trouble with her mother. It's nothing that a visit from me won't cure but it's also not something I'd expect my guests to endure."

Tucker laughed.

"So you and Vivi have the whole house to yourselves tonight. I've instructed the cook to make spaghetti Bolognese for dinner. Serve it with the Sangiovese. Make yourselves at home."

"Thanks." Anticipation pricked his nerve endings. He and Olivia would be alone? They hadn't had two minutes alone since that kiss...

Maybe it was time they did?

Knowing Olivia was already nervous around him, he decided not to tell her. When she went to the pool, he returned to his room to read emails and make calls.

He checked on dinner before showering and changing

into trousers and a white shirt, which he left open at the throat. No tie. No sport coat. Nothing to make her feel— what had she said? Less than?

When she arrived in the dining room he had the Sangiovese breathing. She immediately noticed only two places had been set at the table and she stopped a few feet away from her seat.

Her gaze swung to his. "Just you and me?"

Downplaying the significance of that, since he didn't want her running before they had a chance to talk about that kiss, he walked over and pulled out her chair. "It seems Maria's gotten herself into some trouble with her mother. Constanzo has to smooth ruffled feathers."

She laughed lightly as she sat. "It's kind of funny to think of Maria as being in trouble with her mom. She doesn't seem like the kind of woman who answers to anyone."

"Everybody answers to someone."

She laughed again. "Yeah. With my parents I think I know that better than anyone." She paused until he sat at the place across from her. "You do know they came to check up on you the day they visited New York?"

This time he laughed. "I'm sure I made a stellar impression." But even as he said that, an odd realization came to him. He'd never met a girlfriend's parents. Not one. Because he didn't really have girlfriends. He had dates—lovers.

"Good enough that my parents trusted me to go to Italy with you." She winced. "Of course, I had to do some persuading, but in the end they trusted you."

He sucked in a breath. Strange feelings tumbled around in his gut. No parents in their right minds should trust their beautiful, naive daughter to him—

Unless they expected him to behave like a gentleman? To them, Olivia wasn't a "date" or a "lover". She was their daughter. Their little girl and they would expect him to treat her as such.

The maid brought their salads and garlic bread. After she was gone, Olivia tasted her salad and groaned. "That is fantastic. I'm going to have to diet when we get home."

"Then you probably don't want to know that our main course is spaghetti Bolognese."

She groaned again and set down the garlic bread. "I'll focus on the salad so I have room for the spaghetti."

They ate in silence for a few seconds, then she glanced around. "My mother would probably love Italy."

More talk of her parents, more of those uncomfortable feelings. "Really?"

"My mom likes things with roots. Family recipes. Older houses. She researched our house after she and Dad bought it. Found relatives of the woman who had owned it, and got some of the family recipes." She took a bite of salad, chewed and swallowed. "She said preparing those dishes was like keeping that family alive, too. She respects the sense of continuity."

He smiled, but discomfort graduated to awkwardness. He didn't even know who his parents were. He'd tried to find them a few years back, but there were no clues. He was a baby left alone in a church. Generic blanket. Department-store bottle and diapers. There was no way to find them. He had no parents, no pictures. No old family recipes. No sense of continuity.

"That—" He paused. Not having a normal family had always bothered him from the perspective of not having a support system. But from the way Olivia talked about her mother it was clear she was her friend. They were close. Loving. Impossible for him to comprehend. "That sounds nice."

"It is nice." She laughed. "She's quite the mother hen."

He poured more wine. "What about your dad?"

"Oh, he's our big teddy bear. He doesn't say a lot but we always know he loves us, you know?"

He didn't. He'd never *known* anyone loved him. In fact, in spite of the declarations of a few lovers, he didn't think anyone had actually loved him.

"He's also a card player. When we lose electricity in an ice storm, he always starts a candlelight game of Texas Hold'em or rummy."

Which explained why she had been so comfortable playing rummy with Constanzo the day she'd met him.

"Your dad gambled with you?"

"We'd play for candy."

"Sounds nice." Again. He could envision her family huddled around a table, playing a game by candlelight. Laughing. Just enjoying each other's company. The thought twisted his heart but teased his imagination.

"What about holidays?" He really shouldn't ask. Hearing her stories only reminded him of what he didn't have, but he couldn't resist. In the same way she tempted him, so did thoughts of a family. He'd longed for one as a child, considered the possibility of having one when he tried to track down his parents, then closed the door when he couldn't find them.

Now here he was longing again, just like a little boy with his nose pressed up against a candy-store window.

"My mom's favorite is Easter. She loves pastel colors. Hiding Easter eggs. Going to the Easter-egg hunt sponsored by the volunteer firemen. And though most Americans don't wear hats anymore, she still gets a new one every year for church on Easter Sunday."

He laughed and took a sip of wine.

"But even though she likes Easter the best, my dad's the Christmas freak. Have you ever seen those movies where people try to outdo each other with outdoor lights?"

"I've seen a few."

The spaghetti came. The aroma filled the room and she inhaled deeply. "Wow. That smells fantastic."

"Constanzo promised you some really good food in return for sharing that leftover Chinese food. So far he's made good on his promise."

She winced. "He probably thought I was such a dork. I didn't even have a plate for him. He had to eat out of the box."

"I think he was too hungry to care. Besides, a lot of people like eating food out of boxes. It reminds them of their childhood."

"Does eating food out of boxes remind you of your childhood?"

His chest tightened. He should have realized that she'd turn this discussion to him. She was too polite to monopolize a conversation.

"I don't remember a lot of my childhood."

"I'm sorry. I probably shouldn't have brought that up."

"It's fine." It wasn't. He'd convinced himself to believe his lonely childhood had strengthened him, made him into the strong man he was today, but strength wasn't the only quality a person wanted to have. Knowing her had resurrected his longing for a connection, a place, a real place where he wasn't just wanted and respected, but where he could be himself.

"I'm sure growing up in foster care had to have been difficult."

"It was."

"I shouldn't have brought up Christmas."

"It's fine. Really." He cleared his throat. To salvage his pride, he couldn't let her feel sorry for him. "Some foster families really tried. But they don't get a lot of money from the government to care for the kids they take in so they can't do everything. As a foster child, you adjust."

The room fell silent again. He toyed with his spaghetti.

Worried that she still felt bad, he caught her gaze. "But I had some nice Christmases."

Her face brightened. "Did you?"

"Yes. Two. One year when I was about six I really wanted a certain video game. My foster parents already had the game box in the family room that could play the game, so I asked for it knowing I probably wouldn't get it, but they got it for me."

Her eyes warmed. "That's nice."

He thought back to that day. The one day in his childhood when he actually thought life could be wonderful. "It was nice. But because my foster parents had spent so much on the toy, I didn't get the usual clothes I would have gotten as gifts and my jeans wore thin. I spent the rest of the winter wearing shoes with a hole in the bottom."

"Oh."

He cursed himself in his head. Now he knew why he shied away from honesty. It hurt. And not just him. He could actually feel sorrow pouring from her.

And *that* was why he'd always be alone. Or with women who didn't care to know him. No man wanted a woman he lusted after feeling sorry for him.

"You have to be proud of yourself for how far you've come."

"Yes. Of course, I am." He sat straighter on his chair, closed his heart. Forgot about all those longings for the things she'd had and could tell him about. "But it should also make you realize that if you really want to become successful, you shouldn't let anything stand in your way."

He turned the conversation to a discussion of focus and discipline as they finished dinner then excused himself.

The empty, lonely feeling that followed him to his room was an echo of what he'd sensed with Constanzo, and he realized he and the reclusive old billionaire had a lot in common. His refusal to be vulnerable might be the right choice, but at sixty-five or seventy, he was going to wake up one day and find himself every bit as alone as Constanzo was now.

But in some lives there was no choice. Opening up and being honest simply couldn't be done.

Two days later, with Antonio settled and Constanzo thinking he *might* like to be the one to tell Antonio he was his father, Vivi and Tucker left Italy. After their dinner alone, he'd become quiet. So she wasn't surprised when he handed her work to do on the long flight to New York City.

Hours later they landed at the private airstrip and transferred to his limo. He instructed the driver to take her home first. After a quick, impersonal goodbye, she climbed the three flights of stairs.

When she stepped into her apartment, she was bombarded by hugs and questions from Laura Beth and Eloise. She managed to sidestep the more personal aspects of her trip by focusing on Antonio, her work with a gallery owner and an artist, and her pool games with a billionaire who really would have taken her money if she'd been foolish enough to bet with him.

She told them about the beautiful Italian countryside and then spilled over into a gushing report on Bordighera, which, she told them, they would have to visit—if they ever got enough money to go on a vacation.

She slept like a log, woke groggy, but capable of working, and headed to the office dressed in the gray trousers and pink shirt. No blazer this time. June had turned into July and it was getting hot.

When she arrived at the office, Tucker was already there, head bent over papers on his desk.

She stood by her chair, confused. In a little over a week she and Tucker Engle had gone from being something like adversaries to—

She didn't know what. Almost friends? He'd apologized for pushing her into talking about something that was none of his business. Hell, she'd told him about something that was none of his business. They'd sat by a swimming pool and talked like normal people.

He'd kissed her.

Then they'd had that wonderful private conversation over the spaghetti Bolognese. He'd told her things about his past. Personal, intimate things. Things that showed her that deep down he was a nice guy, a good guy. Not somebody born to money who abused people. Not somebody she had to fear. But somebody she could trust. Somebody special.

And now they were just supposed to go back to the quiet?

She glanced into his office again. His head was still down. His focus clearly on his work. Wasn't he even going to say good-morning?

Apparently not.

It was sad, painful. Especially considering that that conversation hadn't just shown her she could trust him. It had also caused her to like him. The real him.

Maybe too much.

She turned, slid her backpack beneath her desk. A file sat beside her desktop computer. She opened it to find the financials she'd been reviewing the night before. She lowered herself to the office chair, turned the pages to her stopping point, found the legal pad on which she'd been jotting notes and did what she was supposed to do: looked for inconsistencies. Hot spots. Potential trouble.

But her heart broke. She'd never met anybody like him. Never had an adventure like the one she'd had in Italy. And now they were back to not talking.

Two hours later the elevator bell sent a spike of noise into her silent space, causing her head to snap up. Ricky Langley and Elias Greene walked out. Though disgust rolled through her when she saw Elias, he smiled apologetically. She smiled politely and turned to grab the phone to alert Tucker that they were in her office.

But Tucker was already standing in his doorway. He greeted them without as much as a glance in her direction and closed the door behind them.

She sat back in her chair with a huge sigh. Not speaking *might* work to get them past the awkwardness of their near miss with friendship and their kiss, but it wouldn't do anything to stop her longing for more. If she closed her eyes, she could see the blue Italian sky. The rolling hills. The green grass. The cobblestone streets. The villa gallery.

Her opinions had been important. Antonio had listened to her advice. Constanzo had treated her like an equal. And Tucker had kissed her.

She traced her fingers over her lips. Every time she thought about that kiss, they tingled. Her whole body came to life as if remembering every single detail of the way his lips felt pressed to hers, the way his tongue felt taking possession of her.

Now here she sat in an office so quiet she could hear her own breathing.

Tucker's meeting with Elias and Ricky lasted an hour, then he took the pair to lunch. She ate a peanut butter and jelly sandwich and drank a bottle of water.

Knowing she had to withdraw money for the week, she left the office in search of an ATM. She punched in her account number and waited for her balance to appear. When it did, it was twelve thousand dollars over what she expected.

Twelve thousand dollars.

Crap. Somebody somewhere had made a mistake and she'd have to fix it.

Knowing she had sufficient cash to cover a meager withdrawal, she retrieved the money she needed and returned to the office to call the bank.

"This is Olivia Prentiss. My checking account number is—" she rattled off her number "—I seem to have too much money. Twelve thousand dollars too much money. You might want to check that out."

The service representative chuckled. "Thank you for calling us. I'm pulling up your account now." She paused. "Hmm...I see a twelve thousand dollar deposit from a company called Inferno." Another pause. "Do you know them?"

She sucked in a breath. "Actually, I work at Inferno." She grimaced. It would probably be better to tell Human Resources about the mistake and let the company handle it. "Never mind. I'll check it out with my boss."

She disconnected the call and was ready to dial the extension for HR, but a strange thought popped into her head. What if it had been Tucker who'd dropped the twelve thousand dollars into her bank account?

And if so, why?

She went over everything that had happened in Italy and stopped when she remembered that kiss. The rush of excitement. The rightness. The swirl of need. The way he took possession of her.

And the cash in her checking account felt like a glaring, horrible insult—a blackmail payment. *Forget everything that happened in Italy.*

Waiting for him to return, she tried to focus on the financials, but the money in her checking account haunted her.

The second the elevator doors opened, she said, "So, what? Were you afraid I'd tell somebody you kissed me? Or afraid I'd tell somebody the things you'd told me while we were eating spaghetti?"

Tucker's face scrunched in confusion. "What?"

"The twelve grand. Is that payment so I'll keep my mouth shut?"

He rubbed his fingers across his forehead as if totally

unable to believe what she'd said then he pointed at his door. "My office. Now."

She rose from her seat, her head high, and followed him. He fell to the chair behind the desk. She primly sat on the chair in front of it.

"That kiss meant nothing."

Her heart kicked against her ribs. Just when she thought she couldn't feel any worse, he proved her wrong.

"Well, thanks."

"You can't have it both ways, Miss Prentiss. Either you're insulted enough by the kiss to think I'd need to pay you off, or you liked kissing me."

Heat rose to her face.

He sighed. "The order to get the money into your account went out before we went to Italy. The day we left, HR called and told me there was too big of a disparity between Betsy's salary and yours. We couldn't give you a raise to take you up to Betsy's salary since you won't earn that much in Accounting, so we chose a bonus. Your direct deposit is equivalent to an extra thousand dollars a week while you're filling in for her."

Her mouth hung open. Everybody had told her Betsy would be out eight weeks, ten tops. Now suddenly it was twelve? Twelve weeks with a guy she liked, a guy she'd confided in, a guy she'd kissed…a guy who now hated having her around?

"I can't take it."

"Why not?"

"Because it's not right."

"Betsy makes about three times what you make in Accounting. Adding another thousand dollars a week hardly evens the score. It was a compromise number set by Human Resources. Besides, you earned your keep last week."

"I did very little."

"You understood Antonio. You knew to jump in when he needed someone to intervene."

"We haven't told him Constanzo's his father."

"Constanzo wants the chance to tell him himself. We have to respect that."

"I still don't feel right."

He leaned back and steepled his fingers. Vivi surreptitiously studied him, suddenly realizing why she didn't want to take his money. She wanted him to like her and he didn't. She didn't know why he behaved so different in Italy, but they'd talked honestly. Openly. He'd apologized. She'd explained things to him that she'd only ever told Eloise and Laura Beth. They'd connected.

That's what made him different from Cord. *That's* why she liked him. It wasn't the money or his good looks or even the romantic trip to Italy.

They had connected.

"I don't want your money." She lifted her chin. "I want to go back to what we had in Italy."

"We didn't have anything in Italy."

"Yes, we did. We talked. We got close. You kissed me."

"That was a mistake." Tucker looked away, but he knew this was his opportunity to fix the slip up of kissing her and talking to her, to get the stars out of her eyes and get their relationship back to a professional one.

He deliberately caught her gaze again, held it. "Kisses lead to becoming lovers and if I take a lover it's for sex and sex only."

"I don't believe you."

"You don't have to believe me."

"You *liked* talking to me."

"Maybe, but in that conversation I also realized you like connections. Continuity. You want somebody to connect with long term. Somebody to share your life with, I'm not that man."

"How do you know if you won't even try?"

"Because it's not what I want. And I'm rich enough that I don't have to do things I don't want to do."

He saw the light of recognition come to her eyes. They widened with surprise, then dulled with acceptance. In essence, he'd just dumped her.

She rose. "I still don't want your money." Head high, she walked out of his office.

The relief he expected didn't come. Instead, his stomach soured with the truth. No matter how much he wanted her, how tempting her body and how alluring her honesty, he couldn't have her. And it was time they both faced that.

CHAPTER TEN

AFTER DAYS OF intense focus on the financials of a company Tucker ultimately decided not to buy, he switched gears and had Vivi looking at the financials of a company he already owned. The weekend came, and, glad for two days off, she did nothing but read.

On Monday morning, she woke with a headache and by the time she got out of the shower she was so dizzy she could barely stand.

Racing out the door, Laura Beth told her to take the day off. Heading into the shower, Eloise agreed. So she unwound her towel and walked to the dresser for clean pajamas. Almost too tired to lift them out of the drawer, she struggled to get the top over her head and the bottom pulled up to her waist.

Exhausted, she fell face first on her bed. Vaguely, she heard the sound of Eloise leaving for that day's interview but that was her last conscious thought.

At twenty till ten, Tucker Engle sat at his desk staring at the phone. He had no idea why Olivia hadn't come into the office today but he had one of those sneaking suspicions she'd told him about.

She was quitting. After almost complete silence between them for days, their only words to each other questions and answers about that day's work, she'd had enough.

He supposed it was her prerogative to leave Inferno, but no matter how close they'd gotten in Italy, how disappointed she was in his ability to return those feelings, she still had to turn in a notice. Two weeks was customary.

He could have Human Resources call her. But what would he do if she told them she was quitting because he'd kissed her? Or she was quitting because they'd connected in Italy and now he refused to be personal with her?

He didn't think she'd do that, but he also didn't want his private business advertised. So he called Human Resources, got her cell phone number and called her.

He waited four rings before the call went to voice mail. Which probably meant her phone was busy.

He gave her twenty minutes then hit redial. After four rings, it went to voice mail.

Ten minutes later, he hit redial again and it went to voice mail.

Five minutes later, he hit redial. And finally she answered.

"Hello?"

Her weak voice cracked. She sounded like she was on death's door.

Cold fear flooded him. He cursed the feeling. Not just because he wasn't supposed to like her but because he hated anything he couldn't control.

"Are you all right, Miss Prentiss?"

"What?"

The disorientation in her frail voice sent panic through him. But he forced himself to remain professional. "Okay, I'm guessing you're sick."

Nothing.

"Miss Prentiss?"

Nothing.

"Olivia?"

"I'm fine."

No, she wasn't! He could tell from her weak voice that something serious was wrong. He disconnected the call and summoned his driver. The forty minutes it took to get to her apartment increased his panic and he raced into her building. He sighed at the three flights of stairs he had to climb and in the end took them two at a time. When he reached her apartment door, he knocked and knocked. Just as he was considering finding her building superintendent to get a key, the door opened.

Her hair was a tumble of knots. The puffy lids over her glazed eyes drooped. His gaze fell to her soft pink pajamas. The top had thin straps that all but bared her shoulders to him and revealed a plump pink strip of cleavage. The loose bottoms clung to the swell of her hips.

He swallowed hard. He'd never met anyone as naturally beautiful, as naturally built, as she was. And yet she believed she wasn't good enough.

"Well, at least you're not dying."

She looked at him, but said nothing. Tucker wasn't really sure she saw him.

He shepherded her back into her apartment, which was small, but neat and clean. "Which room is yours?"

She pointed back down the hall. That didn't tell him anything, so he let her lead. She passed the first door and turned into the second. One bed was made. The other looked as if a band of feral cats had had a fight under the covers. She fell to the bed with the tousled bedclothes.

Silence fell over the room, the echoing sound of no people. She was alone, sick. Too sick to even get herself a glass of water. And there was no one in this quiet, quiet apartment to help her. The way there hadn't ever been anyone to help him when he was sick. Not that he'd wanted someone to coddle him, but there was an undeniable loneliness, an emptiness to be faced when even a simple cold demonstrated that you didn't have anyone in your life.

He crouched beside her. "What can I do?"

Her face smashed against the pillow, she said, "Go away."

"I'm serious. Can I make you some soup? Get you orange juice?"

"I don't think we have any of those things."

He took out his cell phone. "Not a problem." He called his driver. "Maurice, we're going to need some chicken soup. Find a good deli. Also get a gallon of orange juice, some pain relievers and some flu medications."

He clicked off the call and looked at Olivia. For all practical intents and purposes she was out. He pulled the covers from under her and gently spread them over her. His fingers brushing her soft, soft shoulders caused an awkward fluttering of his heart. His hands paused, fingers skimming the delicate flesh he longed to be allowed to touch, to taste.

He really liked her. But they were so different. And not just about money or social status. He couldn't talk to her. When she tried to get him to tell her about his past, he'd stupidly told her something that had made her feel sorry for him. After that he couldn't tell her anything else. His past hadn't merely been bad; it had left him in the awkward position of being incredibly social in the right crowd and totally unable to be intimate—even with the right person. And *that* was the real reason he wouldn't pursue her. She deserved better.

He walked into the front part of her apartment with a sigh. He'd panicked. Stupidly. Over a case of the flu.

Of course, he hated the thought of anyone being alone and sick. And, more important, he didn't want her to get dehydrated. He needed her to get well enough to return to work. He convinced himself the panic was nothing more serious than his need to have his assistant on the job again. Also giving him a story of explanation to tell Olivia when she questioned him—and she would. He smiled ruefully. She always did.

He opened cupboard doors, looking for tea and eventually found some in the cabinet above a rather fancy-looking coffee machine. For three girls just starting out, they had an odd mix of really, really expensive things and things that appeared to be someone's castoffs.

He prepared the tea and almost took it back down the hall but realized he'd be waking her when Maurice returned with the pain killers and flu meds, and he hated to wake her twice. So he sat on her sofa and drank it himself. Sipping, he picked up his phone and read his emails, but he didn't have a decent attention span, not enough to answer important questions, so he turned on the television.

He sat back on the comfortable red sofa and sipped the tea. By the time Maurice arrived with the soup and medicines, he'd seen two news programs, which he should have considered a waste of time. Instead, he felt more relaxed than he had in years.

He took the soup and meds from Maurice who winced. "You should give her a raise or a bonus or something so she can get into a building with an elevator."

"I tried. She told me I was buying her off."

Maurice's eyebrows rose.

"Trust me. She's an odd, odd woman. And if you're smart you won't try to figure her out."

Maurice chuckled and left. Tucker opened the soup which had cooled during transport. He took that, a spoon, the flu meds and the pain reliever back down the hall to her room. She lay sprawled across the bed, exactly as he had left her.

He marched to the bed. "Come on, now," he said using his outside voice in the hope of waking her. "We can't let you get dehydrated."

She didn't even stir.

He placed the soup and meds on her bedside table, sat on her bed and put his hand to her shoulder, then drew it back as if it had stung him. The softness of her skin always seemed to do him in. But he'd made his decisions. A man who couldn't talk about his past couldn't give a woman like Olivia the kind of love she needed.

But he glanced at her face, her eyelashes fanning against cheeks red with fever, her usually smiling lips a straight line and he wanted to touch her. To help her. He had to do this.

He slid his hand to her shoulder again. "Hey, sick person. I'm here to help you."

The warmth of her fever heated his fingers and hit him right in the heart. She needed him. It almost physically hurt to think of her alone and so sick she could barely blink. So he might as well admit it and do what he'd stayed here to do.

He slid farther onto the bed, put his hands beneath her shoulders and lifted her into a sort of sitting position, leaning against him.

"What do you want first? Soup? Pain meds? Flu meds?"

"Flu meds."

He opened the package and filled the little cup to the appropriate measuring point. But by the time he turned to give it to her she was asleep again. He put the cup to her lips and nudged until she woke and drank. She also took a few sips of juice, but that was it.

He left the room thinking he should go back to the office now. There was nothing else he could do for her. She was fine—safe in her bed—but alone.

The emptiness of being alone rose up in him. Having no one who cared when he was sick. Having no one who really knew him, really cared about him. He couldn't leave her with nothing but the ringing silence of this apartment to keep her company.

With a sigh, he returned to the red sofa, took off his jacket, loosened his tie and turned on the TV again.

Two hours later she staggered into the living room, a blanket wrapped around her.

He shot off the sofa. "Miss Prentiss! Are you sure it's wise for you to be out of bed?"

She made her way over to him. "At this point I'm not entirely sure I'm going to live." She sat on the sofa. "The only reason I have strength enough to get out of bed is the medicine you gave me. Thank you for that, by the way."

He slowly lowered himself beside her. "You're welcome."

"And for coming over."

"I couldn't stand to think of you alone and sick."

She glanced at him. Her eyes told him that she remembered the things he'd said on the trip to Italy, about being a foster child, a baby left in a church in only a blue blanket. A little boy who had once gotten a Christmas gift and that had come at the expense of clothes he'd needed.

She cleared her throat. "Yeah. I get it."

Discomfort turned his muscles to stone. He *hated* that she felt sorry for him. He could not handle pity. And maybe that's why talking to her had scared him more than thoughts of seducing her? People who knew his past might respect him for how he'd changed his life, but deep down inside most people also pitied his humble beginnings. That's why he'd choked on the words and couldn't tell her any more than he already had. He didn't want to be pitied. Especially not by her.

He rose from the sofa and grabbed his suit jacket. "Let's not make a big deal out of it. Are you well enough for me to go back to the office?"

She nodded. "Yes."

"I had Maurice get you chicken soup from a deli. You should eat that and drink plenty of fluids."

She nodded.

He hesitated. With the threat of discussing his past gone, it again felt wrong to leave. She appeared to be well. At least well enough that he knew she could take care of herself, but it just didn't feel right leaving her.

"Are you sure you don't want me to stay and play cards or something?"

She laughed. "You play cards?"

"I do all kinds of normal things."

"I have always suspected as much."

He shook his head. "Even sick you're a smart-ass."

"You're the boss. You could have gotten rid of me on day one."

Her slightly glassy blue eyes connected with his and his heart turned around in his chest, like a little kid doing somersaults in a swimming pool.

He liked her so much.

He didn't just think she was pretty or had potential. He *liked* her. That was why he didn't get rid of her, always felt different around her, more alive.

But he didn't share his past with anyone. Ever. He'd tried with her and only ended up evoking her pity.

He stuffed his cell phone in his pocket. "I'll see you when you're better." He walked to the door, but faced her again. "You should call HR tomorrow morning if you're not coming in. They like to keep track of things like that."

He walked out of her apartment, closed the door behind him and squeezed his eyes shut.

He had been perfectly fine, perfectly happy until she'd come into his life. Now he yearned for things he couldn't have…things he'd long ago adjusted to never having.

He wished with every fiber in his being that Betsy could get better so Olivia could return to Accounting and maybe, just maybe, he could forget all this.

A week after her four-day flu, Vivi sat in Tucker's office, straight as an arrow.

Though he'd very sweetly cared for her the first day she

was sick, when she'd recovered, she'd returned to a silent workplace, a venue for nothing but labor. He wouldn't accept her thanks for caring for her. He didn't want to discuss it. He didn't look at her. Gave her assignments piecemeal, as Mrs. Martin had said he would, and absolutely didn't give any explanations for anything.

She couldn't even measure the disappointment. But she got the message. He didn't want any misunderstanding. He'd cared for her because she was alone. He knew what it was like to be alone, and didn't want to see anybody suffer that fate, but he did not like her.

So why the hell did she continue to like him more and more?

In the silence of his enormous office, the ring of his phone sounded like a bomb going off.

He glanced up at her. "Very few people have this private number. I have to take this."

She nodded and sat back.

He picked up the phone. "Tucker Engle."

"Oh, Tucker!"

"Constanzo? What's up?"

"It's Antonio. He is, as you say, freaking out."

"Did you tell him you're his dad?"

"No! He's just going nuts about the show."

He glanced at Olivia. "Miss Prentiss is here with me. I'm going to put you on speaker."

He hit the button and Constanzo immediately said, "Vivi! You should be here. You calm him down."

"You can calm him down, Constanzo."

"I can't." The passion in his voice vibrated through the room.

Vivi laughed. "You can. You're just freaking out, too. Take a breath, calm down."

"No, you take a plane, come to me. Help me."

Tucker sat forward. "Actually, that's a very good idea."

Vivi's gaze shot to him. Though she loved being in Italy and working with Antonio, after the way Tucker had behaved these past few weeks his suggestion that she leave felt like a kick out the door.

"I'll have her on the plane in two hours."

"Thank you, my dear friend Tucker!"

He disconnected the call and Vivi stared at him. "Are you trying to get rid of me?"

He wouldn't look at her. "You handle Antonio very well. It's only good common sense to send you over there."

"Antonio is a grown man. So is Constanzo. They could deal with this."

He finally glanced up. "You think?" When she said nothing, he tossed his pen to his desk. "Once again, you underestimate your abilities." He shook his head. "This deal is extremely important to me. Antonio has to be cool, calm and collected when we tell him Constanzo is his dad. You calm him down."

Because she knew that was true, she said nothing.

"I know you're playing it by ear here, but you really are good with people."

After weeks of no conversation, his praise was like balm to her desperate soul. "Thanks."

"But with everything going haywire, it looks like we can't tell Antonio that Constanzo is his dad until the show is over."

"You want to preserve the show?"

"You don't? It's the one solid thing Constanzo is doing for Antonio. Even if he's angry after we tell him Constanzo is his dad, he'll have the showing to look back on. Something that proves to him his dad believed in him. You can't get a much stronger connection than that."

"You're right."

"So you're in Italy for the next two weeks, until the show opening. I'll have the driver here in ten minutes. He'll take you to your apartment to pack and you can be in the air in two hours as I promised."

With that he went back to work.

Vivi slowly rose from her chair, her heart lodged in her throat. She turned away as tears filled her eyes. She really didn't want to go to Italy without him.

She didn't want to go anywhere without him. Do anything without him.

The horrible truth was…she loved him and he was sending her away.

CHAPTER ELEVEN

EAGER TO GET his office back to normal, without a wonderful woman sitting a few feet away, tempting him to try a relationship he knew couldn't work, Tucker immediately called Mrs. Martin in Human Resources, requesting another accountant. In ten minutes, Ward Bancroft stood in front of him.

With dark hair and dressed in a black suit, black shirt and silver tie, the kid was a mini version of Tucker, without the green eyes. His eyes were a watered down whiskey-brown that reminded him of a weasel.

"So, Mr. Bancroft, are you ready to work?"

"Absolutely. You tell me what you need and I'll have it for you in ten minutes."

He eased forward on his chair. Even though he appreciated a bit of enthusiasm, he preferred dignity. "Some assignments require more attention than ten minutes."

"Oh, absolutely! I'm sorry!" To Tucker's horror he seemed to get even more enthusiastic. "You tell me what you need and I will do it in the best possible way."

"Terrific." He shuffled the papers on his desk until he found the background-information sheet he needed. "This company could potentially be a great project. But the financials look a little too good to be true." He handed the sheet across the desk. "I want you to tear their annual statement apart, see what they're hiding."

He nearly snapped to attention. "Yes, sir!"

He headed out of the office and Tucker said, "Close the door on your way out."

"Absolutely," he singsonged.

As the door closed behind him, Tucker rolled his eyes. But at least his office felt back to normal. No pretty blue-eyed strawberry blonde, tempting him to talk, to laugh, to like her.

He'd never wanted anything the way he wanted her. But they were wrong for each other. And it was *her* he was protecting from the pain that would result if they tried a relationship and it failed. She'd been through enough in her life without him putting her through something else.

By noon, the sounds of the silence of his office began to close in on him, but, luckily, he had a lunch out with Elias and Ricky to discuss the details of a new ad campaign created by the ad firm Tucker had hired.

Rick and Elias rose as he approached the table and so did the pretty blonde seated by Elias.

"Melinda Fornwalt, this is Tucker Engle."

She smiled and shook his hand. Painted up the way Maria usually was, Melinda might be pretty but since working with Vivi he sort of liked women with less makeup. Or maybe natural beauty?

"So this is Tucker Engle? The guy who made you rich."

Tucker held back a smile. Her voice and manners screamed socialite, somebody who lived the life of charities and theatre and loved it. He suspected Ricky had brought her on board to give the company the touch of class it was lacking.

"Yes and no. I paid to get controlling interest in their company but they were the ones with the idea. They made themselves rich."

She sat and the men sat.

"Still, you're quite the entrepreneur."

He removed his napkin. "Not really. My forte is buying existing companies. I'm more like a renovator than a carpenter."

She laughed. "Not just handsome and smart, you're funny, too."

His eyes narrowed. Was she coming on to him? She might be the kind of woman he typically dated, but for some reason or another, her flirting made him uneasy. No. Not uneasy. He didn't like it. At all.

"I'm sorry. I didn't catch your position with the company."

Elias cleared his throat. "She's not really with the company. She's with me."

He almost said, "And you tolerate her flirting with other men?" But he stopped himself if only to keep the situation civil. Unfortunately, as quickly as he thought that, he also imagined Vivi rolling her eyes about Melinda dating Elias and flirting with Tucker. And being correct. The woman was after Elias's money. That is, if she couldn't catch a bigger fish while going out with Elias.

He caught Ricky's gaze. "I'm guessing that means we won't be discussing the ad campaign you received."

Ricky shook his head as if to say he didn't know what was going on, but Elias blanched. "We can still talk about it."

"I never discuss business in front of people who don't have a financial interest in the project." He rose. "In fact, since we have to reschedule anyway, I think I'll go back to my office."

As soon as he was out on the street, he was sorry. Not only did he not want to go back to the overly keen Ward, but he was hungry. The scents of food beckoned but the one that caused him to stop came from the Chinese restaurant.

The last time he'd eaten Chinese, he'd been with Vivi's family. It had been a strange lunch, but he kept remembering how embarrassed Vivi had been. If there was one thing Vivi wasn't, it was a gold digger.

He shook his head. She was so determined to prove herself. So honest. So much fun. And that kiss in Italy had knocked him for a loop.

He didn't want to miss her, but he did. And not because Ward Bancroft was hard to work with. Because he liked Vivi—Olivia.

Just remembering her telling him to call her Olivia, caused his heart to jolt. He liked who he was with her. He especially liked talking to her. Honestly talking to her. And he'd sent her thousands of miles away.

The grassy fields of Italy relaxed Vivi, but working with Patrice and Antonio invigorated her. Even though the pair argued constantly, Vivi always seemed to be able to see a compromise position. They got more work done in two days than Patrice and Antonio had managed in the two weeks she'd been gone.

After a fattening supper of homemade butternut squash ravioli and two hours playing rummy with Constanzo, she took a long, hot shower and shimmied into a pair of pajamas, ready for sleep.

But as she tucked the covers to her chin and closed her eyes, the company cell phone rang. Tucker had given it to her in the last seconds before she left the office to pack for her trip. He'd said he didn't want to lose this deal and she was to call him if anything changed or if she needed help.

She didn't need help...but maybe he needed her?

Or maybe he just missed her?

Her heart skipped a beat. Two days out of each other's company and she'd missed him. Was it so unbelievable to think he might have missed her?

She grabbed the phone and said, "Hello."

"I think my new assistant wants my life."

Though his voice was serious and maybe even a tad desperate, she couldn't help it. She laughed.

"The little snot even dresses like me."

She sat up, made herself comfortable against the headboard. She could have taken him to task for not speaking to her in the weeks before Constanzo called her back to Italy. She could have reminded him he'd told her he didn't want to get personal because he couldn't be the man she wanted. She could have asked him if he really thought she could just drop her hurt feelings and talk to him now as if nothing had happened.

But she didn't. His life had been difficult, and maybe she needed to cut him some slack, give him some time to work out how he felt.

"You always told me you didn't care what I dressed like as long as I could do the job."

"He does everything too fast."

"And you're afraid he's missing things?"

"Absolutely." He groaned. "That's his word. Absolutely. I ask for a report, he says, absolutely. I ask for coffee, he says absolutely."

"He's driving you nuts."

"He truly is."

"Want some advice?"

"It's why I called."

Her lips lifted into a happy smile. He trusted her. That's why he'd told her the little snippet of his past on spaghetti night. That's why he'd sent her to Italy without him. He might not *want* to like and trust her but he did. He'd come to a problem he couldn't solve and he'd turned to her.

"Call him in and tell him to relax. Or do what you did with me. Take him to a meeting. Make sure he knows he's to be seen and not heard. Remind him that a good assistant is nearly invisible."

"I didn't tell you that." His voice had calmed, almost warmed.

She settled more deeply into her pillow. Maybe he really had missed her, too? Or maybe it was just easier talking long distance? "Not in those words. But after the signing you told me that you appreciated that I hadn't said anything."

"And you extrapolated the rest?"

She thought about that. "Yeah, I guess."

"That's why you're good with people. You don't just read between the lines, you read the right subtext between the lines." He paused only slightly before he said, "How's Antonio?"

"I don't think Antonio is the problem. I think it's Patrice. She likes schedules and timetables. Antonio sort of marches to his own drummer."

"Have you gotten him to put on a shirt?"

She laughed. "He always wears a shirt now."

"Yeah, but is it buttoned?"

The tone of his voice sent a little jolt of hope to her lonely heart. "Are you jealous?"

"No. More like confused. Wondering if I'd get better deals if I stopped wearing ties and showed off a little chest hair."

She laughed with delight and Tucker settled more comfortably into his seat in the limo. He'd missed her terribly. It was wrong, and calling her probably wasn't fair to her, but he'd needed to hear her voice. He'd happily jumped on the excuse of needing advice about his new assistant.

"Seriously, how's it going over there?"

"Actually it's going very well. Antonio considers Constanzo his benefactor and by default a mentor. He seems to like and trust him. I'd say we could tell him now that Constanzo's his dad, except I don't want to screw up his showing."

"I agree. That show needs to go well."

"Especially since Antonio's invested in it. This isn't just his career. Painting is his life. I want to tread lightly here. I want to do this right."

The limo pulled up to Tucker's building. "Then we'll do it right." Maurice opened the door. "Trust your gut, Miss Prentiss. So far you seem to be doing very well."

He stepped out onto the street and inhaled the fresh New York City air after a rain storm. The empty, hollow feeling he'd been carrying around in his gut since she'd left had disappeared. He'd gotten the advice he'd wanted about his new assistant and received an update on her circumstances. There was nothing more to say.

"Good night, Miss Prentiss."

He disconnected the call and headed to the penthouse of his Park Avenue apartment. The quiet of the elevator rattled through him, reminding him again that in his sixties he'd be Constanzo Bartulocci.

When the doors opened on his slick white, black and chrome apartment, the silence was deafening. He unexpectedly wished he'd kept Olivia on the phone for another ten minutes, at least until he had a drink in his hand and the sports channel on TV. But that was foolish. Stupid. He couldn't have her. As he'd told her, he couldn't be what she wanted. And he was going to have to control this.

Tomorrow. For tonight, he was glad he'd called. Glad she'd made him laugh. Glad she was doing well.

The next day, he did as Olivia had suggested. He took Ward Bancroft to a lunch meeting. He told him it was not his job to talk, but to be available to find information and to observe. At the meeting, the kid was so quiet one wouldn't have even known he was there.

In the limo on the way back, Tucker complimented him on a job well done and Ward virtually glowed.

Every assignment he gave him that afternoon was com-

pleted with the utmost care, and he had a much more professional tone with visitors.

Of course, most of his visitors had liked Olivia better,
but that was beside the point. He had companies to run,
jobs to be done, investments to be investigated. He and his
assistant were not there to have fun.

Still, riding up the elevator to the penthouse that night,
he pulled out his cell and speed-dialed Olivia.

"Hello."

"You sound freshly showered."

"Now how would you know that?"

He smiled shrewdly. He wasn't the only one who could
handle people. "I don't. I took a wild guess and led you
into a statement that confirmed it. *That's* how I deal with
people."

"I prefer my direct approach."

"I sort of like being sneaky."

"No kidding."

The elevator ride wasn't interminable. The doors opening on his penthouse apartment didn't feel like the boring,
silent gates of hell yawning open before him. He slid out
of his jacket and walked to the bar.

"I did what you suggested with Mr. Bancroft and today
he was as sharp as a brand-new pencil."

"That's great."

After pouring two fingers of Scotch, he fell to a furry
white chaise. He put his feet up. Put his shoulders back.
Sipped his favorite malt liquor and savored.

"We work like a well-oiled machine. He knows the right
questions to ask. He doesn't ask stupid things. I think I've
found a keeper."

His happiness was met with resounding silence and
he stared at the phone for a few seconds before she said,
"That's really good for him. And you. I guess."

"Miss Prentiss, you've done nothing but whine about

wanting to be in Accounting since the day I dragged you kicking and screaming out of HR. Why would the news that I found someone who fits the position upset you?"

"Nobody wants to be so easily replaced, Tucker."

"You haven't really been replaced. Technically, you've moved on."

"To become a babysitter?"

"To become a manager. A business manager for Antonio."

"I hardly feel like a business manager."

"What do you think mangers do? They solve goofy nit-picky problems."

Her cautiously optimistic voice tiptoed across the Atlantic to him. "So I'm a manager?"

"And you could suggest to Constanzo that he hire you permanently for his son."

Her breath hissed over the phone. "Are you trying to get rid of me *completely*?"

"No." His own breath stumbled. What *was* he doing? "I just… It's just… Well, some people are made to be assistants and some people are meant to be…more."

"You're telling me I'm made to be more?"

"Of course, you're meant to be more. Look at you. In a few weeks, you've gone from working for the head of your company to jet-setting around the globe and infiltrating the art world." He paused, let his ice clink around the walls of his glass. "Olivia, have you ever asked yourself what *you* wanted?"

"I want to be a success."

"And you believed an accounting degree was the best way to get there?"

"Can't run a company if you don't know the basics of the numbers behind it."

"So you want to run your own company?"

She hesitated. "I guess…someday."

"You've shown a talent for being able to get people to do what you want them to do. That's your service...or your stock-in-trade. Now you merely have to figure out who your customer base would be. Then you have to market yourself."

He finished his drink. "Think it through tonight and I'll call you tomorrow. We'll make some decisions."

He hung up the phone and walked back down the hall to his big empty master suite with the equally big and equally empty master bathroom. But tonight, he didn't notice those. Though his home was empty, inside he was full, busy, thinking about Olivia. Her talent. Her skills. How he could help her become the person she wanted to be.

The next day, as she sweet-talked Antonio and persuaded Patrice, Vivi thought about what Tucker had said about becoming a business manager. But she thought more about the fact that he was back to speaking to her casually, as if they were friends.

All day she wondered what she'd say to him. As she signed for deliveries, debated placement with Patrice, soothed Antonio and constantly updated Constanzo, she thought about the job—what she was really doing for Antonio.

When Tucker called that night, after she'd showered, slid into her very best pajamas and snuggled into her pillow, she said, "I think I'm actually a mother."

He laughed.

"Seriously. Constanzo's like the big lovable dad. Patrice is the grouchy middle daughter who wants everything her own way and Antonio's the spoiled baby boy."

"Managers are a lot like mothers—babysitters—what have you, because there are some people who need a 'career' mother. You, as a business, have to find a focus so you learn that world and how to navigate in it."

"Makes sense."

"Do you want to manage artists like Antonio? Or singers? Or rock bands?"

"Is this how you did it?"

"Did what?"

"Decided what to do with your life?"

He got more comfortable on his bed. Tonight he'd showered and put on silky navy blue pajama bottoms before he'd called her. He wasn't entirely sure why he'd left off the top, except he knew it had something to do with Antonio, even though she couldn't see his chest over the phone—damn. They should be video calling! He had two fingers of Scotch on ice and his day had gone fairly well.

Yet he'd still looked forward to this call like a kid at Christmas.

He winced. All but two of his Christmases had been abysmal.

The reminder brought him back to reality. He wasn't supposed to like her. He was helping find her place in the world as a way to repay her for her help with Antonio. "My decisions about what to do with my life had more to do with getting a roof over my head and keeping food in my stomach."

"Was it bad?"

He hesitated. For as much as he didn't want *anybody* to know this part of his life, didn't want anybody to pity him, had been unable to talk about it with her at Constanzo's, he suddenly had an uncontrollable desire to tell her. Probably because they were on the phone and he couldn't see her face, her reactions, her pity.

"A person can sleep on a bench and go without supper and forget about it in a few days. But the feeling of being the only person in your world, having no mom, no dad, no brothers, no sisters… That doesn't ever go away."

"I have a great family."

"Thanks for rubbing that in."

She laughed and for some reason or another, in his mind's eye, he pictured her tucking her feet beneath a soft pink robe as she snuggled into her pillow. "No, silly. I'm suggesting you spend time with them."

"So I can see how the other half lives?"

"So you can see that you'd blend in. My dad's the easiest person in the world to become friends with." She paused. "If you golf. Do you golf?"

Confusion sprang up inside him. How would it feel to be part of her family? "I've made some of my best deals on the golf course."

"Thank God. And my mother loves everybody. Though Cindy can be a pain in the butt like Patrice."

"Ah, thus the comparison to the bossy sister."

"And Billy's the spoiled little brother like Antonio. Now that you know all that, you'll fit right in. You can come to our house for every Christmas, Thanksgiving and Easter dinner for the rest of your life."

His heart stuttered. He'd received other invitations, of course. A wealthy man never spent a holiday alone unless he wanted to. But the picture that formed in his head warmed him. He could see himself going into Olivia's home, armed with gifts, accepting hugs from her crazy family and rubbing his hands in anticipation over a tray of fresh snickerdoodle cookies.

He shook his head to clear it. It was one thing to wish for a second that he belonged, quite another to indulge the fantasy. It was time to get this conversation back to planet earth.

"And what happens after you get married? Your husband isn't going to want your ex-boss showing up every holiday."

"What if I marry you?"

The thought paralyzed him so quickly he felt like he'd vibrated to a stop.

"Marry me?"

"You're not completely unacceptable or hopeless. A few more lessons in communicating like a normal human being and I might actually like you."

Male pride surged. There was no way he'd let her get away with that. "You already like me."

"A tad."

"A tad?"

"Okay, more than a tad. But you like me, too."

It was another perfect opportunity to disabuse her of any romantic notions. Yet instead of forming words to correct her, he felt his own mouth forming the words he shouldn't say.

"A bit."

"Uh-huh. You keep telling yourself that. We like each other and you know it."

Though her presumptuousness should have annoyed him, her words settled over him like a soft blanket. She was bossy and nosy but usually right and he liked her. If he wasn't careful, she'd drag his entire life and all his secrets out of him one phone call at a time.

He changed the subject. "Did I tell you I found another company I might like to buy?"

"You find a new company every day. But in a few weeks you may be on the hook for about a billion bucks to buy out Constanzo. Do I have to put a lock on your checkbook?"

He laughed. "I'd just go to a bank and get a line of credit."

"You are a bad boy."

He laughed again, loving how normal she made him feel. "I want you to know, Miss Prentiss, that whatever you decide to do with your talent, I'm going to fund it. We'll call you a start-up. You'll get capital. I'll lend you a few advisors for marketing. And this time next year you could be a superstar manager."

"Once again, it feels like you're trying to get rid of me."

"You wouldn't let me give you the bonus. And you may end up being the force that gets me Constanzo Bartulocci's fortune. I think I owe you."

"I like the sound of that."

He shook his head. "Good night, Miss Prentiss."

"Good night."

The next day when he called her, he immediately got them down to business. "I spoke with Constanzo today about hiring you to manage Antonio."

Her breath caught. "What?"

"You're in. You've already started. I'm funding you. You now have a client."

Instead of protesting that he was trying to get rid of her, she laughed. "I'm a company?"

"You are a company."

"Thanks."

No one word had ever split his heart the way her sincere thanks had. The feeling was like warm rain or a soft snowfall on Christmas morning. Something you didn't even know you wanted until it was there.

He whispered, "You're welcome."

The phone line grew quiet and he suddenly wanted to tell her just how much he liked her. But he stopped himself. He wasn't sure either one of them was ready for that. But he couldn't deny that every day, every phone call, he wanted to tell her just a little bit more. And he knew that if he didn't stop calling her, one of these days the cat would be out of the bag.

"Just remember, you still work for me until after Antonio's show. Constanzo understands that until this whole process is done, you're an employee of Inferno."

She laughed. "I understand that I still work for you. I remember that my primary mission is to make sure this show goes well so we can tell Antonio that Constanzo is his father."

"Good."

The line grew quiet again and fear suddenly engulfed him. Now that she had a business, his support and a client, what if she didn't want *him* anymore? Maybe in giving her a soft place to land he'd given her a way out. He wasn't exactly the easiest guy to love. She could take his money and run now.

"Did I ever tell you about the time my mom bought me a puppy for Christmas?"

That brought him up short. Confused, he said, "No."

"Well, if I tell you that story, you have to tell me one, too."

Even as relief poured through him, another kind of fear raced in behind it. With every step of honesty they took, they got a step closer to discovering the truth. Did they belong together? Were they good for each other? Or was he just so tired of being alone he was clinging to the first person with whom he could be honest?

He didn't know. But he did know she made him laugh, made him feel whole.

"You remember the story about the video game. My stories might start happy but they end miserably."

Ignoring that, she broke into a long story about a puppy bought for her one Christmas that had fallen in love with her dad instead of her. "To really understand the story you have to remember my dad is bald."

"I remember."

"So one morning my mom wakes up and the dog is sleeping on my dad's pillow, right above his head and it looked like he had hair. She screamed bloody murder until she realized it was just the dog."

Tucker laughed. "That's the stupidest thing I've ever heard."

"Yeah, my family can be pretty silly." She paused a second. "Now your turn."

"Okay." It had taken him the length of her entire story, but he'd finally remembered something he could tell her. "In second grade, I won my first spelling bee."

"First?"

"I was champ every year after that. No matter where I lived or what school I went to, I won my division of that spelling bee."

"So that was the beginning of your overachieving."

He sniffed a laugh. "Yeah. I guess."

The warmth of feeling normal flowed through him again, and from that moment on, he knew he'd call her every night.

Though he didn't have a clue in hell where they'd end up, he was fairly certain one of them or both of them was going to get hurt.

CHAPTER TWELVE

THE DOORBELL AT Constanzo's house rang for the fiftieth time the morning of Antonio's opening and Vivi rushed to get it. Busy with preparations for the elaborate party after the gallery doors closed, the staff had better things to do than sign for deliveries.

The uniformed man handed her a box and a clipboard and pen. She juggled them, until Maria Bartulocci appeared at her side. Not one to let an enormous party given by her incredibly wealthy uncle occur without her input, Maria had arrived two days before and she'd taken over the planning.

"Here. I will help."

Handing the box to Maria, Vivi scanned the delivery information and realized the box was for her. She signed the sheet, gave it back to the deliveryman and closed the door.

"It's for me."

Maria held it up as if weighing it. "Too heavy to be flowers."

She grabbed the card and ripped it open.

We can't have the prettiest girl there in anything but the best. Tucker.

Maria rolled her eyes. "My God, he's a sap."

But Vivi's heart about exploded in her chest. Not because he'd sent her a dress, but because he wasn't running from what was happening between them. Something real.

Some wonderful. Their nighttime chats had become longer and more personal. They'd stopped talking like a boss and assistant and begun talking like friends, but she could feel there was something more behind it.

Still, she wasn't about to tell Maria that.

"He knows I'm poor. I'd told him I'd have to squeeze out a few hours to go into town today to find something to wear." Because she desperately wanted to be beautiful for him. To feel like the woman he saw when he looked at her. "This is his way of being a good boss, making sure I have everything I need for my job."

Maria laughed and batted her hand as she led Vivi up the stairs. "He likes you. Not like he would like me—for fun. He likes you for you." She shook her head. "I don't want that. But you do."

"I do." Vivi couldn't deny that. She wanted their chats to cross the line from friendship into relationship. And if she let herself, she could almost believe this dress was Tucker's way of doing that.

"Then we'll have fun with this."

They took the big box down the hall to Vivi's lilac-and-white bedroom. The second she set it on the bed, Maria pulled the ribbon to unravel the bow. Vivi lifted the lid.

Inside was a raspberry-colored chiffon dress.

A laugh escaped. Raspberry was the color of the bathing suit she'd worn their first day in Italy.

Something soft and warm surrounded her heart. He was telling her he remembered details, maybe everything that had happened between them.

Maria eyed her askance. "What?"

She wasn't about to tell Maria this either. Especially if she was reading all the signals wrong. Plus, this wasn't something she felt like sharing. She just wanted to hug the information to herself. Hug the dress to herself. Be a simple, silly girl falling in love.

But she couldn't. She had absolutely no idea how Tucker felt about her.

She turned to Maria with a short smile. "Nothing. I just love the dress." She pulled it out of the box. "Do you think it will fit?"

"I think a man like Tucker knows his way around a woman's curves."

Maria's snarky comment barely registered as she fought the urge to hug the dress. She'd found a calling. Something that gave her a sense of self-worth that went beyond proving herself to a bunch of people in Starlight, Kentucky, who no longer mattered. She was on the global stage, helping one of the most talented new artists in the *world* start his career.

And Tucker liked her.

She knew he did. She didn't want to deny herself the pleasure of believing it.

"So we play with your hair and makeup until we get it perfect," Maria said, but Vivi stepped away from her.

"I thought you were helping arrange the pool area for tonight's party."

"They will be fine without me."

"No," Vivi said, laying the dress across the bed. She slipped off her T-shirt and slid out of her jeans. "Once we make sure this puppy fits, we're both going back to work."

"You are no fun, Vivi."

"No. I keep my promises, Maria. And as long as I'm working with Antonio and you're anywhere near Antonio, you're going to keep your promises to him, too."

Vivi slipped into the dress, which fit perfectly. Strapless, it caressed her breasts and torso to the waist where it belled out into a frothy skirt that stopped three inches above the knee.

The dress fit so perfectly Vivi shivered. When had he studied her so well, so often?

"I have a necklace that would look wonderful with that

dress," Maria said, racing out the door. In two minutes she was back, holding a thin chain with a simple round ruby.

Vivi gasped. "I couldn't!"

"Please," Maria scoffed. "I got this from a man I now hate. If you lost it, it would be a favor."

Vivi shook her head. "You're bad."

"I am terrible," Maria happily agreed as she secured the necklace on Vivi and turned her to face the mirror.

Vivi touched it reverently. "It does look wonderful."

"*Sì*. You will wear this tonight." She unclasped the necklace and set it on the dresser for Vivi to find that evening. Then she casually ran her finger along the clean wooden vanity top, as if unconcerned. "Why do you have this interest in Antonio? If you like Tucker, why do you follow Antonio around like a little dog?"

"Because Constanzo wants me to." She wouldn't tell her that Tucker had already talked to Constanzo about making this a full-time job. Sweet and generous as she could be sometimes, Maria had a hard side, a scary side. "And my boss wants to do whatever pleases your uncle. No matter how much fun this seems to be, the bottom line is I still work for Inferno and I do whatever Tucker tells me."

Maria said, "Uh-huh," but Vivi got a bad feeling. No longer interested in Vivi or her dress, Maria flitted out of the room. Vivi removed the dress and reverently laid it across the bed. Tonight she would look perfect for him.

Tucker didn't time his arrival to be so close to the actual show opening, but delays had caused him to leave late enough that he'd changed into his tux on his plane and didn't bother going to Constanzo's. He took the limo directly to Patrice's villa gallery.

White lights had been strung across the second-floor balcony and the leafy trees that lined the cobblestone walk that led to the front door. With fifteen minutes to spare before the actual opening, he strode up the walk and slipped in the front door.

His favorite Antonio painting—blue wildflowers in the sea of green grass beneath a pale blue sky—sat on an easel in the center of the foyer, teasing attendees with a sample of his talent. A glance into the rooms on the right and the left showed the elaborate displays of more of Antonio's work.

He heard the clack, clack, click of shoes on marble and he spun toward the sound, but all he saw was a swatch of pink.

That was the dress.

After two weeks of talking on the phone, growing closer and closer, he was finally going to see her.

His heart racing, he headed in the direction that he'd seen the blur of pink, but by the time he reached the room, she was gone. He stood in the area filled with Antonio's paintings as catering staff brought trays of appetizers to the long thin tables lining the walls.

Shoving his hands into his pockets, he glanced around. What was he doing? He never, ever chased a woman—

But he caught a glimpse of the pink dress again and that crazy combination of warmth and excitement tightened his chest, warmed his blood. He couldn't resist this any more than he could hold back a rising tide.

"Olivia! Vivi!"

She stopped.

As she turned to face him, her lips lifted slowly. Her eyes warmed. His heart stumbled and he realized he'd been waiting two long weeks to see that smile.

"I'm so glad you're here."

So was he. The happiness that rose inside him was so intense it couldn't even be described.

"Everything's falling apart."

His joy deflated like a popped balloon. "You want me here because everything's falling apart?"

She winced. "Yes."

It wasn't exactly what a man wanted to hear when he hadn't seen the woman he desired in two weeks. But he told himself not to panic. First, she was under a lot of pressure. Second, it was good to hear she needed him. Really good. She could be so self-sufficient, especially with Antonio, that it was reassuring that she turned to him.

He put his hands on her bare shoulders to steady her. The velvet smoothness of her skin shuddered through him but he held her a few inches away so he could take in the vision she made in the frothy dress. Tall and lean, with graceful arms and shapely legs, she wore the little pink creation as if it were made for her. Her thick strawberry blonde hair had been caught up in a curly creation that allowed tendrils of hair to tickle her neck and tease his imagination. Makeup enhanced her blue eyes. The sprinkle of gloss on her lips tempted him to kiss her.

He couldn't kiss her, not publicly, not when he wasn't entirely sure what was happening between them. But even if the world was crumbling around them, he needed to acknowledge that she was the prettiest thing he'd ever seen.

"You're beautiful."

Her eyes lit. The corners of her lips kicked upward. And his Vivi was back. "What? This old thing?"

"Hey, that old thing cost a bundle."

"And I appreciate that you thought of me. I was just about to steal a minute away from the chaos and go into town to find something to wear when this arrived." She stood on her tiptoes and kissed his cheek. "You're the best boss ever."

Frustration knotted in his chest. He wanted a kiss, a real kiss, for his thoughtfulness, and she had bussed his cheek. Still, he was the one who needed to keep their relationship simple until he figured out what he really wanted.

"And I'll pay you back."

"You can't pay me back." The words were out before he could stop them. He'd already decided to tell her the dress cost five hundred dollars, rather than the five thousand he'd spent. But his damned male pride swooped in and stole those words. He longed to be allowed to spoil her. But she wouldn't let him. And his own fears stopped him, too.

Once, just once, he wanted to relax and let go. Do what he wanted, just because he wanted to.

He softened his voice. "I won't take your money if you try to pay me back."

She smoothed her hand across the soft chiffon. "It's too much."

"For whom? Do you realize what's exorbitant to you is like pocket change to me?"

Her gaze snapped up. "So this is pocket change?"

"Essentially. But it was also my way of celebrating your success. Other people send champagne. I sent a dress."

Their eyes met and temptation tugged at him again. He wanted a kiss so bad his chest hurt from it. But life wasn't always fair or easy. He wished he could look into those big blue eyes and know everything would be okay if they crossed the line from friends to lovers. But he couldn't and neither could she.

As if disappointed, she stepped back, wringing her hands. "Don't celebrate too soon. Maria knows something is up."

"And?"

"And you do know Maria, right? She's a busybody."

"We can handle her."

"You think? She expected to inherit Uncle Constanzo's wealth…or at least to live off the gravy train for the rest of her life. With a son, an heir, in the way…do you really think she's going to take this calmly?"

She stopped suddenly. Her lips lifted into a smile of

pure pleasure. As if only now really seeing him, she said, "Wow. Look at you."

He smiled.

"You look fantastic."

"I do, don't I?" A man didn't get to thirty-four, and have the brain to acquire wealth that exceeded the gross national product of most small countries, without knowing his assets.

Her gaze dipped. "A little vain tonight?"

"It's hardly vain when it's the truth." He stepped closer, slid his arm around her waist, forced her gaze to his. Her eyes met his with a longing that mirrored the feeling churning in his gut. He knew this was risky or maybe too soon. But the need to touch her simply overwhelmed him.

"Besides, we look good together. Very good."

"Tucker!" Maria's voice echoed along the high ceilings of the villa entrance.

He released Vivi and spun around. Maria raced toward him. She caught his upper arms and planted a kiss on each cheek. "So are you going to tell me what's really going on here?"

He peeled her hands off his upper arms and turned her around. "Go fix your lipstick. Olivia and I have work to do."

When she was gone, Tucker sighed heavily. "We've got to get Constanzo to tell Antonio tonight. This can't wait till morning."

She bit her lower lip. "It has to be after the show. Antonio can't take that kind of surprise before his big moment."

"Okay. How about after the show but before the party at his house? We'll get them in the same limo and not let anyone else in."

"Okay."

"Which means we have to warn Constanzo that he'd better prepare his speech for Antonio, and to watch out for Maria."

She nodded.

He caught her hand. "Let's go find him now."

They searched the first floor of the gallery and found him with Antonio who looked ready to throw up.

"Doors open in ten minutes," Vivi reminded Antonio. He looked amazing in his black tuxedo but not as good as Tucker. Tucker wore formal attire as if he'd been born to it, but she knew he hadn't been. There was so much about him that was special, intriguing, and she suspected she was one of only a few people he trusted with his secrets. "But you don't have to show up right away unless you want to. If I were you, I'd give people a chance to look around, then you could kind of slide into the crowd and introduce yourself."

"You will be with me?"

She glanced at Tucker. She wanted to be with *him*. She wanted to walk the gallery with him and tell him every silly nitpicky story of how each displayed painting had been chosen. How Antonio and Patrice had argued over placement. How she'd intervened and stopped fight after fight.

Instead, she said, "I'll stay by your side all night if that's what you want."

He caught her hands, kissed the knuckles. "It's what I want."

Tucker said, "Super," as Constanzo nervously said "Great."

Vivi let go of Antonio's hands. "But for right now, why don't you go up to Patrice's apartment and just chill. Find a soccer game or something on TV. I'll come and get you a half hour after the doors have been opened."

Constanzo volunteered to walk upstairs with him, but Tucker caught his arm. "Vivi and I need to talk to you for a second."

He motioned Antonio to go on without him. "I'll be right behind you." When Antonio was gone, he faced Tucker.

"You don't think it's a good idea for me to stay with my son when he so clearly needs me?"

"I think it's a great idea," Vivi said. "Especially since I think Maria is catching on."

"Catching on to what?"

"Catching on to the fact that there must be a reason you're going to all this trouble for Antonio," Tucker said.

Constanzo fell to an available chair.

Vivi stooped beside him. "She knows you too well. All along she's thought you were going overboard for this project. But today she came right out and asked what was going on."

"We think you need to tell Antonio before the party."

Constanzo's gaze shot to Tucker. "Here? At the showing?"

"How about in the limo on the way home?"

He nodded. "*Sì.* The party can be ruined. But the showing must be perfect."

The two floors of Patrice's villa quickly filled with art enthusiasts and Constanzo's friends. Guests spilled out in the gardens. Waiters wove through the crowd with champagne.

A half hour into the event, Vivi left Tucker and went to Patrice's apartment and retrieved Antonio. She guided him to Constanzo who took him from one circle of friends to the next. Seeing how confident Constanzo was with his guests, she could have stolen away at any time, but she'd made a promise to Antonio and she kept it. Still, she didn't stay on the sidelines. She was as much a part of this event, of Antonio's success at this event, as anyone. So she talked with Constanzo's guests, sipped champagne and in general made Antonio as comfortable as she could.

Tucker watched, growing more and more agitated. He wanted to be with her tonight. He'd missed her. Even though they'd talked every night, it wasn't enough. In fact, sometimes talking to her without seeing her had been torture.

He was here. She was here. They should be together. She shouldn't be with Antonio. She should be with him.

His mental temper tantrum stopped him. He wasn't just eager to see her. He wasn't just longing to see her. He was possessive. And being possessive was dangerous. Every person who'd ever come into his life had left him.

He did not want to be hurt again.

But with every second that ticked off the clock, and every move she made with Antonio from one crowd of art enthusiasts to the next, his heart beat a little harder, a little faster. If this was jealousy he hated it. And if this was jealousy didn't that mean that he felt a little more for Olivia than he'd let himself believe?

Still, could he trust her with his heart? Trust her never to leave?

As the night wound down and guests began heading to Constanzo's, he watched Olivia commandeer a limo for Constanzo and Antonio. She kissed Antonio's cheek. "Congratulations on a wonderful show. I'll be at the house as soon as everything is closed up here."

As Antonio climbed into the limo, she kissed Constanzo's cheek. "Good luck."

He sucked in a breath. "I will need it."

"No, you won't." She straightened his bow tie. "You'll tell him the truth. His mother came to you once and disappeared." She kissed his cheek again. "You can do this."

As Constanzo's limo pulled away and another drove up, she turned to walk into the gallery.

Tucker glanced back at Olivia and then at the limo. If he timed this right, he could wheedle the last limo for himself and Olivia. He could finally have the ten minutes of peace and privacy he'd wanted since they'd arrived.

He opened the limo door slowly enough that the first

couple slid in just as the second couple walked toward the
limo door. He managed to pair couple after couple into
limos until, exactly as he wanted, a limo pulled up as Olivia
walked toward him. She carried the raspberry-colored wrap
that matched her dress in one hand and a small purse in
the other.

He opened the door for her with a smile. She accepted
his courtesy with a nod and her own smile, and slid inside.
He slid in beside her.

"I thought I'd missed you while I was in New York, but
that was nothing compared to the torture of watching you
all night."

"Watching me was torture?"

He laughed. "Watching you was fun, but I didn't want
to watch you. I wanted to kiss you."

Her eyes widened. "Really?"

He drifted closer. "Yes. I can't say for sure you'll never
leave me. I can't say for sure what I feel for you is love.
But I do know I can't ignore what I feel. I wanted you desperately."

Olivia's eyes widened. "Really?"

"Really?" He paused, realizing his mistake. The last man
she'd been involved with had attacked her. He hadn't even
thought of that in weeks. Hadn't taken that into consider-
ation when he thought about the possibility of loving her.

What if she wasn't ready?

CHAPTER THIRTEEN

On the drive to Constanzo's, Tucker turned the conversation to Antonio's showing. Olivia didn't know whether to breathe a sigh of relief or yell at herself. She'd waited two weeks to see him and now suddenly she was afraid?

He'd never hurt her the way Cord had, but that was because he could hurt her in a worse way. She loved him. And he confided in her, got her jobs, bought her dresses. None of which meant he loved her. For all she knew, he wanted sex. And the way she felt tonight, she'd be a very easy target. But what would happen in the morning?

When they arrived, he got out of the limo and turned around to help Olivia out. She smiled, trying not to be panicky.

He tapped her nose affectionately. "Let's find Constanzo."

Then he took her hand and her heart stuttered. Sweet and loving, the gesture soothed her jumping nerves. He wasn't a guy she had to be afraid of. She loved him. Trusted him.

They found Constanzo on the patio by the pool beside Antonio as if holding court.

Careful not to disturb the artist or his group of admirers, she pulled Constanzo away from the small crowd. "How did it go?"

He laughed. "Antonio was a bit surprised." He winced. "Shocked actually, but we agreed to work this out."

She squeezed his forearm. "That's so exciting."

He nodded. "And I have you to thank." He faced Tucker. "And you. It looks like we'll be in some heavy-duty negotiation starting tomorrow."

Tucker shook his hand. "I look forward to it."

With that, Constanzo rejoined his son. Antonio turned to him with a smile and Vivi's heart melted. They had done it.

Tucker faced Olivia. "So."

She stepped toward him. "So?"

"I think we're free."

She ran her hand down his lapels. With things settled with Constanzo, and because Tucker had held her hand, hadn't kissed her, hadn't rushed her, everything suddenly felt okay. She loved this man, and she believed in her heart of hearts he loved her. She could not be a coward.

"You're about to start the biggest negotiations of your life. That's not freedom. That's work."

"Yeah. But I can do these negotiations in my sleep." He grinned. "I kinda owe this to you."

"You bet you do."

He slid his hands to her waist. "I could think of about thirty ways I could repay you."

Need sizzled through her. She'd never been more ready or more afraid. But she knew she had to do this. Conquer her fears. Be with the man she loved. "You're inventive."

"I like to think so." For Tucker, everything suddenly seemed easy, right, and he didn't care that they were in a crowd. He dipped his head and kissed her. The kiss was slow and sweet, like nothing he'd ever experienced. It wasn't just physical. It was personal, emotional, intimate—if only because she knew him. And he knew her. He'd never realized two serious, broken people could be so playful, so happy. And that's what he really owed to Olivia. His soul.

Her purse began to play out a lively beat. She pulled

away, opening it. "It's the cell phone you gave me." She caught his gaze. "I thought only you had that number."

"It's company property. Human Resources has it, too."

She rummaged to find the phone. "What could they want?"

Before she could get it out of her purse the call went to voice mail, but a few seconds later her phone buzzed with a text.

Looking over her shoulder, Tucker saw it was from her mom.

Call me. Emergency.

She immediately punched a number into the cell phone. "Mom?"

Tucker watched Vivi's face fall as she listened to her mother and his heart kicked against his ribs.

"What kind of accident?"

Filled with a fear he'd never experienced, Tucker stood impotently, waiting. When she disconnected the call, her eyes glistened with tears.

"What happened?"

"My sister was driving in the rain, a deer ran out in front of her and when she swerved to miss it, she hit a tree."

"Oh, my God."

"My mom said they aren't sure how bad it is. Cindy's in surgery right now—" Her lips trembled. She pressed her fingers to them. "I have to go home."

He pulled Vivi against him with one arm, then retrieved his cell phone from his pocket and hit a speed-dial number. "Jonah, get the plane ready. File a flight plan for the airport closest to Starlight, Kentucky. Have a car ready for us when we land."

Huddled into his shoulder she said, "I don't want to take your plane. You might need it while you're here."

"You're not taking my plane. *We're* taking my plane."

She pulled away so she could look at him. "You're coming with me?"

"Yes." Though it astounded him, he couldn't let her go alone. He didn't have a sister or a brother to be able to relate to her feelings, but maybe that was the point. Knowing how priceless siblings could be, he couldn't let her suffer the thought of losing one of them alone.

With an explanation to Constanzo, they left the party as unobtrusively as possible. Exhausted from the long weeks she'd had with Antonio, Vivi fell asleep on the flight. Tucker found her a blanket and pillow, marveling at how different this trip was from their first flight to Italy. With so much work to do for his negotiations with Constanzo, he could have gone back to his makeshift desk. Instead, he sat on the seat beside her, letting her lean against him while she slept.

When they landed in Kentucky, he woke her.

"Where are we?"

"If my calculations are correct we're about two hours away from your home." He clicked a few buttons on his smart phone. "And there is no limo service here so Jonah rented a car for us."

They got out of the plane at the small public airport. There was only one rental car agency. When he walked up to the counter, he gave them a credit card, signed a few forms and they presented him with keys.

Still wearing her frothy pink dress, Olivia drew all kinds of strange looks from passersby. Behind her in his tux, he got his fair share of odd glances, too.

"We should probably find Jonah, get our bags and change."

"I don't want to waste time."

Tucker caught her by the shoulders. "This isn't a waste of time. We need to get into comfortable clothes. We need to get something to eat. Maybe a bottle of water. We have a two-hour drive ahead of us. Call your mom. See how things are going. If there's no news, we have plenty of time to change."

She closed her eyes. "I'm afraid to."

"You? Olivia 'Vivi' Prentiss? A woman who yelled at her boss? You're afraid?"

"I never yelled at you. I just made a few points strongly. And this is different. This is my sister. I don't want to talk on the phone. I need to be there."

He turned her in the direction of the door where they'd pick up their rental car. "If you're okay, I'm okay. But we are stopping somewhere for water."

She was out the door before he'd even said water. He ran after her to find Jonah just outside the door, holding their bags. He located their rental car, Jonah tucked the luggage in the trunk and he and Vivi slid into the front seat.

Before they left, he used his phone's GPS to find the best route to the hospital and they drove away from the municipal airport.

He tried to think of something hopeful to say, but nothing came to mind. He almost said, "Everything's going to be fine," but he didn't know that it was. He considered telling her to hang in there, but that sounded stupid.

He glanced over at her. She leaned back against the headrest, her eyes closed in misery, her usually happy face drawn in grim lines. Pain sliced through his heart. He couldn't stand to see her this way.

"Please call your mom." The words came up from the deepest part of him. "For all we know, there could be good news."

She opened her eyes slowly and retrieved the cell phone from her purse. She punched in the numbers. Her voice wobbled when she said, "Mom?"

There was a pause that filled the car with reverent silence. Finally she said, "How she can still be in surgery? That's over eight hours now."

She quieted again as her mother spoke. Tears filled her eyes. And he wanted to kick himself for insisting she call.

"So they're saying the surgery could go on for twelve hours? Four more hours?"

Another pause.

"We're on our way. Tucker's driving. There's nothing to worry about."

Her little bit of confidence in his driving at least gave him the feeling he was doing something. He tried twice to get her to talk. Once about Antonio. Once about how he'd negotiate with Constanzo. But she barely listened. She didn't care. And he didn't blame her.

When they finally made it to the hospital, he parked the car and held on to her elbow as she tried to frantically race into the building. They stopped at the information desk and were told the number of the floor for the surgical waiting room. They stayed quiet as they rode the elevator.

As the doors opened, she raced out. He followed at a slower pace. He'd been inept in the car. Clueless about what to say. He could only imagine how he'd boggle things if he tried to talk to her family.

He stepped into the waiting room in time to see her in a group hug with her mom and dad and younger brother. Her parents wept as her brother tried to keep a stiff upper lip. And Vivi, his Olivia, just fell apart.

Total uselessness rattled through him. He knew nothing about families, knew nothing about this kind of loss, had no idea what to say or do.

After what felt like forever, she pulled away from the group. She faced him, her eyes red rimmed, her nose runny and his heart broke again as impotence filled him. Shaming him. Scaring him.

What the hell did a person say or do at a time like this?

"Mom, Dad, Billy…" Her breath shuddered in and out, a remnant of her crying. "You remember my boss, Tucker Engle."

Though it felt incredibly odd to be called her boss, he stepped forward to shake her dad's hand.

Vivi sniffed a laugh. "I think right now I need that bottle of water you offered me at the airport."

"Okay, one water. Would anyone else like anything?"

Her mother said, "I wouldn't mind a coffee."

Her dad ran his hand along the back of his neck. "Coffee would be good for me, too."

Billy said, "I'll take a soda." He moved away from the group. "But I'll also show you the way to the cafeteria. Coffee from the vending machines is worthless."

As they walked out the door, he nearly breathed a sigh of relief, not sure if he was glad to be getting her parents decent coffee, or glad to be getting out of the room.

"So you brought Vivi the whole way from Italy."

"It's kind of easy when you have a private plane."

Billy snorted. "I guess." He paused, caught Tucker's gaze. "You know, my sister really likes you."

Another wave of relief poured through him but on its heels came an odd sense that he'd never felt before. Olivia liked him in his world. Now, here they were in hers and he was faltering.

"I like your sister, too."

They grew silent again. Hospital sounds crept up on Tucker. Beeps of monitors. Swishes of machines. The scuffing sound of nurses' rubber-soled shoes. Hushed conversations.

And here he was in a tuxedo.

They stopped at an elevator and Billy pushed the button. The doors opened. As they entered, Billy hit the light for the second floor.

He cleared his throat. "So you're what? Sixteen?"

"Not quite sixteen."

"Do you have plans for college?"

He snorted derisively. "To do what? Move away like Vivi did?" He shook his head. "I know she had her reasons for wanting to leave. But around here, unless you're going to be a teacher, you're better off getting some experience as a construction worker or miner."

"Is that what you want?"

Billy glared at him as if he were crazy. "What I want is to live near my family. No fancy college degree is going to help me do that."

The elevator bell pinged. They headed to the cafeteria in silence. He poured the coffees from tall containers at a drink station and retrieved sufficient sugar and cream for an army as Billy grabbed a soda and two waters. He paid for it with a bank card and they returned to the elevator, where they were silent. With the exception of telling Billy he liked his sister, he seemed to always say the wrong thing.

They finally reached the waiting room. He handed Olivia's parents their coffee. Billy gave him one of the waters. Everyone said thanks and the room grew stone-cold silent again. For an hour.

Thirsty, he'd guzzled his water then wished he hadn't because now he had nothing to do with his hands.

When the doctor finally walked into the room, everybody jumped off their seats.

The doctor held up his hand when everybody but Tucker began to talk at once. "She's fine. Great actually. We had to put a few pins in her leg, and she'll be closely monitored for the next twenty-four hours, but I'm very optimistic. There weren't any internal injuries and her head CT came back normal."

Olivia's mother dissolved into tears. Olivia fell to a chair. Her dad shook hands with the doctor, who left.

After drying her tears, Olivia's mom caught her hand.

"You should go home. Change." She laughed a little. Skimming the hem of the poofy skirt of Olivia's dress she said, "This is a pretty little thing."

She smiled across the waiting room at Tucker. "Tucker bought it for me."

Her mother's gaze took a slower, more serious stroll across the room, latching on to his. "Really?"

He'd never realized mothers could be so protective, so suspicious of even simple things, but there was no denying the look on Loraina's face. "Your daughter was responsible for the first showing of a very important new artist in Bordighera, Italy. As an employee of Inferno, she needed to look the part."

"Fancy."

"I wish you could have been there, Mom. It was great. The artist is Antonio Signorelli. His work is fantastic. His dad wanted to foot the bill for a showing so I had to work with him and a woman who owns the gallery and keep Antonio from freaking out." Her eyes grew soft, dreamy. "It was great. The most fun I've ever had."

Her mom clutched her hand. "That does sound great."

She rubbed her fingers along the flounce of her skirt. "Bet I look silly."

"No, you just look like a concerned sister." She glanced at Billy. "But I think Billy should go home. And you, too. And your boss." She said boss in the oddest way, a way that made Tucker feel totally unwelcome. "Get changed. Get some rest. Dad and I will stay. When she wakes up, we'll call you and you can come back to see her."

Rising, Olivia nodded. She hugged her mother and dad, and collected Billy and they headed out of the room.

Tucker caught her hand, if only because he needed to feel her again when she was relieved, happy. "So, all this is good news."

She smiled up at him. "Yes."

Billy made a snorting noise.

Tucker decided to ignore him. He wasn't quite sixteen. His sister had nearly died. His other sister, someone he clearly loved and missed, was home for a few days. He was bound to be a little emotional.

When they arrived at the Prentiss residence, an old two-story house that had a well-kept front yard and blooming flower beds, Tucker brought their suitcases inside. Olivia put on jeans and a T-shirt but Tucker had only dress pants and white shirts. Laughing at him, she drove him to the local discount department store. He didn't wear his tie or jacket but when he walked into the store in black tuxedo trousers and a white silk shirt, he knew he looked silly.

They found jeans and T-shirts and he bought two of each. They checked out and stopped at a fast-food restaurant next door to buy dinner.

She was happy and sweet with her brother as they ate. But after they returned to her parents' house and he changed into the one of the jeans and T-shirts, right before his eyes, she seemed to wind down.

"You need to go to bed."

She yawned. "I want to stay up so I can go to the hospital when my sister wakes up."

"How about if you sleep and I wake you?"

"How about if we both sleep and put the cell phone on my pillow so we can hear it when she calls?"

She headed toward the stairway which he assumed led to the bedrooms.

Positive he'd heard wrong when she'd said "'we' could hear the alarm," he motioned to the living room. "I guess I'll sleep on the sofa."

She stopped, turned. "I was hoping you'd come upstairs with me."

Everything inside him spiked. Their eyes met. He knew what a huge deal this was for her. A sign of trust. He'd like nothing better than to sleep with her, not for sex but for connection. He didn't want to be separated. He didn't want her to be alone. He didn't want to feel alone, ostracized.

But these profound feelings ignited his desire for her, a desire so intense that he didn't trust himself.

"I can't sleep in your bed."

She took a step toward him. "I promise to be good."

He laughed. "I don't."

She looked up. Time seemed to stop again. "It's okay." She drew in a slow breath. "It's what I want. I need to be close to you."

The words humbled him. He'd never had anybody need him, depend on him for anything other than money or work. Still, he also knew it was wrong. He didn't want to mention the past. He didn't want to bring up the worst time of her life. But he had to get them to slow down again or they'd both regret it.

"If and when we make love, I want it to be slow, special. Not a frenzy of emotion neither one of us can control."

She licked her lips, looked like she would argue, but she finally said, "Okay."

"So I'll sleep on the couch."

"What if we both sleep on the couch?"

Relief sliced through him. He glanced into the living room at the oversize floral sofa. "It's big enough for two people."

"And with Billy roaming around there's no privacy." She walked her hands up his T-shirt. "So you'd have to be on your best behavior."

"I would." As he said the words, he contradicted them by kissing her. The sensations that wove through him awed him. He didn't just like this woman. He'd swear he loved her. Even though he wasn't entirely sure what love was, this new feeling that overwhelmed him couldn't be anything less serious than love.

She slid her hands around his neck, pulling him closer and he deepened the kiss, even as his chest tightened and his breathing grew shallow. A month ago, he'd never thought any further with a woman than lust. Today he wanted everything.

She broke the kiss, took his hand and led him to the sofa. He sat first, reclined and patted the space in front of him. She lay down beside him, spoon fashion.

Wonder trembled through him. He was in love with a woman who was equal parts remarkable and vulnerable. Beautiful and kind. Someone who'd been hurt enough that her mother still behaved like a panther protecting a cub.

And as much as he knew he was in love with her, he also realized he didn't know the first thing about loving her.

CHAPTER FOURTEEN

TUCKER FELL INTO a deep sleep. What seemed like only seconds later, the sound of a door closing woke him and he bolted up on the sofa. Rays of the sun poured in through the shear curtains. Olivia's mom stood in the doorway to the living room, her arms crossed on her chest.

"Good morning."

Olivia bounced up in front of him." Good morning, Mom. Sorry." She winced. "This isn't what it looks like."

"Uh-huh."

She said, "Is Cindy awake?" But before her mom could answer she added, "Of course she is or you wouldn't be home. Why didn't you call us?"

"She woke in the middle of the night. The nurses fussed and she couldn't really talk so we decided to let you all get a good night's sleep." Her gaze drifted to Tucker. "She'll be awake again this morning. You can go to the hospital now."

Olivia jumped off the couch. "Let me get a shower and change."

With that she bounded out of the room and Tucker found himself alone with her mom. Seconds noisily ticked off a grandfather clock in the corner. Neither said anything.

Finally, Loraina turned to leave the living room. "I'll make some coffee."

He ran his fingers through his hair. She thought the worst. She had from the moment he'd walked into the hospital waiting room with Olivia. If she were anyone other than Vivi's mom, he wouldn't care. But he did care. He had to care.

He rose and made his way to the kitchen where Loraina stood by a counter preparing coffee.

They were silent for several minutes. When he couldn't take the quiet anymore, he said, "Nothing happened last night."

She didn't even turn from the coffeemaker. "Of course not. I trust my daughter."

He leaned against the counter. "So do I."

She whipped around to face him. "Oh, do you now? You think that means something. That *you* trust her? My daughter's a sweet, precious woman."

"I know how sweet and wonderful she is. In these past few weeks, she's been very good for me."

She sniffed a laugh. "I'm sure she has but are you good for her?"

The kitchen door swung open and Olivia entered. Her hair wet and a big purse over her shoulder. She'd obviously taken the fastest shower in recorded history. "I grabbed a few things that Cindy might want."

"Did you get her iPod?"

"Doesn't she have her phone?"

Her mom shook her head. "It was lost in the accident. I'm going into town this afternoon to get her a replacement with her old number. But if she wakes I think she'd like to at least have her music."

Olivia turned. "I'll get the iPod."

When the door closed behind her, the kitchen became silent again and stayed silent. What could he say to persuade the mother of the woman he had fallen in love with that he was good for her? Should he tell her he'd given her a job? Was helping her start a business? He didn't know much about mothers but he didn't think this one cared about jobs. Especially since the very doubt she was expressing was the same doubt he had himself.

She handed a cup of coffee to him just as Olivia returned to the kitchen.

"Bring that with you," Olivia said, pointing at his coffee. "I want to get going. In fact, I was thinking we should grab breakfast at the hospital and eat in the waiting room."

When they got into the rental car, Olivia took his coffee so he could insert the keys. He wanted the coffee but what he really wanted was a hug and a kiss. He wanted to think she needed them as much as he did. But suddenly everything seemed wrong. Out of place. So he forgot about holding her and the wonderful sensation of having her in his arms, turned the key and got them on the road. Then he took back the coffee.

"A little desperate for caffeine?"

"Actually I'm starving."

"We'll get something as soon as we check on Cindy." She directed him to make two turns that took him to a highway that took them to the hospital.

As he drove, he sipped the coffee which was strong but surprisingly good. When he parked the car, she hopped out. He guzzled the rest of the delicious coffee, left the mug in the car's cup holder and followed her.

The information desk directed them to the ICU where her dad awaited. He hugged Olivia, then smiled at Tucker.

Tucker stepped back, wondering if he'd be smiling after his wife told him he'd slept with his little girl on their sofa.

Though nothing had happened, he knew Vivi's story. Knew that these were the people who'd loved her through the attack that had nearly resulted in a rape. They were protective and to them he was a predator.

"The nurses were taking her vitals, so I came out. You can go in when they give us the all clear."

They sat quietly on plastic seats in a small waiting room.

Tucker leaned back, trying not to feel out of place, unwanted. When the nurse came in, Olivia jumped up. "Let's go."

He hesitated. Everything that had happened in the past few days suddenly seemed surreal. Not only did he believe he had fallen in love, but Olivia's family didn't like him. And now he was being invited to the ICU bed of her sister.

At the very worst possible time in their lives, he'd nudged his way into this family without a second thought.

And he hadn't for one minute felt he belonged here.

"Coming?"

He rose from his seat but didn't take the steps to the door. "You go."

Her head tilted. "What?"

"I'm a complete stranger and your sister is very sick. She doesn't want a stranger at her bedside. You go alone." He turned to her father. "Or let your dad go back in."

Her father's eyes lit with agreement, so Tucker sat again. They left the waiting room and he watched the door to the ICU swallow them up.

Then he sat back, closed his eyes.

He didn't belong here.

Vivi stepped inside the small curtained-off area where her sister lay. Her breath stalled when she saw the cuts and bruising and the metal thing around her leg that connected to pulleys and kept it elevated.

"My God, she looks terrible."

"The nurses tell us she's actually doing very well. In a few days her pain killers will be reduced. She'll be awake longer than two minutes and she'll be able to talk to us."

She walked to the bed, slid her hand along the cool sheet. "So this is good?"

Her dad smiled. "Very good. We'll take it one day at a time. You just have to be patient."

"Oh, I'm the most patient in the land."

"Yes, you are." He walked over and surprised her by enveloping her in a hug. "We've always been proud of you."

"Yeah, well, this morning Mom might not agree. She came home and found Tucker and me sleeping on the couch."

Her dad frowned. "I thought he was your boss."

"He's a little more than my boss, Dad."

Her dad's mouth fell. "Oh, Vivi. After everything you've been through, please do not tell me you'd get involved with a guy who would—" he paused, as if trying to figure out what to say and finally settled on "—use you."

Vivi gasped. "He would never use me!"

"Really? Big-city guy like that? A guy with money? A guy accustomed to getting what he wants and then walking away when he grows tired? You're sure he won't use you?"

She groped for something to say, something that would make him see that Tucker wasn't using her, but when she went back over all their time together, she couldn't really think of anything definitive. Everything they did together somehow involved work. Lots of it even involved him getting a shot at Constanzo's company.

She swallowed then shook her head to clear it. So much had happened in the past few days that her thinking was muddled. She knew Tucker. Better than anybody.

"He's a good guy, Dad. And I won't do anything stupid."

"Okay." He laughed nervously and brushed his fingers along the back of his neck. "You I trust. Him not so much. You just keep a good head on your shoulders."

She stayed the fifteen minutes she was allowed then walked out of the ICU with her dad. When they returned to the waiting room, they found Tucker and her mom sitting silently.

Loraina rose. "Your shift is over," she said with a smile before placing a kiss on her dad's cheek.

"Are you sure you want to stay all day?"

"I feel lucky getting days, since you're stuck with nights."

Her dad wrapped his arms around her mom's waist. "I don't mind."

It was the kind of exchange Olivia had seen every day of her life. Simple, normal, day-to-day love. She glanced at Tucker and saw he'd looked away.

The odd feeling tumbled through her again, making her stomach queasy. She'd worried at Antonio's party that they were taking things too fast, worried that he might only want sex from her. In her desperate need for connection the night before, she'd even offered herself to him, but he'd been a gentleman. In the light of day, though, everything looked different. She was working her way into his world. But he seemed nervous in hers—as if he didn't want to be here.

"You go home, too, Vivi."

When Tucker heard those words coming from Loraina, he almost jumped off his chair, eager to leave this quiet, tense place. But he caught himself and rose slowly. Olivia may not want to leave.

"We don't want to go, Mom. We'll keep you company."

She glanced at Tucker. "Are you sure?"

Olivia said, "Yeah. Cindy's doing fine. But we all want to be here for her."

He started to sit again, but Loraina gave him another one of her looks and he stopped himself. They didn't need him. They didn't want him. He was absolutely in the way. And seeing Olivia's life up close and personal, he understood why Loraina had asked him if he was good for her.

He wasn't. Olivia might know just the right words to say to him to make him happy, or comfortable, but he didn't know what to say to her. They'd really only "talked" for two weeks—and that was on the phone. They'd "been in love" one day—a little over twenty-four hours. He needed to give her space and maybe he needed a little more time to think all this through.

"Maybe I should just go."

Olivia's gaze jumped to his. "Go?"

"Yeah. There's really nothing for me to do here. And I probably have eight zillion emails."

"Really? You're leaving for emails?"

He glanced at her mom, then back at her. "You guys need your privacy."

Her eyes dulled. She smiled shakily. "You're fine here with us."

"I'm in the way."

She studied him a few seconds then said, "You know what? Let's take a walk."

He motioned for her to precede him and when they got far enough away from the waiting room she said, "What's really going on?"

"Olivia, your family is in crisis. I have huge, wonderful enormous feelings for you, but I don't belong here."

"Of course, you do!"

"Olivia, take a look at your parents. They don't want me here."

"I'll talk to them."

His heart skipped a beat. "No! My God, their daughter is lying in a hospital bed. If I leave, the extra stress I add will go and you won't have to talk to them."

Even as he said the words, new fear tightened his chest. What if something he said, something he did, put a wedge between her and her family? What if being with him took away the thing she had that he'd always longed for: a family?

"I need you here."

He shook his head. "No, you don't. You need your family. And they need you."

Suddenly they were at the elevator. Considering it a sign, he pressed the button. She walked over to him, placed her hands on his chest in a gesture he was coming to expect from her, something that made him feel he was hers. Special, precious to her. Her parents might not like him but she did. A lot. She might even love him.

But he'd lived through the last twenty-four hours with her. The best he'd done was get her to this hospital. He hadn't known words of consolation. Didn't fit into her family. Hell, the truth of it was, he might not fit into *any* family. And the very worst possibility was that his inability to fit might drive a wedge between her and the family she adored. The family who adored her.

No matter how he analyzed this, he wasn't good for her.

"Of course, I need my family. But I'd also like you to be here."

He clasped her hands and inched them away from his chest. "Don't you see how different we are?"

"Yes. We both saw it from the day we met. That doesn't mean we're wrong for each other."

He drew in a slow breath. Closed his eyes then popped them open again. Though it shredded his very needy heart to say it, he knew it was the right thing to do. "Yes. It does."

Her eyes filled with tears. "No! It doesn't!"

He realized then how much she cared for him. He also knew that with her sister struggling, she wasn't thinking logically. He had to be the strong one. The smart one. The brave one. Because without her, he had nothing. But without him, she still had family. A brother. A sister. A mom. A dad. A brand-new career in a world full of people who would love her. People she'd get along with easily. Not someone she'd have to struggle with the way she always struggled with him.

"I have to go. I'm not letting any grass grow under my feet with Constanzo."

The elevator pinged. The doors opened. She stared at him with a look of complete confusion.

He almost said, "I love you. I honestly believe you are the first person I've ever loved. And I will miss you so much that I may always feel it."

But, in the end, he knew that it would hurt her or give her false hope about a relationship that was bad for her. So he walked onto the elevator, hit the down button and refused to look at her as the doors closed behind him.

CHAPTER FIFTEEN

VIVI STARED AT the elevator door shell-shocked. He wasn't just leaving. In the space of twenty-four hours of being with her family he'd decided they didn't belong together.

That she wasn't good enough.

She tried to tell herself that was wrong. But as she made her way through the day, keeping up appearances for her family who had enough to worry about, she realized she'd dragged him to a backward small town, made him buy jeans at a discount store and promised him a breakfast he hadn't gotten.

All while her disapproving parents looked on.

What if seeing her roots, where she'd come from, who she really was, had shown him the real her? What if he'd been looking at her through rose-colored glasses, thinking she was something she wasn't…or what if all this time he'd actually been making her into the woman he'd wanted her to be?

Pain gripped her heart, stopped her breathing. Just as he was revamping Jason Jones, he'd been revamping her, creating his perfect woman. He'd eased her into a whole new career, bought her a dress that turned her into a socialite look-alike. Of course he was changing her into the woman he wanted her to be.

She was such a fool not to see it. He didn't love her. He loved the woman he was turning her into.

Her dad wasn't right, but he wasn't wrong either. Tucker might not be the kind of guy who would use her and then dump her. But he was the kind of guy to take someone with potential and turn them into what he needed.

Now that he'd seen the real her, her real life, her roots, he'd probably realized the changes wouldn't stick. And she knew he wouldn't be coming back.

She'd lost him.

If she'd ever really had him—and she didn't think she had. He loved the woman he'd been making her into. Not her.

Tears filled her eyes and she let them fall. She'd almost made as a big of a mistake with him as she had with Cord.

Tucker flew back to Italy and made arrangements for Constanzo to send a car to his private airstrip for him. Though he couldn't sleep or work on the flight, he refused to think about Olivia. He wouldn't even consider that he had abandoned her because he hadn't. She had loving parents, a little brother who wasn't so little and a sister who would soon be leaning on her. She didn't need him. But even if she had, he would have screwed it up. She needed, *deserved,* someone she could depend on, someone she could trust. He was not that guy.

And her parents had seen that.

He walked down the steps, out of his plane and over to the limo. The driver opened the door and when he slid inside he kicked Constanzo's ankles.

"Constanzo? You didn't have to meet me. I would have been fine traveling to your house alone."

"Why are you here?"

"To negotiate, remember?" He scowled. "Unless you're backing out of our deal."

"I don't back out of deals. But you shouldn't be here. Vivi is in trouble and you are here with me…talking business."

"I don't want any grass to grow under our feet."

"You are deserting her!"

"I'm not!"

He wasn't sure how the shout had escaped but it infuriated him. He was better than this. Smarter than this. He'd fallen in love with a woman who deserved a better partner than he could be. It broke his heart. But he had to move on. He couldn't shout or scream or rail at the unfairness of it. He had to move on.

He drew a long slow breath, reaching for his trademark calm. "I'm sorry."

"I'm not. It's the first real emotion you've ever shown around me." He sniffed a laugh. "Unless one counts the emotion I see on your face when you look at Vivi."

He turned his head, glanced out the window, unable to hold Constanzo's gaze anymore.

"You love her."

"It doesn't matter. I'm not good for her. I don't fit in her family. Worse, her family's in crisis and I froze."

"So?"

"So?" He gaped at Constanzo. "So she needed somebody strong and reliable and I had no clue what to say or do. I'm damaged. You know that. I didn't have a normal family life."

"There is no such thing as a normal family life. And I'm sure no one expected you to be strong or reliable. They just wanted you there."

He snorted. "Trust me. They didn't."

Constanzo drew back. "Are you whining?"

"I'm not whining. I'm facing truth. She has a sweet, wonderful family. I grew up in foster homes with moms who made me pack my own lunch and sometimes cook my own dinner. No one ever talked to me about life. I had to figure out personal hygiene from books. I don't know anything about real bonds. While Olivia's family kisses and hugs and talks, I have no idea how to relate to them."

"Tucker! You spent about ten hours with them! You've only known Olivia six or eight weeks. Getting along with people, even the woman you love takes time. Did you think this would be easy?"

"I—" Falling for Olivia had been easy. Natural. Her parents were a totally different story. "I don't want to be so much at odds with her parents that I put a wedge between her and her family. I don't want her to lose what I never had. That would be the ultimate selfishness."

"You won't take her away. You will learn to get along with them."

"Right."

"When you first met Vivi, you didn't know how to deal with her."

He said nothing. But remembered how awkward she'd made him feel.

"But eventually you figured it out."

"She forced me to figure it out."

"She'll help you fit."

"She shouldn't have to help me fit." Hatred of his start in life rolled through him on a hot ball of anger. All he'd ever wanted was to be normal and he'd figured out how. How to be bold and wise and never let anyone take advantage of him. None of that worked in a family.

"Weren't you helping her fit into your world?"

"Yes. But that's different."

"Why?"

"Because my world isn't something everybody understands. Family life is."

"Oh, Tucker. You are making a huge mistake. Go back. Try. Otherwise, you'll be me in thirty years. Except I don't think you have an illegitimate son to find. Someone to give your life meaning. Do you want to be me? Searching out people like you and Vivi who keep you company only because they sort of have to?"

The picture that came to mind surprised him. It wasn't a vision of himself thirty years from now. It was a vision of himself thirty days from now when he returned to his sterile penthouse. Alone. His cold office. Empty. Without even the chance of seeing Olivia in the halls of Inferno because she would be globe-hopping with Antonio. Or looking for new clients. Or going to galleries, studying the art.

Without him.

And he'd even be paying for it.

"You have a chance for a whole new life. You simply have to face a few weeks of mistakes as you adjust to having a family." He leaned across the seat and squeezed Tucker's hand. "A real family. Your family, if you marry her."

He sniffed a laugh. "She already asked me to marry her once."

Constanzo laughed with delight. "She's a girl who knows what she wants and goes after it. Maybe you should take a page from her." He patted Tucker's knee. "Get back on the plane. Humble yourself a little bit. The world is at your feet. A real life is at your feet. Not just Olivia's mom and dad and sister and brother...but kids. Your kids. A dark-haired boy. A strawberry blonde little girl."

He swallowed. He could picture it. He could actually see himself at a swing set. Or teaching his kids to swim. Or taking them to the opera and tickling them awake when they fell asleep. He could see Vivi running a household and having a career. He could see himself slowing down. Traveling with her. Sharing her exciting new career.

"Go home, Tucker. We can talk deal anytime. Right now Vivi needs you."

As if the driver had been listening in on their conversation, the limo door opened.

He stared at it, for the first time in his life seeing freedom and happiness only a few steps away.

A few steps and an eight-hour flight.

Followed by a two-hour drive.

And even those could be a waste if Constanzo was wrong and Vivi didn't want him. Didn't trust him to help her through this. Didn't trust him with her heart.

Two days later, Vivi left the hospital with her head down. They'd had a good day. Cindy had laughed—though it had caused her ribs to hurt so they'd upped her pain meds and she'd fallen back into a deep sleep and hadn't again awakened for hours.

Which had been very bad for Vivi. Because when the room was quiet, she had plenty of time to think about Tucker.

She couldn't believe she'd been so foolish as to fall for him, to believe he was different, that he'd love her in spite of her flaws, her wounds. But the ache in her very soul was proof that she had been. She'd fallen in love with a man who didn't love. He changed people. Molded them to be what he wanted so he didn't have to change.

Oh, she understood why. His upbringing had made him cautious and aware that people could hurt him. So he played it safe all the time.

But hadn't she proven she'd never hurt him?

Even if she had, he hadn't paid attention. He'd still tried to change her. Tried to make her into his perfect woman. He didn't want her. He wanted someone he thought was perfect.

She reached the curb, lifted her head to look both ways before crossing the parking lot and stopped dead in her tracks. A few feet in front of her, leaning against a beat-up rental car, wearing the discount department-store jeans, was Tucker. He had his arms crossed on his chest, his butt on the car's hood and his legs extended as if he'd been wait-ing a long time.

She started walking again, heading for her own car, de-termined to ignore him, but—

Well, there wasn't any reason for him to accidentally be in Kentucky. He'd come to see her. And, damn it, if the flutter of her heart was anything to go by, she desperately wanted him to have come back to her. The real her. Not his perfect woman, but the woman with a sister in the hospi-tal, parents who were worried and a sarcastic little brother.

She changed directions and walked toward him. He lifted himself from the hood.

"I'm sorry."

She smiled slightly, not sure how to take that. Was he sorry he'd left? Sorry he'd tried to change her? Or did he feel what she'd felt? That walking away had torn out his soul.

She'd spent every minute of their time together giving him the benefit of the doubt, believing the best about him, only to be hurt. She couldn't believe the best this time, couldn't make excuses for him. He had to speak. And he had to say the right things.

She looked across the parking lot, at the green, tree-covered mountains behind him. "I think you're going to have to do better than that."

"Sorry's not good enough?"

"Nope."

"Not even from someone who loves you?"

Though her heart raced and her arms longed to swing around him and hold him close so he could never get away, she said, "You don't love me. Otherwise, you wouldn't have gone."

"I left because I love you so much I think you deserve better."

She sniffed a laugh. "Right. That's why you tried to change me."

"Change you?"

"You elevated me from meager accountant to manager, someone who can be seen in public with you. Especially in a five-thousand-dollar designer dress. Something I couldn't have afforded for myself but something appropriate for me to be seen in with you. Almost as if I wasn't good enough the way I was."

"Oh, Olivia. Oh, God. Is that how you saw that?"

Her lips trembled but she continued to gaze off into the distance. He put his fingers on her chin, forcing her to look at him, reminding her of the first time he'd touched her and how she'd known, in that very second, that there was something different about him…about them.

"I wasn't trying to change you. Just help you. I would put the world at your feet if I thought you wanted it." He sucked in a breath. "You're perfect, wonderful. Just the way you are. I'm the problem here."

"You?"

"Your family loves you. Stands by you. Acts a bit like a bunch of barracudas assigned to protect you. And I'm… broken, Olivia. I'm the one who might not be good enough for you."

"But you love me?"

"Yes. Scarily. I want you—want a relationship with you—so badly that it terrifies me."

Her lips quirked. "I think if you do it right, love's supposed to be scary."

He barked a laugh. "What?"

"Well, people in love share secrets, form bonds, sacrifice." She smiled. "You've been spoiled a long time."

His hands slid to her waist. "Spoiled?"

She stepped closer. "Buying yourself everything you wanted."

He laughed, nestled her against him. "I have."

"But you couldn't buy me."

He grew serious. "I know."

"Yet you still won me."

He caught her gaze. "Have I?"

"Oh, come on. Where's the great Tucker Engle, guy who sees all, knows all?"

He smiled. "You love me."

"So you'll win over my parents. You'll make mistakes. Occasionally, you'll say you're sorry."

He winced.

She playfully slapped his arm. "Saying you're sorry isn't that hard."

"I don't know. Your mother's a tough cookie."

She laughed. "Kiss me, you idiot. We're going to make this work."

He kissed her then and she melted against him. Because they were going to make this work. Not just because she loved him but because they were good together, honest, in the way people who'd had softer, easier lives couldn't be. They'd appreciate every minute of every day together, have kids, build a family.

And he'd never be alone again.

EPILOGUE

WHEN THE LIMO pulled up to Constanzo's home, Olivia raced to meet it. She didn't wait for the driver to come around to open the door, she opened it herself.

"Welcome to Italy, Mom and Dad!"

Her dad slid out of the limo first then reached in to help her mom out. "Beautiful place. The trees remind me of home."

She hugged him, then her mom. "I thought the same thing."

Her mom glanced around. "I can see why you'd want to get married here."

Cindy ran out the front door with a squeal. As maid of honor and groomsman, she and Billy had arrived a week early to help with preparations. "I'm so glad you're here."

Her mom caught her in a hug. "Have you been making Billy mind?"

Cindy pulled away with a laugh, her short curly blond hair bouncing in the breeze.

Olivia said, "He's eighteen, Mom. Cut the apron strings. This fall, he'll be attending college in New York, living in his own apartment."

"Only a few floors down from us," Tucker said, coming out to greet her parents. He hugged her mom, shook hands with her dad. "We won't let things get out of hand."

Behind the scenes the driver unloaded their bags. Tucker

directed them into the house. Constanzo stood in the foyer, waiting for them.

"Loraina! Jim! I finally get you to my home."

Jim shook his hand. "Hey, you've never come to Kentucky. I still owe you for beating me at pool at Tucker's."

"I happen to have a pool table in the den."

Olivia sighed. "We're here for a wedding. Not a pool tournament. Tucker, tell them no tournaments."

He said, "No tournaments," but he laughed.

Olivia took her mom's arm. "What do you want to see first? The pool? Your room? Antonio's studio?"

"Oh, I don't want to disturb Antonio."

Antonio walked up the hall, drying his hands on a cloth. "You won't disturb me." He walked over and kissed Loraina. "You're my biggest fan. You never disturb me."

"Then give me ten minutes to get out of my traveling clothes and we'll go to your studio."

Cindy said, "I think I'm going to help the cook with lunch."

Jim sidled up to Constanzo. "Once I change I'll meet you at that pool table."

"I will be there."

In seconds, everybody had scattered, leaving Tucker and Olivia alone in the foyer.

"If you want, I can scold them about playing pool."

She smiled. "No. Let them." She glanced off in the direction Constanzo had hustled. "It's nice to see them getting along."

"It's nice to see us all get along."

She slid her arms around his waist. "People are people. Give us enough time and we can all find common ground."

"Speaking of common ground." He placed his hand on

her tummy. "Have you told your parents yet about the ultimate common ground?"

She laughed. "No. I thought we'd get through the wedding first then tell them they're going to be grandparents. One exciting step at a time."

He kissed her. "One happy step at a time."

"Yeah. One happy step at a time."

* * * * *

REUNITED WITH
HER ITALIAN EX

LUCY GORDON

PROLOGUE

Venice, the most romantic city in the world.

That was what people said, and Natasha was becoming convinced that it was true. Where else could she have met the man of her dreams within hours of arriving, and known so soon that she was his and he simply must become hers?

Sitting in a café by a small canal, she looked out at the sun glittering on the water. Nearby she could see a gondola containing a young man and woman, wrapped in each other's arms.

Just like us, she thought, recalling her first gondola ride in the arms of the man who had changed the world in moments.

Mario Ferrone, young, handsome, with dancing eyes and a rich chuckle that seemed to encompass the world. She'd met Mario just after she'd arrived in Venice on a well-earned holiday. He'd insisted on showing her the city. As his brother owned the hotel where she was staying, she'd briefly thought this a professional service, but that idea soon changed. There was an instant attraction between them, and nothing had ever seemed more wonderful than the time they spent together.

Until then, there had been little in her life that could

be called romance. She was slim, pretty, humorous, with no difficulty attracting admirers. But where men were concerned she had an instinctive defensiveness.

It went back to her childhood, when her father had abandoned his wife and ten-year-old daughter for another woman. Until that moment Natasha's life had been happy. Her father had seemed to adore her as she adored him. But suddenly he was gone, never to get in touch again.

Never trust a man, her mother had told her. *They'll always let you down.*

She'd been content to heed the warning until Mario came into her life and everything turned upside down.

Her own reactions confused her. Her heart was drawn to Mario as never before to any other man. Sometimes her mother's voice echoed in her mind.

No man can be trusted, Natasha. Remember that.

But Natasha felt certain that Mario was different to all other men—more honest, more trustworthy, more faithfully loving.

Last night he'd kissed her with even greater fervour than before, murmuring, 'Tomorrow I want to…' Then he'd stopped, seeming confused.

'Yes?' she'd whispered. 'What do you want?'

'I can't tell you now…but tomorrow everything will be different. Goodnight, *mi amore.*'

Now here she was in the café where they often met, waiting for him to appear and transform her world yet again.

She almost ached with the yearning to know what he'd meant by 'everything will be different'. Was he going to propose marriage? Surely he must.

Oh, please hurry, she thought. How could Mario keep her on tenterhooks when it mattered so much?

Suddenly, she heard his voice call, 'Natasha!' Looking up, she saw him walking by the canal, waving to her from a distance.

'Sorry I'm late,' he said, joining her at the table. 'I got held up.'

She had a strange feeling that he was on edge.

'Is everything all right?' she asked.

'It will be, very soon,' he said.

His eyes never left her and every moment her conviction grew that tonight they were going to take the next step—whatever it might be.

He took her hand. 'There's something I've been trying to tell you for days but—'

'Trying? Is it so hard to tell me?'

'It could be.' His eyes met hers. 'Some things just aren't easy to say.'

Her heart was beating with anticipation and excitement. She knew what he was going to say, and she longed to hear it.

'That depends how much you want to say them,' she whispered, leaning close so that her breath brushed his face. 'Perhaps you don't really want to say this.'

'Oh, yes, you don't know how much it matters.'

But I do know, she thought happily. He was going to tell her how much she meant to him. In a moment her life would be transformed.

She took his hand in hers, sending him a silent message about her willingness to draw closer to him.

'Go on,' she whispered.

He hesitated and she regarded him, puzzled. Was it really so hard for him to reach out to her?

'Natasha—I want to tell you—'

'Yes—yes—tell me.'

'I'm not good at this—'

'You don't need to be good at it,' she urged, tightening her clasp on his hand. 'Just say it—'

'Well—'

'Traitor!'

The screamed word stunned them both. Natasha looked up to see a woman standing by the table, glaring at them. She was in her thirties, voluptuous, and would have been beautiful but for the look of livid hatred she cast on Mario.

'Traitor!' she screamed. *'Liar! Deceiver!'*

Mario's face was tense and pale as Natasha had never seen it before. He rose and confronted the woman, speaking angrily in Italian and pointing for her to leave. She screamed back at him in English. Then turned to Natasha.

'It's about time you knew what he is really like. One woman isn't enough for him.'

She raved on until Mario drew her into a corner, arguing with her vigorously. Natasha could no longer hear the words but there was no mistaking the intensity between them. The dark-haired woman's rage grew with every moment.

'He's a liar and a cheat,' she screamed in perfect English.

'Mario,' Natasha said, 'who is this woman? Do you really know her?'

'Oh, yes, he knows me,' the woman spat. 'You wouldn't believe how well he knows me.'

'Tania, that's enough,' Mario said, white-faced. 'I told you—'

'Oh, yes, you told me. Traitor! Traitor! *Traditore!'*

For a moment Natasha was tempted to thrust herself between them and tell Mario what she thought of him in no uncertain terms. But then her impetuous temper flared even higher, driving her to a course of action even more fierce and desperate. While they were still absorbed in their furious encounter, she fled.

She ran every step of the way to the hotel, then up to her room, pausing at the desk to demand her bill. Nothing mattered but to get away from here before Mario returned. It had all been a deception. She'd believed in him because she'd wanted to believe, and she should have known better. Now she was paying the price.

'You were right,' she muttered to her mother's ghost. 'They're all the same.'

The ghost was too tactful to say *I told you so*, but she was there in Natasha's consciousness as she finished packing, paid her bill and fled.

She took a boat taxi across the water to the mainland, and from there she switched to a motor taxi.

'Airport,' she told the driver tensely.

Oh, Mario, she thought as the car roared away. *Traitor. Traditore.*

CHAPTER ONE

Two years later...

'I'M SORRY, NATASHA, but the answer's no, and that's final. You just have to accept it.'

Natasha's face was distorted by anger as she clutched the phone.

'Don't tell me what I have to do,' she snapped into the receiver. 'You said you were eager for anything I wrote—'

'That was a long time ago. Things have changed. I can't buy any more of your work. Those are my orders.'

Natasha took a shuddering breath as yet another rejection slammed into her.

'But you're the editor,' she protested. 'Surely it's you who gives the orders.'

'The magazine's owner tells us what to do and that's final. You're out. Finished. Goodbye.'

The editor hung up, leaving Natasha staring at the phone in fury and anguish.

'Another one?' asked a female voice behind her. 'That's the sixth editor who's suddenly turned against you after buying your work for ages.'

Natasha turned to her friend Helen, who was also her flatmate.

'I can't believe it,' she groaned. 'It's like there's a spider at the centre of a web controlling them all, telling them to freeze me out.'

'But there is. Surely you know that. The spider's name is Elroy Jenson.'

It's true, Natasha thought reluctantly. Jenson owned a huge media empire that until recently had provided her with a good living. But he'd taken a fancy to her and pursued her relentlessly, ignoring her pleas to be left alone. Finally he'd gone too far, forcing her to slap his face hard enough to make him yell. One of his employees had seen them and spread the story.

'Everyone knows you made him look a fool,' Helen said sympathetically. 'So now he's your enemy. It's a pity about that quick temper of yours, Natasha. You had every right to be angry but…well…'

'But I should have paused before I clobbered him. I should have been calm and controlled and thought about the future. Hah!'

'Yes, I know it sounds ironic, but look at the price you've paid.'

'Yes,' Natasha said with a heavy sigh.

As a freelance journalist her success had been dazzling. Magazines and newspapers clamoured for her sassy, insightful articles.

Until now.

'How can one man have so much power?' she groaned.

'Perhaps you need to go abroad for a while,' Helen suggested. 'Until Jenson forgets all about you.'

'That would be difficult—'

'It needn't be. The agency found me a job in Italy, doing publicity. It would mean going out there for a while.

I was about to call them and say they'd have to find someone else, but why don't you go instead?'

'But I can't just... That's a mad idea.'

'Sometimes madness is the best way. It could be just what you need now.'

'But I don't speak Italian.'

'You don't have to. It's an international thing, promoting the city all over the world.'

'It's not Venice, is it?' Natasha asked, suddenly tense.

'No, don't worry. I know you wouldn't want to go to Venice. It's Verona, the city of *Romeo and Juliet*. Some of that story is real, and tourists love to see Juliet's balcony and other places where different scenes are set. So a group of luxury hotel owners have clubbed together to create some publicity for the place. Of course, I know you're not exactly a fan of romance—'

'It doesn't bother me,' Natasha said quickly. 'I'm not going into retreat just because one man— Well, anyway—'

'Fine. So why don't you take this job?'

'But how can I? It's yours.'

'I really wish you would. I accepted it impulsively because I'd had a row with my boyfriend. I thought we were finished, but we've made up and it would really suit me if you went instead of me.'

'But if they're expecting you—'

'I've been dealing with the agency. I'll put you in touch with them and sing your praises. Natasha, you can't let your life be ruled by a man you haven't seen for two years. Especially when he was a cheating rogue. Your words, not mine.'

'Yes,' she murmured. 'I said that. And I meant it.'

'Then go. Put Mario behind you and put Elroy behind you, too. Seize your chance for a fresh start.'

Natasha took a deep breath. 'All right,' she said. 'I'll do it.'

'Fine. Now, let's get started.'

Helen logged on to her computer and contacted the agency. Moments later, Natasha was reading an email, written in efficient English, offering her the assignment and giving her instructions:

You will be dealing with Giorgio Marcelli. The hotel owners employ him to handle publicity. He looks forward to welcoming you to Verona.

'You see, it's a no-brainer,' Helen said. 'I'll leave you to have a think.'

She departed.

Left alone, Natasha stared out of the window, trying to decide what to do. Despite what Helen said, it wasn't easy to make up her mind.

'Not Venice,' she had asserted and Helen had reassured her, because she knew that nothing would persuade Natasha ever to go back to that beautiful romantic city where her heart had been broken.

Natasha thought back to herself as a very young woman, haunted by her mother's warnings never to trust a man. She had pursued a successful career, devoting her time to her writing, avoiding emotional relationships. Of course she could flirt and enjoy male company. But never for very long. Eventually distrust would make her back away from any man who attracted her.

She'd been glad of it, sure that caution would protect her from suffering her mother's fate. On that she had been resolved.

Until she'd met Mario.

He had affected her as no other man ever had. Together they had walked the streets of Venice, drifting by the canals. In one tiny alley he'd drawn her into the shadows for their first kiss. Despite her attempts to obliterate the memory, it still lived in her now.

Her whole body had responded to him, coming alive in ways she had never dreamed of before. She could sense the same in him, although every instinct told her that he was an experienced lover. Wherever they went, women had thrown admiring glances at him and regarded Natasha with envy. She'd guessed they were thinking how lucky she was to be sharing his bed. That day had never come, although several times Natasha had been on the verge of giving in to temptation.

As the day of her departure neared, Mario had begged her to stay with him a little longer. Blissfully happy, she had agreed.

Even now, two years later, remembering that happiness was the most painful thing of all, despite her frantic attempts to banish it from her memory, her heart, her life.

She imagined his face when he'd returned to the table and found her gone.

Vanished into thin air, she thought. *As far as he's concerned I no longer exist, and he no longer exists to me.*

In fact, the man she'd believed him to be had never existed. That was what she had to face.

Bitterly, she replayed the scene. She'd been so sure that he was about to declare his feelings, but when he'd said, 'There's something I've been trying to tell you for days,' he'd actually been planning to dump her.

He'd probably spent the afternoon with Tania, perhaps in her bed.

She thought he was being unfaithful to her with me.

In fact he was being unfaithful to both of us. That's the kind of man he is.

After fleeing from Venice, Natasha had done everything she could to disappear for ever, changing her email address and phone number.

But one email from him had just managed to get through before the old address was cut off:

Where did you vanish to? What happened? Are you all right?

Yes, she thought defiantly. *I'm all right. I got rid of the only person who could hurt me. And nobody is ever going to do that to me again.*

She'd never replied to Mario, merely instructing the server to block his emails. Then she'd moved in with Helen. If he came to her old flat he would find the door locked against him as firmly as her heart was locked against him.

At night she would lie awake, dismayed by the violence of her response. He had touched her emotions with an intensity that warned her to escape while there was still time. That way lay the only safety.

Oh, Mario, she thought. *Traitor. Traditore.*

Since then she'd devoted herself to work, making such an impression that she came to the attention of Elroy Jenson. The media magnate had propositioned her, certain that a mere freelance journalist would never refuse him. When she did refuse he couldn't believe it, persisting until she was forced to slap his face and bring her successful career to a sudden end.

After that, her life had been on a downward spiral. Her

income had collapsed. Now she could barely afford the small rent she paid on the room she rented from Helen.

The time had come for firm action. And if that meant leaping into the unknown, she would do it. The unknown had its attractions, and suddenly she was ready for anything.

She exchanged brisk emails with Giorgio, the publicity manager. He informed her that she would be staying at the Dimitri Hotel and a driver would meet her at the airport. Two days later she embarked on the journey that might lead to a triumphant new life, or a disaster. Either way, she was venturing into the unknown.

During the flight to Verona she kept her mind firmly concentrated on work. *Romeo and Juliet* was a story that had long touched the world: two young people who fell in love despite the enmity of their families. In the end, they chose to die rather than live without each other.

Legend said that Shakespeare's play was based on real events. The lovers had really lived and died. It would be her job to immerse herself in the story and entice the world to join her.

The driver was at the airport, holding up a placard bearing the words 'Dimitri Hotel'. He greeted her with relief, and ushered her into the car for the three-mile journey to Verona.

'The hotel is in the centre of town,' he said. 'Right next to the river.'

Verona was an ancient, beautiful city. Delighted, she gazed out of the window, enchanted by the hints of another, mysterious age. At last they drew up outside a large elaborate building.

'Here we are. Dimitri Hotel,' the driver said.

As she entered the elegant lobby, a man came forward.

He was in his sixties, heavily built, with a plump, smiling face. He greeted her in English.

'The agency told me there had been a change of plan,' he said. 'Apparently the original candidate couldn't make it, but they say you have excellent credentials.'

'Thank you. I'm an experienced journalist. I hope I can live up to your expectations.'

'I'm sure you will. I'm very glad you're here. I promised the President the lady would be here for him tonight and it's never good to disappoint him.'

He gave a comical shudder which made Natasha ask, 'Is he a difficult man? Scary?'

'Sometimes. Mostly he's very determined. People don't cross him if they can help it. He only bought this hotel just under two years ago and set about changing everything practically the first day. There's been a massive redecoration, and the staff has been reorganised to suit him. Everything has to be done his way. Nobody argues.'

'You called him the President.'

'President of the *Comunità*. It was his idea that a group of hotel owners of Verona, the *Comunità*, should all work together. They thought it would be an easy-going organisation but he said it needed leadership. The others just did as he suggested and named him President.

'A while back one of the other owners thought of challenging him for the top job, but he was "persuaded" not to. Nobody knows how, but neither was anyone surprised.

'When he gives his orders we jump to attention, especially me, because he could fire me any time he likes. I'm only telling you so that you'll take care not to offend him.

'We'll dine with him tonight and tomorrow you will meet all the *Comunità* members. They're looking forward to having you spread the word about our lovely city.'

'But isn't the word already out? Surely *Romeo and Juliet* is the most famous love story in the world?'

'True, but we need to make people realise how they can become involved. Now, I'll show you to your room.'

On their way up they passed two men having a noisy argument. One was clearly in command, yelling, *'Capisci? Capisci?'* so fiercely that the other backed off.

'What does that word mean?' Natasha asked curiously. 'It really scared the other guy.'

'It means "Do you understand?"' Giorgio laughed. 'It's really just a way of saying "You'll do as I say. *Get it?*"'

'It sounds useful.'

'It can be, if you're trying to make it clear who's in charge.' He grinned. 'I've had it said to me a few times. Here's your room.'

Like the rest of the place, her room was elegant and luxurious. A huge window looked out over the river, where the sun shone on the water. The atmosphere seemed peaceful and she took a deep contented breath.

When she'd unpacked she took a shower and began work on her appearance. For this meeting she was going to look her best.

She was attractive so not too much effort was required. Her blue eyes were large and expressive. Her blonde hair had just a touch of red that showed in some lights but not in others.

Natasha pinned her hair high on her head, suggesting businesslike severity. Usually, she preferred to let it flow, curved and luscious about her shoulders in a more relaxed way.

But not tonight, she mused, studying herself in the mirror. *Tonight I'm a businesswoman, here to earn a living.*

She fixed her hair firmly away from her face until she felt it conveyed the serious message she intended. Giorgio had warned her that the owner was a man to be reckoned with, but she could deal with that. She'd meet him on his own ground, a woman to be reckoned with.

'I did the right thing in coming here,' she whispered. 'Everything's going to be fine.'

In Venice, a city where most of the roads were water, motor cars could only come as far as Piazzale Roma, the car park on the edge of town. In the glowing heat of a sunny day, Mario Ferrone went to collect his car, accompanied by his brother Damiano.

'It sounds like your hotel is doing really well,' Damiano said. 'You've got a great future ahead of you.'

'I think I just might have,' Mario said, grinning.

'No doubt,' Damiano said cheerfully. 'After all, look who taught you.'

This was a reference to Damiano's successful career as the owner of several hotels. Mario had learned the trade working in many of them and had finally become ambitious for his own establishment.

'That's right, I learned from the best,' Mario said. 'And having a place in Verona is a help. Several of us hoteliers have got together to promote the *Romeo and Juliet* angle.'

'The city of lovers,' Damiano said wryly. 'That should suit you. You'd hardly believe some of the tales I've heard about you.'

'Not recently,' Mario said quickly.

'No, you've settled down these last couple of years, but before that I remember you gave a whole new meaning to the term "bad boy".'

'Most of us do before we find the right woman,' Mario pointed out.

'True. I wasn't a saint before I met Sally. But you haven't met your "Sally", so what made you suddenly become virtuous?'

'Virtuous? Me? No need to insult me.'

Damiano grinned. 'So is it just a smokescreen?'

'No. I really have changed, not necessarily for the better.'

'Don't say that. You're much improved—quieter, more serious, more grown-up...'

'More suspicious and demanding, nastier sometimes,' Mario said quietly.

'Hey, why do you put yourself down?'

'Perhaps because I know myself better than anyone else does. I'm not the nice guy I used to be—if I ever was.'

'So what made it happen?'

Mario clapped him on the shoulder. 'Don't ask me. It's a long story, and one that—well, that I don't care to think of too often. Let's leave it. I'd better be going. Giorgio has hired a journalist he says will be brilliant at promoting the *Romeo and Juliet* angle. I'm meeting her for dinner when I get back tonight.'

'Best of luck. Goodbye, brother.'

They embraced each other. Damiano stood back, waving as Mario turned out of the car park and across the causeway that led to the mainland.

From Venice to Verona was nearly seventy-five miles. During the journey Mario reflected wryly on his brother's words. Damiano didn't know that one of the turning points in Mario's life had been Damiano's marriage to Sally, four years earlier. Mario had been strongly attracted to Sally, something he'd had to fight. He'd fought it by working in Damiano's hotels in Rome, Florence, Milan, only rarely returning to Venice.

Until then his life had been free and easy. He was young, charming and handsome, with no trouble attracting women. He'd had many girlfriends. Too many, he now realised.

He'd returned to Venice for the birth of his brother's son and found, to his relief, that Sally no longer attracted him, except as a sister. He'd settled into a life of work and pleasure.

Then had come the other great turning point in his life, when he'd met the one woman who could make a difference, drive away the loneliness and give his existence meaning.

Fantasy dictated that she should feel the same and throw herself into his arms. The bitter reality was that she had walked out on him, slamming the door in his face, condemning him to a bleak isolation that was all the worse because he had glimpsed a glorious future, and come so close to embracing it.

Buying the hotel two years ago had been a lucky chance. The owner was eager to sell and accepted a discounted price, and now Mario felt that he was headed for success and independence. If he did nothing else in his life he would triumph in this, he vowed to himself. With that hope to guide him he could banish the pain and bleakness of the last two years.

At last he reached the hotel. Giorgio came to the entrance to greet him.

'It's all set up,' he said.

'Has the lady arrived?'

'Yes, an hour ago. She's not who I was expecting. The

agency made a last-minute change, but she seems serious and professional.'

'I can't wait to meet her.' As they walked across the elegant lobby, Mario looked around him at the place he was beginning to regard as his kingdom. 'You know, I have the best possible feeling about this,' he said. 'We're on the right road, and we're going to reach a great destination.'

'One where the money is,' Giorgio supplied with a grin.

'Of course, but that's not the only thing. Somehow, everything is beginning to feel right.'

'That's the spirit. Get settled in and then I'll introduce you to… Mario? Mario, is something wrong?'

But Mario didn't hear him. His attention had been drawn to the great staircase that led to the next floor. He was staring at it like a man stunned. A young woman was walking down the stairs. She moved slowly, pausing to look at the paintings on the wall, so that at first she didn't seem to notice Mario standing by the bottom step.

When her eyes came to rest on Mario she stopped suddenly, as if unable to believe her eyes.

A terrible stillness came over Natasha as she looked down the staircase, trying to understand what was happening. It was impossible that Mario should be standing there, staring up at her with a thunderstruck expression.

Impossible.

And yet it was true. He was there, looking like a man who'd seen a nightmare come to life.

She tried to move but the stillness enveloped her. Now he was climbing the stairs slowly, as though unwilling to approach her too quickly or come too close. When he spoke it was uneasily.

'I believe…we've met before.'

A dozen answers clamoured in her head, but at last she heard herself say, 'No, never.'

That took him off-guard, she could see. While he struggled for a reply, Giorgio's voice reached them from the bottom of the stairs.

'Aha! I see you two are getting acquainted.' Waving cheerfully, he climbed up to join them.

'Natasha, let me introduce Mario Ferrone, the owner of the hotel and President of the *Comunità*. Mario, this is Natasha Bates, the lady who's going to tell the world about Verona.'

Mario inclined his head formally. '*Buongiorno, signorina*. It's a pleasure to meet you.'

'How do you do?' she said, nodding towards him.

'Let's go and eat,' Giorgio said, 'and we can have a good talk.'

Downstairs, a table was laid for them in a private room overlooking the river. Giorgio led Natasha to the chair nearest the window and drew it out for her.

A waiter hurried in, eager to serve the hotel's owner. His manner was respectful and she was reminded of Giorgio's words:

'When he gives his orders we all jump to attention…'

She'd known him as a cheeky playboy, always ready to laugh and use his charm. It was hard to see the man he'd been then as the stern authoritarian that Giorgio described now. But his face had changed, growing slightly thinner, firmer, more intense. Even his smile had something reserved about it.

Turning her eyes to him briefly, she caught him glancing at her and realised that he was studying her too. What did he see? Had she also changed, becoming older, sterner, less relaxed? Probably. Perhaps she should be glad, for it would make her stronger. And she was going to need strength now.

Giorgio claimed her attention, filling her wine glass, smiling at her with an air of deferential admiration. He had probably been handsome in his youth, and still had the air of a practised flirt.

'How much were you told about this job?' he asked her.

'Only that some Verona hotel owners had got together to promote the city's connection with *Romeo and Juliet*,' Natasha said.

'That's right. It's already well promoted by the council, which works hard to bring tourists here. But the hotel owners wanted to enjoy a bit more of the spotlight, so they formed the Comunità di Verona Ospitalità so that they could make the most of being in the town that saw the greatest love story in the world.

'Shakespeare didn't invent *Romeo and Juliet*. There really were two families called Montague and Capulet, and they did have children who fell in love, and died. It happened in the early fourteenth century. In the next two hundred years the story was told and retold, until finally Shakespeare based his play on the legend. Tourists come here to see "Juliet's balcony" and imagine the balcony scene happening there.'

'Which it didn't,' Mario observed drily. 'The house belonged to a family called Capello, but the council added the balcony less than a hundred years ago.'

'But if everyone knows that—' Natasha mused.

'They know it but they ignore it,' Giorgio said cheerfully. 'People are often tempted to believe only what they want to.'

'How true,' Natasha murmured. 'That's why we're all so easily taken in.'

She didn't look directly at Mario as she said these words, but she had a sense that he was watching her with an air of tension that matched her own.

'And that's what we can make use of,' Giorgio said. 'Juliet's balcony, Juliet's tomb, where Romeo killed himself because he couldn't bear life without her, and where she killed herself for the same reason. Is it true? It is if we want it to be.'

'Oh, yes,' Natasha mused. 'True if we want it to be— until one day we have to face the fact that it isn't true, however much we want it.'

'But that's show business,' Giorgio said. 'Creating a fantasy that makes people happy.'

'And what more could we want than that?' Mario asked.

He raised his glass and drank from it, seemingly oblivious to her. But the next moment he said, 'Tell us something about yourself, *signorina.*'

She turned her head, meeting his eyes directly. 'What did you say?'

'I said I'd like to know about you. I'm sure there is much you could tell us. What are your family obligations? Are you free to live in Verona for several weeks, or is there someone at home who will be missing you?'

'I suppose there must be,' Giorgio said. He assumed a chivalrous air. 'This is a lovely lady. She must have crowds of men following her.'

'That doesn't mean that I let them catch up,' Natasha teased.

'Some women are very good at keeping out of sight,' Mario said.

'Of course,' Giorgio agreed. 'That's the secret. Let them chase after you, but don't let any of them get close enough to know what you're thinking and feeling.' He kissed her hand gallantly. '*Signorina*, I can see you're an expert in keeping your admirers wondering.'

'But just what are they wondering?' Mario asked. 'Will any of them arrive here to assert his "rights"?'

'What rights?' Giorgio demanded. 'She's not married.'

'That's irrelevant,' Mario observed. 'You have only to study *Romeo and Juliet* to see that men and women make that decision within a few moments of meeting. And nobody dares get in their way.'

'When people fear betrayal they can get violent,' Giorgio agreed.

Natasha nodded. 'And if they know for sure that they've been betrayed, there's no knowing how far they'll go to make someone sorry,' she mused, letting her glance rest on Mario.

She was glad to see that he understood the silent message. Before her eyes he flinched and averted his gaze. When he spoke again it was in a voice so defiantly businesslike that it told its own story.

'So we can expect a jealous lover to follow you out here?' he said curtly.

She faced him, reading the chilly hostility in his eyes, answering it with her own.

'On the contrary. You can be certain that nothing will make me leave before my work is finished,' she said calmly. 'Unlike some people, I'm honest about my intentions. I don't make promises and break them.'

'That's not exactly what I asked.'

No, she thought. *You asked whether I'd had the nerve to replace you with another man.*

She gave him her most confident smile, as though his questions merely amused her.

'Let me assure you that I am free,' she said. 'No man tells me what to do, and if anyone tried—' she leaned closer to him '—I would make him regret that he ever knew me.' She added significantly, 'I'm good at that.'

'I believe you,' he said.

Giorgio glanced at them curiously. 'Hey, do you two already know each other?'

'No,' Natasha said quickly, before Mario could speak.

'Really? I feel like I'm watching a fencing match.'

'It's more fun that way,' she said lightly. 'Go on telling me about Verona. Unless, of course, Signor Ferrone has decided he doesn't wish to employ me. In which case I'll just pack up and go. Shall I?'

She made as if to rise but Mario's hand detained her.

'No need for that,' he said harshly. 'Let's get on with the job.'

'Yes, that's the only thing that matters,' she said, falling back into the chair.

For a moment he kept his hand on her arm. 'So we are agreed? You will stay?'

'I will stay.'

CHAPTER TWO

MARIO RELEASED HER. 'As long as we understand each other.'

Natasha drew a tense breath as the bitter irony of those words swept over her. They had never understood each other. Nor could they ever, except on the lines of mutual defensiveness and mistrust.

She turned to Giorgio, assuming her most business-like tone.

'So it's time I consulted with the Publicity Manager. Tell me, what are my instructions?'

'We must go on a trip around Verona,' he said, 'studying all the significant places. Especially the balcony. These days you can even get married in Juliet's house. And afterwards the bride and groom always come out onto the balcony for the photographs.'

'Useful,' she said, taking out her notebook and beginning to write. 'The balcony scene is the most famous part of the story.'

'Yes, people love to imagine Juliet standing there, yearning for her lover, saying, "Romeo, Romeo, where art thou Romeo?"'

'She doesn't say "where",' Natasha objected. 'She says "Wherefore". It means "Why?" She's saying "Why did you have to be Romeo, a Montague, and my enemy?" In Shakespeare's time, if you wanted to know why someone had behaved in a certain way, you'd say—' she assumed a dramatic attitude '"—Wherefore did thou do this, varlet?"'

'Varlet?' Giorgio queried.

'It means rascal. You'd say it to someone who'd behaved disgustingly.'

Giorgio gave a crack of laughter. 'I must remember that. Rascal—*briccone*.'

'Or *traditore*,' Natasha observed lightly.

'Aha! So you know some Italian words?' Giorgio said eagerly.

'One or two,' she said with a fair assumption of indifference.

'I'd give a lot to know how you learned that particular one,' he said cheekily.

'You'll just have to wonder,' she chuckled.

Mario wasn't looking at her. He seemed completely occupied with his wine.

A man appeared in the doorway, signalling to Giorgio.

'I've got to leave you for a moment,' he said. 'But I'll be back.' He laid a hand on Natasha's shoulder. 'Don't go away. I have a very good feeling about this.'

'So have I,' she said. 'I'll be right here.'

When Giorgio had gone, Mario refilled her wine glass.

'Be cautious about Giorgio,' he said. 'He turns on the charm as part of his trade.'

'But of course,' she said cheerfully. 'It's a form of show business. No harm in that.'

'As long as you're not taken in.'

'I'm not. These days, nothing and nobody manages to deceive me.'

He raised his glass to her in an ironic salute.

'This is quite a coincidence,' he said. 'I wonder which of us is more shocked.'

'We'll never know.'

'Just now you were very determined to say we didn't know each other.'

'Would you have said differently?' she asked, watching him.

'No, but I doubt I'd have said it so fast or emphatically. You denied knowing me as though your life depended on it.'

'But we didn't know each other. Once we believed we did but we were both wrong. You thought I was easy to fool or you wouldn't have wasted your time on me. You never reckoned on Tania turning up and showing me what you were really like.'

'I admit I once had a relationship with Tania, but it was over.'

'Was it? I don't think she believed that. She still felt you were hers. That's why she felt so betrayed when she saw us. No, it was me you were planning to leave. That's why you kept hinting about something you wanted to tell me. You said it wasn't easy, but then it's never easy to dump someone, is it?'

He turned very pale. 'Isn't it? You dumped me without any trouble.'

'Dumping you was the easiest thing I'd ever done, but that's because you gave me cause.'

'But the way you did it—vanishing so that I could never find you. Can you imagine what I went through? It was like searching for a ghost. I nearly went mad because you denied me any chance to explain—'

'Explain what? That you were fooling around with

both of us? If you'd been the man I thought you— Well, let's leave it there. You weren't that man and you never could be. It's best if we remain strangers now.'

'*Remain?*' he echoed sharply. But then his voice changed to wry, slightly bitter acceptance. 'Yes, we always were strangers, weren't we?'

'Always were, always will be. That's a very good business arrangement.'

'And you're a businesswoman?'

'Exactly. It's what I choose to be. *Capisci?*'

He nodded. '*Capisco.* I understand.'

'From now on, it's all business. The past didn't happen. It was an illusion.'

'An illusion—yes. I guessed that when you vanished into thin air. And now you've reappeared just as suddenly.'

'Another illusion. I'm not really here.'

'So if I look away you'll vanish again?'

'Perhaps that's what I ought to do.'

'No,' he said with a hint of suppressed violence. '*No!* Not again. You could never understand how I— Don't even think of it. *Capisci?*'

'*Capisco.* I understand very well.'

'Promise me that you won't leave.'

'All right.'

'On your word of honour.'

'Look—'

'Say it. Let me know that I can trust you this time at least.'

'Trust me *this time*? As though I was the one who deceived— You've got a nerve.'

'He's coming back,' Mario said hurriedly, glancing to where Giorgio had appeared. 'Smile.'

She tried to look at ease but it was hard, and as soon as Giorgio reached the table she rose.

'I'm going to bed,' she said. 'It's been a long day for me, with the flight.'

'You're right; get some rest,' Mario said. 'We'll all meet here tomorrow morning at nine.'

They shook hands and she departed at once.

Giorgio watched her go, then eyed Mario wryly.

'What's going on with you two?' he queried. 'You're on edge with each other. For a moment I really thought there'd been something between you.'

'Not a thing,' Mario assured him. 'And there never could be.'

'Pity. Romeo and Juliet were "star-crossed lovers". It could have been interesting to have them promoted by another pair of star-crossed lovers. After all, if a couple is meant for each other but just can't get it together—well, it's not in their hands, is it? They just have to enjoy it while they can, but then accept that fate is against them.'

'Isn't that giving in too easily?'

'It's what Romeo and Juliet had to accept.'

'And then they died.'

'They died physically, but it doesn't usually happen that way. Sometimes people just die inside.'

'Yes,' Mario murmured. 'That's true.'

'I'll call the other members of the group and fix a meeting. They'll just love her. We've found the right person. Don't you agree?'

Mario nodded and spoke in an iron voice. 'The right person. Not a doubt of it. I must be going. My work has piled up while I've been away.'

He departed fast, urgently needing to get away from Giorgio's sharp eyes that saw too much for comfort.

Upstairs, he headed for his bedroom, but paused before entering. The room allocated to Natasha was just across the corridor and he went to stand outside, looking at her door, wondering what was happening behind it.

The evening had torn his nerves to shreds. The woman he'd met had been as unlike the sweet, charming girl he remembered as steel was unlike cream. His heart told him it was impossible that they should be the same person, but his brain groaned and said it was true.

This was the heartless creature who had vanished without giving him a chance to defend himself, leaving him to hunt frantically for weeks until he'd realised that it was hopeless. And her manner towards him had left no doubt that she was enjoying her triumph.

A sensible man would have sent her away at once. Instead, he'd prevented her leaving, driven by instincts he didn't understand, nor want to face.

From behind her door came only silence. He moved closer, raising his hand to knock, then dropping it again. This wasn't the right moment.

Instead of going into his room, he turned away again and went downstairs into the garden, hoping some time in the night air would clear the confusion in his mind. But also doubting that anything would ever be clear again.

Natasha paced her room restlessly. After such a day she should have been ready to collapse into sleep, but her nerves were tense and she feared to lie awake all night, thinking the very thoughts she wanted to avoid.

Mario had blamed her for disappearing without giving him a chance to defend himself, and in so doing he'd touched a nerve.

Perhaps I should have let him say something, she thought. *Why didn't I?*

Because I'm my mother's daughter, said another voice in her mind. *And I can't help living by the lessons she taught me. Never trust a man. Don't believe his explanation because it'll be lies and you'll only suffer more. In fact, don't let him explain at all. Never, never give him a second chance.*

She'd fled Mario because she feared to listen to what he might have to say. Thinking the worst of him felt safer. That was the sad truth.

But now, meeting him again and getting a sense of his torment, she felt uneasy about her own actions.

'No,' she said. 'No, I'm not going down that road. What's done is done. It's over.'

In the last year she'd often suffered from insomnia and had resorted to some herbal sleeping pills. She took them out now, considering.

'I'm not lying awake fretting over him. This is war.'

She swallowed two pills but, instead of going to bed, she went outside for a few minutes. The tall window opened onto a balcony where she could stand and look down on a narrow strip of garden. There were flowers, a few trees and beyond them the Adige River, glowing in the evening light. Now it was easy to slip into the balcony scene and become Juliet, yearning over the man who'd captured her heart before she knew who he was. When she'd realised that she'd fallen in love with an enemy, it was too late.

'Too late,' she murmured. 'The last thing I wanted was to meet him again. I came here to start a new life. *Mario, Mario, wherefore art thou, Mario?* But it had to be you, didn't it? When I'm looking forward to meeting new people, you have to pop up. *Wherefore did thou do this, varlet?'*

In her agitation she said the words aloud. Alarmed at herself, she retreated through the window, shutting it firmly.

Outside, all was quiet. Darkness was falling, and there was nobody to notice Mario standing, alone and silent, beneath the trees. He had come straight into the garden after leaving Natasha's door, wondering if some light from her room would reassure him. What he had seen stunned and confused him. Her whispered words seemed to float down, reaching him so softly that he couldn't be sure he'd actually heard them.

To believe what he longed to believe was something he refused to do. That way lay danger, disillusion—the things he'd promised himself to avoid in future. So he backed into the shadows, his eyes fixed on her window until the light went out and his world was full of darkness.

Promptly at nine o'clock the next morning Mario appeared at the breakfast table, frowning as he saw only Giorgio there.

'Where is she?' he demanded. 'I told her nine o'clock.'

'Have a heart,' Giorgio begged. 'It's only a few minutes after nine. She's not a machine, just a lovely lady.'

'She is an employee being paid a high salary, for which I expect punctuality and obedience to my wishes. Kindly call her room.'

'I've been calling it for half an hour,' Giorgio admitted. 'But there's no reply. Perhaps she doesn't want to talk to us.'

Or perhaps she can't, said a voice in Mario's mind.

He remembered the woman she had been the evening before, bright, completely at ease, ready to challenge him every moment.

Yet there had been something else, he realised. Beneath her confident manner he'd sensed something different—troubled, uneasy. Their meeting had taken them both by surprise. His own turmoil had startled and shaken him, making him struggle not to let her suspect his weakness, the more so because she had seemed free of any weakness.

But then he'd seen a new look in her eyes, a flash of vulnerability that matched his own. It had vanished at once, but for a brief moment he'd known that she was as alarmed as he was.

He remembered how he'd stood under her balcony last night, watching her, sensing again that she was haunted, but resisting the impulse to reach out to her. Her disappearance now hinted at new trouble. If he went to her room, what would he find? The confident Natasha, laughing at his discomfiture? Or the frail Natasha who couldn't cope?

Abruptly he took out his mobile phone, called her room and listened as the bell rang and rang, with no reply.

'If it was anyone else you'd think they'd vanished without paying the bill,' Giorgio observed. 'But we're not charging her for that room, so she's got no reason to vanish.'

'That's right,' Mario said grimly. 'No reason at all.'

'I'll go and knock on her door.'

'No, stay here. I'll see what's happened.'

Swiftly, he went to his office and opened a cupboard that contained the hotel's replacement keys. Trying to stay calm despite his growing worry, Mario took the one that belonged to Natasha's room and went upstairs. After only a moment's hesitation, he opened her door.

At once he saw her, lying in bed, so still and silent that alarm rose in him. He rushed towards the bed and leaned down to her, close enough to see that she was breathing.

His relief was so great that he grasped the chest of drawers to stop himself falling. Every instinct of self-preservation warned him to get out quickly, before he was discovered. But he couldn't make himself leave her. Instead he dropped onto one knee, gazing at her closely. She lay without moving, her lovely hair splayed out on the pillow, her face soft and almost smiling.

How he had once dreamed of this, of awakening to find her beside him, sleeping gently, full of happiness at the pleasure they had shared.

He leaned a little closer, until he could feel her breath on his face. He knew he was taking a mad risk. A wise man would leave now, but he wasn't a wise man. He was a man torn by conflicting desires.

Then she moved, turning so that the bedclothes slipped away from her, revealing that she was naked. Mario drew a sharp breath.

How often in the past had he longed to see her this way? He had planned and schemed to draw her tenderly closer! The night of their disaster had been meant to end like this, lying together in his bed, with him discovering her hidden beauty. But then a calamity had descended on him and wrecked his life. How bitter was the irony that he should see her lovely nakedness now.

She moved again, reaching out in his direction, so that he had to jerk away quickly. She began to whisper in her sleep, but he couldn't make out the words. Only escape would save him. He rose, backed off quickly and managed to make it to the door before her eyes opened. Once outside, he leaned against the wall, his chest heaving, his brain whirling.

At last he moved away, back to the real world, where he was a man in command. And that, he vowed, was where he would stay.

Giorgio looked up as Mario approached. 'No luck finding her?'

Mario shrugged. 'I didn't bother looking very far. Try calling her again.'

Giorgio dialled the number, listening with a resigned face.

'Looks like she still isn't—no, wait! Natasha, is that you? Thank goodness! Where have you been? *What?* Don't you know the time? All right, I'll tell Mario. But hurry.' He shut off the phone. 'She says she overslept.'

Mario shrugged. 'Perhaps the flight tired her yesterday.'

Giorgio gave a rich chuckle. 'My guess is that she was entertaining someone last night. I know she'd only just arrived, but a girl as lovely as that can entertain anyone whenever she wants. I saw men looking at her as she came down those stairs. Did you expect such a beauty?'

'I didn't know what to expect,' Mario said in a toneless voice.

'Nor me. I never hoped she'd be so young and lovely. Let's make the best of it. Juliet come to life. Oh, yes, finding her was a real stroke of luck.'

A stroke of luck. The words clamoured in Mario's brain, adding more bitterness to what he was already suffering. He didn't believe that a man had been in Natasha's room last night, but the sight of her naked had devastated him. He could almost believe she'd done it on purpose to taunt him, but the sweet, enchanting Natasha he'd known would never do that.

But was she that Natasha any more?

Had she ever been?

'I just know what she's doing right this minute,' Giorgio said with relish. 'She's turning to the man next to her in the bed, saying, "You've got to go quickly so that nobody finds you here." Perhaps we should have someone watch her door to see who comes out.'

'That's enough,' Mario growled.

'With a girl as stunning as that, nothing is ever enough. Don't pretend you don't know what I mean. You were fizzing from the moment you saw her.'

'Drop it,' Mario growled.

'All right, you don't want to admit she had that effect on you. After all, you're the boss. Don't let her guess she's got you where she wants you—even if she has.'

'*I said drop it.*'

'Steady there. Don't get mad at me. I was only thinking that if there's an attraction between you, we can make use of it.'

'And you're mistaken. There's no attraction between us.'

'Pity. That could have been fun.'

Slowly, Natasha felt life returning to her as she ended the call from Giorgio.

'Nine-fifteen!' she gasped in horror. 'I was supposed to be downstairs at nine. Oh, I should never have taken those sleeping pills.'

The pills had plunged her into a deep slumber, which she'd needed to silence her desperate thoughts of Mario.

But at the end he'd invaded her sleep, his face close to hers, regarding her with an almost fierce intensity. But he wasn't there. It had been a dream.

'I just can't get away from him,' she whispered. 'Will I ever?'

She showered in cold water, relishing the feeling of coming back to life. Dressing was a simple matter of putting on tailored trousers and a smart blazer and fixing her hair back tightly. Then she was ready to go.

She found Giorgio and Mario downstairs at the table.

'I'm so sorry,' she said. 'I didn't mean to be late but I was more tired than I realised.'

'That's understandable,' Giorgio said gallantly.

Mario threw him a cynical look but said nothing.

'Where's that waiter?' Giorgio asked, frowning. 'I'll find him and he can bring you breakfast.'

He vanished.

'I'm glad Giorgio's gone,' she said. 'It gives us a chance to talk honestly. Last night you stopped me getting out of my chair, and told me to stay. But is that really what you want? Wouldn't you be better off without me?'

'If I thought that I'd have said so,' he retorted.

'But think of it, day after day, trying not to get annoyed with each other, pretending to like each other. Surely you don't want that? I'm giving you the chance to get rid of me, Mario.'

'What about you? Do you want to make a run for it?'

'I can cope.'

'But you think I can't. Thanks for the vote of confidence. We're business professionals and on that basis it can work.'

'You're right,' she said. 'Shake.'

'Shake.' He took her extended hand. 'Perhaps I should

warn you that Giorgio has some rather fancy ideas about
you. He thinks you had a lover in your room last night
and that's why you overslept.'

'*What?* I'd taken some herbal pills to get to sleep after
a strenuous day. A lover? I'd only been here five minutes.'

'Giorgio sees you as the kind of woman who can attract men as fast as that.'

'Cheek!'

'In his eyes it's a compliment.'

She scowled for a moment, then laughed. 'I guess I'll
learn to put up with him.'

Giorgio reappeared with her breakfast.

'Eat up and we'll get to work,' he said. 'I'll get you a
map of Verona.'

'I've got one,' she said, drawing it from her bag. 'I
bought it at the airport so that I would be ready. The more
you plan, the simpler life is.'

'True,' Mario murmured, 'but there are some things
that can never be planned.'

'And you can't always anticipate what they might be,'
she agreed. 'You can try, but—' She shrugged.

'But they always take you by surprise,' he murmured.

'Not always. Just sometimes. It's best to be ready.'

Giorgio looked from one to the other as if his alarm
bells had sounded again.

'It's time we were making plans,' he said. 'I've called
the others in the group, and they're dying to meet you.
We're all invited to dinner tonight at the Albergo Splendido.' He beamed at Natasha. 'It'll be your big night.'

'Then I'd better prepare for it,' she said. 'I'll look
around Verona today so that I can sound knowledgeable
at the dinner. Otherwise they'll think I'm an amateur.'

'Good thinking,' Giorgio said. 'I'll escort you, and we'll have a great time.'

'Now, here—' Natasha pointed to a street on the map '—this is the Via Capello, where I can visit Juliet's house. I'd like to go there first, then the house where the Montagues lived. Finally, I'd like to see the tomb. Then I can work out my plans.'

'We'll leave as soon as you've finished breakfast,' Mario told her.

CHAPTER THREE

THE CHAUFFEUR-DRIVEN CAR was waiting for them, and soon they were on their way around the city.

Natasha already knew a good deal about Verona, having read about it on the plane. It was an old city, much of which went back to Roman times, two thousand years ago. Several places survived from that era, including a huge arena where gladiators had once slain their victims, but now was used for musical performances.

The streets were lined with historic buildings, many hinting at mystery and romance, all seeming to come from a more intriguing and beautiful age. She kept her eyes fixed on them as they drove through the town, trying to absorb its atmosphere.

'We're just turning into the Via Capello,' Mario said. 'We'll reach Juliet's house at any moment.'

A few minutes later the car dropped them at the entrance to a short tunnel. They joined the crowd walking through to the courtyard at the far end, where the balcony loomed overhead. Natasha regarded it with shining eyes.

'It's lovely,' she said. 'Of course I know it was put up less than a hundred years ago, but it looks right. It fits the house so perfectly that you can almost see Juliet standing there.'

'She's actually over there,' Giorgio said, pointing at a figure standing a little ahead, beneath and to the side of the balcony. It was a bronze statue of a young woman.

'Juliet,' she breathed.

As she watched, a woman walked up to the statue and brushed her hand against its breast. She was followed by another woman, and another, then a man.

'It's a tradition,' Mario explained. 'Everyone does it in the hope that it will bring them good luck. That's why that part of her is shining, because it's touched so often. People like to make contact with Juliet because they see her as a woman who knows more about love than anyone in the world.'

'Perhaps that's true,' Natasha murmured. 'But she knows tragedy as well as love.'

Intrigued, she went to stand before the statue. Juliet's head was turned slightly to the side, gazing into the distance as though only in another world could she find what she sought.

Natasha watched as a woman touched Juliet, closed her eyes and murmured something. At last her eyes opened and she stepped back with a smile, evidently feeling that she had received an answer.

If only it was that simple, Natasha thought. *If Juliet really could give me advice I'd ask her about the way my head is whirling, about how I'm feeling, and how I ought to be feeling. But she can't help me because she doesn't exist. She never really did, not the way people believe in her. That kind of love is just an illusion.*

She turned away to find Mario waiting. He moved closer, leaving Giorgio at a distance, and speaking quietly.

'Were you consulting Juliet?' he asked, raising an eyebrow.

'No,' she said. 'She's a fantasy. Nothing more.'

'How very prosaic.'

'I am prosaic, and I'm glad. It's useful.'

'But if you're going to promote the romantic fantasy, shouldn't you believe in it?'

She surveyed him with her head on one side and a faint ironic smile on her face.

'Not at all,' she said. 'It isn't necessary to believe something to persuade other people that it's true.'

'I wonder if you're right.'

A flash of anger made her say quickly, 'You know I'm right. We all know it at heart.'

'So—' he hesitated '—you're telling me that you've toughened up?'

'By a mile. So beware.'

'No need to tell me that.'

'So I've got you worried already? Good.'

For a wild moment he was tempted to tell her of the confused reactions that had rioted in him when he first saw her on the stairs. There had been an incredible moment of pleasure that the sight of her had always brought him, and which even now remained. But it had collided with a sense of alarm, as though a warning bell had sounded, letting him know that she would bring fear and darkness into his life.

But he suppressed the impulse to speak. How satisfied she would be to know that she could still throw him into confusion.

'Don't tell me I'm the only one who's toughened up,' she challenged him. 'Haven't you?'

'No doubt of it. It's called survival.'

She nodded. 'Right. As long as we both understand that, there's no problem.'

For them there would always be a problem. But there was no need of words.

'Now, I have a job to do,' she said briskly.

'Yes, let's look around further.'

Suddenly there was a cry from the far side of the courtyard.

'*Buongiorno, amici!*'

'Amadore!' Giorgio exclaimed, extending his hand in welcome.

The three men exchanged greetings in Italian, until Giorgio said, '*Signorina*, this is Amadore Finucci, a fellow member of the *Comunità*. Amadore, this is the Signorina Natasha Bates, who doesn't speak Italian.'

'Then it will be my pleasure to speak English,' Amadore said, seizing her hand.

She gave a polite response and he carried her hand to his mouth.

'Miss Bates,' he said.

'Please, call me Natasha.'

'Thank you—Natasha. When did you arrive?'

'Yesterday,' Giorgio said. 'Your father has invited us to dine at your hotel tonight.'

'Yes, he told me. I must leave now, but I look forward to seeing you this evening.'

He departed. Natasha eyed Mario curiously, puzzled to find him frowning.

'You're not pleased about this invitation?'

'That's because his hotel is one of the most luxurious in town,' Giorgio said. 'Mario's jealous.'

'I'm not jealous,' Mario said firmly. 'I admit I envy him having a bottomless pit of money to spend on the place.'

'His ballroom has to be seen to be believed,' Giorgio told her.

'Ballroom,' she echoed. 'Romeo and Juliet met in a ballroom.' She turned to Mario. 'Does your hotel have a ballroom?'

'No. None of the other hotels do.'

'Then that gives me an idea. Can we return to the hotel now? I need to get to work.'

'Aren't we going on to Romeo's house?' Giorgio asked.

'I'll do that tomorrow. Today, I have urgent things to do.

'Could you please provide me with a list of every member of the *Comunità*, and their hotels? Then I can check their locations and assess their requirements.'

'I'll see to it as soon as we arrive.'

As they walked back to the car, Giorgio murmured to Mario, 'A woman who knows her own mind. Perhaps we should beware.'

'There's no perhaps about it,' Mario replied grimly.

On the way back to the hotel Natasha took out her notebook and wrote in it swiftly and fiercely. Ideas were coming to her in cascades and she needed to capture them fast. This was the part of any project that she liked best. So absorbed did she become that she was unaware of the journey, and looked up suddenly when the car stopped.

'We're here,' Mario said. He'd been watching her silently.

'I need something to eat,' Giorgio declared. 'Suppose we meet downstairs in half an hour, for a feast?'

'Not me, thank you,' Natasha said. 'Perhaps you could send something up to my room?'

'But we could all celebrate together,' Giorgio protested.

'We can celebrate when I've made a success of this job. Let's hope that happens.'

'It'll happen,' Giorgio said. 'You're going to be just fantastic, isn't she, Mario?'

'No doubt of it,' he said bleakly.

'You're very kind, both of you. Now, excuse me, gentlemen.'

Giving them both a polite smile, she headed for the lift.

Upstairs, she plunged into work, making more notes about the morning before things went out of her head. She was so immersed in her work that at first she didn't hear the knock on the door. It had to be repeated louder to capture her attention.

'Sorry,' she said, pulling it open, 'I got so—' She checked herself at the sight of Mario standing there with a trolley of food.

'Your meal, *signorina*,' he said.

She stared at the sight of the food. Someone had taken a lot of trouble preparing this meal, which Mario laid out for her with care.

'Giorgio told the kitchen to produce their best, to make sure you stay with us,' he said. 'So you have chicory risotto, followed by tiramisù, with Prosecco.'

Her favourite wine. How many times had he ordered it for her in Venice? And he had remembered.

'It's delicious,' she said politely as she ate.

'I'll tell Giorgio you approve. And I brought you this,' he said, handing her a large file.

It was the information she'd requested about the *Comunità*—hotels, owners, background information.

'That man I met today seems to come from the biggest and best,' she said, flicking through it. 'The Albergo Splendido.'

'It was a palace once. You'll like it. You're making a considerable impression, you know.'

'Amadore certainly seemed to think so.'

'Just don't take him too seriously. He flirts with every woman on the planet.'

She gave a brief laugh. 'You warned me about Giorgio; now you're warning me about Amadore. But you don't need to. I can recognise when a man is role-playing. He puts on a performance as the "romantic Italian" because he thinks an Englishwoman is bound to be fooled. I don't mind. He's charming. But don't expect me to fall for it.'

'I suppose I should have known you'd say that,' Mario growled. 'I wonder if you ever fall for anything.'

'Not these days. Never again.'

'And you think that's admirable?'

'I think it's safe.'

'And safety matters more than anything else? Never mind who you hurt.'

She turned on him, her quick temper rising. 'Who *I* hurt? Did I really hear you say that? After what you did?'

'I didn't do what you thought I did, and I could have explained. But you vanished without giving me a chance to defend myself.'

'What was there to defend? I know what I saw.'

'Natasha, why won't you realise that you misunderstood what you saw? Yes, I'd been having an affair with Tania. I'm not a saint. I've never pretended to be. But it was only a casual relationship and I'd started to feel that it must end. Things had changed in my life. I'd met you and nothing looked the same. I had to face the fact that I wanted you, not her.

'So that day I met Tania and told her we couldn't be together any more. But I couldn't make her believe it. When I left her she followed me, and that was how she found us together.

'I went after her, trying to explain that I was sorry to hurt her, but she screamed at me and ran off. I came back to our table, hoping I could make you understand. But you were gone. I tried your phone but you'd turned it off. I went to the hotel but you'd left just a few minutes earlier. Over the next few days I tried your phone, your email, your apartment, but you'd shut off every way of contacting you. It was like you'd ceased to exist.'

'Exactly. I *had* ceased to exist. The girl I was then— naive, slightly stupid, ready to be fooled—vanished into nothing. But now there's another woman in her place— suspicious, awkward, ready to give as good as she gets. She exists. She's me. She's rather hard. You won't like her. Be wise. Get rid of her.'

His face was suddenly tense. 'I think not. I prefer to keep her around and make her face up to what she did.'

'Is that why you got me back here?'

'What do you mean by that?'

'I don't believe it's coincidence that we just happened to meet again.'

He paled. 'You think I manipulated this situation?'

'You could have.'

'And I'm telling you I didn't. How dare you? Perhaps I should accuse *you* of manipulation. Did you persuade your friend to let you take her place?'

'No way. I had no idea you'd be here until I saw you on the stairs.'

'Nor I. Let's get this clear, Natasha. I didn't trick you into coming here. I didn't want to see you again, not after the way you behaved.'

'The way *I*—?'

'You left me feeling as though I was hanging off the edge of a cliff.'

'I know that feeling,' she said softly, with anger in her voice.

'All right. For the moment we have to accept things as they are. We're enemies but we need to be allies as far as this job's concerned. Our fight is still on, but it's a fair fight.'

'Is it? I wonder if your idea of a fair fight is the same as mine.'

'I guess we'll find that out.'

A beep from her mobile phone interrupted him. Answering it, she found a text:

You didn't have to run away. We can sort this out.

There was no name, but there didn't need to be. This wasn't the first text that Elroy Jenson had sent her since he'd shut her out of his media empire. Clearly he'd expected her to cave in and come crawling back.

She had to make him stop doing this.

Swiftly, she texted back:

Forget me, as I've forgotten you.

His reply came at once:

If that were true you wouldn't have run away. Come home. I can do a lot for you.

She groaned, wondering how much more of this she could take. She'd thought that by coming to Italy she could put Jenson behind her.

'What's the matter?' Mario asked. 'Who has upset you?'

'It's nothing,' she said quickly. 'I'm fine.'

'I don't think so. Perhaps you should change your mobile number. Doing that works well because then the guy can't reach you. But of course you know that. Here—'

Before she could stop him he'd seized the phone from her hand and was reading the text.

'Just tell him to— What does he mean, run away?'

'I've been running away from him for months. He's Elroy Jenson, the man who owns a great media empire. It stretches all over the world—England, America, Europe—'

'Yes—' Mario broke in '—I've heard of him. Some of his papers are in this country. Not a man you'd want to antagonise.'

'I used to make a good living writing for his newspapers and magazines, but then he decided that he fancied me. I didn't fancy him but he wouldn't take no for an answer. He kept pestering me until I slapped his face. Unfortunately, some of his employees saw it and the word got out. Since then none of his editors will buy articles from me.'

'And he keeps sending you these messages? Why don't you just change your mobile phone number?'

'I have. Several times. But he always manages to get the new one. He's a powerful man and his tentacles stretch far.'

'Bastardo!'

'If that means what I think it does, then yes. Now I can't earn a living in England and he's coming after me.'

'Thinking you'll turn to him for the money? And he'd like that—knowing that you'd only given in to him out of need?'

'He'd enjoy it. He's that kind of man. But he's going

to be disappointed. I'll do anything rather than what he wants.'

'Anything? Including taking a job with a man you hate?'

'Even that. This job's a lucky break for me. It gets me out of England.'

'But you have to put up with me.'

'Stop being melodramatic. You're not so bad. I can manage. We've put the past behind us.'

He smiled wryly, trying to come to terms with her words. 'You're not so bad' implied a casual acceptance that should have been a relief but felt more like an insult.

'Yes, we've put it all behind us,' he agreed. 'And now we can concentrate on business, which is what we're here for. You need to make a living and I need to repay the bank loans I had to take out to buy this place.'

'That must be a heavy burden,' she said.

'It is. Damiano wanted to help me by lending me some money, and standing guarantor for the bank loan. But I wouldn't let him do either. This is my hotel, and mine alone.'

'I remember meeting Damiano in Venice. And his wife. They were very nice to me.'

'They both liked you a lot.'

In fact both Sally and Damiano had nudged him, saying, 'She's the one, Mario. Go on, make sure of her.'

And when things went wrong they had united again to call him 'The biggest idiot of all time'. It was a remark that still stung him.

'Why wouldn't you let him help you?' she asked.

'I just prefer to control my own life,' he said in a voice that was suddenly hard.

A tantalising memory flickered through her mind:

Mario, two years ago, young, carefree and easy-going. Somehow he had changed into this grimly self-sufficient man who mistrusted the world.

'I prefer it too,' she said. 'You feel safer, like wearing a suit of armour. But is that always a good thing to wear?'

'That depends on who challenges you,' he said.

His eyes, fixed on her, left her in no doubt of his message. Her presence was a challenge, one that he would fight off ruthlessly.

'But you wouldn't need a suit of armour against your older brother,' she said. 'Helping you is surely what older brothers are for?'

'Possibly, but I needed to stop being the younger brother, leaning on him. I told him I could do it alone, so I've got to prove that's true. I simply mustn't fail.'

'And I mustn't fail either,' she said, 'so in future we're going to concentrate on being practical. Please leave me now, and when I've finished my research I'll see you and Giorgio at supper.'

'Good luck with the work,' he said, and departed.

He went quickly to his office and went online. A few minutes' research told him all he needed to know about Elroy Jenson: his creation of a media empire, his money, his far-reaching power.

But it was the man's looks that amazed him. He'd expected a slobbering, middle-aged monster, a man no woman could want to be with unless she was after his money. But Jenson was well built, even handsome, with a riotous head of curly hair. A woman lucky enough to have captured his attention would have every reason to flaunt her triumph.

But not Natasha.

No man impresses her, he thought. *She decides what she wants, and woe betide him if he can't live up to it.*

He glanced at himself in the mirror.

'But could any man live up to it?' he murmured.

Researching the Albergo Splendido, Natasha could easily believe that it had started life as a palace. It was seven hundred years old and magnificently built.

To dine there meant dressing in style. Luckily she'd brought with her a black satin figure-hugging dress that managed to be both decorous and elegant.

Giorgio nodded approval. 'Lovely. You'll make their heads spin. Let's go.'

As they walked to the car Mario said, 'Aren't you making too much of her appearance? Surely it's her efficiency we need to promote?'

'Efficiency alone isn't enough. She's got that extra "something" special, and it's going to make all the difference.'

'I'll take your word for it,' Mario said coldly.

At the hotel Amadore was waiting for them. 'Everyone's here,' he said. 'They're longing to meet you.'

He led her into a room filled with tables at which sat crowds of men and women, who broke into applause at the sight of her.

There could be no doubt that she was the star of the evening. Amadore introduced her to each guest, one by one, giving the name of the person and of their hotel.

'Ah, yes,' she said to one elderly man. 'That's the place where—'

He listened, open-mouthed, as she revealed her in-depth research. She did the same thing with several of the other hotel owners and was rewarded by looks of admiration.

'You see what I mean?' Giorgio murmured to Mario. 'A brilliant lady, clever and hard-working. We've struck gold.'

Mario didn't reply.

When she'd met all the guests she sat down at the head table for the meal, which turned out to be a glorious banquet, adorned with the finest wines.

'Mmm, lovely,' she said, sipping from her glass.

'Everyone thinks of Verona as the site of the love story,' Giorgio told her. 'But it's also surrounded by vineyards. Most of the hotel owners have some sort of investment in vineyards.'

'The wine you're drinking now was produced in my own vineyard,' Amadore said.

'It's delicious,' she said, sipping again.

'Thank you, *signorina*.'

They clinked glasses.

Soon she saw that everyone was looking at her expectantly.

'They're waiting for your speech,' Mario murmured.

'But I can only speak English,' she protested. 'Will they understand?'

'Hotel owners tend to speak English because your country sends us many tourists.'

Mario got to his feet.

'My friends,' he said, 'it has been our pleasure tonight to meet the lady we've employed to promote us to the world. Now let us hear her plans.'

There was applause as Natasha rose. For a few moments she was nervous but the warm, friendly atmosphere enveloped her and she began to enjoy herself as she laid out the ideas that had been forming in her mind.

'Every hotel has something to connect it to the story,' she said. 'Some are near Juliet's house, some near Romeo's house, some are near the tomb.'

'Some of us aren't so lucky,' a man called. 'Our hotels aren't near anywhere significant.'

'Don't be so sure,' she said. 'Remember the scene where Romeo's friend Mercutio is stabbed to death by Juliet's kinsman? That happens outdoors in the street. But which street? Nobody knows for sure, but perhaps some of your hotels are nearby.'

Natasha looked out at her audience, smiling and nodding appreciatively as she spoke. She was fulfilling all their highest expectations. Applause rang in her ears.

CHAPTER FOUR

'Now for the next stage,' Natasha said. 'I'll want to talk to you all individually, and then I'm going to write my first piece explaining how "Romeo and Juliet" are still alive in Verona if people know how to find them. We'll invite them to come here, and stay in your hotels. By that time I'll have produced several more texts.'

'But who will publish these?' called a voice from the floor.

'Anyone she sends it to,' Giorgio called back. 'This lady is a very notable journalist with many connections. She gets published everywhere.'

More applause, but Natasha held up her hand for silence.

'We're not going to take chances,' she said. 'This "article" will actually be an advertisement. We buy a double-page spread and insert our own text and pictures. That way we can be sure of being read. What matters is to get things done the way we want. Of course it will be costly. Advertisements have to be paid for, and perhaps some of you won't want to accept that expense. Let's take a vote. Hands up anyone who's against the idea.'

Not a single hand was raised.

'We'll do it your way,' called a voice.

There were cheers and applause, which went on until they were interrupted by the sound of music.

'That's coming from the ballroom,' Amadore told her. 'Our guests like to dance in the evening.'

'A ballroom is wonderful,' she said. 'The Capulets gave a ball for Juliet and Paris, the man they wanted her to marry, which Romeo gatecrashed to see another girl that he was in love with. Instead he met Juliet and they fell in love within a few minutes. Without that ball it might never have happened.'

'Then come and have a look,' Amadore said eagerly.

Everyone crowded after them as he led her along a short corridor, throwing open a double door at the end, revealing a huge, beautiful room where couples were whirling.

'Perfect,' she murmured.

Amadore took her hand. 'Dance with me.'

Smiling, she let him draw her into his arms and guide her onto the floor. He was an excellent dancer and she responded gladly. When the music stopped another man stepped in to claim her, then another.

At last she found herself facing Mario.

'You've danced with everyone else,' he observed. 'Will it ever be my turn?'

'Not until you ask me.'

'No,' he said. 'I'm not going to ask you.'

But as he spoke his arm went around her waist in a grip too firm for her to resist, even if she had wanted to.

They had danced together once before. One night in Venice, when they had been having supper at an outdoor café in St Mark's Square, a band had started to play and before she knew it she was waltzing in his arms.

'Is this all right?' he'd whispered.

'I'll let you know later,' she had teased.

It had lasted only a few minutes, and she had promised herself that one day she would dance with him again. But the next day they had broken up, and it had never happened again. Until now.

It was unnerving to feel his arms around her, his hand on her waist, holding her close. Her heart was beating softly but fervently. She glanced at him, trying to know if he felt the same. Would he invite her to dance with him again?

But before he could speak they became aware of a middle-aged man on the edge of the crowd, trying to attract their attention.

'Ah, there's Francesco,' Mario said. 'I hoped he'd be here. He owns one of the biggest hotels, and I always like to have him on my side. Let's go and say hello.'

Francesco beamed, greeting Natasha with an embrace.

'It's a pleasure to meet you,' he said warmly. 'Now, let me introduce my daughter, Laura.'

The young woman with him was in her mid-twenties with a beautiful face and an air of confidence that came from being always in demand.

'How have you done?' she said carefully to Natasha.

'No,' her father interrupted her. 'Not like that, *cara*. The English say "How do you do?" not "How have you done?"'

'How do you do?' Laura echoed, smiling. 'Is that right?'

'That is perfect,' her father said.

He spoke proudly and Natasha knew a slight twinge of sadness as a memory came back to her from long ago. She had heard that pride before, in her own father's voice, in her childhood, before he'd abandoned her without a backward glance.

But this was no time to be brooding over the past. She thrust the memory aside, returning Laura's greeting with the appearance of warmth.

Then Laura turned her attention to Mario, saying, 'And how do you do?'

'There's no need for such formality,' Mario said, shaking her hand. 'We already know each other.'

'Indeed we do,' Laura said, glancing at Natasha as she spoke.

Natasha returned her look with interest. She had the feeling that Laura was sizing her up as possible competition.

Then Amadore appeared beside them. 'Do I get another dance?' he asked.

'Of course.' Natasha let the charming hotel owner enfold her in his arms and twirl her gently across the floor.

Out of the corner of her eye she could just see Mario gliding past with Laura, who seemed to be trying to dance as close to him as possible.

'There the women go again,' Amadore said, 'parading themselves to get his attention.'

'Do you mean Signor Ferrone?' Natasha asked.

'Oh, yes. He's a lucky man. Every female makes eyes at him, and the rumour is that he can have any woman he wants.'

So nothing had changed, she thought, remembering how women's eyes had followed Mario during their time together. How they had envied her, being with him. How little they had known how he could make a woman suffer.

'Look at that,' Amadore said, still regarding Mario with envy. 'The way she's pressed up against him is almost indecent.'

Natasha managed to chuckle. 'Oh, come on. A man's entitled to enjoy himself if he can.'

'That's very generous of you. Most women don't take such a relaxed view.'

'I can afford to be relaxed. My life is arranged just the way I want it.'

'You're luckier than most of us then.'

Mario, just a few feet away, glanced at them only briefly before swinging Laura away to the far side of the ball-room. There, he found more female attention to distract him from sights he didn't want to see and thoughts he didn't want to think.

But it lasted only a short time. When he next looked at Natasha she was sitting down scribbling in her note-book. Two men were sitting beside her, while another two looked over her shoulders. As the music came to an end he began to approach her, but Amadore detained him.

'Lovely lady,' he said. 'Every man is interested. Luckily she's not interested in them.'

'She told you that?'

'We were watching Laura making a play for you. I disapproved but she said you were entitled to enjoy yourself. I complimented her on her relaxed attitude and she said she could afford to be relaxed as her life was arranged the way she wanted it.'

'She probably just said that to shut you up.'

'Maybe. But it wouldn't surprise me if back home she has a trail of eager pursuers.'

'You could be right,' Mario growled.

He could see that Natasha had finished making notes, and was rising to move away. He got to her quickly.

'Still working?' he said.

'I've had an idea. I need to talk to everyone again.'

'Then let's return to the dining room.' He offered her his arm, saying, 'You've done well tonight. The contract will be ready soon.'

'Contract?'

'For you to sign. The whole *Comunità* is determined to secure your professional services. Are you willing to stay with us?'

'Yes,' she said softly. 'I'm willing.'

When they were gathered in the dining room again she addressed everyone. 'I think we should take some photographs of Romeo and Juliet. They say a picture's worth a thousand words, and we can send ours all over the world. We'll need to hire actors, then we'll photograph them on the balcony, in the tomb, anywhere that seems atmospheric.'

'We can't pose them on the official balcony,' Mario said. 'There are always tourists there. But this hotel has a balcony that will do.'

It was agreed that they would all meet again when the arrangements were made. Now all Mario wanted was to get away. Nothing had prepared him for being so close to her for hours, and he needed to be alone.

'Sleep well,' he told her as he escorted her to a chauffeur-driven car. 'You've worked hard today and there'll be more tomorrow.' He opened the car door. 'I'll see you tomorrow morning. Goodnight.'

He walked away.

Back in her room, Natasha undressed and went to bed. It had been a successful evening and she should have felt triumphant. Perhaps she would have done if Mario had returned with her, and been here to share her sense of achievement. But he had left her alone while he spent the night somewhere else.

Images of Laura danced through her mind, pursued by Amadore's voice saying '…he can have any woman he wants.'

She tried to shut the thoughts down. She and Mario were no longer part of each other's lives, and she cared nothing where he was now, or who he was with.

She lay down and managed to sleep. When she awoke she could hear a noise in the corridor outside, as though someone was turning a key in a lock. She rose and opened her door just in time to see Mario's door closing.

It was six in the morning.

She half expected him to be late for breakfast but he was there before her, calm, collected and ready for work.

'You were right about hiring actors,' he said. 'We'll have a file of pictures soon. In the meantime I've been making some notes of my own—'

But before she could look at them her phone beeped with another text.

'Is he hounding you again?' Mario demanded.

'No, it's not him,' she said, looking at the screen. Then she drew in her breath sharply. 'Oh, no—no! *Please, no!*'

'What is it?'

'Nothing,' she said sharply.

'Don't tell me it's nothing when it affects you like that. Let me see.'

Without asking her permission, he took the phone from her.

'What's this?' he demanded, reading, *'Sorry, your cheque bounced.'*

'How dare you?' she said furiously, snatching the phone back.

'Who's hounding you for money? Is it him?'

'No, it's my friend Helen, and she's not hounding me. She's been letting me stay in her flat and she got me this job. Before I left I gave her a cheque for my share of expenses. I owe her so much and I've repaid her like this. I didn't mean to. I thought there was just enough in the bank.'

'Right, we'd better get your contract sorted at once. Wait for me here.'

As he left she sat there, deep in gloom. Shame pervaded her and for a moment she wished she could do what Mario had accused her of, and vanish into thin air.

After a few minutes Giorgio appeared.

'The boss says I'm to give you the contract to sign,' he told her. 'Let's go into his office.'

In the office he laid out papers before her. 'Just sign at the bottom.'

She picked up the pen, then paused. 'Wait, are you sure this contract is right?'

'The boss says it is.'

'But I know what the agency offered me—the money was far less.'

'The fee has been changed. The boss says you're worth more.'

Her head was spinning. The new amount was much larger than the one she had been quoted before.

'You need to give me your bank details so that some money can be paid to you today,' Giorgio said.

Dazed, she gave him the necessary information and signed the contract at the bottom of the last page.

'And you must put your initials on the other pages,'

Giorgio told her. 'He wants to make very sure that you're ours and nobody else's. He knows good value when he sees it. Ah, here he is.'

Mario had come into the room, and stood watching as Natasha finished signing. Glancing over the papers, he nodded and handed them to Giorgio, who left the room.

'I hadn't expected so much,' she said. 'You didn't have to do that. But thank you.'

'You have nothing to thank me for, *signorina*,' he said firmly. 'You're vital to this project and I've taken the necessary steps to make sure the *Comunità* keeps your services.'

She nodded, replying in the same formal voice, 'You can be sure that I will remain loyal to the *Comunità, signore.*'

'Excellent,' he said. 'Then we understand each other.'

'I'm sure we do.'

Oh, yes, she thought. They understood each other perfectly, but in ways that could never be expressed in words. He'd moved swiftly to save her from disaster, but in such a way that there was no fear of them growing closer. They were *signore* and *signorina*, and nothing else.

Not long after, she accessed her bank account on the Internet and found that a large sum of money had already been deposited, enabling her to pay her debt to Helen. That was a relief and she was able to enjoy an hour wandering the streets, absorbing the feel of the city.

When she returned she found that the photographs had arrived. Giorgio and Mario were going through them, studying the pictures of young models, seeking one with the perfect combination of beauty and innocence. She joined in and after a while she discovered exactly what she wanted.

Finding Romeo was harder. He had to be handsome, with splendid legs, since Romeo would be wearing tights. At last she found what she wanted.

'Perfect,' Mario said, studying the picture. 'Good-looking and vulnerable.'

'Vulnerable?' Giorgio queried. 'He's one of literature's great heroes.'

'He also fell for everything that was said to him,' Mario observed wryly. 'Not one of the world's great minds.'

'That's what happens to people in love,' Natasha said. 'They set their minds aside and believe what they want to believe.'

'And soon learn their mistake. All right, let's hire these two.'

Giorgio got straight onto the phone, made the contact and arranged for the two young people to appear in a couple of days.

'Paolo and Lucia,' he said. 'They'll be here ready to start on Thursday morning.'

'That's fine,' Natasha said. 'It gives me some more time to work on my ideas.'

The next two days were abuzz with action. Some of the time was spent visiting Romeo's house, and twice Natasha was invited to dine with other members of the *Comunità*. Mario accompanied her on these trips, but did not sit next to her at the dinner table.

She thought she understood. Having tied her down with the contract, both legally and financially, Mario preferred to keep a certain distance between them.

But the money in her bank account was a big relief. There was no doubt that in Mario she'd made a good professional association. She must cling to that thought.

By day they were absorbed in preparing for the photo shoot. Giorgio hired a photographer experienced in taking dramatic pictures. He also found a theatrical costumier.

'She'll join us tomorrow with a big variety of costumes,' he told Natasha. 'Our models can try several until we find the right ones.'

'Juliet will need something exotic for the ballroom,' Natasha said. 'Then an elegant dress for the wedding scene, and a very simple one for the tomb. Right, I'm going to bed. It's going to be a busy day tomorrow.'

'Does anyone know where Mario is?' Giorgio enquired.

'He left an hour ago,' Natasha said. 'He must be busy.'

On the way upstairs she wondered if Mario was in his room, or had he gone to be with the same person he'd probably visited the other night?

Passing his door, she couldn't help pausing to hear if any sound was coming from inside. She blamed herself for yielding to the temptation, but she couldn't help it.

Then she heard his voice. He was on the telephone, speaking Italian in a warm, laughing tone.

'Non è importante. Non è importante.'

She didn't need to know the language to understand what he was saying: 'It's not important'. Mario was reassuring somebody that what was happening now didn't matter to him.

She hurried into her room and locked the door, wishing she'd resisted temptation and vowing to be stronger next time.

Next morning Lisa, the costumier, arrived early. She was a tall businesslike woman who spoke perfect English and went through Natasha's requirements with no trouble.

'Let's hope Romeo is handsome and has a good figure,' she said briskly.

'He looked good in the photo I saw, but I haven't met him yet,' Natasha admitted.

'That's a pity. To be suitable he must be sexy. We need the women to sigh over him and say, "I want some of that".'

'But he'll only be a picture,' Natasha protested. 'We're selling the town, not Romeo himself.'

Lisa chuckled. 'You think that, do you?'

Natasha gave a wry smile. 'Well, it's what I need to believe. But I guess you're right.'

'Share the joke, ladies,' Giorgio called from nearby, where he was talking with Mario.

'You wouldn't understand it,' Lisa told him. 'We're laughing at men, and men never realise how funny they are.'

'That's very true,' Natasha said. 'And if you try to explain they still don't understand.'

Mario gave her an odd glance which she returned with an air of teasing confidence. She felt a certain cheeky pleasure in having disconcerted him. The day had started well. Whatever happened now, she felt she could cope.

They all set out for the Splendido, where everyone was waiting, eager to begin. The next hour was spent going through a variety of garments.

'I like this one,' Natasha said, holding up a long white ballgown. It was simple and elegant, perfect for a girl making her debut in society. 'Juliet can wear this at the ball.'

Giorgio looked impatiently at his watch.

'They should be here by now. What's happened to them?'

He snatched up his phone and dialled. Almost as soon as he was through, an expression of outrage overtook him.

'*Sì? Che cosa? Cosa vuol dire che non posso venire? Oh, dolore bene!*'

He hung up.

'What's happened?' Mario demanded.

'They're not coming. There's been a mix-up with the dates. They thought the shoot was next week.'

'Oh, no, what are we going to do?' Natasha cried. 'It's all set up for today.'

'There's only one thing we can do,' Giorgio said. 'Find another Romeo and Juliet.'

'But we haven't got time to search,' she protested.

'We don't have to search. We've got the duo we need right here.' He threw out his arms towards her and Mario. 'Romeo and Juliet.'

She stared. 'You can't possibly be serious.'

'I'm perfectly serious. You're beautiful enough to be Juliet, and Mario can just about get by as Romeo.'

'It won't work,' Mario growled. 'As though I could—'

'It's got to work,' Giorgio said. 'You're the only two who can do it in the time available. We've got to start right now, otherwise all our plans are in a mess. Come along, you two. Be professional.'

'He's right,' Mario growled. 'We have no choice.'

'Go next door and get changed,' Amadore said. 'Natasha, a maid will come with you.'

She looked around wildly. Surely there must be some other way. But there was no other way. Only this could save her plans for the success she simply had to have.

The maid appeared and took her to the room assigned as Juliet's dressing room. The dress fitted perfectly onto her slender, delicate figure. But her hair didn't seem right, pulled tightly back.

'I think Juliet would wear it hung loose,' she said.

The maid nodded, and got skilfully to work. Natasha watched, only half believing, as the self she knew disappeared and naive, vulnerable Juliet took her place. The merest touch of make-up heightened the impression, and she was ready to go.

As she entered the ballroom heads turned. Giorgio made a clapping movement and Amadore whistled.

She noticed neither of them. Her attention had been seized by the man standing a little further off. Mario had transformed into Romeo, wearing a dark blue doublet and tights. It would need a fine figure to get away with such a revealing costume, but Mario was tall, splendidly built and handsome enough to steal the spotlight.

Suddenly a memory came flooding back to her. Two years ago, during their precious short time together in Venice, they had spent a day on the beach. Her first sight of him, half naked in swimming trunks, had had a stunning effect on her, making her intensely aware that her own swimwear was a bikini, leaving much of her body uncovered.

Oh, yes, she'd thought as she enjoyed the sight of his long, strong legs as he raced across the beach. *Oh, yes!*

After that everything had changed. They spent the day chasing each other, bathing in the sea or stretched out on the sand, and with every moment she wanted him more. She'd feasted her eyes on his smooth, muscular body, seizing every chance to lean closer to him, cherishing the brief moments when her flesh brushed against his.

It had been her first experience of fierce desire and it revealed her to herself in a new light. In the past she had flirted, laughed, teased, but never before had she wanted a man with such fervour. When their eyes met she believed she saw the same intensity in him, and promised herself that soon he would carry her to a new world.

That night they'd parted with only a kiss. She had told herself he was biding his time, waiting for her to be ready to move on.

Three days later they had parted for ever.

Shaking off the memory, she began to walk towards Mario, tense for the moment when she would see his reaction to her. Would the past return to haunt him too? What would she see in his eyes?

At last Mario looked up, saw her and nodded.

'Splendid,' he said. 'Giorgio chose Juliet well.'

His tone was polite but nothing more, and his eyes were blank.

'And you look fine as well, Signor Ferrone,' she said, striving to match him for blandness.

'Well, like Giorgio said, I'll "just about get by".'

'Everybody ready?' Amadore called. 'This way.'

He indicated an archway at the far end of the ballroom. Mario offered Natasha his arm and she took it, saying, 'Thank you, *signore*.'

He leaned closer to her, murmuring, 'Don't call me *signore*. My name is Mario. If you address me formally people will think something is wrong between us.'

'And we mustn't let them think that,' she agreed. 'Shall we go?'

CHAPTER FIVE

THERE WAS A cheer when they came into the ballroom. Lisa nodded, as though to say that Romeo's looks met her high standards.

The photographer studied them with approval and said he would start with portrait shots.

'First I'll take you separately, then together. Juliet, you first.'

'Juliet? I'm Natasha,' she said lightly.

'No, today you are Juliet.'

'He's right,' Giorgio said. 'You don't pretend to be Juliet. You *are* Juliet. You can go back to being Natasha tomorrow.'

'If I want to,' she said, entering into the spirit. 'Natasha might be too boring.'

'That's the spirit,' Giorgio said with a grin.

She turned this way and that, smiled, looked sad, smiled again.

'Now throw your arms out,' Giorgio said. 'Imagine you're looking at someone who's the great happiness of your life.'

She did so, reaching towards the camera with a yearning look.

Mario, watching from the sidelines, turned his head

to avoid seeing that expression on her face. He remembered it too well from the past, and couldn't bear to be reminded of it now that the past was over.

Then he too had to pose for portrait shots.

'This way, that way,' the photographer called. 'Turn your head a little. Good. Now the two of you together.'

The first shot was a formal pose, with Juliet standing just in front of Romeo, his hands on her shoulders.

'Now turn and look into each other's eyes. Keep hold of each other but lean back a little so that I can see both of your faces.'

They obeyed, studying each other seriously, then smiling according to instructions.

'I think Romeo should frown a little,' Lisa called. 'And he should try to look sexy so that we know why Juliet fell for him.'

Mario scowled, annoyed at the comment and even more exasperated by the fact that Natasha collapsed with laughter.

'Don't worry,' she called. 'I can pretend if I have to.'

'And perhaps Juliet had to,' Giorgio said cheerfully. 'Maybe she didn't really fancy Romeo at all. She was pursuing her own agenda. *That's it!* Romeo, that grim look is perfect. Keep it up.'

'Yes, keep it up,' she chuckled. 'Just think how I'm going to thump you later.'

'Juliet, that smile is wonderful,' the photographer called. 'It says a lot about the kind of marriage they would have had if they'd lived. One where he got worked up and she laughed at him. I'm beginning to think nobody ever really understands this pair.'

'No,' she murmured so that only Mario could hear. 'Nobody really understands.'

'He's talking nonsense,' Mario growled.

'He's grandstanding to make us play our parts,' she said. 'It's his job. So we have to do ours.'

'Juliet,' Giorgio called, 'reach up and brush his hair forward a little, around his face.' She did so, hearing the camera click madly.

'That's it—now again—and again—gently—Juliet's longing to caress his face, and this is her chance.'

Natasha told herself that she was merely obeying orders, but she couldn't hide the truth from herself. She wanted to do this—wanted to touch his face, his body, his heart. Even through the lightness of her caress she felt the tremor that went through Mario, despite his attempt to suppress it. She could sense his reaction because it mirrored her own.

But could he suspect the feelings that were going through her at being so close to him? Suddenly, his face had softened. The grim look she saw on it so often faded, leaving a faint echo of the young, gentle man she had loved. His eyes were fixed on her intently but that might be no more than playing his part. If only she could tell.

'Right, that's it,' came Giorgio's voice. 'Now for the balcony scene. Come this way.'

The balcony at the back of the Splendido was decorated much like the one at Juliet's house, and had the advantage of being several feet lower so that Romeo and Juliet could be closer to each other. Mario stood below, reaching up, while Natasha leaned down to touch his hand while the camera clicked away.

'Perfect,' Giorgio cried at last. 'You two are doing a great job. It's wonderful how well you work together.'

They said what was necessary and followed him back

to the ballroom, where another selection of garments was laid out for them.

'Romeo believes that Juliet is dead,' Giorgio said. 'So he comes to the crypt where her body lies. He finds her there, says his farewells and takes his own life. Then she wakes, finds him dead, and she too chooses death. We'll shoot this scene in the cellar.'

With the maid's help, Natasha donned a plain gown and they all went down to the hotel's cellar, where a stone bench had been prepared for her to lie on.

'Ow!' she said, stretching out on it. 'That stone's really hard.'

'Is it really painful?' Mario asked her quietly.

'No, I'll be all right.'

'Let me put something under your head.'

'No, that would spoil it. But thank you.'

He still looked worried but let it drop.

'Walk up to her body,' Giorgio said. 'Look into her face as though you can't believe it's true. Good. Just like that.'

Lying there with her eyes closed, Natasha yearned to open them and see Mario's expression, to meet his eyes. But she must resist temptation and be content with the feel of his breath on her face.

'Lay your head on her breast,' Giorgio instructed.

The next moment she felt him lying against her and gave a slight gasp.

'Now kiss her,' Giorgio said,

She braced herself for the moment his mouth touched hers. It was the faintest possible sensation but she told herself to endure it.

'Again,' Giorgio said. 'Remember, you've lost the only woman in life that you could ever care about.'

Mario kissed her again before laying his head once more on her breast. At last Giorgio called out that the scene was over.

'Now for the big one,' he said. 'The moment when they meet.'

In the ballroom Natasha donned the glamorous gown and watched while the maid worked on her hair. When everything was ready Giorgio guided 'Romeo and Juliet' into position.

'It's during the ball. Juliet is standing there, watching everyone, particularly Paris, the man her parents want her to marry. But then she sees Romeo watching her. Their eyes meet.'

Mario turned his head so that he gazed at Natasha. She gazed back.

'He advances towards her,' Giorgio continued. 'That's right, Mario, a little nearer. He takes her hand, and asks forgiveness for touching her because he says he isn't worthy. But she says he is.'

Now Natasha's hand was clasped in Mario's. He was close to her, watching her intently.

'And Romeo dares to steal a kiss,' Giorgio said triumphantly. 'Go on. Let's catch that on camera.'

Gently Mario dropped his head, laying his lips on hers.

'Good,' Giorgio said. 'But I wonder if we should do it again. Natasha, it might be more effective if you put your arm around him.'

'It's too soon for that,' she said quickly. 'She doesn't yet know how she feels.'

'Nor does he,' Mario said. 'How would Romeo kiss her at this point? Would it be like this?' He laid his lips briefly over Natasha's. 'He might do it respectfully because however much he desires her he fears to offend her.

Or is he a shameless character who simply takes what he wants, like this?'

His arm went around her waist, drawing her against him, while his mouth covered hers firmly and purposefully.

She was stunned. The brief, light kiss he'd given her a few moments ago hadn't prepared her for this. Instinctively, her hands moved to touch him, but she snatched them back, unsure whether she would embrace him or push him away. She understood nothing except the disturbing pleasure of his lips on hers, and the maddening instinct to slap his face.

For two years she'd wanted to be in his arms, dreamed of it while mentally rejecting it in her rage at his betrayal. Now the sweetness of holding him again struggled with fury at his assumption that he could do as he liked and she would have to accept it.

But she could not repulse him. Whatever common sense might dictate, she must appear to react to him blissfully and chance what the future might bring. She let herself press against him, eager to feel his response, and then—

'All right, Giorgio?' Mario cried, standing back. 'Is that what you want?'

Natasha froze, barely able to believe what had happened. It seemed that the feelings that had pervaded her had been hers alone. Had he felt anything beyond the need to get the photographs right? Fury simmered inside her.

'That's fine,' Giorgio said. 'Do it just like that, for the camera.'

Then Mario's hands were on her again, drawing her nearer so that he could lay his lips on hers and hold her against him, unmoving. She could feel the warmth of his mouth, of his whole body, and her own responded to the sensation whether she wanted it to or not. Her anger flared further.

Somewhere in the background she could hear the sound of a camera, clicking again and again until at last Giorgio called, 'All right, that's it. Well done, you two. Now let's think about the next scene.'

'I need a little fresh air first,' Natasha said, quickly slipping out of the nearest door into a corridor.

She ran until she reached a corner behind which she could hide. She must escape Mario lest he suspect that she'd just discovered the power he still had over her.

But when she looked around she found him facing her.

'Did you follow me?' she demanded.

'I thought that was what you meant me to do. Don't you have something you want to say to me?'

'Oh, yes, I have a thousand things,' she said furiously. 'You've got a nerve, doing what you did back there.'

'Kissing you, you mean? But you owed it to me. When we parted you never kissed me goodbye.'

'I never thumped the living daylights out of you either, which I was surely tempted to.'

He seemed to consider this. 'So you think I deserve to have you slap my face? Very well. Do your worst.'

'What are you saying?'

'Go ahead. Slap me if it will make you feel better.'

He jutted his chin out a little and stood waiting.

'Stop talking nonsense,' she snapped.

'I mean it. You can do what you like and I promise not to retaliate.'

'This is all a big joke to you, isn't it?'

He shook his head. 'My sense of humour died the

day you left. In the weeks I spent trying to find you I buried it deep underground. So what now? Aren't you going to hit me?'

'Certainly not. It would be unprofessional. I might leave marks on your face that would spoil the next photographs. The matter is closed.'

He saluted. 'Yes, ma'am. Whatever you say, ma'am.'

'Oh, stop it—stop it! Stop trying to make a fool of me, of yourself, of both of us.'

Suddenly, his manner changed. The wry irony died and a bleakness came into his eyes. 'You silly woman,' he said quietly. 'Don't you realise that we all have our own way of coping.'

'And that's your way? Well, this is my way.'

Without warning, the swift temper she'd vowed to control swept over her, driving her to do something she knew was madness. She seized his head in her hands, drew it down and covered his mouth with her own. At once she could feel his hands on her and sensed the same confusion as she had felt herself—to deny the kiss or indulge it joyfully?

But he was going to indulge it. That was her decision, and she would give him no choice. She slightly softened the pressure of her mouth so that the kiss could become a caress, her lips moving over his in a way she had once known delighted him. She sensed his response in his tension, the sudden tightening of his arms about her.

Now she was ready to taunt him further. The pressure of her mouth intensified, and his breath came faster as his excitement grew. His lips parted as he explored her more deeply. He was no longer merely receiving her kiss but returning it in full, seeking to take command but not succeeding. The command was hers, and she would keep it whether he liked it or not. Her spirit soared. She was winning.

He drew back a little. 'Natasha—'

'Take warning, Mario. Two can play this game. You won't defy me again. If you do I'll make you sorry.'

She felt him tense, saw his eyes full of disbelief as he understood her meaning. Then it was all over. 'You had to do that, didn't you?' he rasped. 'You had to tease me—make me think—but it wasn't a kiss. It was revenge.'

'Revenge can be very sweet,' she said, pushing him away. 'That's one of the things I learned from you. Did you think you were going to get away with what you did back there? You just had to show me that you were the boss, and how I felt didn't count.'

He shook his head. 'You won't believe this,' he said in a hard voice, 'but I kissed you because I wanted to. I'm ashamed of that now because it seems so stupid to imagine that you had any kindly feelings left. But, idiot that I was, I thought some part of you might still be the old Natasha, the sweet-natured girl I loved and wanted to be with.

'But you warned me about that, didn't you? You told me that Natasha was dead. I couldn't believe it, but I believe it now. You did this to get your own back by reminding me of what I've lost.'

'You lost it because you didn't want it,' she said.

'Keep telling yourself that,' he said quietly. 'In the end you may come to believe it. In those days I wanted you more than I've ever wanted any woman. And I could have told you that if you hadn't vanished when you did. You landed us in this desert, not me. You did it by losing your temper and acting without thinking anything through. We didn't have to end up here. We could have been married by now, and expecting our first child. Instead—well, look at us.'

'Stop it! *Stop it!*' she screamed, turning away from him with her hands over her ears.

'Yes, the truth can be very painful, can't it? I could have devoted my life to loving you. Instead, I've come so close to hating you that it scares me.'

'Well, at least that's getting the truth out into the open. You hate me.'

'I didn't say that. I said I came close to hating you. I've never been able to take the final step, but I have a feeling that will come soon.'

She made no reply. The unexpected glimpse he'd given her of his own feelings had set off an aching misery inside her. He didn't hate her, but he would if he could. She wanted to scream and bang her head against the wall.

She turned away but he pulled her around to face him.

'You won't let me tell you my side of it and I think I know why,' he raged. 'Because you're a coward, Natasha. You're afraid to know the truth. If you had to face the terrible thing you did, you couldn't bear it. Everything could have been so different for us if you hadn't condemned me so quickly.'

She didn't reply. Something inside her choked the words back before they could escape.

'If you knew how I planned that day,' Mario said. 'I'd told you that I had something important to say to you. I was going to ask you not to go home, to stay with me, become my love.

'My relationship with Tania was never serious. She was a very experienced woman who surrounded herself with various male "friends". I knew I wasn't the only man in her life but it didn't trouble me because I wasn't in love with her and she wasn't in love with me.

'But when I met you, things changed. Suddenly I no longer wanted "a bit of fun". I wanted something serious and I wanted it with you. Nobody else. Just you. So I met up with Tania and I told her that we couldn't see each other any more.

'She was angry, but I thought she understood. Then it happened. She descended on us; you disappeared. If you could have seen what I went through trying to find you, how deep in despair I was—well, I guess you'd have enjoyed it.'

'I wouldn't have believed it,' she retorted. 'You? In despair, when you played the field so easily?'

'I'd done with playing the field. That life was all over for me. And if I could have explained that—made you understand… But what's the use? You only believe what you want to believe.'

She stared at him, trying to take in his incredible words. It was as though she'd become two people—one recoiling from him, one reaching out, longing to know more.

'Are you two there?' Giorgio's voice came along the corridor.

'We're here,' Mario called back.

'Ah, good.' Giorgio appeared around the corner. 'Time to get changed back into normal clothes. No more photographs today, but we're going to see Romeo's house.'

Natasha escaped to the dressing room and rid herself of the costume. It was a relief to don modern clothes and become herself again. Juliet could be banished, at least for a while.

The longer the better, she thought, staring into the

mirror and brushing her hair fiercely so that it fell down over her shoulders. It looked like spun gold in the afternoon sunlight. Once Mario had made a joke about it; 'my dangerous blonde bombshell' he'd said in a teasing voice.

'I'm not dangerous,' she'd protested.

'You can be when you act on instinct. Some of your instincts could scare a man.'

'Do I scare you?' she'd teased.

'You could if I scared easily.'

Today he'd told her frankly that her headstrong temper had done much to part them.

Suppose I'd stayed to listen to his 'explanations', she thought. *Should I have done that? Should I have trusted him? No! No!'*

She scraped her hair back as tight as it would go. When she was satisfied with her appearance she went down to join them.

Romeo's house was just a few minutes away from Juliet's and could only be seen from the outside.

'It looks like a fortress,' she said, 'with those battlements.'

'A lot of buildings were created like that in those days,' Giorgio said. 'Half of the city was almost permanently at war with the other half, hence the fight between the Capulets and Montagues.'

'Buongiorno!'

A cry from a few feet away made them turn to see a man hailing them. He seemed to be in his forties, tall and strongly built, and Natasha recognised him as a member of the *Comunità* that she had met on the first evening.

'You should have told me you were coming,' he said, giving her a hug.

'I wasn't sure until the last minute,' Mario said.

'Come and have coffee with me. My hotel is just around the corner.'

As they walked there Giorgio dropped his voice to say to Natasha, 'Mario would have avoided this meeting if he could. That's Riccardo, the rival who tried to challenge him for the presidency of the *Comunità*. He's very wealthy, owns more vineyards than any of the others, and likes giving orders just as much as Mario does.'

'You said Mario got him to back off.'

'Yes. Not sure how, but the rumours say some of Riccardo's business dealings wouldn't bear inspection.'

'You mean Mario threatened him?'

'I doubt if it was a blatant threat. That isn't Mario's way. He'll just make a remark that only one man will understand—and fear. Riccardo dropped his challenge very suddenly. Mario isn't a man you tangle with, not if you've got any sense.'

Riccardo's premises were lavish and decorative, even more so than the Dimitri Hotel. Wherever Natasha looked she could see that money had been spent without restraint. It might well appear that Riccardo was a man who could challenge Mario, but after only a few minutes seeing them together Natasha sensed that this could never happen.

Riccardo was afraid of Mario. That was the incredible truth. And Mario was content to have it be so. The young man who had once enjoyed getting his own way by charm now used power to bend people to his will.

He had blamed her for disappearing, leaving him to search frantically until finally he had accepted despair. She had resisted the accusation, but now it troubled her more than she could face. This man scared other people, but admitted that she scared him.

She fell into earnest conversation with Riccardo.

'I want to see the rest of Verona,' she said. 'It's not just about *Romeo and Juliet*. There's more to life than romance.'

'No doubt about that,' Mario agreed.

They clinked glasses.

'Right,' Natasha said. 'I've done my preliminary work. Now I'm going to shut myself away for a while to get everything written. I'll see you in a few days, gentlemen.'

'So we're no longer needed?' Giorgio asked comically. 'You're dismissing us just like that? Ah, it's a hard world.'

'That's how it is,' Mario said, reflecting Giorgio's theatrical manner. 'A woman dismisses a man when she no longer needs him. We just have to accept it.'

They all laughed.

'If I'm not required for a while I'll go back to Venice for a few days,' Mario said. 'Sally, my sister-in-law, is about to give birth again. She had a hard time with her last baby so I think Damiano might appreciate having me around for a few days. I'll stay in touch—*signorina*, Giorgio will take care of you.'

'Thank you. If I have Giorgio, what more could I possibly want?'

Mario left that afternoon, bidding her a polite goodbye in front of everyone else, adding, 'Giorgio can contact me if need be. Goodbye, everyone.'

He fled.

CHAPTER SIX

IT WAS A relief for Natasha to spend the next few days without Mario. She needed time to come to terms with what he'd told her.

If you knew how I planned that day... I was going to ask you not to go home, to stay with me, become my love.

She tried to block out the memory, but it haunted her. Mario vowed he'd broken with Tania because he loved her and was preparing to tell her.

We didn't have to end up here. We could have been married by now, and expecting our first child. Instead—well, look at us.

She tried not to hear the terrible words echoing in her mind. Mario had accused her of believing only what she wanted to believe. And perhaps he was right. If he was telling the truth it meant that she had created the disaster almost single-handed.

To escape that unbearable thought, she submerged herself in work, studying not just Verona itself but its surroundings. It stood in the Veneto, the northern region of Italy that was best known for the city of Venice.

'That's why we speak Venetian here,' Giorgio told her.

'Venetian? Venice has its own language?'

'Certainly, and it's spoken throughout the Veneto. People speak Italian as well, and English is very common because of all the tourists. But you need to know about the Venetian language to really understand this area.'

'And that's what I want to do,' she said, scribbling furiously.

The next day the photographer delivered the pictures of 'Romeo and Juliet' and she studied them closely.

Mario's face fascinated her. When they had met a few days ago, she'd thought he looked older, harsher, more tense. But in these pictures he had changed again, becoming more like the young man she remembered. She thought she could see a softening in his expression as he looked at Juliet, a glow in his eyes which the camera had caught wonderfully.

She had seen that glow before, two years ago. *He must be a very good actor,* she thought. *But I suppose I knew that.*

She spent some time wandering Verona alone, drinking in the atmosphere with nobody to distract her. She found a street she thought might be the place where Juliet's cousin Tybalt killed Romeo's friend, Mercutio. Just a little further on was where Romeo could have caught up with Tybalt and stabbed him in revenge.

Nearby were two *Comunità* hotels, where she was welcomed eagerly. She looked them over, and jotted down notes in readiness for the next despatch.

There were a dozen places to visit, but she had no energy to explore further today. She had coped with the emotional strains of the last few days, but they had taken their toll. Now she was tired and her head ached a little, so she set off back to the Dimitri Hotel.

It was a relief to get back there, order a coffee and sit in the hotel café. She closed her eyes, unaware that a man was watching her a few yards away, taking in every detail about her: her air of despondency, her appearance of being apart from the world, her loneliness.

Suddenly she looked up and saw him.

'Mario!'

'Hello, Natasha.' He went to sit beside her.

'You're back from Venice then?'

'Yes, I arrived ten minutes ago.'

'Is everything all right with your family?'

'Yes, Sally came through it well and now I've got a niece.'

'Congratulations.'

'Thank you. How are things with you? You look very tired.'

'I've had a busy day, but a very satisfying one.'

'Did anyone go with you, to make sure you didn't get lost?'

'Hey, there's no need to insult me.'

'What?'

'I'm not some silly girl who gets lost every time she's in an unfamiliar street.'

'Sorry, ma'am.'

'I could have asked Giorgio to escort me, but I refused. I can manage.'

He had no doubt of her real meaning. She'd needed time alone, free of the tension that was always there between them. He understood because he felt the same.

'You work too hard,' he said. 'You always did. I remember once before, when we first met in Venice, you said you'd been working so hard that you were exhausted. I took you for a ride in a gondola, and you fell asleep.'

He said it with a smile but she recalled that he hadn't been amused at the time. He was used to taking girls for gondola rides, but not used to them nodding off in his company.

'You took me back to the hotel and said goodnight very firmly,' she recalled, smiling. 'You felt insulted at my behaviour. I always wondered what you did for the rest of the evening, but I expect you found someone else who managed to stay awake.'

'I can't remember,' he said firmly.

'Very tactful.'

They both laughed. He couldn't tell her that he'd spent the rest of that evening alone, brooding about her seeming indifference to his attentions. She had intrigued him, and he'd sought her out early next day.

'That was always the way with you,' he reflected now. 'There, yet not there, keeping me wondering.'

'I didn't do it on purpose,' she said. 'You thought I was being a deliberate tease, but I wasn't. I was wondering too.'

And that had been her attraction for him, he realised. Where other girls were often willing, sometimes too willing, Natasha had always been just out of reach. It had driven him crazy but it had kept him in pursuit of her. Until finally she had vanished, leaving him devastated.

How much had she really felt for him? To this day he didn't know, and he doubted he ever would.

But one thing was certain. She was no longer the tense, nervy creature of a few days ago. The woman who had forced a kiss on him as revenge for his kissing her had simply vanished. Now she was relaxed, in command, humorous, alluring.

'I hear that you've been working hard,' he said. 'You've been contacting the other hotel owners to get information, and showing them what you planned to write so that they could approve it. They're very impressed. My stock has risen considerably since I performed the brilliant act of securing your services.' He gave a theatrical flourish. 'Only a genius like myself could have discovered you.'

'But you didn't discover me. It was Giorgio.'

'Hush. We don't say that.' He grinned. 'And neither does Giorgio if he knows what's good for him.'

'I see. The boss gives his orders and we all jump to obey.'

'Some do. I doubt I'll ever see the day when you jump to obey.'

'But you pay my wages,' she reminded him. 'Surely I have no choice but to obey you?'

'All right, all right. You've had your joke.'

'It's not a joke. You're my employer. I know it's Giorgio who directs me, but you're the authority. If you told him to fire me, he'd have to do so.'

'There's no danger of that.'

'Actually, there's something I've been meaning to say to you.'

'What is it?' he asked with a sense of foreboding, for her tone implied a serious matter. 'Go on, tell me. How bad is it?'

'It's not bad at all. I want to say thank you.'

'Thank you? For what?' he asked, sounding nervous.

'For changing my contract so that I'm making more money. I couldn't believe it when Giorgio showed me the new one and said you'd told him to increase it.'

'But you've already thanked me,' he said. 'You did so a few minutes afterwards. I told you then that it was essential to secure your professional services.'

'Yes, you told me that, but you knew how bad my financial problems were. You could have secured me without raising the money. I think there may have been a little kindness involved too.'

He gave a slight smile. 'Kindness? Me? I'm a businessman. I don't do kindness.'

'I think you do. I can remember things in Venice—that little girl who lost her dog, and you found it for her.'

'I was only trying to impress you.'

'And you succeeded. You don't like people to know about your kind and caring streak but it's there.'

'That's practically an insult.'

'Then you'll have to put up with me insulting you,' she said.

'I think I can just about manage that.'

'The thing is—that quarrel we had the other day, when we'd finished having the pictures taken… It just flared up but I wish it hadn't.'

'So do I. I said things I didn't mean.'

'You said I was afraid to face the truth, that everything could have been different if I'd listened to you. I think you meant that and I don't blame you.'

'But do you believe what I told you—about Tania, how I'd already broken with her?'

'Please—please don't,' she gasped. 'It's in the past. It doesn't matter now.'

'Meaning that you still don't believe me.'

'I don't know,' she said in anguish. 'There are so many things battling each other in my mind—'

'I know the feeling,' he said wryly.

'But it doesn't matter.'

'Natasha, how can it not matter? You always prided yourself on being logical, but if you think what happened between us didn't matter you're talking nonsense.'

'I didn't mean that. It mattered then, but not now. The world has moved on. We've moved on.'

'Ah, yes,' he said quietly. 'We've moved on.'

'And I think we were never meant to be together. Something was always fated to go wrong.'

'Now you sound like Giorgio.'

'What do you mean?'

'Just before you arrived, he and I were talking about Romeo and Juliet being "star-crossed lovers". Sometimes a couple is meant for each other but just can't get it together. They just have to accept that fate is against them.'

'Yes,' she said thoughtfully. 'You could say that fate was against us. My problem was that you had more women in your life than you could count. Or that I could count.'

'And mine was that you don't trust any man. I've always wondered why. Was there some other guy who walked out and broke your heart?'

'In a way, yes, but it's not how you think. The man who walked out was my father.'

She fell silent until he said, 'Tell me about him.'

'I loved him, and he loved me, so I thought. And then he just vanished. I never heard from him again. We seemed to be so close but he just wiped me and my mother out of existence.'

As you did with me, Mario thought, but was too tactful to say.

'My mother was so bitter. She told me a million times that no man could ever be trusted, but she didn't need to say it. I felt it for myself.'

'So when we knew each other you were always reminding yourself that no man could be trusted—especially me.'

'No, not especially you. You mattered more than any-one else but—'

'But you instinctively thought I was no different from the rest of them. Except perhaps a bit worse.'

'No, no—it wasn't like that.'

'From where I'm sitting it was exactly like that.'

'And so you've come close to hating me,' she sighed. 'Perhaps I can't blame you.'

'Please, Natasha, forget I said that. I was in a temper. I wanted to hurt you because I resented the way you'd just shown your power over me. The way you kissed me made a point I didn't want to admit.'

'A point?' Her heart was beating fast.

'You showed me that I'm not the strong, independent fellow I like to believe I am. So I hit back with the worst thing I could think of. I didn't mean it and I'm not proud of it. Do you think you can forgive me?'

'That depends.'

'On what?' he asked cautiously.

'On whether *you* can forgive *me*.'

'There's nothing to forgive.'

'Really? What about the way you say I—?'

'Stop there,' he said quickly. 'Whatever I may have said, I take it back. It's over. It's done with. Let us be friends.'

She considered a moment before smiling and saying wistfully, 'That would be nice.'

'It's settled then.'

'Shake?' She held out her hand, but he fended her off.

'No. We shook hands the first night as professional associates. But now we're friends—and friends don't shake hands. They don't need to.' He leaned over and kissed her cheek. 'That's what friends do. And they buy each other coffee.'

'Good. Waiter!'

'No, I meant that I'd buy you a coffee.'

'Stop giving me orders. I'm buying and that's that.'

'Yes, ma'am. Anything you say, ma'am.'

'Mind you, you'll have to do the talking.'

He nodded, gave the waiter the order in Italian, then watched as she paid.

'Have you explored anywhere recently?' he asked.

'I've looked around a bit, but there's still one big place I've set my heart on visiting and that's Juliet's tomb.

'Now it's a museum,' she said. 'It seems to attract as many tourists as the balcony, so I must go there and plan the next article.'

'There's a *Comunità* hotel nearby,' Mario said. 'The Albergo Martinez. You met the owner the other night. We could dine there tonight and hear anything they have to say. Let me call him.'

He took out his phone, made a call and started talking in Italian. While she was waiting, her own mobile phone beeped. Her heart beat hard with horror when she read the text message.

After a few minutes Mario hung up, saying, 'He's expecting us in a couple of hours.'

He stopped suddenly, frowning as he saw her staring into space, full of tension.

'What is it?' he asked. 'What happened?'

'Nothing.'

'No, something's the matter. What is it?'

'No—no—I'm all right. I'd like to go to my room.'

She got up and walked quickly away. Frowning, he followed her, hurrying until he caught up and could take a firm hold of her hand. She didn't resist but neither did she respond, and he had a feeling that she had taken refuge in another world, from which he was excluded.

He accompanied her as far as her door, noting that she still looked pale and tense.

'I'll collect you in an hour,' he said.

'I'll be ready.'

Once inside, she undressed and got into the shower. There was a kind of relief in being doused with water, as though it could wash away the shock that had overtaken her.

The text on her mobile phone had been from Elroy Jenson:

You won't get away from me.

He's driving me crazy, she told herself. *And that's what he wants.*

She wondered why she hadn't told Mario what had troubled her. It should have been easy since she had already told him about Elroy, and he would have been a valuable ally. But something in her was reluctant to reveal more vulnerability. Especially to Mario.

When she had showered she put on a neat dark blue dress, suitable for a polite gathering. For several minutes she teased her hair, trying to decide whether to be seductive or businesslike. As so often with Mario, her mind was filled with conflicting thoughts.

Their conversation had been fraught with double meanings. He'd said, *I wanted to hurt you because I resented the way you'd just shown your power over me.*

But he'd implied the power of a bully, not of a woman. They had made a truce, but the battle was far from over.

When he'd pressed her to say that she believed him now she had been unable to say what he wanted to hear. She longed to believe him, but she couldn't quite make herself take the final step.

But why should it matter whether I believe him or not? she mused. *That's all over. What matters is that we can manage to be friends.*

Nico was watching for their arrival at the Albergo Martinez and came to meet them with hands outstretched. Natasha recognised him from their meeting the first night.

Over supper he described the tomb.

'Juliet was buried in the church of San Francesco al Corso, a monastery,' he explained.

'Yes, it was Friar Laurence, a monk, who married them,' Natasha recalled. 'On their wedding day they went to his cell and he took them to the church to marry them.'

'True. And when Juliet died—or at least she'd drunk the potion and seemed dead—she was taken to the monastery to be buried. These days the monastery has become a museum. You can go to the crypt and see the sarcophagus that legend says was hers.

'The museum also hosts weddings. Many people choose to become united for life in the place where Romeo and Juliet were united in eternity. Of course, if they are seeking a hotel not too far away—'

'They'll be glad to discover yours,' she said in her most professional manner. 'I shall make sure that they do.'

'*Eccellente!* Mario, you've made a fine discovery in this talented lady. Don't let her go, whatever you do.'

'Don't worry; I won't,' he said with a cheerful nod.

'Now, let us go in to supper.'

Supper was served at a large table where many people were already sitting. As they sat down Natasha became aware of something she had seen many times before. From every direction women were casting admiring glances at Mario. It had been there from the beginning, two years ago. It was still there.

And why not? she thought. *He's got the looks to make it happen. And it doesn't bother me any more.*

She soon discovered that the man sitting next to her was an ideal choice. His name was Tonio and he was an academic, specialising in English history. As history had always been one of her interests, she was soon deep in conversation with him, intrigued by his prejudiced arguments.

'You're all wrong about Richard III,' she told him. 'Shakespeare depicted him as a monster but he wasn't really—'

'You English!' he exclaimed. 'You can never believe that any of your monarchs were evil.'

'On the contrary, the evil ones are the most fun. But Richard's evil reputation is mostly a kind of show business.'

'I've studied the evidence and I tell you—'

Heads close together, they stayed absorbed in their argument, with the rest of the table regarding them with amused fascination. All except Mario, who was looking displeased, which surprised Natasha when she happened to glance up. The luscious beauty beside him was paying him fervent attention that a man might be expected to enjoy. But he seemed to be tolerating rather than encouraging her.

'I see Bianca's got her claws into a new man,' said Tonio, sounding amused.

'You speak as though it happens often.'

'With Bianca it does. She likes to cast her net wide.'

'It doesn't look as though he's fallen under her spell.'

'Not now, but give him a little time.'

Bianca was clearly a practised flirt, convinced that any man was hers for the asking. When she patted Mario's face, giggling, he smiled back politely before returning his gaze to Natasha.

'You need to look at it like this,' Tonio said, returning to their discussion. 'King Richard couldn't possibly—'

She plunged back into the argument, enjoying herself for the next half hour, until somebody put on some music and people began to dance. Suddenly Mario appeared by her chair.

'Dance with me,' he said.

'Wouldn't you rather dance with Bianca?'

'No.' He grasped her hand, drew her to her feet and onto the floor.

'I thought you were having a lovely time.' She laughed as they twirled.

'Did you really?' he demanded ironically.

'Being hunted down by a woman who'd gladly have given you anything you wanted.'

'Which would be fine if there was anything I did want from her. But I don't.'

'That wouldn't stop some men. They'd just take anything that's going.'

'I was like that once, when I was young and stupid. I grew up in the end, but by then it was too late.'

He said the last words with a wry look. The next moment the temptress glided past them. She was dancing with another man, but even so she gave Mario a glance that made him tighten his grasp on Natasha.

'Rescue me,' he growled.

'How?'

'Anyhow.'

'All right. Here goes. Aaaargh!'

With a theatrical sigh, she drooped against his chest.

'Oh, how my head aches,' she declared. 'I really must go home.'

'I'll take you,' he said.

Turning to their host, he explained that it was necessary to take Natasha away at once.

'She isn't feeling well,' he said. 'She must go to bed.'

From somewhere came the sound of choking laughter. Mario ignored it and picked Natasha up to carry her from the room. He didn't set her down until they reached the car.

'Thank you,' he said as they drove away.

'No problem. I'm really glad to leave because I need some sleep. Of course, if you want to go back and spend time with Bianca—'

'If that's your idea of a joke, it's not funny,' he said in an edgy voice.

'Sorry, I couldn't resist it.'

'Perhaps you should try to resist it. I'm just a sitting duck as far as you're concerned.'

'All right, I apologise.'

'It was getting very difficult in there.'

'You know what they're all thinking now, don't you?' she chuckled.

'Yes, they think that when we get home we're going to— Well, you can imagine.'

'Yes, I can imagine.'

'And I'm sorry. But that woman was getting embarrassing.'

'Don't tell me you're afraid of her. You? A man who's afraid of nothing.'

'You'd be surprised at some of the things I'm afraid of,' he said. 'Once you were one of them. Now you're beginning to feel like the best friend I have.'

'Good. Then we have nothing left to worry about...'

CHAPTER SEVEN

NEXT MORNING THEY drove to the monastery museum and went down into the crypt, where several other tourists had already gathered, looking at a large marble sarcophagus.

It was open at the top, revealing that it was empty now, but legend said that this was where Juliet had lain after taking the drug that made her appear lifeless. Here, Romeo had come to find her and, believing her dead, had taken his own life, minutes before she awoke. Finding him dead, she had taken her own life.

'I just don't understand it,' said an elderly man, staring into the sarcophagus. 'How could two people so young take their own lives?'

'Maybe they didn't,' said one of his companions. 'Maybe that's an invention of the story.'

'No,' Natasha said. 'It's part of the story because it was inevitable. It's what you do if life has lost all meaning.'

'And that can happen at any age,' Mario said at once.

'No,' the old man said. 'They could have got over each other and found other lovers.'

'But they didn't believe that,' Mario pointed out.

'Youngsters never do,' the man said loftily. 'But when they get older they find out that nothing ever really matters that much. Love comes and goes and comes again. It's ridiculous to believe anyone discovers the full meaning of their life as young as that.'

'No,' Mario said. 'It's ridiculous to believe that such a discovery happens to a timetable. It happens when it's ready to happen. Not before and not after.'

The old man looked at him with interest. 'You sound like an expert, sir.'

'I guess we're all experts, one way or another,' Mario said.

There were some murmurs of agreement from the little crowd as they turned away, following their tourist guide to another part of the museum.

Now that they were alone, Mario watched as Natasha looked into the sarcophagus.

'They married and had one sweet night together,' she murmured. 'But when they finally lay together it was here.'

'They lie together and they always will,' Mario said.

She turned a smiling face on him. 'You know what you've done, don't you?'

'What have I done?'

'Given me a wonderful idea that I can develop for the piece I'm writing. "They lie together and they always will." Thank you.'

He made an ironic gesture. 'Glad to be of use.'

'Would you mind leaving me alone here for a while? I just want to—' She looked around her, taking a deep breath, her arms extended.

She just wanted to absorb a romantic atmosphere without being troubled by his presence, he thought. A dreary inconvenience. That was how she saw him now.

True, she had kissed him, but in anger, not in love or

desire. And hell would freeze over before he let her suspect the depth of her triumph.

He stepped aside to a place in the shadows. From here he saw her stare down again into the tomb, reaching out into the empty space inside. What did she see in that space? Romeo, lying there, waiting for her to join him? Or Romeo and Juliet, sleeping eternally, clasped in each other's arms, held against each other's hearts?

Whatever it was, she had not invited him to be with her, because in her heart she was certain that he had left the dream behind long ago. If he had ever believed in it.

If only there was some magic spell that could enable her to look into his heart and see the truth he had carried there ever since their first meeting. Might she then look at him with eyes as fervent and glowing as she had done once, long, long ago?

He stayed watching her for a while, expecting that any moment she would move away. But she seemed transfixed, and at last he went to her.

'Are you all right?' he asked. 'You seem almost troubled.'

'No, I'm not troubled. It's just the atmosphere here, and what this tomb represents.'

'Surely it just represents death?'

'No, there's more. Finality, fulfilment, completion. They were young; they could have gone on and had lives that would have seemed satisfying. But each meant more to the other than life itself. You put it perfectly when you said people can discover what really matters while they're still young, and then they lie together for ever. This—' she looked around at the walls of the tomb '—this says everything.'

'I think we should go now,' he said. Her fascination with the place was making him uneasy.

'Yes, I've done all I need to do here. I'll spend this evening working on it. Then I'll do a new article and send it around the *Comunità*, so they can tell me what they think. I'm sure their suggestions will be useful.'

'I see you've got all the boxes ticked.'

'I hope so. That's what you're paying me for. Shall we go? We're finished here, aren't we?'

'Oh, yes,' he agreed. 'We're finished here.'

No more was said on the way back to the hotel.

Once there, Natasha hurried up to her room to get to work. She had supper served to her there and did not go downstairs all evening. She needed to be alone to think about the day. Mario's observations at the tomb had left her wondering. The old man had said he sounded like an expert about love. Mario had replied, *We're all experts, one way or another.*

One way or another. Love might be a joy or a betrayal. Which had he meant?

But I don't need to ask that, she thought. *He feels betrayed, just as I do. But how is that possible? Can we have both betrayed each other?*

He'd accused her of refusing to listen to him because she feared the truth, feared to confront her own part in their break-up. She had denied it, but could there possibly be a grain of truth in it?

Surely not, she thought. It couldn't have turned out any differently. Could it?

She had felt her own pain so intensely, but now she was confronted by his pain and it was a bewildering experience.

We'll never understand each other, she thought. *I mustn't hope for too much. Or do I mean fear too much?*

She gave herself a mental shake.

That's enough. I'm here to work and when I've finished my job I'll leave, whatever he says or does.

But the next day everything changed.

In the morning she went exploring again, wandering Verona on foot until, in the afternoon, she reached Juliet's house. There, she looked around the courtyard, meaning to go inside and see the museum.

But something drew her to Juliet's statue, still standing as it had been before, gazing into the distance.

If only, she thought, she could indulge the fantasy of asking Juliet's advice, and imagining an answer. It might help sort out the confusion in her head and her heart.

She didn't know how Mario felt, or how she herself felt. When he had kissed her she'd wanted him so much that it scared her. So she had punished him with a kiss designed to show him what he'd lost. But she too had been reminded of what she'd lost.

Into her mind came Mario's face, looking as he had at the start of the photo shoot. His expression had been— she struggled for the words—cautious, perhaps a little nervous.

She had blamed him for kissing her, thinking him too confident and self-satisfied. But did she blame him too much? Had he been uneasy, secretly wanting the kiss but unsure of himself?

I know how that feels, she brooded. *In my heart I wanted him to kiss me. Perhaps that's why I was so angry when he did.*

She sighed and turned away. Then she stopped, tense.

Mario was standing there, watching her.

'I happened to see you in the street,' he said, 'so I took the liberty of following you. Have you been inside the house?'

'No, I was about to go in.'

'Let's go in together.'

Inside, they looked briefly around the sixteenth-century furniture, absorbing the perfect atmosphere for the legend. Then they climbed the stairs and stepped out onto the balcony.

A young couple was already there, wrapped in each other's arms.

'Sorry,' the girl said, moving aside. 'We just had to come and see it again. We're getting married here next week and all the pictures will be taken out on the balcony.'

'How lovely,' Natasha said. 'The perfect place.'

'We thought so.' They kissed and slipped away into the building.

How lucky they were, she thought, to be so sure of each other, of life, of the future.

Now the light was fading, and there were few visitors. It was easy to imagine herself as Juliet, standing there looking into the night sky, unaware that Romeo was down below, watching her.

'I wonder what it was like for her,' she mused, 'to stand here, dreaming of him, then finally realising he was there, seeing him watching her, not knowing that their love was fated.'

Before he could answer, there was a shrill from her mobile phone. But she ignored it.

'Aren't you going to answer that?' Mario asked.

'No, it can wait,' she said in a tense voice. 'I didn't mean to bring it with me. I don't want to be distracted.'

The phone shrilled again.

'Answer it,' Mario said. 'Get rid of them.'

Reluctantly, she pulled out the phone and answered.

'At last,' said the voice she dreaded.

'You again,' she snapped. 'Stop pestering me.'

'Stop telling me what to do,' said Jenson's voice. 'If I want to call you I shall. Who do you think you are to give me orders?'

'Who do I think I am? I'm the woman who told you to go and jump in the lake. I'm the woman who wants nothing to do with a man as disgusting as you. You should have realised that by now.'

From the other end of the line came a crack of laughter.

'No, you're the one who should have woken up to reality, you stupid tart. You don't know what I could do to you—'

'I think I do. You've made it brutally clear.'

'That was just the start. You don't know how sorry I can make you, but you're going to find out. I know something about you, Natasha, and by the time I've finished you're going to wish you'd treated me with more respect.'

Before she could reply, the phone was wrenched from her hand by Mario.

'Jenson,' he snapped. 'Go to hell. Leave her alone or I'll make you sorry.'

A bellow of ugly laughter reached him down the line.

'Not as sorry as you'll be if you're involved with Natasha,' Jenson bawled. 'She's made herself my enemy, and if you side with her you'll be my enemy too. I have a way with enemies.'

With a swift movement Mario severed the connection.
'Jenson's still pestering you?'

'Yes, he won't stop.' She was shaking.

'All right, let's deal with this,' Mario said. He put his
arms around her firmly, protectively. 'Come on, we're
going back to the hotel.'

Still holding her, he led her back to his car. She almost
collapsed into the seat beside him and sat with her head
in her hands during the drive. To his relief, there was almost nobody in the hotel lobby and he was able to take
her upstairs quickly. As soon as the door closed behind
them he clasped her once more in his arms.

'It's all right,' he said fiercely. 'There's nothing to be
scared of. You're safe here. Jenson is in the past.'

'No, he's not,' she groaned. 'As long as he can reach
me he's not in the past. Changing my number is useless.
He always finds out my new one. That's how powerful he
is. I'm scared. He haunts me. When I get a text or a call
from him it's as though he's actually there. He's already
ruined my career, and I can't be rid of him.'

'You're wrong,' Mario said. 'He hasn't ruined your
career, and he isn't going to because I'm not going to
let him.'

She took some deep breaths, managing to calm down
a little. Mario touched her chin, lifting it so that he could
see her face. For a moment he was tempted to give her a
gentle kiss, by way of comfort. But, instead, he took her
to the bed, still holding her as she sat down, then drawing her head against him again.

'Thank goodness you were there,' she said. 'I couldn't
have coped alone.'

'I know you couldn't,' he said morosely. 'That's why
I grabbed your phone in a way you must have thought

rather rude. If something threatens me I like to know how serious it is.'

'But he's not threatening you.'

'Anything that threatens you threatens me. I told you—I'll deal with it.'

'Thank you.' She clung to him. 'It's lucky it was only a phone call. If he'd turned up in person I think I'd have done something violent, perhaps strangled him.' She made a wry face. 'You're right in what you've always said about my nasty temper.'

'I've never said it was a nasty temper,' he disclaimed at once. 'It's a quick temper. Act first, think later.'

'By which time it's too late to think,' she sighed.

He didn't reply, merely tightened his arms about her.

'It's been a curse all my life,' she said. 'My mother used to say I'd come to a bad end. According to her, I got my temper from my father, and I never heard her say a good word about him.'

'You mentioned him the other day. Didn't they split up?'

'He left her when I was only ten. Just walked out and vanished. It broke my heart. Until then I'd had a wonderful relationship with my father. I was the apple of his eye. But he left my mother for another woman and I never heard from him again.'

'Never? Are you sure your mother didn't keep you apart?'

'No, he didn't write or call. I used to watch the mail arrive and there was never anything from him. I tried telephoning him but he'd changed his number.'

He didn't reply. She waited for him to remind her how she'd done the same thing, but he only hugged her closer.

'You should put all that behind you,' he murmured.

'The past is gone, but you must make sure it *is* the past. Don't let it haunt your life, or it will control you.'

'You sound as though you really know,' she said.

'In a way I do. At one time I owed so much to Damiano that the need to get free and grow up became the most important thing in my life.'

'Grow up?'

'I took a long time to get to that stage.'

That was true, she thought, remembering him two years ago. Now he was so much stronger and more serious that he was almost a different man.

'"Haunt your life",' she murmured. 'My mother never got over him abandoning us. She told me again and again that you could never trust a man.'

'And her words have stayed with you always,' he said softly.

'Not just her words. It was also the way he cut me out of his life, after I'd seemed to mean so much to him. I'd believed in his love, but it meant nothing.'

Mario uttered a soft curse. 'I wish I had him here so that I could sock him in the jaw,' he said. 'But don't let your father—or Elroy Jenson—destroy your life, Natasha. Banish them into the past, turn your back and become the person you really are.'

'Too late,' she sighed.

'It's never too late if it's what you really want.'

She would have given anything to see his face as he uttered those words, but her head was pressed against his shoulder.

'Never too late,' she echoed, resting against him. A feeling of sleepy contentment was overtaking her, and she could have happily stayed like this for ever.

Mario sensed the moment when she began to doze.

He tightened his arms about her, laying his lips against her hair, feeling an unfamiliar warmth go through him. He wanted to hold her close, but not in the hope of making love with her, only to keep her safe.

It was a feeling he'd never known before. When they had first met she had seemed strong, full of confidence, able to challenge the world and emerge victorious.

He found his mind drifting back to his own past. Since the day he'd first begun flirting with girlfriends he had never been attracted by commitment. His girlfriends had all been strong, independent, fancying him but not needing him.

Immature, he thought now wryly. *Boy, was I immature.*

Four years earlier he'd met Sally, the woman who had married his brother, Damiano. His feelings for her had grown so deep that he'd fled their home in Venice for safety's sake.

Later, he'd felt safe enough to return occasionally. His interest in the hotel business had grown. Damiano had been an excellent teacher and Mario's talent had flourished until he could manage to buy and run his own hotel. But he'd remained a playboy, dancing from girl to girl, never choosing anyone who might seriously need him.

Now he realised how much things had changed. Natasha's sadness had touched his heart. She was alone and vulnerable, and the knowledge affected him strongly. The torment he'd endured when she'd deserted him had begun to fade, overwhelmed by her need. She needed a friend to be strong for her, and something told him that he should be that person because without him she had nobody. He tightened his arms, trying to send her a si-

lent message of reassurance. Her breathing was steady
and, although he couldn't see her face, he guessed she
was still dozing.

Probably just as well that they couldn't talk, he
thought. Words could be a trap, especially for a man
like himself, with little verbal skill. He preferred to be
judged by his actions rather than his words.

Since the day she'd arrived he knew he'd been clumsy,
confused. The feeling had been increased by the suspicion that she enjoyed confusing him. He'd fought back,
making matters worse, he now realised. But now he knew
that his own feelings didn't matter. He only wanted her
to feel safe.

He eased her down onto the bed. Her head drooped
to one side and her eyes were closed, as though she'd
slipped away from him into another world. And yet she
was still with him.

And she always would be, he resolved. He'd lost her
once. He couldn't bear to lose her again. He knew he had
to keep her, but for the moment he must be silent about
his decision. They had far to travel before things could
be said openly between them.

Moving carefully, he lay down beside her, still holding her so that her head rested against him. For a while
she was still, but then her arm moved, drifting slowly
across his chest as though seeking him, his help and
comfort.

For a moment he thought that she might awaken and
he could say some of the things in his heart. But then she
grew still again, and he knew she'd slipped back into another world. One where he did not exist, he realised. Did
he exist for her at all?

He looked closely into her face, hoping to read in it

some hint of an answer, but she was fast asleep. Their
time would come, but for now he knew he must be patient. He closed his eyes.

In the early morning light Natasha opened her eyes to
find herself in a strange world, one where her head rested
against Mario and his arms enfolded her protectively.

At once she knew it was a dream. It could be nothing else.

'All right?' asked his gentle voice. 'Are you awake
at last?'

'Am I—what—what am I—?'

Mario saw the dismay come into her eyes as she realised that she was lying in his arms.

'You've had a good night's sleep,' he said. 'So have I.'

'What happened? How did we—?'

'How did we end up lying together? You got a call
from Jenson and it scared you. You were so upset that
it seemed best not to leave you alone, so I came in here
and stayed with you. But don't worry. I was just being a
friend. I haven't done anything I shouldn't.'

She knew at once that it was true. Her flesh was calm
and rested in a way that wouldn't have been true if he'd
touched her sexually. He had merely held her gently, com-
fortingly in his arms, thinking only of her welfare.

'Truly,' he said. 'Stop worrying.'

'I'm not worried. I'm just glad you're here.'

'Glad?' he echoed. 'Really glad?'

'Of course. How could I not be? You said you'd keep
me safe and you did. Oh, if I could only tell you how
good that feels.'

'If that's what you want, that's all that matters,' he said.

Her eyes glowed and he became tense. Desire was

growing in him. He wanted to kiss her smiling mouth, caress her warm body, feel her come to new life in his arms. But he had just reassured her that he had no such temptations, and her reaction left no doubt that this was what she wanted to hear.

He wanted her, but she didn't want him in the same way. That was what he had to accept. It was all he could do for her.

She stirred in his arms and he loosened his hold, thinking she was trying to move away from him. But she turned more towards him, closing her eyes again, sliding an arm around his body and murmuring, *'Mmm!'* as though she had discovered blissful contentment.

And that was what he brought her, he reflected. It was a kind of happiness, and better than the anguish of their first encounter, days ago.

'But there could be more,' he whispered softly into her ear.

'Mmm?'

'If we're patient, there could be more between us, surely? We could take it slowly, and then—maybe—'

'Maybe what?' she murmured.

'I know we still have things to put behind us, and it won't be easy. You didn't treat me kindly, vanishing like that, but, after the way your father behaved, I guess you don't trust any of us. And I hurt you but I didn't mean to. If only you could bring yourself to believe me about that. But you will. One day I just know you will, and then everything will be wonderful.'

'Mmm.'

He gave a gentle laugh. 'I wonder what "Mmm" actually means.'

She met his eyes. 'If I knew—I'd tell you.'

'No, you wouldn't. You enjoy keeping me guessing. All right. I'll play your game because the prize we could win is worth everything.'

'Yes,' she whispered. 'But will we win it?'

'Who knows?' he said. 'We *will* know. We must. But not just yet. Something will happen. It will make everything clear—soon—soon.'

'I guess you understand more than I do. You'll tell me when the time comes—whenever that is.'

She smiled at him in a way that filled him with hope.

CHAPTER EIGHT

'I'LL LEAVE YOU now so you can get some more sleep,' Mario said. 'See you in the morning.'

He fled from the room, downstairs and out into the garden. It was just becoming light and he went to the river, where he could lean over the wall and stare into the water, brooding.

It felt wonderful to have achieved a brief emotional contact with her, but he wondered how completely she understood him. He'd spoken of his hopes for the future, but were they any more than fantasies? She had said that something would happen. But when? How long must they wait to be sure?

He looked back at the building, where he could identify her room from the faint light that still glowed inside. As he watched, the floor-length window opened and she came out onto the balcony.

He backed away into the shadows so that she wouldn't see him, but she didn't even look down. She stood motionless, her eyes turned up to the heavens as though she could find the answer to a mystery in that distant place.

Watching her on the balcony, he thought that this must have been how it was for Romeo, seeing his beloved standing there above him.

On the night she'd arrived he'd gone to stand beneath her window, looking up, longing to see her. And there she had been, reaching out into the night, her body full of anguish, speaking words he had strained to hear. Then she'd gone inside again, leaving him standing alone in the darkness, struggling to come to terms with his conflicting feelings.

Now, here he was again, watching Natasha from a distance, condemned perhaps to be always at a distance, unable to voice his emotions openly.

Romeo's words came into his head. *It is my lady, Oh, it is my love! Oh, that she knew she were!*

'Yes,' he murmured. 'It is my love. Oh, that she knew she were.'

She does know, argued a voice in his head. *You've made it very clear.*

But does she want to know? queried another voice. *Is she ready to accept?*

Her voice was still there in his mind, asking if they would win the prize. That alarmed him, as it meant she could envisage a future apart. The way ahead was still strewn with doubts and problems, and who knew what the answers would be? Or if there would be any answers?

Romeo had reached out from beneath Juliet's balcony, letting her know he was there, telling her of his feelings. But Mario knew that path wasn't open to him at this moment.

Slowly he backed away, retreating deep into the shadows, never taking his eyes off her.

For a while, she stayed looking up into the sky, but then she lowered her head and wrapped her arms about herself, leaning against the wall. Her demeanour suggested confusion, sadness. Mario drew in his breath sharply. He'd tried to ease those feelings in her, and had briefly thought he'd succeeded. But she was still lonely, still vulnerable, and the sight hurt him.

Once he could have reached out to console her openly, revealing everything in his heart, inviting her in, rejoicing in the unity they had seemed to share.

But that unity had been an illusion, with traps along the way, ready to bring them both down. She needed him. He felt this as he had never felt it before, and the longing to fulfil her need was taking him over, heart and soul. But her feelings for him, whatever they might be, were undermined by a caution that barred her from believing that she was his love.

'Oh, that she knew she were,' he whispered again. 'Oh, that I could convince her.'

He slipped quietly away for fear that she might see him.

Inside the hotel, he found Giorgio waiting for him in a state of agitation.

'You were right about her all along,' he said.

'Right about who?'

'Her. Natasha Bates. You suspected something troubling about her as soon as she arrived. You said you hadn't met her before but it was obvious you guessed what a suspicious character she was. And she knew that you sensed it. That's why she's so edgy when you're around.'

'What the devil are you talking about?' Mario snapped.

'We've received an email about Natasha that you must see. It's from Jenson Publications.'

'Show me.'

The email was blunt and vicious:

You should be warned about your employee, Natasha
Bates. She's well known in the media business for her
dishonesty and inefficiency. If you are wise you will dis-
miss her at once.

There was no name attached. The missive merely
came from the Jenson Publications head office.

'He didn't dare put his name to it,' Mario growled.
'But this comes from Elroy Jenson, a miserable, schem-
ing bastard who I'll strangle if I ever get my hands on
him.'

'But suppose it's true,' Giorgio argued. 'You've always
sensed that she was dodgy.'

'Don't you dare say that,' Mario raged. 'None of this
is true and if I ever hear you say such a thing again I'll
make you sorry.'

'All right, all right,' Giorgio said, hastily backing off,
alarmed by the look in Mario's eyes. 'My lips are sealed.'

'Don't say it and don't even think it,' Mario snapped.
'Understand?'

'Understand,' Giorgio said. 'Sorry. It just hadn't occurred to me.'

'Yes, there are a lot of things that hadn't occurred to
me either,' Mario sighed. 'But when they do occur—well,
you just have to face them. This email is a pack of lies.
Jenson came on to her, she rejected him and now he's out
to destroy her out of spite.'

Giorgio nodded as comprehension came to him. 'So
you're on her side?'

'Yes,' Mario said slowly. 'I'm on her side.'

In the past few days he'd felt a desire to care for Natasha, but those moments were nothing compared to the
storm of protectiveness that invaded him now. If Jenson

had been there in person he would have throttled him without compunction.

'Don't tell her about this,' he instructed Giorgio. 'He's trying to scare her and I won't have it.'

'But shouldn't we warn her? She should know she's got an enemy.'

'She already knows. But she also has us, and we're going to take care of her. Not a word. I don't want her upset.'

She had every reason to be upset, he realised. Elroy Jenson might not be following her physically, but he was after her in a far more dangerous way. Through stretching out his tentacles of power across the world, he thought he could still make her suffer for defying him.

But he was wrong, Mario thought angrily. Now Natasha had him to defend her and he would do so, whatever it cost him.

'She mustn't suspect anything,' he said to Giorgio.

'If you say so.' Giorgio sighed reluctantly. 'But can we fend this man off?'

'We can and we will. She's going to be safe.' His face became set. 'I've promised her that and I'm going to keep my word.'

Turning back into her room from the balcony, Natasha returned to the bed and lay down. She had a strange yet pleasant feeling that Mario was still with her, whispering reassurances in her mind, or merely tightening his arms protectively around her, so that she understood.

But was that what he'd meant, or was she just listening to her own hopes? She was still wondering as she fell asleep.

She awoke feeling refreshed, eager to get up and face the day.

As soon as she swung her legs out of bed she knew something was wrong. The carpet beneath her feet was wet. Looking further, she found that the water came from the bathroom and covered most of the floor.

'Oh, heavens, I must have left a tap on!' she exclaimed in dismay.

But when exploring the bathroom she discovered not a tap but a leaking pipe, spilling water directly onto the floor.

Hastily, she called Mario and explained that she'd need a plumber. He arrived a few minutes later and swore when he saw the extent of the damage.

'This must be fixed quickly before it sinks through the floor,' he said. 'Pack your things and get out of here fast. I'll arrange another room for you.'

She was packed and finished in half an hour, glad to escape and leave the room to the plumbers who'd arrived. She found Mario waiting for her downstairs with a table laid for breakfast.

'There's a bit of a problem,' he said. 'It's high season and every room in the place is taken.'

'So I'll find a room somewhere else.'

'Certainly not. I have an apartment upstairs that you can have. I don't sleep there so the bed is free. You can relax in peace.'

'And do some work,' she said, gathering up her laptop.

His apartment was mainly a place of storage, filled with shelves and filing cabinets. She arrived to find a maid making up the bed.

'It's all yours,' Mario said. 'I'll leave you to it. Good-bye for now.'

She worked contentedly, sending her material to a dozen different sources. Then she felt the need for a short break, and crossed the room to switch on the television. But on the way her heel tangled in the carpet and she pitched forward. Reaching out, she grabbed hold of some small shelves, which promptly disgorged their contents onto the floor. With an exclamation, she dropped down and began gathering them up.

Then she stopped suddenly, as though something had grabbed her in a vice. An envelope had opened, spilling out several sheets of pale blue notepaper. On one of them she saw what was written at the bottom: *Your loving Tania.*

Her whole being was consumed by a silent howl of anguish. Tania was still communicating with Mario. After all his promises, his assurances that he had broken with her, that she meant nothing to him, the truth was that he had been in contact with her.

When she thought of how close she had come to trusting him she wanted to bang her head against the wall.

'Fool!' she murmured. 'Fool! You were so wise in the beginning. You should have listened to your suspicions.'

Was he still in touch with her? Or was it an old letter? If so, why had he kept it so long?

Because he's still involved with her, she told herself. *He's been lying all this time.*

With frenzied hands she pulled the letter open and began to read it. As she read she grew still. When she got to the end she went back and read it again. And then again, trying to believe the incredible words Tania had written.

Don't keep me at a distance. I know you told me it was over because you wanted to be with that Eng-

lish girl, but look what she did when she found out about me. She wouldn't have vanished if she'd really loved you. I thought you'd realise that and come back to me. Why won't you take my calls or answer my emails?

Don't keep rejecting me, Mario. Natasha can't possibly mean that much to you.

Your loving Tania

She read it again, murmuring the words aloud, as though in this way she could manage to convince herself that they were real.

Everything Mario had told her was true. He had broken with Tania, as he'd vowed. She had refused to accept it and kept hounding him, but it seemed that nothing would make him take her back.

'I should have believed you,' she whispered. 'Oh, my love, I should have trusted you. But why didn't you show me this? Then I would have known the truth.'

She noticed that the letter was written in English, and remembered how Tania had spoken mostly in English with the odd Italian word thrown in. Doubtless, English was her native language, and perhaps her closeness to Mario had helped his mastery of English.

Which is lucky, she thought. *If Tania had written in Italian I couldn't have understood, and I wouldn't have missed this for the world.*

A noise outside warned her that Mario was coming. Swiftly she gathered up the papers and thrust them back onto the shelf, except for the Tania letter, which she thrust into her pocket. She would want to read that again, many times.

Natasha was back in front of the computer when he came in.

'Did you manage to sort the plumbing problem?' she asked.

'Yes, it's all taken care of. It'll be a couple of days before you can move back in but, thanks to you, I was alerted in time to avoid total disaster. How are you getting on?'

'I've managed to do quite a lot of work. Now I feel like taking the evening off. I think I'll have a stroll by the river.'

'Am I allowed to come with you?'

'Why not?'

It was a joy to have his company now that she could see him in a new light. All the pain and tension of the past two years had vanished, leaving only happiness and hope.

The light was fading as they left the building and crossed the street to the river. He slipped his arm around her shoulders, and she stretched hers about his waist. Clinging together, they strolled along the bank until they reached a café by the water, and he indicated for her to sit down. Waving a waiter over, Mario spoke to him quickly in Italian and moments later the waiter returned with a bottle of wine.

'I have a reason for bringing you here,' Mario said. 'This place buys all its wine from a shop that stocks products from my vineyard.'

'The best, naturally,' she said.

'Naturally. Everyone knows about Verona's romantic reputation, but its fame as a great wine centre tends to get blocked out.'

'I've been reading a little about it recently,' she said.

'There are wine tours, aren't there? We might do a little publicity for them too.'

'Good idea. You can turn your talents on to Vinitaly. That's a wine festival that happens every year in spring.' He grinned. 'There's a lot more to Verona than you think.'

'I'm sure there is. I look forward to discovering all its secrets.'

He raised his glass to her, saying, *'Ti vol un altro goto de vin?'*

'Is that Venetian?'

'You know about Venetian?'

'Giorgio told me. The more I know, the better.'

'It means would you like some more wine?'

'Yes, please. It's delicious.'

She sipped the wine, enjoying its excellent taste and the feeling that things might be going well at last.

He watched her, wondering at the smile on her face, unwilling to ask about it. There might be more pleasure in wondering.

When at last they rose and walked on he put an arm around her shoulder, saying, 'Are you all right? Not too cold?'

'I'm all right,' she said, looking up. 'Not too cold, not too anything. Everything's perfect.'

He gave a soft chuckle. 'Does that mean I haven't offended you recently?'

She looked up at him teasingly. 'Not that I can think of.'

'You can usually think of something.'

They smiled and moved on.

She barely noticed where they were going. It was like being in a new world. Nothing was the same. His voice had a note of warmth that she had never noticed before, and his eyes held a gleam that promised much.

'It's lovely out here,' she sighed.

'Yes,' he murmured in her ear. 'It's lovely, and you're lovely.'

'You have to feel sorry for Romeo and Juliet, who could never take this kind of walk, just enjoying being together and letting the world drift by.'

'I guess we're luckier than they were.'

She turned to look up into his face. 'Yes,' she said. 'We're lucky. We were always lucky, if only we'd known it.'

His fingertips brushed her face gently. 'I always knew it,' he said. 'Now I know it even more since I had to endure life without you. I thought I'd never see you again, and the future was nothing but a terrible blank. But then you were there again and I had my life back. Suddenly, there was something to hope for.'

'Yes, for me too,' she said. 'But sometimes I can be afraid to hope.'

'Better not to hope at all, than hope and have it destroyed,' he said.

'No, I don't believe that. Wonderful things can happen when you least expect it. You have to be ready for the best as well as the worst, and then— Oh, Mario, Mario!'

She was silenced by his mouth over hers.

'Be minc,' he whispered. 'Tell me that you're mine.'

'I always was. I always will be.'

'Do you really mean that?'

'Yes—yes—'

'Say it again. Make me believe it.'

'I'm yours—all yours—yours—'

'For ever. I won't let you go. I warn you, I'm possessive.'

'You couldn't be too possessive for me,' she assured him.

His answer was another kiss which she returned with fervour.

A group of young people passed by, cheering and clapping at the sight of them.

'It's too public out here,' she said.

'Yes, let's go home.'

They slipped back into the hotel without being seen. She was glad. What was happening now was for them alone.

He came with her as far as the apartment, then stopped at the door, regarding her uncertainly.

'Don't go,' she said, holding him in a gentle but determined hug. 'Stay with me.'

'Natasha, do you mean that?'

'Yes, I mean it.'

'But don't you realise that—if I stay—no, you don't realise. I mustn't stay.'

'Yes, you must,' she whispered. 'I say you must, and I won't let you refuse me.'

It hurt her to see how tense and vulnerable he seemed. After all the hostility that had simmered between them he couldn't believe that she was really opening her arms to him; even perhaps opening her heart. It was what he wanted but something he couldn't dare believe too easily, and she longed to reach out from her heart and reassure him.

'Trust me,' she murmured. 'Things move on. Nothing stays the same for ever.'

'Are you telling me that something really has changed?' he asked.

'In a way. I've learned to be more understanding. I was always so sure I was right, but now—now I feel like a different person. I have so much still to learn.'

She took a step back through the door, holding out her hand.

'Come in,' she said. 'Come with me—stay with me.'

He still could not understand her, but he put his hand in hers and followed her in perfect trust.

'Yes,' he said. 'Take me with you. Let me stay.'

His mouth was on hers, making her rejoice with heart, mind and body equally. There was pleasure but there was also a fierce possessiveness. She wanted him and she was determined to have him. She had waited as long as she could endure and now she was determined to enjoy her conquest.

With the door safely closed against the outside world, Mario felt able to yield to his longing and take her in his arms. Yet doubts and confusion still whirled about him.

'I don't believe this is happening,' he whispered. 'I've dreamed of it so often, so hopelessly.'

'Not hopelessly,' she told him. 'I've dreamed too. Dreams can come true. Let us believe that.'

'Yes, while I have you in my arms I can believe it.'

She drew his head down, kissing him with fervour and passion, rejoicing in his response. Gradually he began to move towards the bed, easing her down onto it so that they lay together. When she felt him start to undo her clothes she was there before him, pulling open buttons, inviting him to explore her.

He accepted the invitation, tentatively at first, caressing her gently, almost uncertainly. But as his hands discovered the soft smoothness of her skin their touch became more fervent, more intense, sending tremors through her. She reached out to him, now working on his buttons so that his shirt fell open and she could explore him in her turn.

Once, long ago in Venice, she had dreamed of this. But fate had denied her dream, banishing her into a wilderness where there was no love, no hope, no Mario.

Now, at last, the moment had come and it was everything she'd wanted. His caress was tentative, almost as though he feared to touch her.

She understood. In the depths of her heart joy was warring with disbelief, scared that this might not really be true, that she would wake to find it a delusion. And it was the same with him. Instinct too deep for thought told her this was true. After so long their hearts and minds were as one, just as their bodies would soon unite.

He laid his face against her. She drew him closer, wanting this moment to last.

'Yes,' she murmured. 'Yes.'

'Yes,' he echoed. 'Natasha—are you sure?'

'I'm sure of everything—sure that I want you—'

He gave a faint smile. 'Are you sure I want you? Or shall I try to convince you?'

'I don't need convincing.' She returned his smile in full measure. 'But don't let me stop you.'

'Whatever you please, ma'am,' he murmured, intensifying his caresses.

Her pleasure rioted, but more than pleasure was the joy of knowing that they were close again. The man she had loved long ago had been stolen from her, but now she had him back. And she would never let him go again. The world might turn upside down. The heavens might fall, the seas overflow, but she would never release him from her arms and her heart. On that she was resolved.

He worked eagerly on her clothes until nothing was left. Then he removed his own garments and they were naked together. He took her into his arms, kissing her mouth, her face, her neck, then going lower to smother her breasts in kisses. She took long breaths of delight at the storm growing within her, longing for the moment when he would claim her completely. When it came, it was everything she'd hoped.

CHAPTER NINE

As THE FIERCE excitement died they lay quietly, holding each other, coming to terms with the new world in which they found themselves. Gradually they fell into peaceful sleep, lying motionless together until the room grew lighter and the new day had come.

Mario was lying with his face hidden against her neck, but then he raised it and looked down at her.

She met his eyes, seeing in them a look of loving possessiveness that made her heart skip a beat.

'Natasha,' he murmured, almost as though trying to believe that it was really her. She knew how he felt, for she was feeling the same herself. She had told him they must believe that dreams could come true.

'I've wanted this from the first moment,' he whispered. 'But I'd given up hope. And then suddenly—beyond my wildest dreams—why?'

'The time was right,' she whispered. 'Couldn't you feel that?'

'I've often felt it, but I was always wrong before. Suddenly—everything became different between us.'

'Everything became as it should be,' she said. 'This is how it was always meant to be.'

'You really mean that? Natasha, I'm not deluding my-self, am I? Things are really all right between us?'

'How can you ask me that? After the way we've spent the last night, don't you think everything is all right?'

'Oh, yes.' He gave a wry smile. 'But I didn't mean that. I meant the other things that have come between us and separated us in the past. You didn't believe what I told you about Tania, that I'd broken with her because I'd met you and you were the one I wanted. Please, please say that you believe me, that you trust me at last.'

'I trust you, my darling. I should have trusted you long ago, but I was blind. It was like being lost in a maze. Every time I thought I'd found a way out it just led to more confusion.'

She promised herself that one day soon she would tell him about Tania's letter, and the way it had con-firmed everything he said. But she didn't want thoughts of Tania to intrude just now. She wanted only Mario, the warmth, beauty and contentment they could find together.

'You trust me,' he echoed as though trying to believe it. 'And you're mine.'

'I'm yours.'

'For always?'

'Always and for ever.'

'Then everything's perfect.'

'Not quite,' she said. 'Don't you have an "always and for ever" promise to make me?'

'Of course. I just didn't think you needed to hear it said. I'm so completely yours that—'

He was interrupted by the sound of his mobile phone. Sighing, he answered it, speaking in Italian. Natasha didn't understand the language, but she understood that the caller was Mario's brother, Damiano.

'*Come stai, fratello?*' Mario said cheerfully. '*Come è Sally e il bambino?*'

After listening a moment he gave Natasha a thumbs-up sign.

'They've set the christening for this weekend,' he told her. 'I'm going and they want me to take you.'

'They want me? But how—?'

'Yes or no?'

'Yes. Oh, yes.'

'Damiano—Natasha *dice di sì. Va bene!*' He hung up.

'I don't understand,' she said. 'How did they even think of inviting me?'

'You mean how did they know you were here, and we'd found each other again?' He became a little awkward. 'When I went there for the birth a while ago I may have mentioned you briefly.'

She gave him a glance of wicked humour. 'Yes, I can imagine what you said. "That pesky woman has turned up again, when I thought I'd got rid of her."'

'Something like that,' he said with a grin.

'I'd give a lot to have been a fly on the wall.'

'You'd probably have had a good laugh. I talked about you non-stop. When I told them how amazed I was when our publicist turned out to be you, Damiano roared with laughter. And Sally wanted to know everything. She thinks it's a great joke to see me conquered by a woman.'

'But I haven't tried to conquer you.'

'Of course. If you had tried I'd have fought back and we wouldn't be talking like this now. But you caught me unaware, and I was finished before I knew it.'

And before I knew it, she thought. His words struck a disturbing chord within her.

'I remember everything so vividly,' he said. 'Our first meeting—you were sitting in the restaurant of Damiano's hotel when I came in. You were so lovely I just stopped and stared at you. Suddenly you looked up and saw me. And you smiled. Such a lovely smile, as though I was the only person in the room—in the world.

'I didn't understand straight away what had happened to me. But I did know that suddenly the world was focused on you.'

'And you came and sat down at the table,' she remembered. 'You said that you worked in the hotel and were offering your services—'

'That was just an excuse to talk to you, find out all I could about you. Were you married, was a man coming to join you? I hung on your every answer as though my life depended on it. And now I realise that my life did depend on it. And then—'

'What is it?' she asked, for he suddenly seemed troubled.

'It all happened again, didn't it? When you came here I asked you the same questions the first evening.'

'You said would a man turn up to drag me home?' she remembered.

'Yes, it sounded like the practical questions of an employer, but in fact I had this terrible need to know if there was someone in your life, just like the first time. It shocked me. I couldn't believe it had happened again—'

'With a woman you hated,' she said gently.

'I didn't hate you. I told myself I did because I needed to believe it. That was my defence and I clung to it. But things change and—well—'

'I wonder how much things change,' she murmured. 'Or do they only seem to have changed because *we* have changed?'

'Maybe we've changed in some things but not in others.'

'I wonder which is which.'

'We might find that out in Venice.'

'Mmm. So Sally thinks we're a joke. Yes, it's like fate played a joke on us. Sometimes I almost fancy I can hear laughter echoing from the heavens at the way we fell for it.'

'We didn't fall for it,' he said, drawing her close. 'We won. Fate lost. When Sally sees us together she'll understand that we're having the last laugh.'

'You really want me to come to Venice with you?'

'I think it's important that we go back there together.'

She understood. By returning they would confront their memories and that would help to show them the way forward.

'Everything that happened there looks different now,' she said.

'Yes,' he agreed gladly. 'So different. So much happier. The sooner we go the better. Then we can have a few days before the christening.'

At once he called Venice again, to say they would be arriving that evening. Then he stopped, regarding Natasha uneasily.

'Sally says one room or two?' he said. 'What's your choice?'

She was suddenly struck by inspiration. 'I'd like the same room I had last time.'

'That's a single room.'

'Perhaps we should be a little discreet.'

He seemed about to protest, but then understanding dawned and he turned back to the phone. At last he hung up.

'She's fixing it.'

'Does she think I'm crazy?'

'No, she said it made a lot of sense to put the clock back. I don't need to ask what that means, do I?'

'I don't think you do.'

'Let's get packing.'

Not long after, they bid farewell to Giorgio and set off for the Verona railway station to catch the train. It was just over seventy miles, and an hour and a half passed before they found themselves on the causeway that led over the water from the mainland to Venice.

She remembered the last time she had made this journey, leaning out of the window to see the beautiful buildings grow closer. How excited she'd been during that journey, how thrilled at the thought of spending time in the magical city.

At Venice station Mario hailed a water taxi and soon they were on their way to the hotel on the Grand Canal.

'There it is,' he said, pointing forward. 'Remember?'

'Yes, I remember,' she breathed.

It was a magnificent building, a converted palace that seemed to sum up everything that was glamorous about Venice. As soon as they entered Damiano and Sally came to meet them. Damiano and Mario slapped each other on the shoulders in brotherly fashion, while Sally embraced Natasha.

'It's lovely to see you again,' she said. 'And Pietro has really looked forward to your return. He says when you were last here you used to talk to him about football.'

'That's right. And last night England played Italy.' Natasha chuckled. 'Luckily, Italy won.'

Pietro appeared. He was in his early teens, already looking strikingly like his father, and full of beans.

'Did you see the match?' he challenged at once, after which perfect communication was established between them.

'How's Toby?' she asked, meaning Pietro's spaniel, who had helped bring Damiano and Sally together.

'Here he is,' Pietro said eagerly, drawing his furry friend forward.

She greeted Toby, received his welcoming lick and looked up to find Mario watching them with a pleased smile, as though everything was working out as he'd hoped.

Then Sally took them to see the two children she'd borne her husband—little Franco, nearly three years old, whose birth had nearly cost her life, and Elena, the little girl she'd borne recently.

'Supper's in half an hour,' Sally said.

As promised, Natasha had the same room as before which, at first, gave her a slightly weird ghostly feeling. But it soon faded against the different, happier, reality of the present. Mario's room was just a few feet along the corridor, and soon he appeared to escort her downstairs to Damiano's private dining room.

It was clear to Natasha that she was being welcomed into the family. During the meal that followed she was toasted as an honoured guest.

'Wait till you see the church where we'll have the christening,' Pietro said. 'It's where Mamma and Papà got married.'

'That was quite a ceremony,' Mario recalled. 'Toby was there too, practically one of the witnesses.'

'I'm sure he performed his role perfectly,' Natasha said.

As she spoke she tickled Toby's head and was rewarded with a *woof!*

It was a happy evening. A sense of peace came over her as she realised yet again the true purpose of this trip: to put right the mistakes and misunderstandings of the past.

Only Sally's brother Charlie was missing, which Sally explained with sisterly frankness. 'Out making himself objectionable again.'

'What kind of objectionable?' Natasha asked, laughing.

'Women, gambling—you name it, he can do it. Mind you, he's not as bad as he was. Mario helped reform him a bit.'

'Me? Reform?' Mario squeaked. 'That's practically an insult.'

'Well, Damiano told me you had a "guardian angel" side, and you did keep Charlie on the straight and narrow—more or less. Time for bed, anyway.'

The party broke up. Mario announced that he and Natasha wanted to take a walk. The others nodded in perfect understanding and slipped away.

'A walk?' she queried.

'Maybe. Maybe not.'

'What was the idea—?'

'I wanted to be sure of being alone with you. Let's have a coffee. Not here—in the restaurant.'

It was almost closing time and most of the restaurant tables were empty. At once she knew why he'd brought her here. There in the corner was the table where she'd sat at their first meeting. He led her over, showed her to a seat and sat beside her. A waiter brought them coffee.

'You were just here by the window,' he said. 'I watched you for a few minutes, trying to believe my eyes, rather like that guy over there.'

He pointed to a young man standing just inside the door, his eyes fixed on another table just a few feet away from them, where sat a young woman in her twenties. She was beautiful, and she was alone.

'I can guess what he's thinking,' Mario said. 'He's working out a good excuse to approach her.'

'You can't know what he's thinking.'

'Oh, yes, I can. When I look at him I see myself. In fact, I see every guy trying to summon up the courage to approach a woman he knows is going to matter more than any other. Look, there he goes.'

As they watched, the young man approached the girl and gestured to ask if anyone was sitting with her. She shook her head and he took a seat.

'Does he work here?' Natasha asked.

'No, he'll have to think of another excuse. He doesn't seem to be doing too badly.'

Amused, they watched the couple for a few minutes. Then Mario said with a touch of unease, 'There's something I keep wanting to ask you.'

'What is it?'

He hesitated, then said, 'What happened to you after we parted? I know you worked hard and Jenson gave you a bad time, but was there—anything else?'

'You mean another man? But I've already told you about that.'

'You've told me you're not married, you haven't settled down with anyone, but that's not what I meant.'

She gave a gentle chuckle. 'You mean am I secretly yearning for someone? Take a guess.'

'No, I can't see you yearning for someone who didn't return the feeling. But surely in the last two years you must have had some sort of romantic interest.'

'No. Apart from the horrible Jenson I've been alone. Which is a kind of freedom,' she added wryly.

'I know exactly how that feels.'

'Don't tell me you've been alone,' she teased. 'Every woman who passes gives you yearning looks.'

'But what matters is to be wanted by the one you yourself want,' he said. 'The others don't count.'

'That's true,' she said softly.

'So you're telling me there was no other man?'

'Hmm!' She appeared to consider this before saying gently, 'I suppose I could always say that it's none of your business. How about that?'

'It's certainly one response.' He gave her a wry smile. 'I could go and bury myself under the bedclothes because I couldn't cope with you snubbing me. Or I could get blind drunk. Or I could say that your lovers definitely are my business. And always will be. So now what?'

His eyes met hers, gleaming with a mixture of humour and intensity that struck her to the heart.

'My lovers,' she mused. 'I wonder just what you've heard.'

'Not a thing. After you vanished I tried to hunt you down for a little while, but when you never made contact with me I thought—well—' He gave a slight shrug.

'You thought, "To hell with the silly English girl! If

she wants to play it like that let her go and jump in the lake.'"

'Well, maybe once or twice, but I didn't mean it,' he said, colouring.

'Oddly enough, I did end up in a lake shortly afterwards. It was a pleasure trip and the boat collapsed.'

'*What?* Were you hurt?'

'No, I just I got wet. Hey, I wonder if you made that happen. Strange to think we were in touch all that time and didn't know it.'

'Possibly. You were never off my mind.'

'Nor you off mine. And I did some cursing of my own.'

'I'm not sure I want to know about that,' he said with a grin. 'It could give me nightmares.'

'If we're asking about each other's lovers—what about yours? You must have had plenty.'

'Not lovers,' he said. 'Girlfriends, perhaps. I won't deny that I've enjoyed the company of a certain kind of woman because that way I could briefly forget the way you threw me overboard. But there wasn't anyone that I loved, even for a moment. It was always you, even when I most desperately didn't want it to be you.'

'Couldn't get rid of me, huh?' she teased.

'No matter how hard I tried.' He gave a warm laugh. 'You're a pesky woman. I told you a hundred times to get out of my heart but you just said, "Nope. Here I am and here I'm staying."'

'That sounds like me.'

He looked up suddenly. Following his gaze, she saw the other couple rise from the table and depart, hand in hand.

'I guess he got lucky,' Mario mused.

'Or maybe she did.'

'I didn't get lucky. Damiano called me to look after another customer and when I returned you'd gone. If only you could have heard me cursing.' He drained his coffee. 'Let's go.'

Upstairs, he came with her as far as her door.

'Remember last time?' he asked.

'Yes, we said goodnight at this door. I went inside and you went away.'

'I didn't really go away. I stayed out here in the corridor for ages.'

She opened the door and stretched out a hand to him.

'No need for that this time,' she said.

He took her hand at once, eagerly letting her draw him inside, then going into her arms, which she opened to him. It was she who drew them to the bed, he who followed her lead, but slowly, as though aware that they were rewriting history. Once they had wanted each other without satisfaction. Now they embraced satisfaction eagerly, joyfully.

There was physical pleasure in their caresses, but more than that was the joy of rediscovering each other. To retread the road, each seeing the other with new eyes, exploring new diversions, making wonderful discoveries; these were things they had never dared to dream of.

Afterwards, as they lay together in each other's arms, Natasha gave a sudden soft chuckle.

'What is it?' he demanded. 'What did I do that makes you laugh?'

'Don't get defensive. You could make me laugh and still be "macho".'

She laughed again and he frowned, demanding, 'So what is it?'

'It's what Sally said about you having a "guardian

angel" side. That's the last thing I'd ever have suspected about you. A rebel, a pain in the butt, a pesky clown— any of them. But a guardian angel? Or any kind of angel. I doubt it.'

His annoyance faded and he kissed her forehead. 'Thanks. I see you really understand me.'

'You don't mind being called those things?'

'Not at all. I'd have minded being called an angel. That would have been insulting. But I think "pain in the butt" rather suits me.'

'Definitely,' she said, kissing him. 'Now, I'm going to sleep. You've exhausted me for the night. Goodnight, "guardian angel".'

She snuggled against him and in a few moments she was asleep.

Guardian angel, he thought. *That's almost funny, considering how I hated you only recently. But somehow things took a different turn.*

He rested his head against her and in a few minutes he too was asleep. After several hours he awoke to find her eyes still closed and her head on his shoulder. When he ventured to move slightly her arms tightened, as though even in sleep she needed to keep him close.

He clasped her back, offering her the embrace she needed for reassurance.

Romeo's words drifted through his mind again. *It is my lady...oh, it is my love. Oh, that she knew she were.*

But she does know, he mused. *If she knows anything by now, it's that I love her.*

He kissed her gently, murmuring, 'You are my lady. You are my love.'

She sighed and nestled closer, smiling as though she'd heard him and been reassured. He leaned against her, happy and willing to sleep again, but then a noise from his phone disturbed him.

'Curses,' he muttered. 'My mobile phone. Where is it?'

Undressing hastily, he hadn't noticed it fall to the floor. Now he eased himself gently away from Natasha and leaned down to pick up the phone. Connecting, he found a text from an unknown number:

You're taking a bigger risk than you know. She's mine. Get lost.

For a moment he was simply bewildered. Who could the message be from? But then the answer came to him like a clap of thunder.

Elroy Jenson. The man who'd vindictively destroyed Natasha's career because she'd dared to defy him. The man who'd spied on her from a distance, watching where she fled to escape him. The man who still had his claws in her, and would deepen them if he could.

He was swept by such rage that his head was dizzy and the whole world seemed to turn black.

'No,' he whispered. 'She's not yours. She's mine. She's *mine*. She always was. *And she always will be.*'

Behind him, Natasha stirred, murmuring, 'Is something the matter?'

'No,' he said. 'Go back to sleep. Nothing's the matter. Nothing at all. Your guardian angel will deal with it.'

CHAPTER TEN

'How are you enjoying Verona?' Sally asked Natasha at breakfast next morning.

'I love it.'

'And Verona loves her,' Mario said. 'She's doing a great job for our hotels.'

'Perhaps she can come here later and do something for Venice hotels,' Damiano said.

'What a lovely idea,' Natasha said. 'I'll take a stroll around Venice this morning.' She glanced at Mario before saying slowly, 'Just to remind myself what it's like.'

He nodded.

After breakfast they slipped out into the narrow alley that ran by the hotel.

'You walked this way alone the first time,' he reminded her. 'But I wasn't far behind you.'

'I know.'

'You know? You mean you knew it then?'

'Yes, I told the receptionist where I was going, and you were nearby. When I came out I heard your footsteps behind me.'

'So you always knew I was following you?'

'No, but I hoped you were. I went into a shop to give you a chance to catch up. But you didn't.'

'I was tempted. When you stopped I worked out a plan to go into the shop casually and just "happen" to meet you. But I lost my nerve, so I waited a bit.'

'Lost your nerve? You?'

'You have that effect on me.'

'I'll remember that. It could be useful.'

'Be honest. You already knew that you scared me stiff.'

Laughing, they went on their way.

At last they came to the Grand Canal, the great S-shaped stream of water that wound through the city. Boats of every kind filled it. Just coming up was a *vaporetto*, one of the great water buses that transported passengers all over the city. Small water taxis were everywhere, but also the boats that everyone came to Venice to see, gondolas. Natasha looked eagerly at the slim, elegant conveyances, propelled by a man with one oar.

'You were standing here when you saw your first gondola close up,' he remembered.

'And I couldn't think how a gondola could go straight when it was only being rowed on one side,' she said. 'You told me that that side bulged more than the other, so the water took longer to slide past. I didn't understand, so you said I should take a ride in it. You hailed the gondolier—like you're doing now.'

The boat was gliding to a halt beside them. Gently, he handed her in and they settled down together. It felt wonderful, just as it had the first time.

'Aaaaaah.' Sighing with pleasure, she stretched out, looking around her at the little canal and listening to the singing coming from around the corner. 'It's lovely, but this is where I fell asleep.'

'That's right. You couldn't have made it plainer what you thought of me, Natasha—Natasha?'

She was lying back with her eyes closed. *Just like last time*, he thought.

The gondolier regarded him sympathetically. 'Some men are just unlucky, *signore*,' he said, speaking in Venetian dialect.

'True,' Mario said wryly in the same language. 'But some men are also luckier than they know. The problem is finding out which you are.'

He watched Natasha carefully for a moment, then leaned forward and kissed her. When she didn't react he repeated the kiss more forcefully.

'Hello,' Natasha said, opening her eyes.

'Hello. Sorry if I disturbed you.'

'Tell me, when I fell asleep the first time, did you kiss me then?'

'Don't you remember?'

She smiled up at him in a way he guessed was meant to drive him mad. She was certainly succeeding. Did she know that? Did she enjoy it?

'I'm not sure,' she murmured.

'Then let me remind you.'

He laid his lips gently over hers again, leaving them there for several moments.

The gondolier grinned. His job exposed him to a lot of enjoyable sights.

Natasha relaxed and put her arms about him. Although she had been asleep for their first ride, two years ago, she was sure he hadn't kissed her then because she would have remembered. Now she gave herself up to pleasure.

Afterwards, they sat leaning against each other, watching the little canals drift past. She had a mysterious sense that the journey might go on for ever, and wished that it would. But all too soon they drew up outside the hotel. Once inside, they became involved in the preparations for the christening, and for the rest of the day she barely spent a moment alone with him.

Next morning everyone set out for the church where the christening would take place. It was only a short distance away, so they went on foot.

'It's a big family occasion,' Mario said as they walked through the alley that approached the church. 'Damiano's first wife died giving birth to Pietro. One reason he married Sally was to give that kid a mother.'

'You mean it was a marriage of convenience? They seem so devoted to each other.'

'They are. They thought it was a marriage of convenience, but in fact they were really in love. They just hadn't realised it.'

She looked into her wine glass, murmuring, 'That can happen when people don't understand their own feelings.'

'So I've heard. It must be quite a stunning discovery.'

'Yes,' she said. 'It is. There's no recovering from it, or from blaming yourself for how stupid you were.'

'Would you call yourself stupid?'

'Mad, imbecile,' she said. 'Even worse than that. But a lucky fate gave me the chance to put things right.'

He raised his glass. 'Here's to fate.'

They clinked glasses.

'So did they realise they were in love?' she asked.

'It dawned on them eventually. She had a bad time when Franco was born. She might not have come through it. I thought Damiano would go out of his mind with fear and grief. He wasn't keen on Sally having another baby, but she really wanted it and he gave in.'

He gave a brief laugh. 'Few people know the real Damiano. To the outside world he's a ruthless businessman. But once that front door shuts behind him, he's a willing slave to his wife.'

'Oh, really?' She gave him a cheeky look. 'Is that how you judge a good husband? If he's her willing slave?'

'Who knows? Perhaps you'll have the chance to find out.'

There were already plenty of friends and family in place, smiling when they appeared and made their way along the aisle. Sally walked with her new baby in her arms, Damiano carried their toddler, Charlie and Mario walked together, while Pietro accompanied Natasha, holding her hand. Again she had the happy feeling of being part of the family.

It grew even better at the party that evening. Mario introduced her to everyone in the crowd, most of whom seemed to have heard of her already.

'We've all looked forward to meeting you,' said one elderly man.

'Just be a little patient,' Mario told him. 'You'll hear something soon.'

'What did that mean?' she asked as he drew her away.

'Just that people think we're a couple. Do you mind that?'

'Not at all,' she assured him. 'But what is he going to hear soon?'

'Why don't we go and talk about that?'

He drew her slowly out of the room, waving farewell to the other guests, who cheered them in a way that left no doubt that they were expecting to hear about a wedding very soon. Somehow, Mario had given that impression.

Once inside her room he kissed her before saying, 'I may have said more than I should have done without asking you first. But we so clearly belong together that people accept it.'

'And if you could have asked me first?'

'I'd have asked you to set the date for our wedding.'

'Yes, you really should have mentioned it to me.'

'Are you mad at me?'

'I'll let you know that later.' She drew him to the bed. 'For the moment I have other things on my mind.'

'So have I.' He was already working on her clothes.

We did the right thing coming here, she thought. *It's made things better, as nothing else could have done. The past is over. It didn't happen. We are free.*

Free. The word seemed to echo, casting hope over the future. As they made love she kept her eyes on his face, finding that he too was watching her, sending a silent message that she understood and returned with all her heart.

And he too understood. She recognised that from the long sigh of happiness and fulfilment he gave as they lay in each other's arms afterwards.

'If only we could have known,' he whispered.

'It was too much to hope for,' she replied. 'Even now I daren't hope. It's too good to be true. Something will happen to make things go wrong.'

'Nothing will go wrong,' he said firmly. 'I won't let it.'

'Oh, you think it's all up to you, do you, big man?'

'Right this minute I feel powerful enough to dictate everything in the world. You hear that?' he yelled up at the ceiling. 'Nothing is ever going to go wrong between us again. I insist on it. I order it.'

'Who are you giving orders to?' she chuckled.

'The little green men who try to dictate to us. From now on, I'm in charge.'

'Oh, yeah?'

'Not of you,' he said hastily. 'Just of them.'

They collapsed with laughter, rocking back and forth with delight.

Afterwards, Natasha was to remember that moment, a triumphant assertion of joy and confidence before catastrophe descended on them once more.

Next morning Mario suggested a walk through Venice.

'It was a good idea to come back,' he said as they strolled. 'The people we were then don't exist any more, and this way we've got rid of them.'

'I'm not sure I want to get rid of them,' she observed. 'There were things about you I think I'll cling to. You've always been the best-looking man for miles around. I'm not changing that.'

'Thank you, ma'am.'

He began to draw her in another direction, but she resisted.

'Why can't we stay here?' she asked.

'Because of that place,' he said, indicating an outdoor café. It was the one where they had had their quarrel.

But it need not have happened, she thought.

So many times she'd wanted to tell Mario that she knew the truth after reading Tania's letter, but somehow the moment had never been right. But perhaps this was the right time and place.

'Why don't you buy me a coffee there?' she said.

'Don't you realise what that place is?' he demanded.

'Yes, it's where we made our huge mistake and lost each other. Perhaps it's time to put it right.'

'I thought we'd already put it right.'

'Yes, but there's a little more to do. Come with me.'

She led him to the café and found that by a strange chance the same table was available.

'This is where we sat,' she said as they sipped coffee.

'Until we were interrupted, but that won't happen this time,' he said firmly. 'That woman is out of our lives for good.' He became suddenly tense. 'What's the matter? Why are you smiling like that? Don't you believe me?'

'Yes, I believe you.'

'Do you really? You believe that I was telling you the truth? You trust me? I would never deceive you. Tell me that you believe that.'

'I do. I believe everything you've told me. I know you're an honest man and you always will be.'

'You mean that? You really mean that?'

'Every word.'

He took her face between his hands and spoke softly. 'If you could imagine what it means to me to know that we're close enough for you to have learned to trust me.'

'I only want to tell you—' She stopped, silenced by a nervous feeling that she did not understand.

'You only want to tell me what? That you love me. That's it, isn't it?'

'Oh, yes, that's it.'

'Then that's all I need to hear.'

'But, Mario—'

His lips on hers silenced her. He was kissing her fiercely, powerfully, yet devotedly, longingly. She surrendered to the pleasure, knowing that this, and only this, was the whole of life.

At last he released her. She could tell that he was shaking and his breath came unevenly.

'My darling,' he whispered. 'What is it that you needed to say?'

'Nothing. It doesn't matter.'

Nothing mattered enough to break the spell of this moment. She took hold of him again, returning the kiss fervently. Around them the other diners laughed and cheered, and the waiter cleared his throat. Without looking at him, Mario pulled some money from his pocket. The waiter seized it and vanished.

'Let's go,' Mario said. 'This isn't the place for what we have to do.'

'*Have* to do?' she murmured against his lips.

'We have urgent business to attend to,' he whispered. 'Can't you feel it?'

'Yes—oh, yes.'

Seizing her hand, he rose and hurried away. She followed him joyfully. The words she'd planned to say could wait. Nothing mattered now but to be with him, in his arms, his bed, his life.

Together they ran through the streets of Venice, down alleys, over bridges, eager to get to the hotel, where they could achieve the fulfilment that awaited them, that they longed for.

At last they reached the hotel, hurrying through the entrance and across to the lift.

Sally appeared, calling, 'Ah, Mario, can I talk to you—?'

'Not now,' Mario called back.

They vanished into the lift, clinging to each other as it carried them up.

'Nearly there,' he said hoarsely.

'Yes, nearly there.'

She knew he meant they were almost at his bedroom, but to her the words meant far more. The glorious destination that had waited for them since the moment they'd met—they were nearly there.

They had reached the room. He flung open the door, drew her inside and began to undress her at once. She responded instantly, wrenching off his jacket, pulling open his buttons, tearing off his shirt.

They fell onto the bed, still working on each other's clothes until they were both naked and ready for each other.

'You're mine,' he said huskily. 'Now and for ever.'

'Yes—yes—'

She was dizzy with passion and delight, wanting him more than she had ever wanted anything in her life. Their previous lovemaking had been wonderful, but this one was pervaded by an extra sense of triumph.

She reached for him, offered herself to him, claimed him, and sensed his delight not only through his movements but by the glow in his eyes. His lovemaking was tender, emotional, and at first this was enough. But soon she wanted more. She was his, heart and body, and with every movement she demanded that he accept the gift and return it. When he claimed her finally she cried out with joy.

Afterwards, lying contentedly in his arms, feeling the warmth of his flesh and the gentle power of his embrace, she knew that she had come to the place that was always meant for her, and where she could live happily for the rest of her life.

She had meant to tell him about the letter, but things

beyond her control had swept her up. Was that an omen? she wondered. Should she try to tell him now?

'My love,' she murmured.

'My love,' he echoed, 'if you knew how wonderful it is to hear you call me that. I am your love and you are mine.' He stroked her breast. 'I was afraid this would never happen,' he whispered.

'It's not the first time we've made love,' she reminded him.

'No, but it's the first time we've made love like this, with all doubts settled, all fears gone, everything open and clear between us. When you told me that you trusted me I felt as if I'd gone to heaven.'

'Yes,' she whispered. 'I feel like that too.'

'And we must keep it that way. We lost two years, but we mustn't lose any more time. We must marry as soon as possible.'

'Marry,' she said in wonder.

'I told you yesterday that we should set the date. You didn't give me an answer. Are you trying to put me off?'

She glanced down the bed at their naked entwined figures. 'Does it look as if I'm trying to put you off?'

'I just want to be sure of you. Say yes. Say yes.'

'Oh, yes. Yes, with all my heart.'

'Now we've found each other,' he whispered, 'nothing can ever come between us.'

He kissed her again before saying, 'I've just remembered—you had something you were trying to say to me.'

'Did I?'

'Yes, it sounded urgent but I kind of distracted you.' He grinned, recalling the way he'd grasped hold of her and made her run.

'I suppose you could call this a distraction,' she agreed, smiling.

'So what were you going to say?'

Natasha's head was whirling. This was the moment she'd planned to lay bare the secret, but suddenly everything seemed different. To speak of it now would be to let Tania intrude on them again, and she was determined never to let that happen.

'Natasha?' he murmured.

'Mmm?'

'Are you awake?'

'Er...no. I—must have dozed off again. Did you say something?'

'I asked you what you'd been planning to tell me.'

'I can't remember. It's gone out of my head now, so it can't have meant much.'

'It's just that you made it sound important.'

'No, it couldn't be.' She touched his face. 'Only one thing is important now.'

'And that's us,' he agreed. 'You're right. Nothing else matters. Come here.'

She did so, taking refuge in his arms and his love, so that the rest of the world ceased to exist.

The letter didn't matter, she decided. This was how it would always be.

She opened her eyes next morning to find Mario regarding her anxiously.

'You did mean it, didn't you?' he asked. 'You really will marry me?'

'No,' she teased. 'I was just making fun of you. Oh, don't look like that. Of course I meant it. Would I have said it otherwise?'

'I can't be sure with you. You always seem to have a surprise to spring on me. I get nervous waiting for the next one.'

'Oh, really?' She regarded him with wicked humour. 'Let's see now. I could always thump you.'

'But that wouldn't be a surprise. You've already thumped me so often in different ways.'

'So maybe it's time to find another way. How about that?' She delivered a light pat on his shoulder.

'Ouch!' he cried comically. 'Now I'm in agony.'

'Good. Then I'll know how to bully you in future.'

She patted him again and they both burst into laughter.

'I don't believe this is real,' he said against her neck. 'Nobody could be as happy as I am now. It's an illusion.'

'No, we're going to teach the world what happiness looks like.'

'Mmm, that sounds nice. Can I thump you back?'

'Permission granted.'

He rolled her onto her stomach and lightly patted her behind. 'You be careful,' he said, 'or I'll do it again.'

'Is that a promise?' she chuckled.

'It's whatever you want.'

He was right, she thought, nestling contentedly against him. Nobody was allowed to be as happy as this. It must be an illusion. And she would do everything in her power to make it last.

CHAPTER ELEVEN

ENTERING THE BREAKFAST room downstairs, they found Damiano, Sally and Pietro waiting for them. They all looked up, eager for news.

'Have you got something to tell us?' Damiano asked. 'Sally seemed to think you might have.'

'You mean after she tried to talk to me yesterday and we dashed upstairs?' Mario said. 'Sorry, Sally. It was urgent.'

'Well, I gathered that,' she chuckled. 'So come on, tell us.'

'We're going to be married,' he announced. 'Natasha has decided she can put up with me.'

Pietro cried, 'Yippee!'

Sally hugged Natasha, and Damiano declared cheerfully, 'Welcome to the family, Natasha. We're all delighted that you're going to take charge of Mario and turn him into a sensible man.'

'Thanks, brother,' Mario said, grinning.

'By the time you discover your mistake it'll be too late,' Mario added. 'He'll have put the ring on your finger.'

'And I'll never let her take it off,' Mario said.

'You must marry here in Venice,' Sally said. 'After all, it's where you met. It'll be such fun to arrange.'

'That's very nice of you,' Mario said, 'but I think there's another place that would be more right for us. In Verona, we can marry at Juliet's house.' He glanced at Natasha, who nodded, smiling.

'Romeo and Juliet,' Sally mused. 'But you two can't be Romeo and Juliet. You're having a happy ending. I suppose there's still time for something to go wrong, but it won't.'

'No, it won't,' Mario said. 'We're together, and now nothing is going to go wrong. She is my Juliet, and Verona is the right place for us.'

Sally insisted on having a party for them that evening. Her warmth was a special blessing to Natasha. Her life had been lonely, with no relatives but her bitter mother. Now, suddenly, she had a brother and sister, and a cheeky nephew in Pietro.

They laughed and danced their way through the party, spent the night nestled together, and set out for Verona the following morning.

When Giorgio heard the news he roared with delight. 'Romeo and Juliet made it at last! What a story.'

'It's not exactly a story,' Mario protested.

'It is to me. You hired me as your publicity manager, and I'm going to do my job. When you've fixed the date we'll get some pictures.'

'The date will be as soon as possible,' Mario said.

'It'll have to be a Monday morning,' Giorgio told him. 'All wedding ceremonies are held then because the house has to be closed to tourists while it's happening. Then we'll have the reception here in the afternoon, and everyone in the *Comunità* will come.'

Later that day they went to the City Hall to make the booking for two weeks' time, and learned what they could about the wedding procedure. The actual ceremony would take place inside the building, with photographs taken afterwards, on the balcony.

Giorgio was in his element, planning to broadcast the information as far and wide as possible.

'This isn't just a wedding,' he said gleefully. 'It's the biggest publicity opportunity the *Comunità* has ever had. You really must make the best of it.'

'That's fine,' Mario said. 'I'm happy for everyone to know that I've secured the best bride in the world.'

But Natasha drew him aside, feeling some concern. 'Jenson will get to hear of it,' she said.

'Good!' Mario declared at once. 'I want him to know that his bullying has achieved nothing. That should stop his nonsense.'

'But suppose it doesn't?'

'Then I'll make him sorry he was born. Don't tell me you're still afraid of him. You're going to be my wife. There's nothing more he can do.' He took her in his arms. 'Trust me, darling. You have nothing more to fear from him. I told you I'd scare the living daylights out of him, and I have.'

'You scared Jenson? But how?'

'By slashing his advertising revenue. There are several media outlets I've been able to persuade to drop their adverts. Some here, some owned by friends of mine elsewhere. It should be enough to put the wind up him.'

'You did that for me?' she breathed. 'Oh, thank you— thank you.'

Blazing with happiness, she threw her arms around his neck.

'I told you I wouldn't let you be hurt,' he said. 'And I won't.'

'So you really are my guardian angel?'

'Angel? Not me. But I can put the wind up people when I want to.'

Chuckling, they embraced each other.

'It's such a weight off my mind,' she said. 'To know that he won't trouble me again.'

Now her most urgent arrangement was choosing a wedding dress. At Giorgio's orders, several gowns were delivered to the hotel for her to try on. She chose one of white satin, cut simply and elegantly.

'Perfect,' Giorgio declared when he saw it. 'It'll look great in the pictures. We must get started on them quickly.'

It seemed strange to be taking wedding pictures before the wedding, but they were to be part of Giorgio's publicity campaign to promote Verona as a wedding venue.

'The photographer will be here tomorrow morning,' Giorgio said. 'He's the same one who took the pictures of you as Romeo and Juliet. We'll put the two sets of pictures out together. Romeo and Juliet became Mario and Natasha.' He grinned. 'Or perhaps they always were.'

'Forget it,' Mario said. 'This story isn't going to end in a tomb.'

He was looking so handsome, Natasha thought as they posed together. For one picture she stood just in front of him, his hands on her shoulders as they both faced the camera. For another shot they danced together.

'Don't look so stern,' Giorgio called. 'Gaze into each other's eyes. Look romantic.'

'But why?' Natasha teased. 'We're getting married. That's not romantic; it's deadly serious.'

'Stop that,' Mario said. 'I'm quite scared enough without you scaring me more.'

She began to laugh. He joined in and Giorgio yelled with delight at the picture it produced.

'That's perfect,' he said. 'That says it all.'

As he'd predicted, the two sets of pictures worked splendidly together. When circulated to the rest of the *Comunità*, they produced a flood of excited congratulations.

There was one reaction Mario vowed to keep to himself. The text from Jenson was as spiteful as he'd expected, and he was thankful that Natasha didn't see it.

I've warned you but you didn't take any notice. Now see how sorry I can make you.

He checked the phone number of Jenson's organisation and dialled it.

'I want to speak to Elroy Jenson,' he told the receptionist.

'I'm sorry. Mr Jenson isn't accepting calls today.'

'He'll accept mine. Tell him Mario Ferrone wants to talk to him.'

A pause, some clicks, then a harsh masculine voice came on the line. 'What do you mean by calling me?'

'Ah, Mr Jenson. Good.' Mario leaned back in his chair. 'You know exactly who I am. You don't like me, and you're going to like me even less when I've finished.'

'You're wasting your time,' Jenson's voice came down the line.

'I don't think so. I think you'll find that some of my recent actions have been very significant.'

'What recent actions?' Jenson's voice contained a sneer but Mario thought he also detected a hint of nervousness.

'You'll be hearing from your Italian publications, wondering why whole batches of advertising have been suddenly cancelled.'

'Don't think you can scare me,' Jenson snapped. 'A few hotels and vineyards—'

'It'll be rather more than that. I've got friends working on this, friends you know nothing about but whose tentacles stretch great distances abroad. You'll be losing advertisements left, right and centre. And when they want to know why—I wonder what you'll tell them.'

'That's no concern of yours!' Jenson raged.

'Everything that concerns my fiancée concerns me, as you'll find out if you don't stop your nasty ways. You wrecked her career out of spite because she wasn't interested in your cheap advances and too many people got to know about it. Well, now the whole world is going to know about it.'

'What do you mean?' Jenson snarled.

'The digital age is a wonderful thing. A few texts and emails and the world will know what a pest Elroy Jenson is: a man so conceited that he felt no woman had the right to reject him, and with so little self-respect that he could never leave her alone afterwards.'

'There are laws of libel,' Jenson snarled.

'There's no question of libel. Once those texts you've sent her are revealed there would be no question everyone will know the truth.'

'Texts? I don't know what you're talking about.'

'Don't waste time trying to deny it. I've got records of every word you sent, and where they came from. I can reveal every word and prove it. The world will rock with laughter at you. And if you resorted to law you'd just keep yourself in an unpleasant spotlight longer.'

'What are you after? Money?'

'No, I just want you to leave Natasha alone. One more text or call from you and you've had it. Do you understand me?'

'You're very good at making threats,' Jenson snapped with his best effort at a sneer.

Mario grinned, feeling that he could risk a little vulgarity.

'I'm good at a lot of things,' he said. 'Which is why she chose me over you.'

'Why, you—'

'Goodbye. Go to hell!'

Mario hung up. Then he stared at the phone, trying to come to terms with his own actions. He was neither a violent nor a cruel man, but the need to conquer Jenson had brought out a side of him he'd never needed to use before.

But it was for her, and for her he would do anything. That was the effect she had on him, and now he realised that part of him had known it from the first day.

From behind him he heard a sound that made him turn in amazement. Natasha stood there, applauding.

'Well done,' she said. 'Wonderful! You've really dealt with him.' She engulfed him in an embrace.

'It was easy—just threaten to expose him as an idiot,' he said, returning her hug. 'He's far more afraid of that than losing business.'

'But I don't understand what you said about his texts. Surely you don't really have records of them?'

'Only the one he sent today. I don't have the others, but he doesn't know that and he won't take the chance.'

'No, he won't,' she breathed.

'And he won't dare send you any more because now he knows the risk he runs.'

'You're so clever.' She sighed. 'I never thought anyone could put this business right.'

'But you've got me to protect you now. And that's all I want to do for the rest of my life.'

He enfolded her in a fierce embrace.

'Three days before we're married,' he said huskily. 'I don't know if I can bear to wait that long to make you mine.'

'But I'm already yours. I always have been and I always will be.'

'No doubt about that,' he said, smiling. 'I'll never let you go.'

'That suits me just fine.'

Now things were moving fast. Two days before the wedding, Damiano, Sally and Pietro arrived and took up residence in the hotel's best suite. That evening there was a party attended by them, by Giorgio and by several members of the *Comunità*. Toasts were made to the bride and groom. Then the bride alone was toasted, leaving no doubt that she was the heroine of the hour.

As the evening wore on, Sally announced that she would retire for the night.

'I've got a bit of a headache,' she confided to Natasha.

'Me too,' she said. 'And I think Mario might enjoy chatting if he didn't have to keep breaking off to translate for me.'

Together they bid everyone goodnight and went upstairs. A warm, friendly hug and they said goodnight.

Natasha was glad to be alone for a moment for she needed to think. She must decide what to do about Tania's letter.

There had been a time when she might have told Mario

about it but events had conspired to distract her and now she knew the moment had gone. Her best course now was to destroy it so that it would be out of their lives finally and for ever.

Going quickly into her room, she went to the place where she kept it hidden.

She found the small piece of blue paper and unfolded it.

She read it again, taking in the words that had meant so much, thanking a merciful fate that had given it to her. Now she reckoned she must burn it.

'What's that?' said Mario's voice.

Startled, she looked up and saw him there. He had come in quietly, without her hearing him. Now he was standing with his eyes fixed on the blue paper that she held. With dismay, she realised that he knew what she was holding.

'What's that?' he repeated.

'It's just—'

'Give it to me.'

He wrenched it from her hand before she could protest. As he read it he seemed to grow very still.

'How did you get this?' he asked in a toneless voice.

'By accident. I came across it while I was in your apartment, after my room flooded.'

'And you kept it.'

'I needed to read it again and again. It seemed too good to be true. She says there that you'd told her it was over because you wanted to be with me. So after that I knew—'

'You knew I'd been telling you the truth,' he said slowly.

'Yes. It was so wonderful. After everything that happened, who could have thought it would be Tania who would make things right for us?'

There was a silence.

When he spoke he didn't look at her. 'Did she make things right for us?' he asked in a strange voice.

'She added the missing piece. She told me what I needed to know. After that, everything was different.'

If only he would smile and share her pleasure at the way things had turned out, but instead he was silent, frowning. It was almost as though her words troubled him.

'Tell me something,' he said at last. 'That night we took a walk by the river and when we got home you invited me into your room—had you read Tania's letter then?'

'Yes. I was so happy. Suddenly everything was all right.'

'Why? Because Tania had confirmed I was telling the truth? You knew that because *she* told you? But not because *I* told you?'

'I didn't know you as well in those days. I couldn't be sure what the truth might be. Oh, Mario, why didn't you show me the letter yourself?'

'I meant to. But I was waiting for the right moment.'

'But surely any time would have been right to show me the proof?'

'The proof?'

'The proof that what you were telling me was true. That you really had broken with her.'

A strange, tense look came over his face. 'So you could have believed me when you saw proof. But not my word alone.'

'Mario, I'm sorry about that. I see now that I should

have believed you. But does it matter now that it's been finally settled?'

'Settled.' He repeated the word softly. 'If only I could make you understand—'

'Understand what, my darling?'

'Since you came to Verona I've clung to a happy fantasy, a dream world in which we understood each other. In that world we grew close, loving each other more and more until you finally believed what I told you because you knew me well enough to know that I was true to you.'

'But I do know—'

'Yes, because you've got the evidence in that letter. But in my fantasy you didn't need evidence. You believed me because you loved me enough to trust me completely. We were so close that no doubt could ever come between us.

'That night, when you opened your arms to me, I felt I'd reached heaven. I thought our great moment had arrived at last, the moment I'd been longing for since the day we met. If only you knew how I... Well, never mind. It doesn't matter now.'

'But it does,' she cried passionately. 'Mario, don't talk like this. You sound as though everything is hopeless between us, but it isn't. We've discovered our hope at last. It's taken too long but we've finally found each other. Can't you see that?'

'I want to. If you knew how desperately I long to believe that everything can be all right now, but there's something missing and perhaps it always will be.'

She stared at him, struggling to believe what he was saying.

'Then blame me,' she said. 'I got it wrong; I took too long to understand the truth. But I understand it now.'

'Yes, because someone else told you. Not me. The closeness I thought we'd achieved doesn't exist. It was an illusion I believed because I wanted to believe it.' He gave a grim laugh. 'I remember you saying people believed what they wanted to, and boy were you right! In you I saw what I wanted to see.

'And now? Will we ever have that closeness? I doubt it. You said things were "finally settled". But when is something settled? When you finally have peace of mind?'

And now he did not have peace of mind with her. He didn't say it—but he didn't need to say it. She had thought that all was well between them, but after this would their love ever be the same?

'Do you understand the bitter irony of this?' he asked. 'The next thing is our wedding. We'll stand side by side at a site that commemorates the greatest lovers of legend. We'll vow love, loyalty, trust. *Trust!* Can you imagine that?'

'I do trust you,' she cried passionately.

'Do you? Perhaps you do, perhaps you don't. I'll never really know, will I?'

'Can't you take my word for it?'

He gave a harsh laugh. 'Are you lecturing me about accepting your word? That's the cruellest joke you ever made. I was looking forward to our wedding. Now I'm dreading it. I'm not even sure that I—'

He broke off, almost choking. His eyes, fixed on her, were full of hostility. Suddenly he turned, pulled open the door and rushed out without a backward glance.

'Mario—don't. Come back, *please.*'

But either he didn't hear or he ignored her, heading for the stairs and running down them. At the bottom he turned towards the entrance. Dashing back into the room,

Natasha went to the window and looked down, where she could see him heading down the street until he vanished.

She almost screamed in her despair. The perfect love that offered a wonderful future had descended into chaos. Now a terrifying vista opened before her. Ahead stretched a road of misery, where every hope came to nothing and only emptiness remained.

CHAPTER TWELVE

WHAT FOLLOWED WAS the worst night of Natasha's life.

It was over. Everything was over. She had lost Mario and nothing could ever matter in her life again.

Why didn't I tell him earlier? her heart cried.

But she knew the answer. However he had learned about the letter, he would have hated the fact that she'd relied on it. In his heart he no longer believed that she loved him. And now everything might be over between them. He had even hinted that he might not be there for the wedding.

For a moment she thought of chasing after him, but he'd had time to disappear and she would never find him. Her best hope was to wait for him to return.

She lay down, trying to control her wild thoughts and believe that there might still be hope. For an hour she lay there, listening for some sign of his return, but all she heard was the party breaking up.

Then there was silence and darkness, leaving her with an aching heart and terrified thoughts.

Why didn't he return?

Would he ever return?

She slept for a while and awoke in the early hours. There was no sign of Mario, but perhaps he'd gone to his own room. She slipped out into the corridor and went to his door, where she stood listening for a moment. But there was no sound from within.

Tentatively, she opened the door and slipped inside. The bed was empty. He had not returned.

'Come back,' she whispered. 'Don't let it end like this. Come back to me.'

But another two hours passed with no sign of him.

A terrible sense of irony pervaded her. Suddenly it felt as though she was Juliet again, a star-crossed lover facing the final destruction of her joy.

There was nothing to prepare her for what happened next.

A shrill from her mobile phone made her look to find a text. Incredibly, it was from Jenson.

You think you're clever, setting your lover on me. Take a look at this.

Below it was the address of a website. Studying it, Natasha realised that it was an English provincial newspaper, doubtless belonging to Jenson.

He'd said he knew something about her, implying that he could smear her in print. But she couldn't think of anything she would be reluctant to have known.

She got to work on her laptop, typing in the web address. There on the screen was a printed page with a photograph. A cry broke from her as she recognised her father.

Forcing herself under control, she looked closely at the text. It was dated eight years ago and named the man as Charles Bates. It seemed to be part of a series about people who had been brought down by misfortune. Charles

Bates had turned to crime and gone to prison following a tragic crisis in his life.

He had given the interview two days after being released. As she read what he'd had to say, Natasha felt her blood run cold.

'I blame my wife. I loved her and the girl I thought was my daughter. But then I discovered she wasn't mine. It broke my heart. I ran away as fast as I could go.'

So her mother had betrayed her husband and she, Natasha, was not his child. She struggled to deny it, but lurking in her memory was a quarrel she had overheard between them. Her father had shouted, 'Who was he? Tell me!' And he'd called her mother some terrible names. The next day he had gone.

Another memory returned—Jenson walking into the room as she was telling this story to a fellow employee. How sympathetic he had been, encouraging her to talk. How kind she had thought him, while all the time he was softening her up so that he could pounce on her, while storing the information in case it could be a useful weapon. That was his way. He liked to have weapons against everyone.

Checking back, he'd found that one little item and made a note of it. Mario's action over the advertisements had convinced him he had nothing left to gain, and still he'd lashed out to hurt her for revenge.

Now she saw that years of being warned not to trust men went back to this point. Her mistrust had made her wary of Mario, but it was based on a lie. And that lie threatened the love they shared.

Unless she could find a way to solve the problem.

Suddenly she found words whispering through her head. *I have a faint cold fear thrills through my veins, That almost freezes up the heat of life.*

Juliet had spoken those words, faced with the decision that would change everything. And now Natasha felt the cold fear running through her. She must do something to make Mario return. But what?

'*She* will know,' she said. 'I'll go and ask her.'

Hurriedly, she flung on some clothes and rushed out of the room and downstairs.

Damiano was just crossing the hall. 'Just on my way to breakfast,' he said. 'No Mario?'

'He'll...be a while,' she stammered.

Damiano chuckled. 'Ah, still asleep, is he? I guess you must have exhausted him.'

She managed a smile. 'Something like that. I have to hurry away for a while.'

She quickly went out, seeing the hotel driver just outside. She approached him.

'Please take me to the Via Capello.'

In a moment they were away. She didn't notice Giorgio standing in the doorway with a puzzled frown.

For the whole journey she sat tense, watching Verona glide past her, wondering what the city would mean to her in future. The place where she and her Romeo had achieved their happy ending? Or the place where the star-crossed lovers had been forced to accept that their love was never meant to be?

At last they drew up outside the Casa di Giulietta and she got out.

'Shall I wait for you?' the driver asked.

'No. I don't know how long I'll be. Thank you, but go back.'

He drove off, leaving her standing there. Then she went to the house, which had just opened for the day. A doorman greeted her, recognising her as a bride who was booked in a couple of days ahead.

'You'll find everything just as you're hoping for,' he called cheerfully.

'I'm sure I will,' she called back politely.

But would her wedding be as she was hoping for? Would anything in her life be right again?

As always, Juliet was standing in the courtyard. Natasha headed for the statue, glad that for the moment they were alone.

'I never asked your advice before,' she said. 'I believed you were just a fantasy. But now my whole world is upside down, and maybe you're the one person who can help me.

'What can I do? I made a silly mistake but I was confused. I didn't want to hurt Mario. I just couldn't understand what it would mean to him. Now he thinks I don't really love him, but I do. How can I make him believe that?'

Silence.

'Oh, please, you must help me. You know more about love than anyone. Tell me what I can do.'

She pressed her hand against her chest.

'You understand that, don't you?' she said to Juliet, who also had a hand on her breast. 'You know what it's like to press your hand over the pain, hoping to make it go away. But it doesn't go, and you become frantic trying to think of something that will help. I can't think of anything. What can I do?'

She took a step closer to Juliet, seeking to look her in the eye. She told herself not to be fanciful, otherwise she might have imagined Juliet's soft voice saying, *He's as troubled and unsure as you are.*

I know. He's suffering terribly and it's my fault. I thought the worst of every man because of my father, but now I realise that I shouldn't have done.

Discovering that you'd read the letter hurt him. He hasn't completely recovered.

Nor have I.

You're coping better than he is.

Truly? What can I do now?

Be kind to him. He is confused.

But what is it that confuses him?

You. You always have, although he would never admit it.

Does our love really have a future?

Who can tell? You can only hope.

And hope might come to nothing. That fact had to be faced. She would return to the hotel and find him not there because he no longer wanted her. It was over. He would never return.

Tears filled her eyes, blurring her vision so that the street around her seemed to become a swirling mass. She groped her way forward, missed the edge of the pavement and crashed to the ground. She was intensely aware of pain going through her head before she blacked out.

The first person Mario met on his return was Damiano.

'So there you are!' his brother exclaimed. 'I thought you were still upstairs, sleeping it off while Natasha was away.'

'Away?'

'She came downstairs a few hours ago. She went off somewhere in a hurry.'

'Went somewhere? You mean she's gone? Where?'

'She didn't say where she was going. Just walked out and didn't come back. You don't mean there's something wrong, surely? The two of you are getting married tomorrow. She's probably making last-minute preparations for the wedding.'

'Yes, of course,' Mario said in a voice that was deliberately blank to hide the storm of alarm that was rising within him.

'I expect she's preparing a special surprise for you.'

Yes, Mario thought desperately. Natasha was preparing a surprise for him, and he had a dreadful feeling that he knew what the surprise was.

'Oh, no!' he breathed. 'How could she do this to me?'

'What do you mean?' Damiano demanded.

'She's done it again.'

'Done what again?'

'What she did before—leaving without a goodbye, when I wasn't there to see. Disappearing into thin air like she'd never existed.'

'I'm sure you're wrong about that,' Damiano protested.

Mario tore his hair. 'You have no idea,' he raged. 'She vanished and I spent weeks looking for her before I realised that I'd never find her because she'd shut me out of her life.' His voice rose in anguish. *'Now she's done it again.'*

Nobody had noticed Giorgio entering the hall. He stood watching Mario with a puzzled frown.

'What's happened?' he asked at last.

'Have you seen Natasha today?' Mario demanded.

'Yes, I saw her get into the car with the chauffeur a few hours ago. He was only gone half an hour.'

'Fetch him,' Mario said.

Giorgio went out and returned with the chauffeur.

'Where did you take her?' Mario demanded.

'To the Via Capello.'

'And you brought her back?'

'No, she told me not to wait for her.'

'So she's gone,' Mario muttered. 'She's gone.'

He turned away so that they shouldn't see his face, which he knew must betray his pain, greater than any he'd known in his life before. He'd wanted so much to believe in her. Since their quarrel the night before he'd brooded over what lay before him. A life with her, always worried about the strength of her love? Or a life without her?

He'd paced the dark streets for hours, trying to understand his own heart. By the time he'd arrived home he knew that Natasha mattered more than anything in the world. However hard it was for him, he would do what he had to for their love to succeed; the thought of losing her was unbearable.

And he had arrived to find her gone.

He wanted to howl with rage, but even more with misery. She had betrayed his love, abandoned him, while knowing what it would do to him.

'Why don't you look in her room?' Damiano said. 'If she's really gone she'll have taken everything with her.'

'All right,' Mario said heavily.

What was the point? he thought. He would find her room deserted and the brutal truth underlined. Moving mechanically, he went up to her room and opened the door. Then he grew still.

The wardrobe was open, and inside it he could see her clothes. Pulling open drawers, he found more clothing.

'She hasn't gone for good,' Damiano said, coming in behind him. 'Or she would never have left all this behind.'

'But where did she go?' Mario asked hoarsely.

'The chauffeur said he took her to the Via Capello,' Giorgio said. 'Surely she went to Juliet's house.'

'Yes,' Mario said at once. 'I understand that now.'

Everything was becoming clear to him. Natasha had gone to consult Juliet, and now she would know how the two of them could put things right.

One thing was clear. He must join her as soon as possible. He headed for the front door.

'Hey, Mario,' Giorgio called. 'Where are you going?'

Mario paused and looked back at him. 'I'm going to find my lady,' he said.

As he drove himself to the Via Capello the words haunted him, as they had many times before. *It is my lady. Oh, it is my love.*

'"Oh, that she knew she were,"' he murmured.

At last Juliet's house came in sight. He parked and ran down the street to the alley that led to the courtyard. There was no sign of Natasha. All he could see was Juliet, staring ahead, coolly indifferent to her surroundings. He placed himself in front of her.

'Was she here?' he demanded. 'Did she come to you and ask your help? Did you help her?'

No response. Nor had he expected one. Nobody else could help them now.

He wandered through the house, seeking her without success. In one room he stood looking around him, reflecting that this was where their wedding was supposed to take place, and wondering what the future held.

Once more he returned to Juliet. A small group of tourists had gathered in front of her, pleading for her attention.

'It's very tempting to talk to her, isn't it?' a woman said to Mario. 'We came here earlier and there was a lovely young woman talking to her as if it really mattered. But I don't think she had any luck because as soon as she left she got hurt.'

'Hurt? How?'

'I'm not sure what happened. She just seemed to lose her balance. She went down hard and hit her head on the pavement. The last I saw, she was being taken to the hospital.'

Barely able to speak, he forced himself to say, 'You said she was a young woman. What did she look like?'

'Pretty, blue eyes, blonde hair.'

'And how did she seem?'

'Not sure, really. She wasn't moving. I suppose she might actually have been dead.'

He swallowed. 'Thank you for telling me,' he said hoarsely.

It took him ten minutes to get to the nearest hospital. There, he tore inside and up to the desk.

'A young woman was brought in this morning,' he gasped. 'She had a fall in the Via Capello. I must see her.'

The receptionist made a phone call and a nurse appeared.

He followed her into a small side ward and held his breath at the sight of Natasha lying on the bed. Her eyes were closed and it seemed to him that she was frighteningly still.

'Is this the person you are looking for?' the nurse asked.

'Yes, this is the person I was looking for.'

'Please tell me who she is.'

'Her name is Natasha Bates.'

'And who is her next of kin?'

'I am. I'm her husband. At least, I will be in a few days. If she lives.'

He had to force himself to say the last few words, but the fear was more than he could endure.

'We don't yet know how seriously she's hurt,' the nurse said. 'She's still unconscious, but hopefully she'll soon come round.'

He moved to the bed, looking down at Natasha lying there. She seemed different to the strong, determined young woman he remembered: smaller, more frail and vulnerable.

A sudden fearsome echo haunted him: Romeo coming to Juliet in the tomb, seeing her lying there, silent and motionless, believing her dead. He tried to fight the thought away but he had a terrified feeling that she would leave him unless he could prevent her.

'Natasha,' he said, taking a chair beside the bed. 'It's me, darling. Can you hear me?'

She neither moved nor spoke.

'Are you there?' he begged. 'Please tell me that you're there.'

His heart sank. Her breathing told him that she was still alive, but in another sense she wasn't there. She was living in another universe, one where she might be trapped for ever.

'You went away from me once,' he whispered. 'I thought I would go mad at your rejection, but you came back and we found each other. Then today I thought you'd abandoned me again, and losing you was even worse than before.

'What happened was my fault. I couldn't bear discovering that I'd been living in a fantasy, that you loved me less than I'd thought. But if that's true—' he hesitated '—if the love is mainly on my side, then…then I'll live with that as long as I can have you. Do you understand? I'll accept any conditions as long as I don't lose you again. Even if—' he shuddered '—even if you never really wake up, but stay like this always, I won't leave you. I'll care for you and love you for years and years, until the day we can be finally together for ever.'

He leaned closer to murmur into her ear, 'Don't leave me. I'm yours in every way and I always will be. Natasha? Can you hear me?'

'Yes,' she whispered.

'I followed you all the way to Juliet's house. You went to ask her help, didn't you?'

'Yes.' She whispered the word so softly that he wasn't sure he'd heard properly.

'What?' he asked eagerly, leaning closer.

'She was very kind to me.'

He was suddenly sure that they understood each other. He must seize this moment, lest there should never be another.

'I tried too,' he said. 'But she stayed silent. I reckon she was telling me to see the truth for myself.' Inspiration came to him. 'And the truth we have to understand is that we love each other more than we can say in mere words. We've always known that, but we've never managed to face it before. But now the time has come and if I do nothing else in the world I have to make sure that you know.'

He kissed her again softly before murmuring, 'You are my lady. You are my love. Oh, that you knew you are.'

'Am I?' she whispered. 'Am I truly?'

'You know you are. And you will always know that you are.'

'How can I believe it? It's too good to be true.'

'Then I'll have to spend my life convincing you. I was so afraid you wouldn't wake up.'

'I was in such a strange place. I couldn't tell which way to turn, but suddenly you were there, beckoning me.'

'I always will be. I'll never let you go.'

The nurse appeared. She checked Natasha's pulse, read the machines and smiled at the result.

'This is what we hoped for,' she said. 'It's not serious. A few days' rest and you'll be back on your feet.'

When she had left they hugged, looking deep into each other's eyes, reading the depths for the first time. But now no words were spoken. No words were needed. Soon Natasha's eyes closed and Mario held her while she slept, thinking blissfully of the years ahead when he would hold her many times in his arms and always in his heart.

The wedding had to be delayed for two weeks, but at last the time came when they entered Juliet's house and made the vows of lifelong love and fidelity. Once, many years before, another couple had vowed the same, only to see their happiness cut short. But Natasha and Mario had no fear.

After the ceremony they went out onto the balcony, where Giorgio had arranged for a photographer to be clicking his camera madly. But the bride and groom were barely aware of him. They saw only each other.

'Just us,' he said as they held each other later that night.

'Not quite just us,' she murmured. 'There were two other people there. Couldn't you sense them?'

'Yes, they were there, watching over us as they've always done. And perhaps they always will.'

'No need,' she said. 'From now on we'll watch over each other.'

'Do you really think we can?'

'Yes, we can.' She turned in the bed, taking him in a fervent embrace.

'Come here,' she said. 'Come here *now*.'

* * * * *

THE FORBIDDEN
PRINCE

ALISON ROBERTS

For Becky

With all my love

CHAPTER ONE

So THIS WAS what freedom felt like.

Raoul de Poitier sucked in a deep breath as he paused to get his first proper glimpse of the view he'd climbed about two thousand steps to find.

He had the whole world at his feet.

Well...he had what looked like a large part of the Amalfi coast of the Mediterranean down there, anyway. Far, far below he could pick out the tiny blue patch that was the swimming pool on the roof of the hotel Tramonto d'Oro where he'd stayed last night. Beside that was the tiled dome and spire of the ancient church against the terracotta tiles and white houses of the small coastal town of Praiano.

Beyond the village, the waters of the Mediterranean stretched as far as the horizon, a breathtakingly sapphire blue as the sunlight gentled its way to dusk. Somewhere out there was his homeland—the European principality of *Les Iles Dauphins*.

Another deep breath was released in what felt like a sigh, and with it came a pang of...what... homesickness? Guilt, perhaps?

His grandfather was ill. His heart was failing and it

was time for him to step down from ruling his land. To hand the responsibility to the next-in-line to the throne.

His grandmother would be anxious. Not only about her beloved husband but about the grandson she'd raised as her own child after the tragic death of his parents.

'I don't understand, Raoul. A holiday...yes. Time to prepare yourself for what is to come. For your marriage... But alone? Incognito? That's not who you are.'

'Maybe that's what I need to find out, Mamé. And this is the last chance I will ever get.'

No. The pang wasn't guilt. He needed this time to centre himself for what was to come. To be sure that he had what it took to put aside his own desires if that was what was required to protect and nurture a whole nation, albeit a tiny one. He was thirty-two years old but he hadn't been really tested yet. Oh, there'd been formal duties that had got in the way of private pleasures, and he had always had to curb any desire to push the boundaries of behaviour that might be frowned on by others. But, within that reasonably relaxed circumference, he'd been able to achieve the career that had been top of his chosen list—as a helicopter pilot in his country's first-rate rescue service. And he'd had his share of a seemingly infinite supply of beautiful women.

All that was about to change, however. The boundaries would shrink to contain him in a very tight space. Almost every minute of every day would be accounted for.

He had always known it would happen. He just wasn't sure how ready he was to accept it. Somehow, he needed to find that out. To test himself, by himself, which was why this had to be in a place where he knew no one and no one knew who he was.

Was it homesickness, perhaps? Because he was feeling a new and rather extraordinary sensation of being alone? No. He'd dealt with homesickness many years ago when he'd been sent to the best schools that Europe had to offer and, while the love of his family and homeland would always draw him back and enfold him, he loved to travel.

It was relief, that was what it was. He had won this time. A reprieve from thinking about the overwhelming responsibility of being in charge of a nation, along with the daunting prospect of a marriage that had been arranged when he'd been no more than a child. A union that would bond two similar principalities together and strengthen them both.

Raoul turned away from the view of the sea. Les Iles Dauphins was out of sight and he was going to try and put it out of mind for just a little while.

He was free. All he had was in his backpack and he could choose any direction at all, the time he would take to get there and how long he would stay when he did. As of yesterday, nobody knew where he was and he was confident that nobody would recognise him. His hair grew fast and he'd deliberately missed his last cut. His beard was coming along well, too. With his dark sunglasses, he could pass for any European tourist. Italian, French... Spanish, even.

He could feel the corners of his mouth curve. If he'd had a guitar case on his back instead of his backpack, he would probably have looked like a flashback to the sixties. He was completely alone for what felt like the first time in his entire life. No family, no friends and, most importantly, no bodyguards or lurking paparazzi. He had won the freedom simply to be himself.

He just needed to find out who that was, exactly, because he had a feeling there were layers to his personality that had been buried for ever. Even his earliest memories involved a performance of some kind. Of behaving in a way that would never have been expected of others.

How many five-year-olds could take part in a national ceremony to mourn both parents and not cry until they were finally alone in their own beds and presumed to be sound asleep? Who had childhood friends chosen for them and, even then, had to be careful of what was said? What young adult knew how much had been sacrificed by a generation that had already raised a child and shouldn't have had to start all over again? The burden of a debt that could never properly be repaid had never been intended but it was there all the same.

He had never been drunk enough to do anything inappropriate or create a scandal by dating indiscreet women. He had excelled in his university studies and military training and, until he'd taken this leave, had shone in his role as a helicopter pilot for a service that provided both military transport and emergency rescue services.

Sometimes, it felt like his life had been recorded by photographs that had been staged for public consumption and approval. A picture-perfect life of a happy prince. And the next album would have all the pomp and ceremony of his coronation, then his wedding and then the births of the next generation of the de Poitier royal family.

The happiness was not an illusion. Raoul loved his life and knew how incredibly fortunate he was but his curiosity of the unknown had teased him with increasing frequency of late. Was there something solid that formed the essence of who he was as a person? Something that would have been there if he hadn't been born a prince?

He had four weeks to try and find some kind of answer to what seemed an impossible question and the only plan he had come up with was to see if he could find a challenge that would be testing enough to make him dig deep. He had set out with no more than the bare essentials of survival in a backpack—a phone, a fake ID, limited funds and a change of clothes. This demanding climb up a mountain to the track that led from Praiano to Positano was just the first step on a very private journey.

Or maybe it wasn't quite that private.

Frowning, Raoul stared at the narrow, winding track ahead of him. He could hear voices. One voice, anyway.

Faint.

Female.

'Aiuti... Per favore aiutatemi...'

The vertigo had come from nowhere.

Utterly unexpected and totally debilitating.

Tamika Gordon was clinging to the side of a cliff and she didn't dare open her eyes. If she did, the nausea would come back, the world would start spinning again and there would be nothing to stop her falling into that terrifyingly sheer drop onto rocks hundreds of feet below. But keeping her eyes shut didn't wipe out the knowledge that the unprotected edge to this track was no more than the length of her arm away.

The panic that led her to cry for help was almost as terrifying as the yawning chasm below.

Mika didn't do panic. She'd been told more than once that she was 'as hard as nails' and she was proud of it. It was a badge of honour, won by surviving. Of course she was tough. Who wouldn't be when they'd been dragged up through a succession of disastrous foster homes and then had ended up on the streets as a teenager? She'd fought for everything she had achieved in her twenty-nine years on earth so far and she'd been confident she could cope with whatever life chose to throw at her.

But this…this was totally out of her control. She'd fought it for as long as possible with sheer willpower but the symptoms were physical rather than mental and they had increased in ferocity until she'd reached a point of complete helplessness—reduced to a shivering blob of humanity clinging to a couple of tufts of coarse mountain grass. It was beyond humiliating. She'd be angry about it as soon as she got out of this and the terror had a chance to wear off. *If* she ever got out of this…

She hadn't seen anyone else on this supposedly popular walking route so far. Maybe that was her own fault. She'd chosen to set off from Praiano much later in the day than most people because she knew the light would be so much better for taking photographs. And maybe she'd spent too much time down at the monastery halfway up the steps, taking photographs with her precious new camera and scribbling notes in her pristine journal.

How long would it be before it got dark?

'*Help*...' She tried English this time instead of Italian. 'Can anyone hear me?'

Her voice wavered and tears stung as they gathered behind her eyelids. This recognition of a despair she hadn't felt since she'd been too young to protect herself had to be the worst moment of her adult life.

'I'm coming... Hold on...'

She wasn't alone. There was hope to be found now. A glowing light in the darkness of that despair. It was a male voice she'd heard, the words short, as if he was out of breath, and in the space after those words Mika could hear the sound of shoes crunching on the sparse gravel of the track.

He was *running*?

When there were only a few feet between the steep wall of the cliff above and that appalling drop into nothingness below?

The speed of the footsteps slowed and then stopped.

'What is it?' A deep voice with a faint accent that she couldn't place. 'Are you hurt?'

Mika shook her head, her eyes still tightly closed. The overwhelming relief at not being alone any more made speech impossible for several breaths.

'Vertigo,' she managed finally, hating how pathetic her voice sounded. 'I... I can't move...'

'You're safe,' the man said. 'I'll keep you safe.'

Dear Lord...had anybody *ever* said that to her? Being so helpless had made her feel like a small child again, so it was too easy to imagine how it would feel to have somebody say those words to that frightened little girl. To feel fear and desolation start to drain away as if a plug had been pulled. To have an insight into how different her life might have been if somebody had said that to her, back then, and meant it. If somebody had been there to protect her. To love her...

How humiliating was it to have her outward breath sound like a child's sob? She'd learned long ago that weakness was something to be hidden very deeply.

'It's okay,' the man said. 'You're going to be fine. How long have you been stuck?'

'I...don't know.' It felt like for ever.

'Are you thirsty? I have water.'

She heard a shuffling sound and then a zip opening. She was thirsty but to accept a water bottle would mean opening her eyes, and what if the spinning started again? Sobbing in front of a stranger was bad enough. Imagine if she threw up?

'It's okay. I don't need a drink.'

There was a moment's silence. 'What's your name?'

'Mika.'

'It's a pleasure to meet you, Mika.'

This time her breath came out as a huff of something closer to laughter than tears. Her rescuer had very nice manners. He sounded as though they'd just been introduced at a cocktail party.

'I'm Ra...um... Rafe.'

She had only been speaking to him for a minute or two, and she didn't even have any idea what he looked like, but the hesitation seemed out of character. Did he not want her to know his real name? Was it possible that she was about to step from the frying pan into the fire and put her faith in an axe murderer? Or a...a rapist?

It might have been five years ago but the fear was always too close to the surface. If he hadn't chosen that precise moment to touch her, she could have dealt with it. It wasn't like the vertigo; she could persuade herself to think rationally and conquer it.

But he touched her arm and moving away from that touch was too instinctive to avoid. Mika let go of her tufts of grass with every intention of trying to run but her legs were still shaking and she lost her footing. Desperately trying to stop the skid, she reached for the grass again, but it slid through her fingers. Her foot made contact with something solid and she pushed against it but that, too, slid out of touch. She landed on her hands and knees, aware of a sound like rocks falling that provided a background to the soft but vehement curse that came from her rescuer.

And then silence.

Cautiously, Mika sat back on her heels as she tried to process what had just happened.

'Are you all right?'

'Yes. I'm sorry. I... I slipped.'

'Hmm...'

She could feel him watching her. 'Did I...um...kick you?'

'No. You kicked my backpack. It went over the cliff.'

Mika's eyes opened smartly. '*What?* Oh, no... I'm *so* sorry...'

'Better the pack than you.'

It seemed extraordinary but he was smiling at her. A smile that made the corners of his eyes crinkle. Dark eyes. Dark, shaggy hair and a dark jaw that had gone well past designer stubble but wasn't quite a beard. And he was big. Even crouching he seemed to tower over her.

Weird that the fear that had prompted this unfortunate development was ebbing away instead of increasing. Maybe it was those eyes. This man might be in a position of power over her right now but he wasn't any kind of predator. He looked...nice. Kind?

You're safe. I'll keep you safe.

'Did it have anything important in it? Like your wallet?' A churning in her stomach reminded her not to try looking over the edge of the cliff.

'There's no point worrying about that right now. The light's going to fade before long, Mika. I need to get you off this track.'

Mika nodded. She scrambled to her feet, her own light pack still secure on her back. If she didn't look into the chasm, maybe she would be okay. She looked towards the solid side of the cliff, reaching out her hand to touch it as well.

'I'm trying to decide which way would be best. You've come a long way onto the open part of the track already. It's probably better to keep going towards Positano rather than go down all those steps when it's getting darker.'

Mika swallowed hard and then nodded again. 'That's where I'm living at the moment. In Positano.'

'The track is quite narrow. Do you want me to walk ahead of you or behind?'

'Ahead, I think... I can watch your feet. If I don't look at the drop, maybe the dizziness won't come back.'

It worked...for a little while...but, try as she might, Mika became more and more aware of the emptiness on the left side in her peripheral vision. Using her free hand to provide a kind of blinker also helped for a while but it wasn't enough. Her stomach began to fold itself into spasms of distress and her brain began a slow, sickening spin. She tried to focus on the boots in front of her: smart, expensive-looking leather hiking boots. Thick socks were rolled down above them and then there were bare legs, muscles under olive skin outlined with every step.

'How's it going?'

Mika dropped the hand she was using as a shield to look up as Raoul turned his head when she didn't respond immediately. She tried to smile but changing the focus of her vision seemed to have made the spinning sensation worse.

'Here… It might help to hold my hand.'

It was there, right in front of her, palm downwards and fingers outstretched in invitation.

And it was huge.

Not the hand, although it had long, artistic-looking fingers. No. It was the idea of voluntarily putting her own into it that was so huge. Five years was a very long time not to have allowed the touch of a man's skin against her own.

But the need to survive was an overwhelmingly strong motivation. Strong enough to break a protective barrier that was inappropriate in this moment. She put her hand in his and felt his fingers curl around hers. She could feel the strength of the arm attached to that hand. The solidness of the body attached to the arm. The confidence of each step that was being taken.

He was half a pace ahead of her, because there was no room to walk side by side, but the hand was all that mattered.

He was holding her.

And he would keep her safe.

* * *

She was a fighter, this Mika.

And there was something wild about her.

She was certainly unlike any woman he'd ever met before. For a start, she was out here all by herself, which advertised independence and courage, but she was tiny. Her head barely reached his shoulder, which probably made her look younger than she really was—an intriguing contrast to those big, dark eyes that made you think she'd seen far more than her age should have allowed for. She had spiky dark hair, which should have seemed unattractive to someone who'd always favoured long, blonde tresses, but he had to admit that it suited Mika. So did the clothes that looked more suitable for a walk on a beach than a mountain hike—denim shorts that were frayed at the bottom and a loose white singlet, the hem of which didn't quite meet the waistband of the shorts.

The shoes weren't exactly suitable either, being well-worn-looking trainers, and it looked as though her feet were bare inside them, but the surprise of that choice had been well and truly surpassed when Raoul had noticed her tattoo. The inked design looked tribal—like a series of peaked waves encircling her upper arm just below armpit level. No. Maybe even that observation had been trumped by spotting the tiny charm on the simple silver chain around her neck.

A dolphin…

The symbol of his homeland. What would she think if she knew that she was wearing something that gave her an instant connection to everything he held most dear in his life?

But it had been that instinctive flinch from a touch

that had been intended as no more than reassurance that had really given him the sense of wildness about her. It wasn't just the physical appearance that said she made her own choices or the fact that she was alone in a potentially dangerous place. It was that wariness of the touch, the hesitation in accepting contact from another human, that had been revealed by her body language when he'd offered to take her hand.

The trembling he'd felt when she'd finally accepted the offer.

Or perhaps it was the way she'd been doggedly following him even though it was clearly an enormous struggle. She'd been as white as a sheet when he'd turned to check on how she was doing. He could see that she was pushing herself beyond her limits but he could also see the determination that she wasn't going to let it defeat her. Anger, almost, that she'd been beaten into submission. Like a wild creature that had been trapped?

Another hundred metres along this goat track of a path—past a rustic wooden sign with Praiano written on one side and Nocelle on the other—and Raoul could feel that the trembling in her hand had ebbed. The holding had all been on his part to begin with but now he could feel a return pressure from that small hand he was holding and it made him feel…good.

Protective. She hadn't wanted him to touch her but she'd allowed it when she'd reached the end of her endurance.

She was trusting him and he wasn't going to break that trust. He would look after this wild creature of a woman until he was absolutely sure she was okay.

'Don't worry,' he told her. 'It'll wear off as soon as you don't have that drop beside you.'

'I know.' It sounded like she was speaking through gritted teeth.

'It's nothing to be ashamed of,' he added. 'Vertigo is like altitude sickness. It makes no difference how fit or strong you are. These things just happen.'

A tiny huff of sound suggested that Mika didn't let things just happen to *her* and Raoul felt a flash of empathy. Imagine if it had happened to him. If he'd set out to discover the qualities in himself that would allow him to face his future with confidence and he'd been left helpless and totally dependent on the kindness of a stranger...

Oddly, he felt almost envious of Mika. Maybe it took something that dramatic to strip away every layer that life had cloaked you with. To face that kind of fear would certainly reveal any strengths or weaknesses. Maybe the kind of challenge he needed was something like Mika had just faced—something that you would never choose voluntarily.

But you couldn't create one. Like the vertigo he'd told her about, it either happened or it didn't.

He *was* facing an unexpected development, however—a small thing, compared to Mika's challenge, but how on earth was he going to cope with losing that backpack? The clothing and toiletries didn't matter but he'd lost his wallet, passport and phone. It would be easy enough to place a call from a public telephone to request help but, even if his grandmother said nothing, he would hear the subtext of 'I told you so'. Going incognito to be a nobody in the real world was not something a prince should do. It wasn't who he was.

Failure wasn't an option. He just needed to come up with a new plan. Maybe he'd find inspiration by the time this walk was over.

The sigh he blocked after a few minutes of nothing remotely inspirational occurring seemed to transfer itself to Mika, as she pulled her hand from his.

'I'm okay now.'

He'd been so lost in his thoughts that Raoul hadn't noticed how the track had changed. They weren't on a cliff edge any more. The path had widened and there were trees on either side.

A glance at Mika and the change he saw in her appearance was startling. She was still pale but the tension in her face and the panic in her eyes had gone. And, if that hadn't made her look different enough, her mouthed curved into a grin that he could only describe as cheeky.

'Stupid, huh?'

It was impossible not to grin back.

'Not at all. Like I said, it can happen to anybody.'

'It's like a switch has been flicked off. Now that I can't see the cliff, I'm fine.' She ducked her head and when she looked up again there was something soft in her eyes. Something that made Raoul feel a flush of warmth like the tingle you got when you held cold hands out to a fire.

'Thank you *so* much. I… I think you might have saved my life.'

'It was my pleasure.' The words were quiet but he meant every one of them. Oddly, he needed to clear his throat after he'd uttered them. 'Let's hope there are no more open parts to the track.'

'I don't think there are. We should get to the village

of Nocelle soon and then it's just a whole lot more steps down into Positano.' Mika raised her eyebrows. 'I wonder if the police station will still be open.'

'Excuse me?'

'So you can report the loss of your backpack. In case someone finds it.'

'I think that's highly unlikely. It didn't look like the kind of cliff anyone would be climbing for fun.'

'I can't believe I did that. I feel awful.'

'It doesn't matter. Really…'

For a few moments they walked in silence. Dusk was really gathering now, and it was darker amongst the trees, so coming across a small herd of goats startled them both. The goats were even more startled and leapt off the track to scramble up through the forest, the sound of their bleating and bells astonishingly loud in the evening stillness.

'Sorry, goats,' Mika called, but she was laughing. She even had some colour in her cheeks when she turned towards Raoul. 'I *love* Italy,' she told him. 'I might live here for ever.'

'Oh? You're not Italian, then?'

'Huh? We've been talking English since we met. What makes you think I'm Italian?'

'When I first heard you call for help, you spoke in Italian. And you've got a funny accent when you speak English.'

'I do *not*.' Mika sounded offended. 'I can get by in Italian pretty well but English is my first language.'

'So you are from England?'

'No. I'm half-Maori, half-Scottish.'

'You don't *sound* Scottish.'

'I'm not. I'm a Kiwi.'

Raoul shook his head. She was talking in riddles. Her smile suggested she was taking pity on him.

'I come from New Zealand. Little country? At the bottom of the world?'

'Oh...of course. I know it. I've seen the *Lord of the Rings* movies. It's very beautiful.'

'It is. What about you, Rafe?'

'What about me?' He was suddenly wary.

'Rafe isn't your *real* name, is it?'

The wariness kicked up a notch. 'What makes you say that?'

'You sounded like you were going to say something else when you introduced yourself, that's all. Do you have a weird name or something?' That cheeky grin flashed again. 'Is Rafe short for Raphael?'

Relief that he hadn't been unexpectedly recognised made him chuckle. 'Um...something like that.'

'Rafe it is, then. Are *you* Italian?'

'No.'

'How come you speak English with a funny accent, then?'

He had to laugh again. 'I'm European. I speak several languages. My accent is never perfect.'

'It's actually pretty good.' The concession felt like high praise. 'Are you here on holiday?'

'Yes. You?'

'No, I'm working. I'm doing my OE.'

'Oh-ee?' The word was unfamiliar.

'Overseas Experience. It's a rite of passage for young New Zealanders.'

'Oh...and is it something you have to do alone?'

'Not necessarily.'

'But *you* are doing it alone?'

'Yep.' Her tone suggested she wouldn't welcome any further questions about her personal life. 'Oh, look—civilisation.'

Sure enough, they had reached the outskirts of the mountain village. There was no real reason to stay with Mika any longer. She had completely recovered and she was safe. But Raoul was enjoying her company now and he had to admit he was curious. Mika was a world away from her homeland and she was alone.

Why?

They walked in silence for a while as they entered the village of Nocelle. Raoul's eye was caught by big terracotta pots with red geraniums beneath a wooden sign hanging from a wrought-iron bar advertising this to be the Santa Croce *ristorante* and bar. Extending an invitation was automatic.

'Can I buy you a coffee or something to eat? I don't know about you, but I'm starving after that hike. We could get a bus down to Positano if it's too dark to use the steps later.'

The invitation had been impulsive—a polite thing for a gentleman to do. It was only after he'd voiced it that Raoul realised how much he actually wanted Mika to agree.

He wanted to offer her food, not just because he was reluctant to give up her company—he wanted to look after her for a little while longer. To recapture that heart-warming sensation of winning the trust of somebody who needed his help although they would have preferred not to accept it.

It was just to make absolutely sure she was okay, of course. Nothing more. Hooking up with any young woman on this trip was an absolute no-no and, besides, he'd never be physically attracted to somebody like Mika. She was a tomboy, possibly the complete opposite to any woman he'd ever invited into his life or his bed—those picture-perfect blondes that knew how to pose for an unexpected photograph. Maybe that explained the fascination.

She was looking almost as wary as she had when he'd offered his hand to help her along the track and suddenly—to his horror—Raoul realised it might be better if she declined the invitation. He could feel the smile on his face freeze as he discreetly tried to pat the pocket on his shorts. He might have enough loose change to cover a bus fare for them both but it was highly unlikely that he could pay for a meal.

He was still smiling but Mika seemed to be reading his mind. A furrow appeared on her forehead.

'Your wallet *was* in your backpack, wasn't it? You don't have any money, do you?'

'Ah…'

'What about your passport? And do you even have a place to stay?'

'Um…' The echo of the 'I told you so' vibe that he would very much prefer to avoid made him straighten his spine. 'I'll find somewhere.'

He found himself nodding. A short, decisive movement. Maybe this unfortunate occurrence was actually a blessing in disguise. Exactly the kind of challenge he needed to find out what he was made of. Whether he could cope with a bit of genuine adversity.

'Do you have any friends around here?'

The nod morphed into a subtle shake, more of a head tilt, as the question unexpectedly captured Raoul on a deeper level. He'd never lacked for people desperate to be his friends but experience had taught him that it was all too often due to his position in life rather than any genuine personal connection. He was probably as wary of making friends as Mika was about letting someone offer her assistance. Of letting someone touch her. It was impossible to know, in fact, whether he had any real friends at all because he'd never been in this position before.

Being ordinary.

Meeting someone who was judging him on who he *really* was—as a man and not as a prince.

'Doesn't matter. You've got one now.' Mika's face lit up with that impish grin but it faded quickly to a much more serious expression. 'You saved my life, mate.' There was still a gleam in her eyes that didn't match her sombre expression. 'I'm afraid I can't subscribe to the Chinese tradition of becoming your slave for life to rcpay the debt but…' Her face scrunched into lines that suggested serious thought. 'But I can buy you dinner.' The grin flashed again. 'I might even splash out on a cold beer.'

Raoul couldn't take his eyes off Mika. Witnessing the confidence that was returning now that her frightening experience was over was like seeing a butterfly emerge from its chrysalis. The way her expressions changed so quickly, and the lilt of her voice with that unusual accent was enchanting, but perhaps the most extraordinary thing was the effect that smile had on him.

He wanted to see it again. To make her laugh, even…

And she'd declared herself to be his friend. Without having the faintest idea who he really was.

Oddly, that made him feel humble. It gave him a bit of lump in his throat, if he were honest.

'Come on, Raphael.' The pocket rocket that was his newest friend was already heading down the cobbled street towards the arched entrance to the restaurant. 'We'll eat and then we'll figure out what you're going to do. If you're starving, it's impossible to think about anything but food, don't you think?'

'Mmm...' But the lopsided grin—almost a wink— that had accompanied her use of what she thought was his real name made Raoul smile inwardly.

It was a rare experience indeed for him to be teased. He had no siblings, and apparently it hadn't been the done thing for others to tease a prince, even in childhood.

He liked it, he decided.

He liked Mika, too.

CHAPTER TWO

IT WAS ONE of the things that Mika loved about Italian villages—that she could rock up to a place like this, in shorts and a singlet top, probably looking as weary and in need of a shower as she felt, and still be welcomed with a smile and gestures that suggested they had been waiting for her arrival.

The change when Raoul entered the restaurant behind her was subtle but unmistakable. Instead of a welcome guest, Mika suddenly felt like a…*a princess*?

'This way, sir, please; this is the best seat in the house. And you're lucky. You get to catch the last of this magnificent sunset.'

The whole wall of the restaurant was glass and the building seemed to be perched on the side of the mountain. It was the same view they'd had from the top of the Footpath of the Gods, only now the Mediterranean was on fire with red and gold light, and the islands way up the coast were dark, mysterious humps. It was a similar drop over a cliff right beside them, too, with no more than a low, railed fence outside the window and a roof or two of houses well below on the steep slope.

The slight quirk of Rafe's eyebrow along with the expression in those dark eyes was remarkably eloquent.

He wanted to know if she was okay to be sitting, overlooking the drop. He would be more than happy to forgo the view if she wasn't and he would request a change without embarrassing her by referring to her recent disability in public.

It made Mika feel even more like a princess.

No. It made her feel the same way that taking hold of his hand on the track had made her feel.

Protected.

Safe.

She had to clear her throat to get rid of an odd lumpy sensation before she spoke.

'This is gorgeous,' she said. 'Perfect.'

The white linen tablecloth was more of a worry than the view, in fact. Along with the silver cutlery, and the way their host flicked open a huge napkin and let it drape over her bare legs told Mika that this was nothing like the café she currently worked in. Was it going to be horrendously expensive? She remembered those nice boots Rafe was wearing. How well he spoke English when his accent advertised that it wasn't his first language. How the *maître d'* had instantly recognised somebody that deserved respect. Mika suspected that Rafe had come from a far more privileged background than hers. He was probably quite used to eating in restaurants that had linen tablecloths and silver cutlery.

Thank goodness she'd been paid yesterday.

'I will bring you the menu,' the *maître d'* said, reaching out to light the candle on their table. 'For drinks, also? We have a wide selection of the finest wines.'

It was Mika's turn to raise an eyebrow in Rafe's direction. At least, that was what she intended to do, but as soon as her gaze met his she completely forgot and found herself smiling instead. Was he as amused by this as she was? Here they were, looking like scruffy tourists, and they were being offered a selection of the finest wines.

'A glass of your house red, perhaps,' Rafe said.

'I'll have a beer, please,' Mika added. 'A really cold lager.'

With a nod, their waiter turned away. Mika glanced back at Rafe and this time her eyebrows did rise. He looked as though he was assessing something important. Something to do with herself? His face looked quite serious as he turned his head.

'Excuse me,' he called. 'I've changed my mind. Can you bring me a beer, too, please?'

It was a bit silly to feel so pleased about a simple change of drinks but it was as if Rafe was sealing their friendship in some way. Telling her that he liked her choice and was prepared to follow it.

She liked him, she decided. It was a bit disconcerting that merely his presence could alter an atmosphere in a room, as if he had an aura of some invisible power, but she didn't feel threatened by him in any way. Quite the opposite—and that was probably as disconcerting as how ridiculously good-looking that glow from the sunset through the window was making him seem.

Nobody was *that* perfect.

To cover the tumble of thoughts she had no intention of exploring, Mika opened her bag to take out her camera.

'I've got to get a photo of this sunset,' she told Rafe. 'How stunning is that?'

'It's amazing,' he agreed. 'I bet we could see as far as Capri in the day time.'

Mika wished she'd read more of the instruction booklet for her camera last night. She had to hope the settings were appropriate for the level of contrast out there.

'Nice camera,' Rafe said when she'd finished snapping.

'I know.' Mika sighed happily. 'It's a Nikon D4. Sixteen-point-two megapixels. It's my new baby,' she added quietly. 'I've been waiting a long time for this.' The first step to a new career. A new life.

'You're keen on photography?'

'Mmm.' Mika was scrolling through the photos she'd just taken. The dream of becoming a travel writer and supplying great photos to accompany her stories was too new and private to share. 'Look...' She tilted the screen of the camera towards Rafe. 'These are the ones I took of the monastery on the way up the mountain.'

He leaned forward and reached out to hold the other side of the camera as she kept scrolling.

'These are great. I just stopped long enough to look at the view but you've captured so much more. That close-up of the stonework in the arch... And that hand-painted sign: *Convento San Domenico,*' he read aloud. '*Sentiero Degli Dei.*'

'Ah...you've walked our famous path.' The waiter delivered tall, frosty glasses filled with amber liquid. '*Sentiero Degli Dei*—Footpath of the Gods. It is beautiful, isn't it?'

'An experience I will remember for ever,' Mika answered truthfully.

Was the touch of Rafe's foot against hers under the table accidental? No. Judging by the gleam of mirth in his eyes, he was sharing a private understanding that the experience was not what the waiter might be assuming. It had been the lightest of touches…how come she could feel it all the way up her leg? Into an almost forgotten spot deep in her belly, even.

Mika put her camera down to pick up the menu that had come with the drinks. 'At least I got some good photos before it hit me. And I have my notes.'

'You took notes? What kind of notes?'

Oh, help… Mika had spotted the prices beside some of the dishes, like the *pesce del giorno*. Had they sent out their own boat to select the best fish the Mediterranean had to offer?

'Um, oh, interesting things. Like, there's a bit of confusion over whether that's a monastery or a convent. The church, *Santa Maria a Castro*, was there first. It was donated to the Dominican Friars in 1599 and they were the ones who built the convent. And…um…' She turned a page in the menu, distracted by the rumbling in her stomach. 'What are you going to have to eat?'

'Do you like pizza?'

'Of course.' Mika bit her lip. Did he really want to eat street food when there was so much more on offer? Or was he choosing the least expensive option because she had revealed too much when she'd said she'd waited a long time to get her flash camera? Had he guessed that she'd had to put so much effort into saving up for it? She could feel herself prickling defensively. She didn't need looking after financially. She didn't need looking after at all, in fact. Today had been an anomaly and it wasn't going to happen again.

'It goes with beer,' Rafe said smoothly. 'And they're usually so big I don't think I could eat one on my own.' He shrugged. 'I just thought that maybe we could share. How about this one? It's got wild mushrooms, asparagus, caramelised onion and *scamorza*. Do you know what *scamorza* is?'

'It's a cheese. Similar to mozzarella.'

'Sounds delicious.'

It did. And suddenly it was what Mika wanted to eat more than anything else on the menu. That the shared meal would be so affordable was merely a bonus.

Were they being watched by the staff? That might explain why—despite other tables being occupied—Rafe only had to glance up to have the waiter coming to take their order. But Mika couldn't help the feeling that this man was used to having control of his life. That he was one of that golden breed of people for whom things happened easily.

He had a problem now, though, didn't he?

He'd lost everything, she reminded herself.

And it was *her* fault.

Raoul could feel himself relaxing.

There'd been a moment when he'd thought the game was up because the *maître d'* had recognised him when he'd followed Mika into this small restaurant, but it seemed that it had simply been deference to his being Mika's male companion—an outdated assumption that he was in charge?

Whatever. It wasn't lost on Raoul that being in Mika's company, with people assuming they were a couple, was actually a layer of going incognito that he could never achieve on his own. Not that he would ever use someone like that, but it was an unexpected bonus. Like her company. Not only was she so easy to talk to, but every new snippet he was learning about her was adding to an impression that he was with a rather extraordinary person.

He didn't even have to say anything to communicate with her. Just a glance from those dark eyes, that seemed too big for the small face that framed them, had been enough to answer his concern that she might not want to sit beside a window that looked out over the kind of drop that had triggered her vertigo. The deliberate nudge of her foot had rewarded him with another glance and that one had cemented a bond. They were the only people in the world who knew about Mika's unfortunate experience up on that mountain track and it was going to stay that way. As far as anyone else was concerned, the journey would be memorable for ever because of the extraordinary view or the accomplishment of a not inconsiderable physical challenge.

How often did you find somebody that you could communicate with like that?

He'd seen it—between people like his grandparents, for instance—but they'd been together for decades and adored each other.

He and Mika were complete strangers.

Although, that strangeness was wearing off with every passing minute as he got to know more about her.

He'd glimpsed a dream by the way she handled that camera and a note in her voice when she'd told him that owning it had been a long time coming. Was she planning a new career as a photographer, perhaps? He already knew how determined she was by the way she'd handled her desperation at being in the clutches of vertigo, so he was quite confident that she would find a way to achieve any dreams she had.

Weirdly, it made him feel proud of her...

He'd also seen her pride. He'd deliberately searched for the least expensive item on the menu because it was obvious that Mika didn't have unlimited funds. He'd picked up on that, when she'd said she had waited a long time to own that precious camera, as easily as he'd been able to absorb communication from a glance. And he'd seen the way she'd reacted. It had reminded him of that curious little creature he'd come across for the first time when he'd been at his English boarding school— a hedgehog that curled itself into a ball to protect itself so that all you could see were prickles.

But Mika had relaxed again now. And she could *eat*... There was real pleasure to be found in the company of a female who actually tackled food like a boy. There was no picking at a low-calorie salad for Mika. She was attacking her big slices of pizza with so much enthusiasm, she had a big streak of tomato sauce on one cheek.

This was so different from anything he'd ever experienced. The only note of familiarity was the offer of the best table the restaurant had to offer—and another table would have been found, of course, for the discreet security personnel who were never far away. Photographers would have been shut outside for the moment but his female companion would have excused herself possibly more than once, to make sure she was ready for them later, to touch up her make-up and check that there were no stains on the figure-hugging evening gown she was wearing.

Imagining any of those elegant women he'd dined

with in the past with food on her face made it virtually impossible to hide a smile. Raoul also had to resist the urge to reach out and wipe it clean with his napkin. Or maybe just his thumb. He could imagine how the prickles would appear again if he did, though. He already knew Mika quite well enough to know that she would not appreciate being treated like a child.

'It's good, isn't it?'

'*So* good.' Mika eyed the remaining slices of the pizza but reached for her beer first. She frowned at Raoul when she put her glass down. 'What's funny?'

The smile had escaped. 'You've got a moustache.'

'Oh…' With the back of her hand, Mika erased the foam above her lip. The gesture captured the streak of tomato sauce as well. 'Better?'

'Mmm.' But Raoul was still smiling. He'd never sat a table with a woman who would use her hand rather than a napkin and it was quite possible he'd never enjoyed a meal quite this much, either.

'Tell me more about this OE you're on… Do you have an itinerary?'

'Not really. I find a place and a job and work until I've saved enough to go somewhere else. I'll be here for a while longer after investing in that camera, but it's a good job and I love it here, so that's okay.'

'What's your job?'

'I'm in hospo.'

Raoul blinked. Maybe his English wasn't as good as he'd thought. It took only as long as that blink for Mika to realise his lack of comprehension and rescue him.

'Hospitality. I'm a waitress in a café down in Positano.'

'And that's a good job?'

'It is when you're travelling. It's easy to get work and nobody's too bothered about permits or anything. You can get paid in cash, too. It's what most people do on their OE. Part of the rite of passage, even. Everybody should work in hospo at least once.'

'Why?'

'Because it changes the way you see the world. You get to see the best and worst of people in ways you wouldn't believe. And it changes how you see people who work in the kind of jobs that usually make them invisible—you know what I mean?'

Raoul nodded slowly but his interest had been piqued. How many people were there in his world that quietly came and went, making life easier for himself and his family? Advisors and bodyguards. Cooks and cleaners. He'd never served anyone so he had no idea what life would look like from that kind of perspective. He was ashamed to realise he hadn't even given it much thought.

Until now…

So that kind of job could change the way you saw the world… Was that what *he* needed to do?

There was only one slice of pizza left.

'You have it,' Raoul said.

'No, it's all yours. You're a boy. You need to eat more.'

'How about we go halves?'

Mika's face lit up. 'Okay.' She tore the big triangle into two pieces and then eyed them up.

'That one is bigger,' Raoul pointed out. 'You have it.'

Mika hesitated for a moment then she picked up the larger piece and took a big bite out of it before putting it down again.

Raoul snorted with laughter. 'Okay, now they're the same. I choose this one.' He picked up the piece that now had a semicircle of tooth marks where the point of the triangle had been, his hand grazing hers as it passed. Or maybe it hadn't actually touched her skin—it just felt like it had—because she didn't move hers further away. His gaze met Mika's over the slice as he bit into it...and there it was again...

That feeling of a connection he'd never felt before.

Was this what having a real friend was like?

Oddly, it was as exciting as that first flutter of physical attraction could be.

Mika washed down the last of her pizza with the last swallow of her beer. She sighed with contentment and then leaned back in her chair.

'Right, mister. What are we going to do with you?'

The expression on her face was a mix of concern and a determination to fix things. She was fiddling with the charm on her necklace in a way that suggested it was an automatic accompaniment to a process of deep thought.

The irony wasn't lost on Raoul.

'Why do you wear a dolphin charm?'

Mika's fingers stilled. She was staring at him with those huge eyes and Raoul felt that he'd stepped over a boundary of some kind. He'd asked a question that had personal significance and, right now, she was weighing up whether or not to trust him with an honest response.

'It's a symbol,' she finally said softly. 'Of being wild and free. And...and happy.'

The wistful note in her voice went straight to Raoul's heart and struck a very unexpected chord.

Mika was searching for happiness, as everybody

did, but she was already almost as wild and free as one of the beautiful creatures his homeland had been named for. She didn't have to step into a life that was pretty much set in stone—a life that meant personal happiness was unimportant compared to the greater good. If happiness was there, as it had been for most of his life, it was a bonus.

Raoul envied her. Okay, there was a twinge of sympathy that she hadn't yet found her ultimate happiness, but she was free to create it. To go anywhere and do anything that might help her reach her goal.

As if she knew she might have revealed too much, Mika lifted her hand away from the charm and pushed her fingers through her already spiky hair.

'What are you going to do?' she asked bluntly. 'I can't go home and leave you out on the streets. Not when it's my fault you're in this predicament.'

'What would you do, if you were me?'

She probably didn't notice that her fingers strayed back to the dolphin charm. 'I guess I'd find somewhere to stay and then I'd find a job. If you can get one like mine, you get at least one meal a day thrown in as well. It all helps.'

Raoul nodded. Something was falling into place in his head. Impressions and ideas that had been accumulating over the course of this dinner. He'd set out on this private journey to learn about himself but what if he was approaching his quest from the wrong angle? What if he actually needed to learn about *other* people? The invisible kind, like those in service? Or the individuals amongst a mass like the people he would very soon be ruling?

He could get himself out of his predicament with a simple phone call.

Or, he could embrace his situation by deciding that fate had provided an opportunity that would have been unthinkable even a few hours ago. He could see if he had the personal fortitude to face being homeless. Penniless and without even the prospect of a job. How many of his own people had faced a challenge like this at some time in their lives?

He'd been silent for so long that Mika was chewing her lip and frowning, as if she was trying to solve the problem of world peace rather than his own immediate future.

'Have you ever worked in hospo?'

He shook his head. 'Never.'

'Oh…it's just that our café is really busy with the start of the high season. I reckon you could get a job there too.'

'I could try.'

'You wouldn't cope if you've never done it before. With no experience, probably the only job you'd get would be washing dishes.' Her eyes widened. 'The dishie we've got was talking about moving on yesterday. I'll bet Marco hasn't found a replacement yet.'

Washing dishes. Had he *ever* had to wash dishes? Meals away from his residential apartment at university had always been in restaurants, like meals away from the mess during his time with the military. As for the palace…he hadn't even been near the kitchens since he'd been a small child in search of an extra treat.

Dishwashing was possibly one of the most ordinary jobs there was out here in the real world. And wasn't 'ordinary' exactly what he'd set out to be in this time away from his real world?

'I... I wouldn't mind washing dishes.'

Mika's nod was solemn. It was her turn to be silent for a while now. At last she spoke, and he could see by the way her throat moved as she swallowed first that she was making a huge effort.

'I owe you one, Rafe...for today. There's a couch in my room that you can sleep on tonight...as long as...'

She wouldn't meet his gaze. There was something important that she didn't want to say. Something about her body language reminded him of the hedge-hog again. She was poised to curl into a ball to protect herself. With a flash, he realised what it could be and the thought was horrific. Had she been hurt by a man? Did that explain the way she'd reacted when he'd touched her? How hesitant she'd been to take his hand even when she'd been desperate?

'Mika...' He waited until she looked up and, yes, he could see uncertainty. It wasn't fear, exactly, because there was a fierceness that told him she was well prac-tised in defending herself. But she was clearly offering him something that was well out of her comfort zone.

He resisted the urge to touch her hand. Eye contact was more than enough, and even that he kept as gentle as he could. 'We're friends now, yes?'

Mika nodded but she wasn't quite meeting his gaze.

'You're safe with me. I give you my word.'

She looked straight at him, then, and for a heart-beat, and then another, she held his gaze, as if she was searching for confirmation that his word was trust-worthy.

That she found what she was looking for was revealed by no more than a softening of her face but Raoul could feel the gift of her trust as if it was solid enough to hold in his hands.

His vow was equally silent.

He would not drop that gift and break it.

CHAPTER THREE

WHO KNEW THAT military training would end up being so useful in the daily life of an ordinary person?

It meant that Raoul de Poitier was conditioned well enough that yesterday's strenuous exercise had been no more than a good workout. It also meant that he'd been able to sleep on a lumpy old couch that was actually a lot more comfortable than sleeping on the ground.

He'd tapped into a bit of initiative in making the best use of available resources, too. Mika had a laptop computer and he'd borrowed it for long enough to send an email to his grandmother to let her know he was safe but not to expect to hear from him for a little while.

Mika had been busy with her technology for a while after that, downloading photographs she had taken that day, her busy tapping suggesting she was adding notes to the images. Her frequent glances away from the screen told him that she wasn't entirely comfortable having him share this small space; the idea to turn the couch around so that the back of it faced into the small room came to him in a flash of inspiration. The effect of the change had been to create the illusion of a wall and, once he was lying down—with his legs bent and his knees propped on the wall—he couldn't see Mika in the single bed that was only a few feet away. Any tension ebbed as it became apparent that the arrangement would give her more privacy as she worked and then slept.

The bathroom facilities were shared with all the other occupants of the rooms on that floor of the old boarding house. That had been more of a shock than Raoul had expected after a lifetime of a sparkling clean, private *en suite* bathroom always having been available but, on the plus side, there was no queue at this early hour of the morning.

Mika wasn't due to start her shift in the café until eight a.m. but it opened at six a.m. and she was taking him in to meet the owner, Marco, in the hope that there might be some work available for a new dishwasher. She'd used the bathroom first and came out in her uniform of a short black skirt and a fitted short-sleeved black shirt. It was an outfit designed to cloak a member of the army of invisible people and, when Mika tied on a pretty white apron with a frill around its edge, he realised the uniform was probably also intended to make her look demure.

The shirt certainly covered the tattoo on her arm but Raoul doubted that anything would make Mika look demure—not with that aura of feistiness, combined with the impression of intelligence that one glance at her face was enough to discern.

'It's a horrible job,' she warned Raoul. 'A dishie has to be a food-hand as well and help with the food prep to start the day, with jobs like chopping onions and making sauce, and then he has to keep up with all the dishes as soon as service starts, and that's not easy.'

'I'm sure I could get up to speed.' How hard could it

be to do such menial work? This was the twenty-first century. Even a small establishment would have commercial dishwashing machines, surely?

Mika turned a corner as they headed downhill towards the beach. They walked past a series of shops still shuttered and sleeping in the soft light of a new day.

'Dishies get yelled at by the chefs if they get behind,' Mika continued. 'The waitresses hate finding they've suddenly run out of cutlery or something and the *barista* will have a tantrum if he runs out of coffee cups.'

'Who's in charge?'

Mika looked up to grin at him. 'Marco *thinks* he is but everybody has to keep the head chef happy. A dishie is right at the bottom of the pecking order, though. He has to keep *everybody* happy.'

Raoul wondered where the waitresses fitted into the pecking order. He would do his best to keep Mika happy if he got this job.

It was a surprise to realise how much he *wanted* to get this job. It wasn't simply the opportunity of gaining a different perspective on life   the idea of it was beginning to tap into a yearning that went way back.

Didn't every kid dream of being invisible at some time? And maybe that fantasy had more meaning to those who grew up under a very public spotlight. He would be visible to the people he worked with here, of course, but it felt like he would be stepping into an alternative reality. Nobody who knew him would expect to see him in this kind of work and that would be enough to make him blend into the background, even if they took notice of the people who spent their lives in service of some kind.

'Here it is.' Mika began to cross the cobbled street to a shop front that had canvas awnings over the footpath. The name of the café was printed on the dark terracotta canvas in big, white, cursive letters—*Pane Quotidiano*—the 'Daily Bread'.

A short, middle-aged man with a long, white apron tied around an ample waist was lifting wrought-iron chairs from a stack to position around small tables. '*Buongiorno*, Marco.'

'*Buongiorno,* Mika. Why are you so early?'

'I've brought a friend—Rafe. He needs a job. Is Pierre still here?'

Marco threw his hands in the air and his huff of breath was exasperated. 'He walked out yesterday, would you believe? Demanded his money and that was that.' Raoul was receiving a shrewd glance. 'You got any experience?'

'I learn fast,' Raoul replied in Italian—the language Mika was speaking with impressive fluency. 'Try me.'

Marco had his hands on his hips now as he assessed Raoul.

'He speaks English,' Mika put in.

'And French,' Raoul added. And Dauphinesque, but that was hardly likely to be useful to the majority of tourists this café served, and he had no intention of giving anybody such a clue to his nationality.

'Makes no difference.' Marco shrugged. 'All he needs to know is how to follow orders and work hard.'

'Try me,' Raoul said again. He should probably have added 'please' but, curiously, it rankled that he was being assessed and possibly found wanting. Not something he was used to, that was for sure.

'One day,' Marco said grudgingly. 'You do a good job, I will hire you. Mess up and you won't get paid for today.'

A glance at Mika gave him another one of those lightning-fast, telepathic messages. This was a good deal and, if he wanted the job, he'd better grab the opportunity.

Marco was clearly confident he had an extra set of hands for the day, at least.

'Finish putting these chairs out,' he told Raoul. 'And then come back into the kitchen. Mika? Seeing as you're here so early, make me a coffee.'

'One macchiato coming right up.' Mika didn't seem bothered by the crisp order. She was looking delighted, in fact, by the way this job interview had panned out. She gave Raoul a quick thumbs-up sign as she disappeared into the café behind her boss.

His boss, too, if he could prove himself today. Raoul lifted a couple of the heavy chairs and carried them to the table on the far side of the outdoor area. As he went back for more, he caught sight of himself in the windows that hadn't yet been folded back to open up the café to catch the breeze and what he saw made him catch his breath and look again.

He'd had to comb his hair with his fingers this morning so it was more tousled than he'd ever seen before. He'd rinsed out his only set of clothes and hung them over the tiny line outside the window of Mika's room, so they were clean enough, but so wrinkled it looked as if he'd slept in them for a week. He'd noticed that the stubble on his jaw had felt a lot smoother yesterday but now he could see that it was beginning to look like a proper beard.

Nobody was going to recognise him. He barely recognised himself.

He wasn't a prince here. Nobody had even asked him for a surname. He was just an ordinary guy called Rafe. And Rafe was on the way to finding his first paid employment.

Maybe he was delighted as well.

The trickle of breakfast customers had grown into a steady stream of holiday makers who preferred a relaxed brunch. Mika's section today covered all the street tables so she had the added hazard of stepping around dogs lying by their owners' chairs as she delivered plates of hot food or trays laden with coffee orders. Tables were being taken as soon as people stood up to leave so they had to be wiped down fast, and a new carafe of chilled water along with glasses provided.

She was almost too busy to wonder how Rafe was coping out the back but he entered her thoughts every time she cleared a table, being careful to scrape the plates and put all the cutlery on the top. Carrying the piles to the kitchen, she found herself scanning shelves to see where they were running low on supplies.

'We're going to need more water glasses soon. And don't forget the lemon slices and sprigs of mint in the carafes.'

'Okay.' Rafe had a huge apron on and a dish brush in his hand. He started to push a pile of plates further towards the sinks so that Mika had room to put hers down.

'Careful…' Without thinking, Mika caught his hand.

'Margaret's left cutlery between the plates. That whole pile could topple and smash on the floor.' She could feel the heat of his skin beneath her fingers. Had it been soaking in hot water for too long to feel as if it was burning her? Hastily, she pulled her hand away and scooped up the knives and forks on her top plate to put them into the big, sudsy bucket on the floor. Pierre, the last dish-washer, had trained her not to drop them too fast and splash his legs.

'Thanks.' Rafe cast an eye over his shoulder and lowered his voice. 'I don't want to annoy him again. He had to show me how to run the dishwasher twice.'

Mika smiled. 'Gianni's bark is worse than his bite. He's a pretty good chef.'

'*Service…* Table eight.'

'Oh, that's me…' Mika turned swiftly, uncomfortably aware that she'd been distracted. 'Behind,' she called in warning on her way to the pass, as one of the other waitresses backed through the swing door with another tray of dirty dishes. Would she have room to dump them on the bench? Rafe was going to have to work faster if he wanted to get this job. He might not even get a break, at the rate he was going.

There were plenty of water glasses on the shelf the next time she settled new customers and every carafe was decorated with mint and lemon. This was good. Rafe hadn't been exaggerating when he'd promised Marco that he was a fast learner. Mika delivered another tray of coffees to the table where her boss was sitting—as usual—with a couple of his mates, right on the footpath, so he could greet anyone else he knew and keep an eye on how the whole café was functioning. If things got really crazy, he would pitch in to help, or sometimes he would just wander around to check that everybody was enjoying their time in Positano's best café. He had the best job, which was fair enough, given that he was the owner of the establishment.

Poor Rafe had the worst job but he seemed to be managing. Mika stopped worrying about him as the day sped on. It wasn't her problem if he didn't like the work or didn't get offered a paid job, was it? She'd repaid her debt by giving him dinner and a place to stay last night. Finding him work was just a bonus.

Except...

She liked him. And she liked having him around. Instead of grumpy Pierre, whom she had to be careful not to splash, she could look forward to a smile every time she carried dirty dishes out the back.

It was growing on her, that smile.

The other waitresses must be getting smiled at too, she decided. There was a faint undercurrent of something different amongst her colleagues today. They seemed to be putting more effort into being charming with the customers. Was it her imagination or was Margaret, the English girl who was here to improve her Italian, making more frequent trips to the kitchen than usual? She'd spotted Bianca reapplying her lipstick more than once and Alain, the gay barista, had even gone to collect clean coffee cups himself instead of calling for one of the waitresses to do it.

No surprises there. Hospitality workers were usually young, travelling and eager for any fun that came their way. Rafe was new.

And gorgeous...

It was his eyes even more than that smile. The warmth in them. And that wicked gleam of humour.

Would she ever forget the way he'd looked at her over that slice of pizza that she'd already taken the huge bite out of? It had been a silly joke but he'd bought right into it and for a heartbeat, as she'd been caught in his gaze, she'd felt like she'd known him for ever.

Like he was her best friend. Or the brother she'd never had.

'Sorry?' Mika had to scrabble to retrieve her pad from the pocket of her apron. She pulled her pencil from behind her ear. 'Was that one seafood risotto?'

'Two.' The customer glared at her. 'And the linguine with lobster. And side salads. And we need some more water.'

'No problem. Coming right up.'

Mika stepped over a sleeping poodle, dodged a small child and turned sideways to give Margaret room to carry a tray past her.

'Thanks, hon.'

Margaret had a nice smile, too. And long blonde hair. And legs that went on for ever under that short skirt.

Mika ducked into the kitchen to put the order for table six under the rail above the grill. She glanced sideways to see Rafe scraping plates into the rubbish bucket. He had promised that she was safe with him and he certainly hadn't done anything to undermine that promise last night. They were friends. He hadn't given her so much as a glance that might have suggested any kind of attraction and that was exactly what she'd wanted.

So what if he was tempted to hook up with Margaret? Or Bianca? Or even Alain for that matter? It was none of her business and she wasn't bothered.

With a sigh, Mika collected another carafe of water and headed back to table six.

It wasn't completely true, was it?

She *was* bothered.

It was that smile that was doing it. Other people smiled at her and it could make her feel good but there was something about Rafe's smile that made her feel much better than good. It felt like her body was waking up after a long, long sleep and that every cell was tingling in the bright light of a brand new day. She was over-sensitive to the slightest touch, like the way his hand had barely brushed hers in taking that piece of pizza last night. Or the heat of his hand when she'd laid her fingers over the back of it to stop him unbalancing that pile of crockery.

The tingling bordered on being painful. And it was confusing. She didn't *want* to feel this way but there it was. Like that horrible vertigo, it had just appeared from nowhere.

And, now that it was here, she didn't really want it to go away, either. It was making her feel so…alive…

Forty euros.

Raoul stared at the notes in his hand. For more than ten hours of back-breakingly hard work, it was a pittance but, having had no more than enough for a bus fare in his pockets at the start of the day, it looked like a small fortune.

It was a clever ploy of Marco's to give him cash at the end of his day's trial as well as offering him as many shifts as he wanted to take in the café. If he hadn't had actual money in his hand right now, it would be very tempting not to show up tomorrow.

Military training hadn't set him up very well for this particular challenge. His hands felt waterlogged and swollen and he had tiny cuts from not handling the cutlery well enough that would probably sting later. His back ached from so many hours standing and, even though he'd wolfed down a meal when he'd finally been given a break, he was starving again already.

'You did it.' Mika was waiting for him outside the café and her expression made him think of a proud mother collecting her child from their first day at school. 'Go you.'

Suddenly Raoul felt proud of himself, too. 'It was a close call. When I forgot to warn Gianna that I was behind him and he dropped a whole pizza, I thought I was going to get fired on the spot.'

Mika shrugged. 'Worse things happen. Pierre had a huge stack of dishes crash onto the floor and smash when he started.'

'Did he have to pay for them?'

She shook her head. 'If Marco had expected that, he would have lost his worker as well as the dishes. People working in hospo don't usually have that kind of money and employers can't afford to chase them.'

'Why not?'

'It's easy employment. Casual. If we get paid in cash, we don't have to worry about paying tax, and employers can get away with paying less than minimum rates. It works for everyone.'

Raoul was frowning as he walked alongside Mika. Taxes were essential because they paid for things like hospitals and schools but he could understand why having part of an already low wage removed would add insult to injury. What was the minimum acceptable rate to pay people in his own country? And how much tax were they expected to pay?

He should know things like this.

'What's wrong?'

'Nothing…why did you ask?'

'You sighed. It sounded like you had the weight of the whole world on your shoulders.'

'Oh…' He'd have to be a bit careful what he thought about while he was with Mika. 'I'm a bit tired, I guess. It's been quite a long day.'

'I know how to fix that.'

'Oh?' The sound was wary. Considering that Mika had been racing around working just as hard as he had been for the same length of time, she looked remarkably chirpy. Raoul hoped she wasn't going to suggest an evening in a nightclub when he knew that all he would want to do later would be to sleep.

And he might need to find a place to sleep. Mika had only offered him a night on her couch.

'Do your feet hurt? Is your back sore? Have you got a bit of a headache?'

'Ah…yes, yes and yes.'

Raoul was beginning to wonder how long he might have the fortitude to keep it up, in fact. He'd never spent such a concentrated length of time doing such menial tasks. How horrified would his grandmother be if she knew? How astonished would his people be if they found out? In public opinion, it would be beneath his station in life—the work of servants.

But what made *him* so special, other than an accident of birth? Equality was a core value of the constitution of his land. Other people did this kind of work and some did it for their entire working lives. And Mika had worked just as hard today, hadn't she?

She was nodding, as if agreeing with his unspoken thoughts. 'Me too. And I know the cure.'

'Wine?' Raoul suggested hopefully. 'Sleep?'

Mika laughed. 'A swim. It's what I usually do when I have time after work. I collect my bathing suit and jump on a bus to Praiano and go down to my favourite beach. Want to come with me?'

'I don't have a bathing suit.'

'You could just wear your shorts. It would save washing them later.' Mika's head turned, scanning the tourist shops they were passing that were still open. 'You should get another tee shirt, though. Let's have a look.'

Raoul had to stop as well but he shook his head. 'I can't afford a tee shirt. It's my turn to buy dinner tonight and…and I need to find somewhere to stay. I'll need money for that, too.'

'But you've got somewhere to stay.' Mika seemed to have gone very still, her hand touching the rack of tee shirts on the footpath. 'If you don't mind the couch.'

Raoul blinked. 'You want me to stay?'

'I know it's not ideal but it's only for sleeping, and you're only here for a few weeks. I'm either at work or out exploring for the rest of the time. I'm happy to share if you are.'

She was making it sound as if it was fine if he liked the idea but she wouldn't be at all bothered if he decided otherwise. Her attention seemed to be on the shirts as she began to ruffle through them. Her tone and body language didn't quite fit with the flash of something he'd seen in her eyes, though. It wasn't any kind of come-on—she'd made it quite clear she wasn't interested in anything more than friendship—but there was something that made him think she would like him to agree to the plan a lot more than she was letting on.

Was Mika *lonely*…?

Part of him was more than a bit horrified by the idea of continuing to live in one room and share a bathroom with who knew how many other people, but was it because he was spoiled and soft or was it more to do with always having to be over-vigilant as to what others might think? When you lived in the public eye you had to behave perfectly at all times because you never knew if you were under observation by a journalist or the paparazzi. For as long as he could remember, he'd never been able to be impulsive and just do what he happened to feel like doing. Or even let how he was feeling show on his face sometimes.

But now he could. Nobody was watching. If his reluctance stemmed from the fact he was spoiled, it would do him good to toughen up. And if it was because of what others might think, well, there were no rules he had to follow other than his personal morality right now. What would happen if he really let his guard down?

'Maybe one more night? We can talk about it again tomorrow. Right now, I love your idea of a swim.'

Mika nodded. 'Stay here. Buy a tee shirt and maybe some shorts to swim in. Look, this might help…' She put her hand in her pocket and when it came out she was holding a small handful of gold-rimmed silver coins. 'I always put all my tips in the communal jar but…' Her shrug made light of any residual guilt. 'I thought we might have something to celebrate tonight.'

'No way.' Raoul put his hand over Mika's to close her fingers firmly around the coins. Such a small hand. He liked the way his could enclose it completely. 'You earned that. You keep it.' His voice was stern. 'You've got to stop paying for things for me, okay? I'm beginning to feel like a gigolo.'

Mika was smiling as she pulled her hand free and put the coins back in her pocket, but she avoided meeting his gaze, and Raoul gave himself a mental shake. Gigolos were rewarded for services that he had no intention of offering, and that would be the last thing Mika wanted anyway.

'I'll be back in ten minutes.' Mika was already walking away from him and it felt like a rebuke. Perhaps even a subtle reference to sex was dodgy territory that he needed to steer well clear of. 'Happy shopping.'

A gigolo?

With those looks and that charm, there would probably be any number of rich older woman who would be happy to have Rafe at their beck and call. While Mika knew that the comment had been no more than a joke, it had sexual connotations that had put her well out of her comfort zone.

Had she turned into some kind of prude in the last few years?

Or was it because it was Rafe who had said it and that was tapping into feelings she wasn't sure how to deal with yet?

And why had she been so quick to renew the offer of having him sleep on her couch? Did she want that painful prickle of awareness to get worse? Was she trying to test herself in some way?

Maybe she was but it wasn't something she wanted to think about because, if she did, she'd find somewhere to hide. She could find the concierge of this boarding house, perhaps, and see if there was an empty room that Rafe could rent.

Tomorrow would be soon enough for that. Right now, she needed to hurry, to change out of her uniform and put her bikini on under her favourite shorts and singlet top. She swapped her soft, black tennis shoes for lightweight sandals and draped her towel over her arm. With her camera hanging from her shoulder, she was ready to go and find Rafe.

She'd made this trip for a swim after work many times already but how much better was it to have company?

Company that was now wearing a huge white tee shirt with *I heart Positano* emblazoned on the front. Rafe didn't look the least bit embarrassed to be wearing it.

'It was on the sale rack,' he told her. 'An absolute bargain.'

'Mmm…' Mika's lips twitched. 'Fair enough. I heart Positano, too. Oh…there's our bus down the road. We'll have to run.'

The bus was crowded and they had to stand but the journey was short enough for it not to matter. Mika led him down the cobbled alleyways in the heart of Praiano and many steps that led down to a beach that had no sand. There were rows of sun loungers to hire, like on every European beach, but they were on a huge, flagged terrace, and further back there were tables and chairs spilling out from a beachside café. Rock music was also spilling out and the place was crowded with young people.

Mika made a beeline for a couple of empty loungers and she put her camera on one and covered it with her towel. Then she kicked off her sandals and peeled her singlet top off. Taking her shorts off in front of Rafe gave her an odd feeling, as though something had thumped her painlessly in her belly. A sideways glance showed that he wasn't taking any notice, however. He was too busy pulling off his new tee shirt. The sight of all that bare skin created ripples from the thumping sensation that felt like small electric shocks. It sent Mika swiftly to the edge of the terrace where she could dive straight into the deep, cool water.

The sea had always been her ultimate comfort zone. It was her place of choice to unwind and to think clearly, and it was definitely the best place to burn off angst of any kind, whether it was emotional, physical or—like now—possibly a combination of both.

She knew Rafe had dived in right behind her but Mika wasn't here to float around or play, like most of the other young couples in the water. She set out for the pontoon that was moored a hundred metres or so offshore. And when she became aware that Rafe was keeping pace, she doubled her efforts. This was a race she knew she could win.

'Where did you learn to swim like that?'

The words were hard to get out because Raoul was unexpectedly out-of-breath by the time he heaved himself up onto the pontoon. Mika was already sitting on the edge, her feet just touching the water.

'My mother always said I had dolphin blood.' Mika

didn't seem at all out of breath. 'I grew up by the sea and apparently I could swim even before I could walk properly.'

Raoul smiled, liking that idea. Yes…there was something about Mika that reminded him of the creatures his homeland was named for. Confident and a little bit cheeky. Graceful… He'd seen Mika moving around the café today, twisting and turning her body to ease through small spaces or avoid obstacles. Friendly but still wild. Yes, you could touch them sometimes, but it was an honour to be allowed to do so.

They were both sitting on the edge of the pontoon, facing the shore, where they could see the crowd in the popular bar growing. They could still hear the music from here and it was a quieter number—a folk song that was wistful enough almost to create a sensation of yearning…

A need to feel less alone by connecting with another human being…

'I don't remember my mother very well,' Raoul said quietly. 'She died, along with my father, in a plane crash when I was only five.'

People were always shocked that he'd been orphaned so early but the glance Mika gave him had no pity in it.

'I wish I'd never known mine very well,' she said. 'Maybe it wouldn't have hurt so much when she abandoned me.'

Raoul was definitely shocked. '*Abandoned* you? How?'

'She took me into the city for the day. Put me in the play area of a big department store and just never came back.'

'How old were you?'

'I was five, too. I'd just started school.'

Wow... To have lost a parent at such a vulnerable age was something that he'd never found he had in common with anyone. Ever. Even now, he could remember how lost he'd felt. How empty his world had suddenly become.

Had Mika had loving grandparents to fill such an appalling void? A small army of kind nannies, tutors and so many others, like cooks and gardeners, who would go out of their way every day to make a small, orphaned prince feel special?

'What happened? Who looked after you?'

'The police were called. I got put in the hands of the social welfare people and they found a foster home.'

'Did the police find your mother?'

'Oh...eventually. She turned up dead about ten years later. Drug overdose. Maybe she thought she was doing me a favour by shutting me out of her life.'

'What about your father?'

'Don't have one. My mother never told me anything about him other than that he was Scottish. A backpacker she'd met in a bar somewhere. I have no way of tracing him. No idea of where I came from, really.'

'I'm sorry...'

'Don't be. It has a good side. I'm as free as a bird. Or a dolphin, maybe. I can't imagine living away from the sea. I had to do that in a couple of foster homes and I hated the cities.'

Raoul was silent for a long moment. He could trace his family back to the twelfth century when their islands had become a principality. He knew every drop of his bloodline and almost every square mile of the place that was where he came from and where he would always belong.

How lost would someone feel not to have that kind of foundation? Did he really envy the freedom she'd had in comparison to how precisely his own life was mapped out?

Was that what Mika was looking for—a place where she felt she belonged? A life that offered the safety of a real home? How much heartache had been covered by that casual reference to 'a couple of foster homes'? How often had she been passed from home to home? Abandoned again and again?

The sun was low now and Mika's nut-brown skin seemed to have taken on a golden glow as Raoul's silent questions led him to turn his head towards her. Her bikini was white—small scraps of fabric that left very little to the imagination.

It wasn't his imagination that was his undoing, though.

Mika had her hands shading her eyes from the glare of the setting sun so she didn't see him looking at her. She might be tiny, Raoul decided, but she was most definitely perfectly formed. And *real*… It would probably never occur to Mika to make her breasts larger or wear killer heels to make herself look taller and sexier. He couldn't imagine her plastering her face with make-up, either. She didn't need it, with those amazing eyes of hers.

She was…gorgeous.

He'd come to the conclusion that Mika was an extraordinary person within a short time of knowing her and learning about her rough start in life somehow didn't surprise him.

What did surprise him—and not in a good way—was the strength of the attraction he was feeling towards her right now. Had either of them really been aware of how close to each other they were sitting? He would only have to relax his arm a little for their shoulders to touch. He could feel the warmth of her skin just thinking about it.

His hands tightened on the edge of the pontoon as he realised how much he *wanted* to touch Mika. He pressed his lips together to try and stifle the urge to kiss her.

Given the uncanny way they could communicate with no more than a glance, it was unfortunate that Mika chose that moment to lower her hands and turn her head.

For too long, she held his gaze. Too long, because Raoul knew that she was aware of him physically, too. That the attraction might well be mutual.

It couldn't happen. Not when, in a matter of a few short weeks, he had to step back into his real life and prepare to marry the woman he'd been promised to for almost as long as he could remember. The engagement was about to become official, which had to put an end to any sexual adventures, and surely he'd had enough over the years, anyway?

He'd never known anybody like Mika, though, had he?

Maybe being homeless and poor wasn't going to be the ultimate challenge that would tell him whether he could be the ruler his people deserved. Perhaps *this* was going to be the biggest test. Could he put aside his personal desires in order to do what he knew was the right thing to do?

It would be shameful if he couldn't.

The tumble of his thoughts took no longer than the shared glance. It was Mika who broke the eye contact, and she did it so abruptly, Raoul was left wondering if he'd imagined what he thought he'd seen. Or had she been shocked by what *she'd* seen?

'Hot chips,' she said.

'What?' The randomness of the words cleared his mind with a jolt.

'Bernie—the guy who runs the bar on the beach. He's English and I think he was in a band that did quite well back in the seventies. He makes the best hot chips I've ever tasted. Everyone comes here for his fish and chips, and I've just realised that I'm absolutely *starving.*' Her grin held all the cheek he was coming to expect from Mika. 'I seem to remember you saying something about it being your turn to buy dinner?'

'I did. And it is.'

'Race you back, then…'

It was a huge relief to sink into the chill of the seawater. As good as a cold shower, in fact.

He could do this, Raoul decided. He could enjoy the company of the first genuine friend he'd ever made without ruining that friendship with sex. That way, Mika wouldn't end up being hurt, and it could be possible that the friendship might never be completely lost. Sure, Mika would get a shock when she found out who he really was, but by then maybe she would know him well enough to understand and forgive the deception.

This feeling of connection to another person was too special to lose.

Raoul had a distinct feeling that he might never experience it again.

CHAPTER FOUR

HAD SHE IMAGINED it?

That buzz of physical awareness she'd seen in Rafe's eyes when they'd been sitting side by side on the pontoon, in the glow of a sunset, the other night...

Maybe it had just been a product of a combination of things. The gorgeous sunset, how relaxed a swim in the sea could make you feel after a long, hard day at work, and the fact that they were both as close to naked as public decency allowed. If—for a moment in time—Rafe had fancied her, he had done nothing to confirm any interest since.

And Mika would have noticed the slightest indication because she'd been so nervous about it. Emotionally, she'd run as hard and fast as she could when she thought she'd seen it. She'd tried to wash away the confused jumble of feelings by swimming hard enough to beat Rafe back to the shore, and had kept the conversation deliberately impersonal as they'd eaten the fish and chips that Rafe had declared the best he'd ever tasted after she'd snapped a few photos of the fading sunset and their surroundings. One of Rafe, too, that he hadn't even seen her taking.

He'd been standing watching that sunset—one hand

shading his eyes, the other holding the damp towel he had insisted she used first. His hair had been still wet and drops were landing on his shoulders to trickle onto that bare chest. There'd been something poignant in the way he was staring out to sea and even through the lens of her camera the beauty of this man had been enough to give Mika that curious sensation in her belly again— the thump and the electric tingles of physical attraction.

The action had been instinctive. Something had told her that there could well be a time she'd want to re-member this day and this man who'd stirred these feel-ings she thought she'd lost for ever. It was an action that had taken only a split second and was as private as the reasons she had taken it.

It had been only a momentary blip in the impersonal atmosphere that Mika had been determined to foster as a safety buffer zone, and the tactic had worked so well that it had cemented what seemed to have become a pattern. They did their long shifts at the café, went for a swim after work, ate a meal that they took turns paying for and, by the time they got home after dark, they were both so tired that sleep was essential before another early rise.

Had the tactic worked *too* well?

A couple of days later, Mika realised that her ner-vousness had evaporated. That she had to conclude that she *had* imagined any desire on Rafe's part.

And, if she was really honest, there was a part of her that was…what?…disappointed?

Frustrated, even?

If things had been different—if *she* was different— that moment on the pontoon could have played out in a very different way.

She would have seen that look in Rafe's eyes and fallen into it instead of running away. They would have held that eye contact as they'd slowly closed the distance between them and then…then she would have felt Rafe's lips against her own…

The way she had so many times in those unguarded moments of the last few nights when she'd been slipping into sleep and could hear the sound of Rafe's breathing only a few feet away. The intensity of her body's reaction to the fantasy kiss had been enough to make her think that she'd never wanted anything as much as she wanted Rafe to kiss her.

But it wasn't going to happen, was it? Oh, he still seemed to be enjoying her company. He still smiled just as readily. But there was something different about the way he looked at her. Or *didn't* look at her. Yes, that was it. There was a wariness that hadn't been there before. That connection that she felt when her gaze met his was missing…because he never held her gaze long enough for it to kick in.

Because he was avoiding it?

Had he seen her fear?

Mika's thoughts seemed to be a series of questions that were becoming increasingly unsettling.

Would she react the same way if she had another chance?

Did she *want* another chance?

Part of her seemed to. Otherwise, she wouldn't have had a quiet word with Marco yesterday to ask if Rafe could have the same day off as she had this week. She wouldn't have told him about her plan to explore the valley of the ancient mills in Amalfi and slipped in that casual invitation for him to join her if he had nothing else he wanted to do with his day off.

They wouldn't be here now, standing in the central square of Amalfi beside the cathedral stairs, gazing at the narrow, cobbled streets and trying to decide which one would take them uphill to where they would find the entrance to the valley.

A woman walking a small dog glanced at Rafe and paused. Smiling, she asked if they needed any help.

'Please,' Rafe answered. 'We're looking for the way to the Valley of the Mills.'

'Ah…the *Valle dei Mulini*… Go up the main street here, which leads into *Via Pietro Capuano*…'

Mika was listening to the directions but she was also watching the body language in front of her. Did Rafe know the effect he had on women? Of course he did, she decided. How could he not know?

He could have anyone he chose, couldn't he?

Was it no more than a fantasy that he might choose *her*?

The answer to that was simple. Of course it was. He saw her as a friend, nothing more. And maybe this was the best thing that could have happened for her—the reason why fate had made him appear in her life. She could play with the possibility of something physical developing in her mind, and perhaps that was the step she needed to take so that she would be ready when someone came into her life that she was attracted to—someone who wanted to be with *her*.

Someone other than Rafe…

'Did you get all that?' The woman and her dog were walking away. Rafe's glance was unreadable.

'Yep. Let's go.' Oddly, the excitement of this adventure had faded a little for Mika.

'We go past the paper museum. You want to go there, don't you?'

'Mmm…' Mika was slightly ahead of Rafe now. 'It won't be open yet, though. I'll go on the way back. You don't have to do the museum, though, if they're not your thing.'

They walked in silence until they'd passed the museum and reached a set of steps going uphill. Rafe went ahead of Mika as they climbed the steps and, by the time they'd walked on for a few more minutes, the silence had become awkward.

'Can we stop for a second? I'd like to take a photo of that lemon grove.'

Rafe stopped. He turned and, for the first time in days, Mika found her gaze properly caught.

'Would you rather be doing this by yourself?'

'What? No…of course not.'

'But you want to go to the museum by yourself?'

'No… I…' Mika retrieved the snatch of conversation from her memory. She'd been feeling out of sorts when she'd thrown that comment in. Aware that the next man in her life was not going to be Rafe… 'It's just that some people don't like museums, you know? I don't want to bore you.'

He was still holding her gaze.

'You would never bore me, Mika.'

Oh, help…that connection was still there, wasn't it?

And that look. She could fall into that, if she let herself.

Maybe she couldn't *help* herself falling…

'Same.' Mika felt her heart skip a beat. 'You're…

good company, Rafe.' She had to break the eye contact because she felt suddenly, inexplicably, shy. She pulled her camera out of its case. 'It's…um…really nice to have a friend to do things like this with.'

'But you'd do it on your own if I wasn't here, wouldn't you?'

'I'd have to.' Mika focused on the terraced rows of lemon trees, the fruit glowing goldlike giant gems against the glossy, green foliage. 'But it's better when you have company. Makes it feel… I don't know… more real?'

'Mmm…' Rafe's nod was thoughtful. 'I get that. They say a problem shared is halved. Maybe a pleasure shared is doubled.'

She kept the camera in her hand as they carried on. There was so much pleasure to be found in this walk. They entered the valley into woodlands where the bird calls were the only sound to break the cool silence and the forest floor was a wash of pink from wild cyclamens. The ruins of the ancient paper mills were tall, mossy, concrete structures with haphazard holes where windows had once been, perched beside the river as it tumbled over huge boulders. The drama of one of the waterfalls they passed was enough to make them pause and sit beneath one of the massive old trees for a few minutes.

So much pleasure…and it was definitely doubled by having Rafe's company. More than doubled…

Mika could have simply sat here and soaked it in but she needed more than photographs to record the journey. She pulled her notebook from the pack Rafe had been carrying for her.

'What are you writing?'

'I'm adding to the research I did online. Putting the things I notice in as well. Like how gorgeous that carpet of flowers was under the trees. I won't have room to include every photo I take.'

'Include in what?'

'My article.'

'You're a *writer*? You never told me that.'

'That's because I'm not. Yet...' That very uncharacteristic shyness resurfaced. Mika didn't tell people her dreams. Was that because she didn't have anyone in her life that she wanted to share them with?

'I want to be a travel writer,' she said quietly. 'I'd like to earn my living by doing things like this all the time, instead of working in cafés.'

Rafe looked impressed. But then he frowned. 'You want to spend your whole life travelling? Never settling down anywhere?'

'Oh, I'll settle somewhere. I just don't know where yet. I know it will be near the sea because of my dolphin blood.' Mika smiled, hoping to make light of revealing something so personal. 'And I think it will be somewhere warm, because that way you can spend more time in the sea, but there's a lot of places in the world that fill those requirements—especially round here.' She closed her notebook and slipped it back into the pack. 'I'm killing two birds with one stone, here. When I find the place I want to be for ever, I think I'll know who I really am.'

Did everyone wonder who they really were at some point in their lives, or was this another extraordinary bond that Raoul had just found with Mika?

He wanted to tell her everything at that point. Who

he was and why he was here. He could share his problems and maybe they would be halved.

Except they wouldn't be, would they? Okay, he could imagine that Mika would understand the need to reveal the strongest, most basic, layers of his personality so that he would know he had a foundation that would serve him well for the rest of his life—because wasn't she doing pretty much the same thing? She was searching for a layer he didn't need but one that was even more fundamental—a place where she felt she belonged.

But, if he did tell her the truth, she would realise he didn't belong here, in her world, like this. She might feel that the dream she had shared with him was insignificant in comparison to his future and she might show her prickles again—the way she had, inexplicably, in suggesting that she could go to the paper museum by herself.

And, if the prickles came out, the pleasure of this day would be dimmed and it was too good to spoil. The serenity of the dappled light in this forest had the echoes of a long and proud history in the ruins of the ancient mills but the bubbling river was timeless. A link to the future and a reminder that nothing stayed the same. Life moved on and changed...

He could accept that with a new sense of peacefulness in this moment and it felt really good.

Being with Mika felt really good, too. Maybe it wasn't just their surroundings that made him feel so much closer to embracing his future. There was strength to be found simply in her company and in the way she faced life and made the most of every moment.

The sensation of feeling so close to another person's

soul—as if his own could reach out and take the hand of hers—was a new thing for Raoul. As if he needed to see if it was real, he turned his head, to find Mika looking up at him. Her eyes were very serious but her mouth had the hint of a curve to it, as if she knew how deep his thoughts had been and that he was happy with where they'd taken him.

The need to connect on more than this weird, telepathic level was so strong Raoul could feel his head drifting. Tipping in slow motion until lowering it a little would be all that was needed to kiss Mika.

Did she know how overpowering the pull was? She didn't break the lock of his gaze and he could see a reflection of his own wonderment at how close it was possible to feel to someone else. And then her lips parted and he saw the very tip of her tongue touch her lower lip.

The shaft of desire was painful.

If ever there was a moment to test himself to see whether he could resist this overwhelming temptation, this was it.

Surely a kiss couldn't be such a big deal?

But it wouldn't stop there, would it?

If he wanted it *this* much, even a touch could be dangerous. What if it ignited something so powerful, he lost control of his best intentions? Exposed a weakness that could make him doubt himself even more?

He had to find out if he had the strength it would take to resist this. Closing his eyes helped because it was a shutter against how it made him feel to be holding Mika's gaze.

Forcing himself to move helped even more because he could get to his feet and walk away to put some distance between them. But the effort was draining and a good part of the peace he'd found ebbed as well. When they got home, he decided, he would have to find the concierge and ask about the availability of another room to rent. How could he sleep so close to her without having to fight that particular battle again and again? How many times could he fight it and not weaken to the point of giving in?

He knew Mika was following him but it was some time before he could break the silence.

'How many articles have you done already?'

'A few. I haven't tried to get any published yet, though. I need a really special one to send to the good magazines.'

'Maybe this will be the one?'

'Maybe…' Mika still had her camera out as they finally left the valley behind and came into the small village of Pontone. She stopped to take photographs of the wide, stone archway they walked through that had antique kitchen utensils and old woven baskets hanging from the walls. They found a picturesque café and sat, sheltered from the sun by big umbrellas, amidst barrels of bright flowers with tumblers of chilled home-made lemonade in front of them as they waited for the lunch they ordered.

'I love this,' Mika said, a while later.

'The salad? Me, too.' They had ordered *insalata caprese,* a salad of sliced mozzarella cheese layered with slices of the delicious bright red tomatoes grown locally, drizzled with olive oil and sprinkled with tiny basil leaves. It had come with crusty, just-baked bread and it had to be the most perfect lunch ever.

Mika laughed. 'It's my favourite lunch, but no, I

mean all of this. This part of Italy. It's the closest I've come to feeling that it's my place.'

'Where else have you been?'

'I went to Scotland first, seeing as it's apparently where half my genetic history came from.'

'Ah, yes…you said your father was Scottish.'

'Mmm…'

There was a hint of something sad in her eyes. Something lost. Raoul couldn't remember his father very well, but he knew exactly who he was and what he looked like, and he could remember how important he'd been in his life. Knowing where your place was in the world was inextricably linked with family, wasn't it?

But Mika didn't have family. She was roaming the world in search of a link to something but, clearly, she hadn't found it in the birth place of the father she'd never known.

'You didn't like Scotland?'

Raoul loved the way her face scrunched up to reveal the impression she'd been left with.

'I loved the oldness. And the accent. I even loved the bagpipes but I didn't love the weather. It was too cold and the sea was so wild. I decided you'd have to be a bit mad to swim there so it wasn't ever going to be *my* place.'

'Maybe you need people to make it feel right. When you find your special person, you'll make a family and then the place will be yours. And theirs…for ever.'

Mika shook her head and her voice was quiet. Cold, almost. 'I'm never going to get married.'

'Why not?' The thought of Mika growing old alone was shocking.

But she simply shook her head again—a warning

that the subject was off-limits. 'It's just not going to happen. I've learned that I'm better off on my own.'

How had that lesson been learned? Raoul wondered, in the slightly awkward silence that followed. He wished he hadn't said anything, now, because they'd lost that easy flow of conversation. Could he fix it?

'What about New Zealand?' he asked. 'Doesn't that feel like your place?'

'I love New Zealand, don't get me wrong, but… there's something about the oldness of Europe that calls me.' Mika seemed as relieved as he was to forget that forlorn blip in the conversation and start again. She grinned, as if embarrassed by being fanciful. 'Maybe I lived here in a previous life.'

Maybe she had. Maybe Raoul had, too, and that could explain why he felt like he'd known her for ever. Why they had this extraordinary connection.

'There's still so much of the coastlines to explore, too. It's exciting…' Mika's face lit up. 'I want to go to the south of France. And Spain. And the Greek islands. And Sardinia and Corsica and…' Her hands were tracing a map of the Mediterranean in the air.

'And…' Raoul only just stopped himself adding *Les Iles Dauphins* to her list.

Mika's eyes widened as she waited for him to finish what he'd been about to say.

'And…you will,' he managed. 'You could be anything at all you really wanted to be, Mika, and…and you're going to be the best travel writer. Your passion will make the pages glow and everyone who reads your articles will want to go to those places. To be where you've been.'

He would want that.

She was smiling at him. A soft smile that had nothing of the characteristic cheekiness he had come to expect. This was the smile of someone basking in unexpected encouragement. Of having their dreams become a little more real because someone else believed in them too.

He would want more than to read her articles, Raoul realised. He would want to go to those places *with* Mika, not after her. And he could make it happen, so easily. He could choose almost any place in the world and the means of getting there would be sorted instantly. A helicopter, a luxury yacht, a private jet... There would be comfortable accommodation waiting at the other end, too, and Mika could have all the time she wanted to do the thing she loved doing, without the prospect of having to get back to a mundane job.

But would she want that?

And wouldn't it change how she saw a new place? Earning a day off, as they'd had to, to make this trip possible, made it so much more valuable. Exploring somewhere by having to use public transport and eating at inexpensive restaurants made everything so different.

Maybe Raoul wouldn't want to go back to having the best of everything so easily available. If he had the choice, perhaps he would choose to go to those places with Mika in the same way they'd set off today. On foot, with no more than a bit of spare change to rely on.

This longing for more days like today had nothing to do with the desire to touch Mika physically, although he could still feel that simmering in the glow of her smile. This was about what it was like simply to be in her company. To contribute to Mika's strength to achieve any dream she held…and to feel like he had someone walking alongside him as he achieved his.

Was this what real friendship was about?

…Love?

Was he falling in *love* with Mika?

No. That couldn't be allowed to happen.

They could be friends. Very good friends. But that was all.

Some people were lucky enough to marry their best friends but he wasn't going to be one of them. His future was mapped out and he couldn't imagine Francesca being his best friend.

He barely knew her. Oh, they'd spent time together—usually at formal occasions—and he knew how beautiful she was, and that she was intelligent and easy to talk to. He could fancy her, even—in the way that any man could fancy a gorgeous woman—but would he ever feel like this about Francesca? That helping her get everything she wanted out of life could be as important as his own ambitions?

He had to hope so.

Maybe Mika had been sent into his life to teach him about what was really important in relationships.

Raoul would never forget this moment.

Or that particular smile…

'What time does the paper museum close?'

Mika blinked as if she had to drag her thoughts away from something that had nothing to do with the article she was planning to write. 'I'm not sure… I imagine we've got plenty of time.'

'Shall we head off now? Just to be sure?'

'Okay…'

Mika hadn't moved a muscle but something in her

tone told Raoul that she was much further away from him than she had been a moment ago, when she'd been smiling at him.

It was an odd thing, this connection he could feel between them. Like the sun emerging from the screen of thick clouds, there were moments when it scorched him; then it would vanish again and the whole world felt so much cooler.

What created the clouds? Was it because he was getting hot enough to feel uncomfortable, so that he pulled them in for protection, perhaps?

Or did Mika feel the heat, too; and was she using them to hide behind?

Whatever was causing those clouds, they were a good thing, because it made this friendship manageable and it needed to be manageable because Raoul was nowhere near ready to risk losing it.

He thoroughly enjoyed the time they spent in the *Museo della Carta* that was housed in a wonderful thirteenth-century mill. Raoul was no stranger to museums and was, in fact, the patron of the largest in his own country; he had toured it many times, usually in the company of a large group local dignitaries and important contributors. He had to look fascinated even if he wasn't and remember to turn a little whenever he shook someone's hand or stopped to admire a new exhibit, so that the best photographs could be taken.

This was a new experience because, for once, he was less important than the exhibits and he found that he was watching Mika as much as the treasures on display, and that made him see things differently and in far more detail. He stared up at the huge wooden mallets that were powered by a hydraulic wheel that could beat rags of cotton, linen and hemp into a pulp.

He stood beside the ancient vat with its murky water that housed the pulp and watched Mika crouch to take a close-up shot of the majolica tiles that lined the vat. Pale blue tiles, with red flowers and delicate green swirls for leaves. Would he even have noticed them if he'd been here alone?

'I'm going to write this up tonight,' Mika announced, as they waited for the bus to take them back to Positano. 'And I'll finish the one about the Footpath of the Gods.'

'I'll get out of your way,' Raoul told her. 'I'm going to find the concierge and see if there's another room available. That way, you'll get plenty of time to write without interruptions.'

The bus was approaching the stop but Mika didn't seem to notice. Her gaze had caught his and those clouds had evaporated again as instantly and mysteriously as they had on every other occasion.

This time, the heat felt different. It wasn't the burn of desire. It felt more like the kind of heat that came with the prickle of shame.

Mika knew exactly why he was going to find the concierge. He wasn't finding his own place to sleep in order to give her more space, he was doing it because he needed to get away from her. And she felt…rejected?

The bus seemed to bring the cloud cover back as it jerked to a halt beside them and Mika turned away to climb on board.

Maybe it would be the last time he got to experience the heat of that connection.

That would be a good thing, wouldn't it? It would

make it so much easier to step back into his own world and his own life when the time came and that wouldn't be very far away. A whole week of his month of freedom had vanished already.

But, if it *was* a good thing, why did it feel as if he'd just broken something rather precious?

CHAPTER FIVE

IT HAD BEEN one of *those* days.

Right from that first customer who'd put his hand in the air and clicked his fingers loudly enough to make Mika freeze as she hurried back to the pass to collect more plates for the table.

'I ordered my eggs to be poached, not fried.' He didn't look at Mika as he spoke. 'Take them back.'

'I'm so sorry, sir.' Mika picked up the plate. 'There's been a mistake. I'll get you a fresh plate.'

'Make it snappy. And I'll have another coffee while I'm waiting. On the house—it's the least you can do for messing up my order.'

'Of course.' Mika looked over her shoulder, thinking that Alain had probably heard the loud voice. His subtle nod told her that he had and his smile offered sympathy at her dealing with a rude customer.

The customer wasn't the only person Mika had to deal with. She knew she hadn't written the order down incorrectly but the person who'd made the mistake wasn't likely to admit it. Not this morning, that was for sure, when they were being run off their feet.

Sure enough, Gianni was furious.

'How could you get something so basic wrong?' he

shouted. 'You think I have time to be cooking another full English breakfast when I've got orders coming out of my ears?' His spatula splattered oil on the dockets lining the rail above the grill.

He'd picked the wrong morning to have a go at Mika. It had already started badly when she'd opened her eyes to remember that she was alone in her room. That Rafe had chosen to be a lot further away from her. Had that been her fault? Had she said or done something to put him off her? She hadn't been able to think of anything. Quite the opposite, really, when she'd gone over and over everything they'd said during yesterday's outing.

Okay, she'd upset him by being offhand about whether she wanted his company to visit the museum, but they'd got past that, hadn't they? More than past it. She could swear that he'd almost kissed her when they'd been sitting under that tree by the waterfall. And the way he'd looked at her when he'd told her that he was so sure she would succeed in her dream of becoming a travel writer. As if he believed in her completely.

As if it was important to *him* that she did achieve her dream.

But having him use that dream as an excuse to find somewhere else to sleep felt like she was being punished for something that she didn't feel was her fault, and now it was about to happen again so this pushed a button harder than it might have otherwise.

'Have a look at the docket,' she told Gianni. 'I didn't write the order down wrong. You *read* it wrong.'

'Don't tell me how to do my job!' Gianni yelled. 'You want to come in here and start cooking? *Do* you?' He'd stepped away from the grill and by the time he fired his last, aggressive question he was right in her face.

Mika stiffened. She knew that Gianni wouldn't hurt her but there were huge buttons being pushed now and it took everything she had to control her reaction. Behind her, she could sense that Rafe had stopped loading the dishwasher. He was staring, probably horrified, at the altercation. The second chef hadn't blinked and he was now busy trying to rescue the food that Gianni had left unattended on the grill. Margaret took plates off the pass and vanished swiftly. Gianni's temper tantrums were nothing new and it was best for everybody not directly involved to carry on with their own jobs. There was no point in escalating things further so Mika tried to push past Gianni's arm to put the offending plate back on the pass. Hopefully he would calm down and do what had to be done to satisfy the customer.

But standing up to him had been a mistake. Gianni grabbed the plate before it got to the bench. Maybe it slipped out of his hands, or maybe he threw it. It didn't matter because the effect was the same. The sound of smashing crockery caused a sudden silence in the busy café and, from the corner of her eye, Mika could see Marco glaring from his table on the footpath.

Rafe was right beside her now and she could feel him bristling. Was he ready to defend her? She shot a warning glance in his direction and followed it up with a firm shake of her head. It would only make things a lot worse if Rafe said or did anything. This was between herself and Gianni. The more people that got involved, the worse the whole day would become for everybody.

'What's your problem?' Gianni shouted at Rafe.

'Can't find the broom? Can't do *your* job, either?' He threw his hands in the air. 'Why do I have to work with such *stupid* people? Nobody can do the jobs they're being paid for.' He turned back to the grill in disgust, narrowly missing a collision with his junior chef who was putting new plates on the pass.

'Service,' he said. 'Table four.'

Mika's table. He'd managed to add a replacement plate with poached eggs to the remaining orders going to table four. Mika let out a breath she hadn't realised she'd been holding. If Alain had already delivered the free coffee as well, this small crisis might be over.

Even the mess. Rafe might have a face like thunder but he had a broom and pan in his hand and was sweeping up the broken crockery and food as she collected the plates, balancing one on her arm so that her hands were free to hold the other two.

In the end, it was no more than a commonplace disruption to smooth service but it had set the tone for the day. All of Mika's least favourite tasks had appeared, one after the other. Having to return an incorrect order was the biggest but others were equally irritating. Like the group of middle-aged women who treated her like their personal servant for the duration of their visit, requesting fussy changes to every dish they ordered, more ice for their water and replacement cutlery for all when one of them noticed a smudge on the handle of a knife.

Then there were the unsupervised toddlers who'd been allowed to smear smashed avocado all over the table, laminated menus and the wooden spokes of two chairs and up-end the sugar dispenser so that the crystals crunched underfoot. Mika knew that cleaning this particular table in time for the next group of customers was going to be a mission that would have her running behind for a considerable length of time.

And now, when the end of her shift was finally in sight, she had a table of young men who were getting progressively more obnoxious with every order of drinks she delivered to their table.

Their attempts to grab her legs was something she was adept at avoiding but the verbal innuendoes were harder to shake off.

'Whatcha doing after work, cutie? We could show you a good time.'

Her smile was tight. 'Are you ready to order?'

'I know what *I'd* like to order...' One of the men licked his lips suggestively as he leered at Mika, his gaze raking her body from head to toe.

She gritted her teeth, her smile long gone. 'I can come back in a minute, if you need more time to decide?'

'Just bring us pizza. And more beer.'

'Yeah...*lotsa* beer.'

The sooner this group left, the better. By then it would be time for Mika's shift to end and she could escape and go for a swim, and maybe she could wash away the unpleasantness of this entire day.

But would she be walking home alone? Back to the silent room she now had all to herself again? Would Rafe decide she might need the space to go swimming by herself, too?

The hollow feeling inside her chest was the worst thing about this bad day.

She was missing him.

If she was honest, she'd started missing him at the

bus stop in Amalfi yesterday when he'd dropped that bombshell about finding the concierge and arranging a room for himself. She hadn't ended up doing any of the writing she'd planned to do. Instead, she'd relived every moment of their day together. Tried to second-guess every glance or remembered tone of voice. Tried—and failed—to understand how she could be so drawn to someone who didn't feel the same way.

It was Rafe who had needed the space—that much was clear.

She'd hardly seen him at work today, either, except for the incident of Gianni's outburst, when she'd made it clear she wouldn't welcome his involvement. Had that been why he'd seemed so preoccupied every time she'd been near the pass? Why he'd kept his back to her, intent on loading or unloading the dishwasher whenever she was depositing a pile of crockery? Why he'd been outside, in the alley for his break at a completely different time from her own? Had she offended him again, the way she had when she'd tried to push him away just a little bit by suggesting he didn't have to go to the museum with her?

When she thought about that, she realised it had been a forlorn effort to protect herself because she knew how much she was going to miss him when he disappeared from her life as suddenly as he'd entered it.

But all she'd achieved was to find herself missing him already, when he was still here. How stupid was that?

It had confirmed something, though. She needed to protect herself. If it felt this bad with him still here, how much worse was it going to be when he was gone for ever?

At least she hadn't fallen in love with him because Mika instinctively knew that that would make the missing unbearable. Not that she had any real evidence to base it on because she'd never been in love. Not the kind of love she'd seen other people experience, anyway. Mika was confident that that would never happen to her because life had taught her both to rely only on herself and to avoid anything that made her more vulnerable than she already was.

Falling in love with someone was to make yourself ultimately vulnerable, wasn't it?

She'd told Rafe that she would never marry and have a family of her own and she believed that. How could she chase a dream of something like that when she had no idea what shape it really was? She wasn't looking for her *person*. A home that she could call her own was the closest she was going to get to finding her place in the world.

This was a physical reawakening, that was all. An attraction that might have been enough to break down a very big barrier, if Rafe had been interested.

The messages she'd received on that score were mixed, to say the least, and Mika didn't like feeling confused.

Feeling rejected was even more of a downer.

She delivered pizzas to the table of young men and followed that up with another order of their drinks, avoiding their wandering hands and letting their crude comments become no more than the background buzz of a busy café. As soon as they'd gone, she could wipe down their table and she'd be finished for the day.

Would Rafe be due to finish then, too?

Maybe she should give him some more of that space

and not even check to see if his shift was going to finish close enough to hers for it to be only friendly for
one of them to wait so they could walk home together.

He knew she'd be going for the usual swim. If he
chose not to join her then at least she'd know for sure
that whatever had been gathering between them was
not going to go any further. She could start pulling
herself together, then. She'd been fine before Rafe had
come into her life. It was ridiculous to be afraid of how
lonely she might be when he left.

The anger had been building all day.

How did someone like Gianni think he had the right
to put people down like that? Mika wasn't stupid. Neither was Raoul, but the bad-tempered chef had left
them both feeling at fault for a situation and its consequences that Raoul was quite sure had been the result of the chef's lack of attention to detail. Part of him
had wanted to put everybody in their place. To reveal
his identity and use the power he could summon with
a click of his fingers that could potentially change the
lives of these people. To get the chef fired. Provide
Mika with enough money to let her achieve her dreams
without having to put up with any of this kind of abuse.

And the way she'd put up with Gianni's tantrum
hadn't been the only thing he'd noticed today.

She'd told him that you got to see the worst of people in a job like this and she hadn't been wrong. Raoul
could see out into the café when he collected pans from
the chefs or replaced water carafes and glasses on their
shelves. He'd seen people clicking their fingers to get
Mika's attention. A group trying to sit down at a table
she was trying to clean had glared at her as if it was

her fault there was sugar or salt that had to be swept up before the table could be wiped clean. And he'd seen a low-life make a grab for her legs as she'd leaned over the table to deliver tall glasses of beer.

It wasn't right that someone like Mika had to put up with being treated like this because she needed a job to live and she just happened to be so far down the pecking order.

Because she was vulnerable.

He hadn't been allowed to stand up for her this morning as she'd faced Gianni's wrath and he'd thought he understood why, even if he didn't agree with it. Hospitality workers were easy to replace and Marco probably wouldn't have thought twice about firing them both if he'd faced the prospect of losing a good chef who'd be far harder to replace. He couldn't do anything about the way people treated her in the café, either, but it fed the anger. Maybe he was angry with himself, too, that he'd quashed the notion of revealing who he was because it would mean the end of this time of being so successfully incognito.

He'd seen that look in her eyes yesterday. That smile, when he'd offered her encouragement to believe in herself and her dreams. Had it been so special because it hadn't happened to her very often in her life? Was she more used to being treated as if she didn't matter? As if it was obvious she'd had to put up with whatever people felt like dishing out so many times in her life it didn't matter if they couldn't be bothered considering how she might feel?

She *did* matter, dammit. Raoul had wanted to help and her gestures had told him she didn't need his help. That she could look after herself, just the way she always had—except for that time when he'd first met her, when she'd been in the grip of something totally beyond her control.

She'd needed him then but he knew how hard it had been for her to accept his help.

To take his hand…

But this was her world and she knew what she was doing. Raoul had never been in a position of having to put up with being treated as being stupid or worthless. He didn't have to be in it now. He could walk out of here whenever he wanted to and step back into a life of privilege. A life where people looked up to him as being important even if he wasn't doing anything to earn that respect. It was the opposite end of the spectrum and it was an eye-opener, for sure.

Maybe he'd learned enough. He'd walked a few miles now, in the shoes of the invisible people, and it would change his perspective on many things. It would make him a better ruler. A better man. It wasn't that he hadn't always had a strong sense of what was right or wrong, but this experience of life as an ordinary person was sharpening his perception of the shades of grey within those boundaries.

It was wrong enough to anger him that Mika had to put up with people treating her so badly, even if she was tough enough to deal with it. When Raoul had caught a glimpse of the table of young idiots who were out to have a good time with whatever feminine company came within reach, it had been the last straw. He hadn't forgotten his impressions of Mika as a wild creature. Or the horrific thought that some man had hurt her in the past. She deserved protection even if she didn't think she needed it. She deserved to know that how she felt mattered.

That *she* mattered.

Raoul had had to fight the urge to march out of the kitchens and warn them to keep their hands and their crass comments to themselves. Or else…

Or else what?

Choosing to reveal his identity and throwing his power around would have been one thing. What if he got into a fight and maybe ended up getting arrested, being forced to admit who he was, and creating a scandal that would embarrass his entire nation? And what about his beloved grandparents? They'd sacrificed retirement to raise him and wait for him to be ready to take up his destiny and maybe doing that had contributed to his grandfather's failing health. How sad would it be to have the final days of their position as ruling monarchs marred by something so unfortunate?

He couldn't do that. Any more than he could act on the attraction towards Mika that was getting steadily more difficult to contain.

It would be easier to leave now.

Safer.

But would it also be cowardly? He'd already been tested in ways he had never imagined he'd be faced with in his quest to uncover his core strengths. If he left now, might he be running away from the opportunity to face an even more intense challenge?

Perhaps it was frustration more than anger that was making his gut churn today.

Frustration that his offer of help had been dismissed.

That he couldn't let Mika know how important she had become to him.

Most of all, that he wasn't being honest with her.

She'd revealed things to him that he knew she'd never told anybody else. Her search for a place where she felt she belonged—the idea that she would know who she was when she found a place to call home. Her dream of using her talents in photography and writing to make a new—better—life for herself.

But she knew nothing of him on such an intimate level.

What she thought she knew was no more than a pretence.

A lie…

He would tell her, Raoul decided as he finally hung up his apron for the day. He would tell her how he felt about her and why they could be no more than friends. He could offer her a new life, perhaps. Surely there would be a way to find her work within the vibrant tourism industry of his own country? Above all, he could thank her for giving him a perspective on life he would never forget, and they could talk about how best he could use his remaining time before he was due to report back and take up the reins of his future.

When was Mika due to finish her shift? The last glimpse into the café had shown her wiping down a very messy table after the rowdy group of young, male tourists had finally moved on.

But now Raoul couldn't see her anywhere. Margaret was looking after that section and Bianca had come in for the late shift.

'You looking for Mika?' Bianca handed an order form to Gianni. 'She just left a couple of minutes ago.'

Without him?

Raoul headed for the alley behind the café. The hope

of having an honest conversation with Mika was fading rapidly but he'd created this new distance himself, hadn't he? He'd put up new barriers—literal barriers—in the form of the four walls of his new, private room in the boarding house.

Mika had felt rejected and she was running away. He couldn't blame her but, if he left things this way between them, it would haunt him for ever.

He needed to find her.

Had she taken the main street as her route home, detoured past the beach or marina to give herself a longer walk, or had she chosen the narrow back alleys that offered far more solitude?

The alleys, he decided. Because that would be the route he would take if he wanted a space away from other people after a bad day and knew it was the fastest route to get to the best part of the day—that swim…

He turned another corner, skirted a bank of rubbish containers and passed the open back door of a restaurant kitchen where he could hear a chef yelling at his kitchen crew. They were shouting back and the noise level should have been enough to cover up a much fainter cry but the sound caught something in Raoul's chest.

His heart…

He knew that sound even though it was so muffled. He recognised that note of distress and it felt like a knife in his own chest.

The place it was coming from wasn't an alley, it was more like a hole in a wall—a bricked space that was a tiny courtyard with rear entrance doors to shops that were already closed and locked for the day.

And, right in the corner of the shaded space, was Mika.

Surrounded by the young men she'd been serving in the café. One of them was holding her from behind as she struggled, his hand over her mouth. Another was trying to put his hand up her skirt as she kicked out at him.

The impression of Mika's face was only in the periphery of Raoul's line of sight as he launched himself into the space but he didn't need a clear look to be painfully aware of what he would see.

He'd seen it before. The terror of a wild creature who had been trapped—unable to save herself from the dreadful situation she had found herself in through no fault of her own.

And this was worse than the vertigo that had left her stranded on a cliff side. This was unthinkably horrific.

The frustration and anger that had been building all day gave Raoul the strength to tackle four men without giving the odds a moment's thought. He had an advantage because they were so fixed on their evil intent that they hadn't seen him coming.

With a roar of pure rage that he didn't recognise as coming from his throat, Raoul grabbed the one who was lifting Mika's skirt by the scruff of his neck and hefted him into the air, before throwing him to one side. In almost the same motion, he swung his arm and let his fist connect to the jaw of one of the leering bystanders.

A blow to the side of his own head blurred his vision and seemed to intensify the sounds around him. The swearing of the thwarted attackers still on their feet and trying to defend themselves. Groaning from the one still on the ground where Raoul had thrown him. A scream from Mika as the man restraining her shoved her aside viciously. More raised voices as other people came running. From the corner of his eye, Raoul could see white aprons that suggested it was the staff from the nearby restaurant who had been alerted to the trouble and he caught the impression of them being pushed, and falling as the young men decided to make a run for it, but he didn't turn his head as he leapt forward with his arms outstretched to catch Mika before she fell and hit her head on the cobbled ground.

He had only held her hand before this moment and he remembered the trembling within the gentle circle of his fingers.

This time he was holding her entire body as tightly as he'd ever held anybody and he could feel the shuddering of someone who'd been pushed past the brink of fear.

Oh, God…had he been too late?

'Did they…? Are you…?' He couldn't bring himself to say the words, and Mika clearly couldn't say anything, but she knew what he was asking and she was shaking her head forcefully. Letting him know that he had been in time to stop the attack.

Just…

The restaurant staff were picking themselves up. More people were gathering in the narrow street. The chef was shouting for someone to call the police and a waitress stepped closer.

'Is she all right? Can I help?'

Mika was shaking her head again, curling closer within the fold of Raoul's arms. He heard her stuttered words and bent his head.

'Home…' she whispered. 'Please…take me home…'

She was so small, it took no effort to scoop her

off her feet and into his arms. She wrapped her arms around his neck and clung like a child.

Raoul pushed politely through the worried onlookers.

'She's okay,' he told them. 'I'll look after her.'

'Who is she?' someone asked. 'The police will want to talk to her.'

'She's my friend,' Raoul told them. He straightened his back, instinctively calling on the kind of presence that he might have had if he'd been arriving at a royal function. He was in control and he expected it to be respected. 'She's safe.'

The crowd parted. In silence, they made space for him to carry Mika onto the open street and carry on up the hill.

He could have put her down then but he didn't want to.

This time, he wasn't going to let her go.

Even when he got to the boarding house and into her room he still didn't let her go. He sat down on the couch he'd slept on for those first nights and he cradled her in his arms and let her cry until the shuddering finally ebbed and he could feel her fear receding.

How ironic was it that Mika could feel so safe with a man's arms around her? When her worst nightmares of men touching her again had come so terrifyingly close actually to happening?

But this was Rafe.

And this felt like the safest place she had ever been in her entire life.

More than that.

Would she ever feel safe again if he wasn't in her life?

Missing him wasn't something that she could protect herself from and it wasn't something that was ever going to get easier. Given her lifestyle, it should be something she had become very used to, but when Rafe left it was going to feel like he was taking a big part of her with him.

Even if she hadn't fallen in love with him.

As calmness won over the shaking and she could breathe without triggering a sob, Mika felt something like a wry smile gathering strength somewhere deep inside.

Who was she kidding?

She might have been in denial about the process of falling but she already loved this man. That physical reawakening had come in the wake of finding someone who had touched her soul.

Someone she could trust.

Her breath came out in a sigh this time instead of a sob. She could find words finally.

'You did it again.'

His arms tightened around her. 'I wanted to kill them. Are you sure they didn't hurt you?'

Mika swallowed hard. 'They would have. If you hadn't found them.' She tilted her head. 'How did you find them? I knew as they dragged me in there that nobody would be able to see from the street.'

'I heard you. Just the faintest sound but I knew it was you. I think my heart heard you rather than my ears.'

Mika could feel tears prickle behind her eyes again but these were very different tears from those in the aftermath of fear.

She would remember those words for the rest of

her life. They had to be the most romantic words she had ever heard.

Had Rafe just told her that *he* loved *her*?

It felt like he had.

One of those tears escaped and she could feel it rolling slowly down until it caught on the side of her nose. Rafe had seen it, too. He used the pad of his thumb to brush it away.

'It wasn't the first time something like this has happened to you, was it?'

Mika blinked, shocked. 'How did you know that?'

Silly question... Somewhere along the line, they'd had one of those lightning-fast, totally private conversations. Like the one where he'd asked if she would be okay sitting beside the view of that drop to the sea and had told her that he would change the arrangements if that would help.

He'd seen her fear even though she thought she'd kept it so well hidden. Had it been that moment she'd pulled away and headed for neutral ground after she'd seen the attraction in his eyes when they'd been sitting on the pontoon?

No. Maybe it had been there right from the start. When he'd touched her and she'd panicked and kicked his backpack over the side of the cliff.

It didn't matter. He knew. And, while it made her heart rate skip and speed up, it didn't make her feel any less safe that he knew.

'This was worse,' she whispered. 'There were more of them...and they were strangers.'

She felt the sudden increase in tension in Rafe's body.

'You *knew* him? Last time?'

Mika swallowed, closing her eyes against the shock she could see in his eyes. 'He was my boyfriend. But I didn't know how angry he could get. That he would think nothing of hurting me…that he would come after me when I tried to get away and force me to…to…'

Rafe's arms tightened around her and Mika could feel his cheek pressed to the top of her head. Then she felt his head turn and she could feel his lips on her hair. A slow, tender press that felt like a deliberate kiss of comfort.

For the longest time, they were silent. Mika knew she didn't have to go into the horrible details. That she didn't have to uncover those dreadful memories and make them fresh again.

It was Rafe who broke the silence.

'I think you're wrong,' he said softly. 'I think what happened to you before was worse than what happened today.'

Mika nodded slowly. 'Because you saved me…'

'No. Because you were betrayed by someone you thought you could trust. Someone that was supposed to care about you and keep you safe.' His breath came out in a sigh. 'I'm so sorry that happened to you, Mika. I'm not surprised you don't trust men.'

Her eyes snapped open. It was important that she could see Rafe. That he could see her.

'I trust *you*,' she said quietly.

'I care about you,' Rafe said. 'You're safe.'

It seemed like the most natural thing in the world that he would kiss her again to seal the truth of those words. It was a gentle kiss but it stirred up everything that had been woken and waiting in Mika's body.

The fear and bad memories were becoming a distant memory. *This* was what mattered. This moment.

This man that she *could* trust.

Her heart was beating wildly as she shifted in his arms. There was one way, she realised, that she could put not only today's horror but the memories that had kept her trapped for so long behind her for ever.

One thing that could restore her faith that there were good men in the world and, amongst them, one that she could trust with not only her heart but her body. If she was brave enough…

'Rafe?'

The subtle quirk of those dark eyebrows was enough to tell her he wanted to hear her question.

'Would you do something for me? Please? Something that will really make me feel safe?'

His eyes darkened. 'Of course. What is it?'

Mika licked suddenly dry lips. The words were so hard to get out that they emerged in no more than the ghost of a whisper.

'Make love to me…'

CHAPTER SIX

FOUR TINY WORDS.

How could they be enough to make it feel as if the bottom of Raoul's world had simply vanished?

As if he was falling and there was nothing he could find to catch hold of and save himself.

He'd started slipping without even realising it was happening. Touching his lips to Mika's head. That gentle kiss on her lips. He'd stepped over a boundary and now he had the choice of which direction his next step was going to take him. He'd been right in thinking that kissing this woman was always going to be more than a small thing. That it would unleash a desire unlike any he'd ever experienced before. Physical control was still possible, of course. He wasn't an animal—like those brutes who'd captured Mika this afternoon. He could stop, if that was the right choice.

This was it.

The challenge that was going to tell him who he really was. What his values really were and whether he was made of the right stuff to rule a country in the best interests of the many thousands of people who would be trusting him to do the right thing.

He'd convinced himself that resisting the attraction he felt towards Mika was that test so why, in this moment after those words had been uttered, and it felt like time was holding its breath, did it really so utterly *wrong*?

As if he didn't really have a choice at all?

Again, he was reminded of when she had taken his hand, up there on the top of that cliff. Of when her trembling had finally ceased and he'd known she was trusting him.

He'd felt taller, then. Powerful in a way that had nothing to do with him being a prince but everything to do with who he was as a man. Nothing would have persuaded him to break that trust.

And, right now, Mika was trusting him with so much more than her hand. She was asking him to take hold of her whole body and, by doing so, he would still be leading her to safety, wouldn't he?

To a place where she could believe it was safe to trust a man. To let him touch her.

Was it so far-fetched to imagine that she was trusting him with her entire future?

Raoul was aware of the part of his brain that was reminding him of the challenge he'd set himself—to put aside his own desires in order to do the right thing— but what *was* the right thing in this case?

It was astonishing how fast a brain could work. How thoughts could coalesce into a split second of time.

If he refused Mika's whispered plea, would she ever have the courage to ask again?

This moment had come in the wake of Mika being forced to face her worst nightmare and now being in a space where she felt safe. With someone she trusted as the closest friend she had available.

It was a no-brainer to hope that this particular combination of circumstances would never happen again. He would never want Mika to be attacked or even threatened ever again.

And if he was really honest with himself—and wasn't the point of this journey he was taking to be exactly that?—the thought of Mika being this close to any other man felt wrong and he knew there was a part of him that would always be envious of that man.

He could feel the whole shape of the small, lithe body he had cradled in his arms. He could still feel the incredible softness of her lips against his own. Mika had no idea how much she was asking of him but Raoul had a very good idea of how huge this gift he could give *her* was.

It was something that nobody else could ever give her, because this moment would never happen again, and she would remember it for the rest of her life. A life that might very well be happier because of this gift.

The choice had already been made, Raoul realised, as he slowly dipped his head to touch Mika's lips again with his own, knowing that this time it was going to be with passion, not an intention to comfort.

He'd been right in that there really wasn't a choice to be made at all. This had nothing to do with whether he was fighting or submitting to his own desires.

This was the right thing to do.

For Mika.

Because he loved her...

Nothing else existed the moment Rafe's lips touched hers and it was nothing like the gentle comfort of that first kiss.

Mika could fall into the overwhelming spiral of feelings that were so much more than a blinding physical need. This was an expression of love, and the combination of what both her body and her heart were experiencing was more than Mika could ever have believed was possible.

Rafe was so gentle with her that Mika knew he would stop in an instant if she gave any indication that she was afraid, or that she'd changed her mind, but neither of those things was going to happen.

She'd been waiting her whole life for this—she just hadn't known it was possible.

This was why people took the risk of being ultimately vulnerable, wasn't it? Because sex could never be like this if you weren't in love with your partner.

Surely nobody else had ever felt quite like this, though? She already had that weird kind of telepathic communication with Rafe that meant an entire conversation could happen in a glance. Maybe it was a natural extension of that connection that meant that every touch said so much as well.

Which was why she could feel his initial hesitation —the edge of gentleness that was still there enough to suggest Rafe needed reassurance as much as she did that this was a safe thing to be doing. It was Mika who slipped her hands under Rafe's tee shirt, to feel his skin beneath her hands and encourage him to take it off. She started to unbutton her own shirt but Rafe caught her hands, catching her gaze at the same moment.

And it was then that everything seemed to come together. The attraction that had been sizzling between them for so long, the desire unleashed by those first kisses and what was being said in that glance.

That this was about so much more than sex…

Mika was aware of the moment when everything else ceased to exist for Rafe, as it had done for her , and she tipped her head back with a sigh as she felt him take over the unbuttoning of her shirt and then the touch of his lips on the swell of her breast. They could both let go now and see just how close to paradise this was going to take them.

And surely it was as close as anybody could ever get in this life?

Mika had no idea when her tears had begun or when they had stopped; she could only feel them cooling her cheeks as they dried as she lay, still within the circle of Rafe's arms, waiting for the moment when she could catch her breath again enough to speak.

And, when she could, there was only one thing to say.

'Thank you,' she whispered.

'Oh…' Rafe still had his eyes closed, and the sound was no more than a soft groan, but Mika could see the way Rafe's lips were curling into a smile. And then he opened his eyes to look straight into hers. 'Believe me, it was my pleasure.'

The smile made everything perfect. It brought Rafe the friend back into the body of Rafe the amazing lover.

It made this real.

Mika hung onto his gaze. There were more words aching to escape. Words she had never said to anyone. Ever.

Oddly, they were harder to get out than the extraordinary request she'd made that had led to this.

But she couldn't *not* say them. Even though they made something else scarily real.

How vulnerable she had just become.

'I...' It was that smile that made this possible. The smile that seemed to underline the warmth and humour in those gorgeous, dark eyes. 'I love you, Rafe.'

Something she couldn't begin to define flared in his eyes but then the lids came down to shutter them and Rafe pulled her more closely against his body. For the longest moment, he simply held her, and Mika could feel the steady thump of his heart against her cheek.

The silence continued for so long that Mika forgot she was waiting for him to say anything. The rhythm of his heart and the warmth of his skin, in the blissful aftermath of their love-making, were lulling her towards what promised to be a deep and dreamless sleep. Or maybe not dreamless.

When Mika woke, it was completely dark and Rafe was sound asleep in the narrow bed beside her, his arm still cradling her head against his chest.

She could hear the words. A low rumble that still seemed to reverberate in every cell of her body.

I love you, too...

Had she heard those words with her ears or her heart?

Maybe it didn't matter. Mika pressed her lips gently against the soft skin at the base of Rafe's neck and then, with a sigh, let herself slip back into sleep.

Life could change in the blink of an eye.

Or over the space of one night.

The world felt different when Raoul woke in the morning. All his senses seemed to be heightened. He could smell the coffee Mika was brewing, having boiled the electric kettle on the only power point her room provided, and he felt more awake long before he tasted it. He could hear the trickle of the water as she poured it into the coffee jug and the tiny sound—a faint hum of pleasure—that Mika made as she glanced up to see that he was awake and acknowledged his company with a smile.

It was the most beautiful smile he'd ever seen. Mika was beautiful. Her skin seemed to glow this morning and he could actually *feel* the touch of her glance against his own eyes. Through his whole body, in fact.

Was *this* how being in love made you feel?

He'd waited until he was sure Mika was asleep in his arms last night before he'd echoed the words she'd said to him.

I love you, too...

They were dangerous words to say aloud because they carried a promise that he knew he would not be able to keep.

Last night had been a gift for Mika.

It hadn't occurred to him how much of a gift he was also receiving but, there it was, sitting inside his chest. Something huge, warm and comforting.

He knew exactly who he was.

A man who could feel this kind of love. Who could protect and nurture. Who could follow his instincts about whether something was the right thing to do, even though there were loud arguments against it, and trust those same instincts that were telling him it would be worth it, despite any inevitable consequences.

He was a man he could be proud of being.

And there was something even bigger that had brought him to this space.

Mika loved him.

She had no idea who he was or where he came from. She barely knew anything about him, but she loved what he was in this moment of time, and that had nothing to do with his elite position in life or his wealth. It was based entirely on who he was as a man.

A man worthy of being loved.

Would she still feel the same way when she found out the truth?

She had to know the truth. Was he really a man worthy of being loved if he was being dishonest?

On the other hand, wasn't he being more honest than he'd ever been in his life before? He had nothing to hide behind. Mika was seeing him as simply the person he was inside, without any of the trappings that were inescapable if you were a member of a royal family.

By a quirk of fate, he had escaped them completely, albeit temporarily.

With a huge effort, Raoul slammed a mental lid on that can of worms. He knew it was wrong—just as much as he'd known that giving Mika the gift of feeling safe to be touched had been right—and he was not impressed with himself for doing it, but he couldn't go down that track just yet.

He would break Mika's trust if he did and that would erase any of the magic that had happened last night.

It would be easy to persuade himself that this continued deception was to protect Mika but he knew he needed it for himself as well. This discovery was too important. This was what he'd set out on this journey to discover—who he was at the very core of his being—and he'd only just found it, this very instant.

He needed time. To hold this precious gift up to the

light and look at it from every angle he could find. To
revel in the beauty of its simplicity and its strength.

To make sure it was real…

'Hey, sleepyhead…' Mika's voice was a smile in itself. 'You'll need to hurry up if you want to have coffee and a shower before we go to work.'

Work.

Washing dishes. The most mundane of employment
but even this felt completely different today.

Knowing that, at any moment, he might catch a
glimpse of Mika coming to the pass to collect plates,
or that she could arrive beside his sink to deposit dirty
dishes and share a glance and a smile, made even the
worst jobs of the day worthwhile. With his senses so
heightened, he could actually hear her voice at times
amongst the cacophony of customers chatting, dishes
clattering and even the chefs arguing. And whenever
they were close enough for their gazes to meet, and
one of those silent, lightning fast conversations to happen, he could feel a swell of what he could only identify as joy.

This was…happiness, that's what it was.

And, okay, it couldn't last—not in this form, anyway—but Raoul needed to hang onto every moment
of it that he could because…

Because it felt perfect.

As though nothing else at all mattered.

Nothing else mattered.

There was nothing that could happen that day that
could dent the astonishing joy that encased Mika like
a private force field. Rude customers and crying ba-
bies, even the small dog that bared its teeth and snarled

whenever she approached that table, did nothing to spoil her day. It made no difference that there were only snatched moments here and there when she actually saw Rafe or could share a glance or a smile. He could have been a thousand miles away and it would have still felt as if he was right by her side.

It was just as well she was so good at her job because every task was being accomplished on an automatic level. Most of her head was filled with thoughts of Rafe. Thoughts that were more like sensations, really, that she could feel right down to the tips of her toes. A memory of his smile. The sound of his voice. The touch of his fingers or lips on her skin...

So this was what it was like to be in love.

It was extraordinary.

Crazy.

She barely knew him but that didn't seem to matter. In a way, it was exciting, because there was so much still to find out. She had taken the first steps on a journey she had never expected to take, but the unknown wasn't daunting, because she wasn't on this journey alone.

Okay...maybe it *was* daunting. There was a rollercoaster of emotions that came with such heightened awareness and, as the day wore on, the dips caught Mika when she was least expecting them. There were aspects of this that were quite possibly terrifying.

What if this wasn't real?

What if Rafe didn't feel the same way?

What if his holiday came to an end and he simply said goodbye and she never saw him again?

An answer to the disturbing whispers came as their

shifts ended and Mika found Rafe waiting for her outside the back door of the café.

'Time for a swim?'

'Oh…yes. I can't wait.'

'Neither can I.' Rafe held out his hand. 'Let's go.'

Maybe it was the way he took her hand, as if it was the most natural thing in the world to do. Or maybe it was his smile or the expression in his eyes. Whatever it was, it made Mika's fear evaporate.

If Rafe vanished from her life without a backward glance, she would have *this* for ever.

The knowledge that it was possible to feel like this.

As if life was perfect and only this moment mattered. That was what she needed to hold onto. This moment.

The future would happen, and it wasn't something she could control in the same way she had been controlling her life, because she had, for the first time in so long, chosen to open herself to being vulnerable. To allow someone else to hold the gift of her heart and her happiness.

CHAPTER SEVEN

THERE WAS NO race out to the pontoon today.

It was tempting to stay close to the rock wall, in fact, with the music from the bar right above them— to simply float in the deliciously cool water and play like other young couples always did here—but it felt too public. As if what they had discovered with each other was too new and special to be on display just yet. It only took a shared glance for that suggestion and agreement to be made and Mika had no idea whether it had been her idea or Rafe's. Not that it mattered.

They swam side by side this time, and their hands touched the side of the pontoon at the same moment. Their bodies bumped together as they sank into being upright, and Mika let go of the pontoon to wrap her arms around Rafe's neck and her legs around his waist as she lifted her face for the first kiss since last night.

For an instant, she was aware of a tiny hesitation on Rafe's part and the dip in that emotional rollercoaster was so fierce it felt like she was leaving her stomach behind as she fell. But then his lips softened on hers and she felt his legs move to keep them both afloat as he let go of the pontoon to wrap his arms around her. It was only a matter of time before the water washed over the top of their heads and they had to surface to breathe, but who knew that kissing under water could be so amazing?

The sea was Mika's ultimate comfort zone. To be in that space, with the added magic that being in love seemed to bestow on everything, made that fraction of time something that she knew she would remember for ever. This would be the moment that she could return to if she ever lost sight of how perfect life could be. This total embrace of the cool water that made the heat of Rafe's skin against hers so intense. How safe it made her feel to be within the circle of his arms. The blinding heat of passion that licked her whole body from just the touch of his lips and tongue.

It lasted for ever, but it was over in a moment, and ended with a tangle of limbs, some frantic kicking to get back to the surface and a lot of laughter as they both hauled themselves up to sit on the solid planks of the pontoon. Again, by tacit consent, they sat quietly to watch the sunset with Mika's head against Rafe's shoulder and his arm draped loosely over hers, his fingers covering her tattoo.

The sunset was as gorgeous as ever but Mika closed her eyes after a minute or two because she wanted to bask in this feeling of such astonishing closeness. It was hard to pinpoint where her body ended and Rafe's started—as if they were two parts of one being. How had she not known that she had been missing another part of herself? That she had never felt complete?

It was the movement of Rafe's fingers on her arm that finally distracted her. Purposeful movement of just a single finger that was tracing the peaks and troughs of the inked design.

'It's the sea, isn't it?'

'Yes. It's a Maori design. The sea—and the land—have a huge spiritual significance in Maori culture.'

'I get that. I come from a country of islands, too. The sea is everything.'

Mika's breath caught. Rafe never talked about where he came from. Or anything else about his past. The only thing she really knew was that he'd been left without parents early in his life—as she had. This was the start, then, of finding out about this man she had fallen in love with.

'What islands? Where are they?'

'Out there…' Rafe tilted his chin towards the expanse of the Mediterranean, now gilded rose-pink by the rays of the sun. He was silent for a long moment and then his words were so quiet Mika barely heard them. 'They're named after the creatures they're famous for. *Les Iles Dauphins.*'

'No *way…*' Mika sat up straight so that she could turn her head to stare at Rafe. His arm fell away from her shoulder and the connection between their bodies was broken.

He stared back at her, an oddly wary expression in his eyes, and weirdly Mika felt a chill run down her spine. She swallowed hard.

'How did I not know that a place like that existed?' Her fingers had gone to the charm around her neck. 'Why didn't you tell me before?'

That wariness was still there but it was softened as Rafe offered an apologetic smile. 'I guess it didn't seem important. I'm here. And you're here. Maybe I'm just living in the moment.'

Which was exactly what Mika had decided she

needed to do. But questions were bubbling to the surface now and she couldn't hold them back.

'How far away are your islands? Do you live there now? How many dolphins are there?'

The curiosity in Mika's eyes was enchanting as her questions tumbled out like those of an excited child.

The moment of dread, when he had been sure she knew about his homeland and had suddenly made the connection and knew who he was, was evaporating.

He had taken the first step towards being really honest with her and it felt good. If he was gentle in the way he carried on, perhaps they could get to a place that would make their inevitable parting less painful.

He took a deep breath as he smiled back at her. 'They're not so far away but they're isolated enough to stay under the radar of the more usual tourist haunts. They're known as a tax haven. There's a thriving industry building luxury yachts. And the waters are a dolphin sanctuary. And, yes, I do live there now but I was away for quite a long time to go to school and university.'

'What did you study at university?'

'Oh…history. Politics. Environmental things…'

Mika's breath came out in a huff. 'Good grief… are you going to be a politician when you grow up?' She shook her head. 'I don't even know how *old* you are, Rafe.'

'I'm thirty-two.'

'Do you have a job?'

It was time to back off. 'I'm kind of between jobs right now. I wanted to try something different.' He'd had no idea, had he, of just how different that something was going to turn out to be?

Mika was grinning now. 'How's that working out for you, then?'

'I'm loving it.'

'But you're not going to be washing dishes when you go home, are you?'

'No.'

'What will you be doing?'

'Too many things, I expect.' He could feel the weight of those duties pressing in on him. The politics. The pomp and ceremony. The lack of personal space and choices. The sense of duty that would be ever-present…

The clock was ticking loudly now. This time was precious. He would never have anything like it, ever again.

Mika frowned. 'Are you a politician already?'

Raoul laughed. 'No…why?'

'Because you're so good at not giving a straight answer to a question.'

It really was time to distract Mika and there was a sure-fire way to do exactly that. By kissing her.

Or maybe he had wanted to distract himself. To remind himself of this extraordinary connection to another person that he had discovered and what it was teaching him about himself. That he wanted to buy a little more time simply to experience this.

Lost in the sheer pleasure of Mika's response, it was a surprise to find how brightly the lights of the bar on shore were shining. It told them how late it was getting but Raoul stole one more kiss. And then he held Mika's face between his hands.

'I don't want to think about my next job right now,' he said softly. 'Can't we just have this time? Just for us?'

Despite the fading light, he saw the shadow that clouded Mika's eyes. But he also saw determination and a smile that made light of any misgivings she might have.

'Okay. But will you answer one more question? Honestly?'

Raoul's heart skipped a beat. 'I would never lie to you, Mika.'

But he had already, hadn't he?

No. He just hadn't told her everything. But what if her next question was the one that ruined this moment? He wasn't ready for that. Not yet.

These memories would have to last him for ever. Surely one more night with Mika wasn't too much to ask for?

That curiosity was still lighting up her face and it was encased in a warmth that made him feel like he could tell her anything and she would accept it. Would forgive him, even. It was a risk but, in that moment, he felt safe enough to take it.

'One question,' he managed. 'Go for it.'

But Mika's face scrunched into thoughtful lines. 'Can I have one question tomorrow, too?'

He had to laugh. 'That's your question?'

'Oh, no…' Mika was laughing too. 'That's not fair. It's not a real question.'

'Why not?'

'Because it's not about *you*…'

There was something shy in her eyes. She was asking to be allowed closer but not quite sure if that was something he wanted. Raoul felt a tiny pang, as if a hairline crack had just appeared in his heart.

'Okay. We won't count that question. And, yes, you can have another one tomorrow.'

'And one the day after that?'

Oh…how tempting was that? The idea of more days. And nights. Of more hours than he could count just to be with her like this…

Mika was nodding as though he'd already agreed to the plan. And she was smiling.

'In that case, I have my last question for today.'

'What is it?'

'Whose turn is it to buy dinner?'

The trouble with questions was that one was never enough.

One question could open a door but then you stepped through it and it seemed like you were in a corridor with more and more doors stretching ahead of you.

Even deciding on that one question was tricky. One minute Mika would know for sure what she was going to ask next, but then she would come up with the potential answer she might get and she would see all those new doors. And she wasn't at all sure she wanted to open them.

Like, if she asked whether he would be going home to his magical-sounding islands as soon as his holiday ended.

It didn't make any difference whether his answer would be positive or negative because there were other doors that might change her life completely if she walked through them.

Like the one that might open if she asked if he wanted her to go with him...

It was too soon to open a door like that. What if the answer was no? That would break the bubble they had found themselves in now and Mika couldn't bear to do that. She had never been this happy.

Rafe hadn't moved back to his own room. Last night, when they'd caught the bus back to Positano after the swim she would always remember for that underwater kiss, he'd stopped when they'd found a pharmacy that was still open. They'd both been a little embarrassed by the purchase of condoms but Mika had been secretly thrilled. The love-making wasn't about to stop.

The fact that she was so happy about that was unbelievable. Was it only a couple of weeks ago that she had been so sure she would never let another man that close to her again? Her life had changed and her future was looking completely different.

Better.

Okay, they'd taken a stupid risk last night, but the moment had been too intense to think about something as premeditated as contraception and the odds were fortunately low enough for both of them to ignore, apparently. Well, not entirely ignore, because they'd had one of those silent conversations that had taken all of a heartbeat the moment that Rafe had picked up the box in the pharmacy and his gaze had met hers.

Is it too late?

It was a safe time, I'm sure of it.

Are you sure? You'd tell me, wouldn't you? If...

Yes, of course I'd tell you. Stop worrying... I'm sure...

She *was* sure but continuing that risk was definitely unacceptable. Mika hadn't yet found the place she would be content to call home. Getting pregnant would bring her journey to a grinding halt. Worse than that, it might scare Rafe so much that he would vanish from her life—the way her own father had. She would probably have to retreat to a place where life was familiar enough not to present extra challenges and that place was half a world away from where she was now.

With Rafe.

She watched as he paid for his purchase. Seeing his profile reminded her of that photo she'd taken the first evening they'd gone swimming together. Shifting her gaze, she took note of the printing machine in the corner of the pharmacy. She could pop in here with her camera card on a break from work and nobody would notice. How good would it be to have a copy of that photo that she could hold in her hand? A small, private thing to treasure.

One day, she would confess and check that he didn't mind, but that was an insignificant question compared to so many others.

So many questions that piled up in a corner because it was too hard to put them in an order of priority and appropriate times to ask were few and far between. There was never a chance to ask a meaningful question while they were at work together and, lying in his arms at night, random conversation was the last thing that came to mind.

This place—in this particular part of the world, with Rafe—was too good for Mika to want to risk changing a thing. In the end, she actually forgot to ask a personal question that day in the precious time between work and bed.

And she decided not to the day after that. Rafe seemed happy to be taking a day at a time—just for them—so maybe she needed to do that, too.

And it was enough for a few days. More than enough. This was a healing time for Mika and every day she felt safer as a little bit more of her protective shell crumbled and fell away. There were no tears in the wake of love-making now. She was becoming more playful and often there was teasing and laughter that added something completely new. Rafe was not only the most amazing lover she had ever found but he was her best friend as well.

The sense of something so solid between them made those doors far less daunting. So much so that there came a point, when a personal question came out so casually, it felt as natural as taking hold of Rafe's hand whenever they walked somewhere, like to the beach or home from work.

'What did you do?' she asked. 'In your last job?'

'I was a helicopter pilot.'

Mika's jaw dropped. His answer had come so automatically she knew he wasn't kidding but it was the last thing she had expected him to say. As far-fetched as him being an astronaut, perhaps. Or a brain surgeon.

'A commercial pilot?'

'No. I was with the military. We ran a rescue service as well.'

'Did you save people?' Mika smiled as she shook her head. 'Silly question. Of course you did. You've saved me twice already—it's second nature for you, isn't it?'

'I wouldn't say that.'

'Will you go back to a job like that?'

'No.'

'Why not?'

'I have another job waiting for me. That's why I needed a break. I wasn't sure how ready for it I am.' He squeezed Mika's hand. 'Are we going for a swim today?'

'Are you trying to change the subject?'

The discomfort in his glance confirmed her suspicion and Mika felt a chill run down her spine. What was he hiding? She hated the sudden tension that seemed to increase the heat of the late-afternoon sun enveloping them.

Her mouth simply ran away with her next question.

'You're not *married*, are you?'

'No.' Her hand was jerked as Rafe stopped in his tracks.

'Have you been in jail recently?'

His breath came out in an incredulous huff. '*No.*' But he was smiling as he tugged her into his arms and silenced her with a kiss. 'Enough questions, already...'

Mika could feel both the need to ask anything and that odd chill of premonition evaporating in the wake of his kiss.

'Okay...but I get to ask another question tomorrow.'

'Maybe.'

'You can't say that. You agreed.'

'Not exactly. And, even if I did, there's a problem with that arrangement.'

'Which is?'

Rafe's smile widened into a grin. 'You can't count.'

They started walking again and a welcome puff of a sea breeze lessened the heat around them. Or maybe it was that the tension had been blown away.

Mika's lips quirked. 'How many times will you make love to me tonight, Rafe?'

'One.'

She glanced up to catch his gaze and they both laughed.

'So I'm not the only one who can't count, then...'

CHAPTER EIGHT

IT WAS RAFE'S idea to do something special on their next day off.

The day was still early and deliciously cool but the clear sky suggested that being close to the sea would be the best way to enjoy the rest of it. Waiting for a beach-side café to open for breakfast, they wandered past the main beach in Positano where the deck chairs for hire were already being set up in orderly rows, colour-coded for the businesses that owned them, and they began to explore the marinas where boats of all sizes and shapes bobbed gently on their moorings.

It was Rafe who spotted the sign advertising a day trip out to the island of Capri. The cost was an extravagance in Mika's opinion but Rafe persisted as they retraced their steps to find coffee.

'You want to see it, don't you? It would make a great subject for one of your articles.'

'I would love to see it. I've been intrigued ever since I saw the outline of those rocks in the distance.'

'The *Faraglioni*? The Three Spurs? They're very distinctive. Did you know you can go right though the gap in one of them?'

'No…really?'

'If we find the right boat, it'll be part of the trip.'

'It's too expensive.'

'It would be my treat. And you need a new subject. You've finished your articles on the Footpath of the Gods and the Valley of the Ancient Mills now, haven't you?'

Mika caught her bottom lip between her teeth. 'I emailed them last night.' She scrunched her nose. 'I can't believe I took your advice and sent them to *National Geographic* and *Lonely Planet*. They only take the best.'

'It's a good thing.' Rafe squeezed her hand to make her pause and then dipped his head to kiss her. 'Always start at the top. Why settle for less if you don't have to?'

'Mmm…' The sound was a sigh of happiness in the wake of that kiss. 'Okay…if you're sure. But you could buy a lot of new clothes with that kind of money. I'll bet you haven't replaced half of what you lost when I kicked your backpack over that cliff.'

'Ah, but I've learned how little you actually need to survive,' Rafe said quietly. 'And, more than that, how good life can be when you keep things simple.'

The look in his eyes told Mika that *she* was the reason life was so good for him right now and the bubble of joy that caught in her throat exploded to send ripples of pleasure right through her body.

'I'll have to go home to get my camera. And my notebook.'

'We've got an hour or so before the boat leaves. I'll go back and make sure we can get tickets while you fetch your camera. We'll still have time for a quick breakfast. Let's meet at the café beside the bus stop.'

Excitement was chasing joy now. 'Race you, then.'

Mika stood on tiptoes to press another kiss to Rafe's lips. 'I'll be back here first.'

She wasn't, because she took a little extra time to throw their sunhats and some sunscreen into her small backpack, but it didn't matter, because Rafe had ordered coffee and croissants and had the tickets in his hand that were a passport to a new adventure. Mika couldn't wait. She was first on the boat to ensure the best position to take photographs and already had her camera in her hands as more and more people climbed aboard. The powerful launch took them swiftly up the coast and Mika started taking a series of shots as the massive spurs of rock the island was so famous for came closer and closer.

The side of the boat was not going to be the best place to record the experience of going through the gap of the middle spur, so Mika edged her way through the group to get to the back. A young man, holding a remarkably similar camera to her own, made space for her beside the rail.

'Nice...' He tilted his head as he looked at her camera. 'It's a D4, isn't it?'

'Yes. What's yours?'

'A D5. It's the latest.' He sounded English. And very confident. 'The best.'

'Wow...'

'I need it for my job. I'm a pro.' He grinned at Mika. 'I'm James.'

'Nice to meet you. I'm Mika.'

The boat was slowing, coming closer to the arched hole. Mika readied her camera but took a sideways glance at her new companion. He was going to get very hot today in those tight, black jeans and tee shirt but he certainly looked professional. The huge lens he had on his camera at the moment made her think of paparazzi.

The passage through the gap was exciting, with the roll of the sea and the height of the ceiling of rock overhead making the walls feel closer than they probably were. Mika tilted her camera, trying to capture it all.

'You need a wide-angle lens.'

'It's on my list. I'm saving up.'

Mika lowered her camera as the boat picked up speed, turning her head to see where Rafe was in the crowded boat.

'Hang out with me for the day and you might earn enough for any lens your heart desires.'

'What?' She turned back swiftly. 'How?'

'There's a rumour that there are some big names coming to the island today for a spot of shopping.' He tapped the side of his nose. 'Can't say who, but they're the hottest ticket there is right now. Get a good shot, and you could sell it for serious cash.'

So he *was* paparazzi. Mika took a step back, shaking her head. 'Thanks for the offer, but I'm spending the day with my boyfriend.' Another glance showed her that Rafe was still in the spot she'd left to come to the back of the boat. And he was watching her. Or, rather, he was staring at James.

James was staring back. 'Lucky guy,' he said. 'My loss.'

'Who was that?' Rafe asked when Mika got back to his side.

She shrugged. 'He said his name was James and he's a professional photographer. Apparently there's a movie star or someone going to Capri today and he wants to get a shot he can sell.' She made a face to ex-press her distaste. 'He said I could make big money if I hung out with him for the day.'

A glance over her shoulder revealed that she was still an object of interest for James. Or was it Rafe he was staring at? Impossible to tell now that he had sunglasses on, and he turned away as soon as Mika spotted him. Or, rather, he waited a heartbeat before he turned away. And he was smiling. Did he want her to know that he was still watching? That he was enjoying whatever game he thought he was playing?

'We picked the wrong day for this, I think.'

There was a note in Rafe's voice that Mika had never heard before. He sounded angry. Disgusted, even.

'Why?' Anxiety formed an unpleasant knot in her stomach. She didn't want this to be a 'wrong' day. She wanted a day like their walk through the valley of the ancient mills when that feeling of being connected to Rafe had become so incredibly strong. He'd fought the attraction, though, hadn't he? He had come so close to kissing her but had pulled away—so much so that he'd moved out of her room.

But now…everything had changed. If they were totally alone in a beautiful place, and returned to that kind of space where there was nothing else but that connection, would it grow even more? And, if it did, where would it take them? Could she ask the questions that would open the scariest doors of all?

Maybe she wouldn't need to ask them. Maybe he would tell her that he didn't want to stop sharing his life with her. Ever…

But, right now, he was scowling.

'Paparazzi are like wasps. When one gets attracted, you know there'll be dozens more. I hate them.'

Mika blinked. 'Hate' was such a strong word—as if he had personal experience of something extremely unpleasant. Or did he hate the principle of privacy being violated? That was more likely. Despite how little she still knew about him, Rafe was clearly a very private person.

And that was fine. Privacy was exactly what she was hoping they could find today.

'We won't hang around the shops,' she said. 'Look, I've got a brochure. There's a map. We could go walking and see something historic. Like this—the *Villa san Michele*. That looks amazing.'

Their boat wasn't the only one docking at Capri and the streets were already crowded. When they made their way to the funicular train to ride up the side of the cliff to the *piazetta*, they were urged on to squeeze in with dozens of other tourists.

Maybe Rafe was right, Mika thought, as she was jostled hard enough to cause momentary alarm. They *had* picked the wrong day for this. But then his arm went around her shoulders and his was the only body she was pressed against, and she felt safe again. They emerged into the square and the crowd thinned as they dispersed towards the cafés and shops. Mika breathed a sigh of relief and unfolded the brochure she was still holding in her hand.

'Let's find the road we need. Looks like the *Via Acquaviva* to start with and then the *Via Marina Grande*.'

'How long will it take to get to the villa?'

'It says about forty-five minutes.'

'It might be a good idea to buy some water and something to eat.' Rafe still sounded out of sorts, and he wasn't looking at Mika. He seemed to be scanning the crowds around them and wasn't happy with what he could see.

'Okay. My turn to pay this time.' Mika touched her shoulder to slip off the strap of her camera case and retrieve the euros she had tucked into a side pocket for easy access. 'Oh, my God...'

'What is it?' Rafe was looking at her now, his brow furrowed with concern. 'What's wrong?'

'My camera... It's *gone*...'

'You didn't put it in your backpack?'

'No. It was over my shoulder. I had it when I got on the train.'

When she'd been jostled hard enough almost to fall.

'You must have dropped it. We'll go back to the station and see if someone's handed it in.'

Mika's sinking heart told her that this was probably too much to hope for. The head shaking of the train officials was bad enough. Being given a lecture about being wary of pickpockets in tourist destinations was worse. She left her details with the officials and a woman assured her that she would pass the information to the police in case the camera turned up elsewhere.

The shine had been taken off the day and it seemed like they were both out of sorts now.

'I'm sorry,' Rafe said. 'Your camera can be replaced but you won't get photos today. You've saved your earlier pictures, haven't you?'

Mika nodded. They were all safely on her laptop. The most precious one of all—that she'd printed into a passport size the other day at the pharmacy—was tucked into the wallet she'd left at home for safekeeping.

And, yes, the camera could be replaced but how long would it take her to save up that kind of money again?

It was a setback, one that could very well ruin this day, but Mika couldn't afford to let that happen—not when she didn't know how many more days like this she would have with Rafe. Where they could find the right time and place that would make it natural to talk about what the future might hold...

With a huge effort she pushed the negative effects of her loss to one side.

'You know what?'

'What?'

'I've still got my notebook. I can come back and get photos another time. Maybe one of my articles will sell and that'll be enough to buy a new camera.'

Raoul could see the effort Mika was making. He knew how hard it was for her and he loved her for that courage and determination in the face of adversity.

That camera was precious. She had worked so hard for it and it represented her dream of a better future.

He would replace it for her. Not only the camera, but he would get every type of lens available as accessories—a tripod too, perhaps, and a beautiful case to carry everything in. He could have it gift-wrapped and delivered as soon as he got home.

When he'd left Mika behind...?

He didn't want to think about that. Not today, when it might be the last day they got to spend together like this. While they were both still invisible as far as his real world was concerned.

In the meantime, he needed to encourage her. To make them both feel better. His own mood still left a lot to be desired. The day had soured for him when he'd seen the way that photographer had tried to hit on Mika. It hadn't been as simple as jealousy, though, had it? His instincts had been validated by knowing that James was a paparazzo. One of the army of watchers that had never been far away for his whole life—a symbol of why he'd never really known what he'd needed to know about himself because he'd always had to be what others expected him to be.

He could be who he really was today, though. Not being able to protect Mika from that theft rankled but he could fix that, in time. For now, perhaps all he could do was offer comfort.

'Someone might still hand it in. We could check in at the police station on our way back.'

A police station was the last place Raoul wanted to go, though. What if they wanted his ID and awkward questions led to him having to confess the truth?

Mika's gaze was steady. Given the way they could communicate, it was more than likely that she could sense his reluctance. Was that why she was shaking her head?

'They've got my details. It's pretty obvious the theft was deliberate so I doubt it'll be handed in anywhere.' She shrugged. 'It's rotten but I don't want it to spoil our day. Let's try and forget about it.'

Her smile was pure Mika, with that edge of feisty cheekiness, but there was a hint of apology in her eyes.

'Have you got enough money for some water and a sandwich or two? Mine was in the camera case.'

Raoul could only nod because he didn't trust himself to speak for a moment. It summed up so much, didn't it? How much he loved her zest for life and the courage she displayed in living it. How little she knew about him to think that paying for a simple meal might be stretching his resources. How much she loved him, that she didn't want their day to be spoiled.

Escaping the crowds of the *piazzetta* and the streets of boutique shops that were luxurious enough to attract the kind of customers that the paparazzi loved to follow was a huge relief but, for a long time, their walk was silent and a little sombre.

Maybe it was the magic of the quiet, residential streets with their pretty gardens and wafting scents of lemon trees and lavender. Or maybe the increasing peacefulness had something to do with the summery sounds and sights of bees busy in the flowers and butterflies drifting past. By the time they had reached their destination, it felt like they had left the unpleasantness of James, the theft and the crowds of tourists far behind. There were so few people at the villa right now that, for long stretches of time, they could wander in peace and admire the beautiful, old house and its breath-taking views.

Mika was enchanted by everything.

'I wish I'd known we were coming here. The brochure doesn't tell me nearly enough—just that it was built by a Swedish physician, Alex Munthe, who came to Capri in 1885.'

'You'll have plenty of time to do some research later.'

'Mmm… Oh I love this quote…' Mika's eyes were shining. 'He said, "My house must be open to the sun, to the wind and the voice of the sea, just like a Greek temple, and light, light, light everywhere". Isn't that just how it makes you feel?'

It was impossible not to smile back. Not to be drawn into the joy Mika was sharing.

'We've got it all today, haven't we? The sun and the wind. I can't hear the sea yet, though.'

'You can see it from almost every window. And, if you can see it, you can hear it. In here...' Mika touched Raoul's chest, laying her hand over his heart. 'It's a song. The most beautiful music ever...'

He put his hand over hers, dipping his head so that his forehead rested on her hair. He knew exactly what she meant and the connection between them had never felt so strong.

Maybe they'd both been born with dolphin blood in their veins...

He could smell the scent of the shampoo she used, something lemony and fresh. And, more than that, he could smell a scent that was unique to Mika. Something sweet but with a hint of spice. Something he knew he would never smell on anyone else.

Something he would never, ever forget.

They got lost wandering from room to room when they were finally ready to explore outside.

One room was the biggest yet.

'It's like a ballroom,' Mika breathed. Her gaze snagged his. 'Let's pretend...'

'Pretend what?'

'That this is our house. That there's a small orchestra just over there and they're playing music, just for us...' Her eyes shone. 'I'm wearing a dress...a really pretty, swirly dress... Dance with me, Rafe...'

She held up her arms like a child asking to be cuddled and there was no way he could refuse the request. And then he started moving. It was obvious Mika had never had the kind of formal dance instruction that he'd had but she was so easy to lead and so astonishingly light on her feet. Even without music, this was a dance he would remember. And maybe they did have music…that song that came from the voice of the sea…

It was Mika who stopped the dance. She pulled away, holding only his hand as she took one more look around them.

'Imagine *really* living somewhere like this,' she whispered. 'How unreal would that be?'

Raoul didn't have to imagine. Many elements of this wonderful old house were very similar to the palace he would soon be returning to, like the intricately tiled floors, Grecian columns and works of art that could grace any museum. His home had a ballroom much larger than this, with an area that could seat an entire orchestra. That the idea of living in such opulence was a fairy-tale for Mika drove home the realisation that he'd been avoiding for so long.

She didn't belong in any part of his world. Even wearing a pretty dress was the stuff of make-believe and that was only a tiny piece of the jigsaw that made up the lives of the people in that world.

The thought was unbearably sad. How could he leave her behind when he couldn't imagine not having her in his life now?

But how could he *not* leave her behind?

Raoul's love for his country and his grandparents was bone-deep. His destiny was already written and it included a marriage that would bring two small kingdoms together and make them both stronger, which would be of great benefit to the people he was about to take responsibility for. He couldn't walk away from any of that. He didn't want to walk away from it but...

But doing so was going to hurt them both.

He could cope. He had to. But to hurt Mika so much? He wasn't sure he *could* do that.

A few days or weeks were nothing in the timeframe of a lifetime. How could snatching this gift of something so perfect have become such a dilemma?

He'd felt his heart crack once before when she'd touched it in an unexpected way and it felt as though that crack was widening with every gasp of astonishment or pleasure that escaped Mika as they kept exploring.

Hand in hand, they walked along the paved pathway beneath vine-covered pergolas supported by columns with splashes of vibrant colour from the flowers in perfectly manicured gardens on either side.

Their path led them past a granite sphinx that Mika had to touch, and that was the moment that Raoul felt that crack in his heart start to bleed.

Such small, clever hands. Such a light, reverent touch—as if she was still dancing.

That made sense. She was dancing her way through her life like some kind of magical creature.

He knew what it was like to be touched by those hands. How it made him feel like he was the best man he could ever be. He'd learned so much about himself in the last few weeks and it was too bound up in how he felt about Mika for the fragments ever to be separated.

When he left Mika behind, was he also going to leave behind the part of himself she'd helped him discover?

They came to a circular viewing point with an uninterrupted panorama of the Bay of Naples.

'You can see for ever,' Mika said in awe. 'I bet you can see *Les Iles Dauphins* if you look hard enough.'

Raoul stood behind Mika because he could see perfectly well over the top of her head. She leaned back against him and he put his arms around her, his breath escaping in a long sigh.

He would certainly be leaving a part of himself with Mika. A large part of his heart. But he had to believe he wouldn't lose what she had taught him. He'd learned things that were ingrained in his soul now. Things about love. Things about life. They would serve him well in the future and he would be a king that his people would be proud of.

Gazing out to the sea and the islands he knew were out there gave Raoul a pang of homesickness and, in that instant, he knew he was finally ready.

It was time he stepped back into his life.

And that meant that any reprieve was over. It was time to tell Mika the truth.

He tried to find a way to begin as they walked back to meet their boat but the words turned themselves over and over in his head and, whenever he caught Mika's gaze, they became an incomprehensible jumble.

It would be better to do it when they got back to her room, he decided. That way he could at least slip away and give her privacy to deal with the shock. How awful would it be for both of them to have to face heartbreak in public?

And it was *so* public. The crowds seemed to have swelled so much it was difficult to navigate through them to get to the train and down to the marina. Whatever celebrities had come to Capri today had certainly caused a stir. There were paparazzi everywhere, and James wasn't the only one on their return trip to Positano. He was still snapping photos. Raoul pulled the brim of the baseball cap he had been using as a sunhat further down his forehead and pushed his dark glasses further up his nose. It was probably Mika that the sleaze was trying to get a picture of but it was making him extremely uncomfortable.

Was this the kind of guy that would step in to fill the gap in her life when he had gone?

The dilemma was doing his head in.

On the one side was his duty that he could never walk away from.

On the other was his love for Mika and the overwhelming desire to be the man he was when he was with her.

There had to be a way through this that wouldn't destroy them.

And maybe there was…

Crazy thoughts were coming out of the turmoil in his head and his heart. He wasn't married yet. He wasn't even formally engaged, although the whole world was expecting the announcement. Would Francesca still *want* to marry him if she knew that his heart was with someone else?

His grandparents adored each other. Wouldn't they be prepared to allow him the same happiness of being married to the one he loved?

He needed more time to think.

Positano seemed to be as popular as Capri for tourists today and, oddly, the *Pane Quotidiano* seemed to be the most popular café. From the end of the street, it looked as if there was a crowd of people queuing to get in.

'What's going on?' Mika sounded worried. 'Maybe we should see if Marco needs extra help. They'll never be coping with that kind of crowd.'

As they got closer, the hairs on the back of Raoul's neck started to rise. He could see the cameras and he knew exactly who all these people were. A glance over his shoulder and he could see James a step or two behind them, and that was when he knew the game was up.

It was too late to try and escape. Mika was holding his hand—obliviously leading him further and further into enemy territory. He could feel her grip tighten as she realised that something unusual was going on. It was normal enough to see Marco waving his arms in the air as he spoke, but for Gianni to be out on the street as well, holding a newspaper? Other staff were filling the doorway, too, watching what was going on—Alain, the barista, and probably all the waitresses working today.

They were easily close enough to hear Marco now.

'He's *not* here. And how many times do I have to tell you that you're barking up the wrong tree? Go away— you're scaring off my customers.'

And then he spotted Mika.

'She'll tell you. *She* knows… He's her boyfriend, for heaven's sake.'

They moved as a pack, shifting their attention, lifting their cameras. Raoul could feel Mika's whole body stiffen as she froze. He could see the fear in her eyes as she looked up at him.

'*Prince Raoul…*' a dozen or more voices shouted in the instant the flashes started exploding around them. 'Look *this* way…'

CHAPTER NINE

NONE OF THIS made any sense.

Blinded by the bright flashes going off right in her face, Mika clung to Rafe's hand. He was pulling her away but her legs wouldn't co-operate. The roaring sound around them was starting to coalesce into recognisable words but it still didn't make any sense.

'*Why?*'

'Crown Prince of *Les Iles Dauphins*...'

'Washing *dishes*...?'

'Who's the girl, Prince Raoul?'

'Does your fiancée know?'

That did it. Like having a bucket of icy water thrown over her head. The word settled into Mika's consciousness and ricocheted around, inside her skull, like a bullet.

Fiancée...fiancée...fiancée...

She ripped her hand from Rafe's grip.

Rafe? Oh, yeah...he'd stumbled over the name when he'd introduced himself, hadn't he? Up there on the Footpath of the Gods, when he'd rescued her. Some instinct had suggested that maybe he didn't want her to know his real name. Who he really was.

But...a *prince*...?

With a *fiancée*...?

She was free of his touch now. The pack of paparazzi was moving in from all sides but Mika was small.

And as hard as nails. It was easy to launch herself at a gap between two of these men, squeeze through and then start running. She didn't realise she was holding her breath until she'd almost reached the end of the street and had to stop, doubled over as her lungs screamed for some oxygen.

Turning her head, she could see that Rafe was coming after her—getting away from the crowd that had now attracted a police presence—but he'd been ambushed by someone further up the street. A slim figure wearing tight, black jeans and a tee shirt...

James?

Her world had turned upside down and Mika had to find safety. Her lungs burning, she started running again and didn't stop until she got to the boarding house and into her room, where she could slam the door behind her and push the bolt into its slot to lock it.

Now what?

Should she throw herself onto her bed and hide her face in her pillow?

The bed that she had been sharing with the man she loved so much...who wasn't the man she'd thought he was...

Should she sink onto the couch and put her face in her hands?

The couch that she'd offered to someone whom she had believed had lost everything and had no money and no place to sleep.

Oh…there was humiliation to be discovered amongst this shock.

If it was true…

But how *could* it be true?

Why would a prince pretend to be nobody? To take on an unskilled, underpaid, physically hard job and work amongst people like herself?

Why would he have chosen to *be* with someone like herself—in the most intimate way it was possible to be with someone?

Instead of choosing either the bed or the couch, Mika stayed exactly where she was, standing in the middle of her small, dingy room. She wrapped her arms tightly around herself and, instead of hiding her face, she stared at the blank wall.

His last job had been as a helicopter pilot.

She'd thought that was as unlikely as him being an astronaut or a brain surgeon.

A huff of something like laughter escaped her throat.

Why hadn't *'prince'* been at the top of that list?

And he hadn't really chosen to be with her, had he?

He'd been determined not to be. Now she could see that hesitation on his part, when she'd believed he had been about to kiss her for the first time in the valley of the mills, in a whole new light.

She'd forced him into it.

She'd *begged* him to make love to her.

Shame was a step down from humiliation. Who knew?

No wonder he hadn't wanted her to ask too many questions. He'd known all along that there was no possibility of any future for them. He'd wanted to have this time *just for them*…

Just for him, more likely. A final fling before he got married.

A bit of...*rough*?

The rattle of her door handle, swiftly followed by a sharp rap on the door, made Mika flinch.

The sound of Rafe's voice sent a spear of pain in its wake.

'Mika?' Her name was a command. 'Let me in. *Now...*'

Things had hit the fan in an astonishingly spectacular way.

The last way Raoul would have chosen.

It would have been bad enough that his identity had been revealed before he'd had the chance to tell Mika the truth but never in a million years could he have imagined how much worse it could actually be.

Clutched in his hand was a copy of the newspaper that James had shoved in his face when he'd stepped out in front of him.

The front page of a national evening paper that had the provocative headline *Prince in Hiding* and a huge photograph.

A photograph he had no idea had been taken and could have only been taken by one person.

Mika.

He remembered the moment. Standing there on the flagged terrace in front of Bernie's bar in Praiano, watching that glorious sunset. After that swim with Mika, sitting on the pontoon and feeling that first, heady realisation that he'd found someone with whom he had an extraordinary kind of connection. He was staring out to sea, with one hand shading his eyes and clearly deeply in thought. With no sunglasses on and his beard still in the early days of its growth, it was no wonder that someone had recognised him.

How much had James been paid for that picture?

How much of a percentage had he offered Mika?

He'd been so smug.

'Say thanks to your girlfriend for me. Here—have this as a memento...'

He'd shaken off the rest of the paparazzi but it wouldn't take them long to run them down. His cover was blown and Mika's life was about to turn into a circus.

But maybe she deserved it...

Raoul banged his fist on the door again.

He'd been betrayed. And he was angry.

'Open the door, Mika. You owe me an explanation.'

The door flew open a second later.

'I owe *you* an explanation?'

Raoul unravelled the newspaper and held it in front of her.

'*You* took this picture, didn't you?'

He'd never seen her look this shocked. Not even in those first few minutes of knowing her, when she'd been in fear of her life on the side of that cliff. Or when she'd been threatened by those men intent on rape.

'How did *that* happen? Oh, my God...it was on my camera...'

For a heartbeat, he believed her. He *wanted* to believe her. But he could see the smirk on James' face as he'd asked him to pass on his thanks. And he knew how well a lot of women could act. They could make men believe whatever they wanted them to believe—

especially when they had eyes like Mika. He'd believed everything she'd told him.

Had trusted her.

And she'd betrayed him. He caught hold of that anger again, like a shield.

'The camera that got so conveniently stolen.' Raoul pushed his way into the room, forcing Mika to back up, slamming the door closed behind him with his foot. 'It must have made a great cover, being jostled in that crowd on the train.'

'What on earth are you talking about?'

'You handed it over, didn't you? To your new friend. *James*. Did you decide that being a travel writer wasn't a fast enough way to get to fame and fortune? Did you realise you had a much quicker route right at your fingertips?'

'You think I was *responsible* for this?'

'He told you that you could make big money if you hung out with him for the day, didn't he?'

Raoul could imagine all too easily what had really been said in that conversation.

'You think a movie star is a big deal? Boy, have I got a story—and photo—that you'd kill for...'

'What is it?'

'Hang on. Let's talk money first...'

Mika was looking stunned rather than shocked now. They hadn't lost the ability to communicate in the space of a single, sharp glance.

She was as angry as he was now.

'Why the hell would I have done that? When I didn't have the slightest idea who you actually were?

'Didn't you? *Really?* Not even when I told you where I came from?'

Raoul remembered that chill he'd felt when he'd told her the name of his homeland—the fear that she might have guessed the truth.

Had she just been waiting for an opportune moment to use that knowledge to change her life?

That was what was so much worse than everything hitting the fan.

He'd been taken for a fool.

He'd believed that Mika was in love with him for who he was as a man and not as a prince.

'I don't believe this. *I'm* the one who should be angry here. *You're* the one who lied to me.' There was a flash of something stronger than anger in her eyes now. Something like despair. 'And you said you never would…'

'I didn't lie to you.' Anger was a great way to obliterate anything like misgivings. 'I just didn't tell you who I was. I didn't *have* to, did I?'

'I didn't give that photograph to James. Even if I *had* known who you were, I would never do something like that.'

'I saw the way you looked at each other.' He'd seen it when she was back by his side on the boat and she'd turned to look at James. 'I saw the way he smiled at you. It's obvious that the deal had been done. That the arrangements for a handover were in place.'

Mika gave an incredulous huff, stepping further away from him.

'And you didn't want to go to the police, did you? I wonder why that was?'

He'd thought it was because she'd sensed his own reluctance, but now the new explanation was too obvious to ignore.

'It's not the first time this has happened,' he snapped. 'Tell me, is it easy for girls to pretend they're in love in order to get what they really want?'

Mika's face looked as if it had been carved out of stone and her voice was chillingly quiet.

'Get out,' she said. 'Get out of my life, Rafe. Or should that be *Raoul*?'

The chill of her voice and the stare he was receiving cut through the anger just enough for something else to surface.

A wash of something that felt ridiculously like... fear.

This was it, wasn't it? The last time he would ever see this woman.

And it made no difference what she'd done. He would still be leaving his heart behind.

A part of himself that he might never find again.

He did have to go, however. He could hear noises on the street below. He had to get out—probably via the fire escape—and then get himself out of sight. Summon whatever assistance he needed to get back to where he belonged. There was far too much more fallout to come from this and he had to front up and deal with it as soon as possible.

He owed his grandparents that much.

He owed his people that much.

Raoul turned. With a flick of his hand he threw the newspaper onto Mika's bed. The bed he'd been sharing with her. A symbol of just how much trouble he'd heaped on himself and those he loved.

Mika spoke as he let himself out of the room and the words followed him like an icy draft as he headed for the fire escape at the back of the old building.

'It's happened to me before, too, you know. Men pretending to be in love with me in order to get what *they* want.'

The slam of the door behind him came a split second after her final words.

'Never again.'

CHAPTER TEN

NO COMMENT...

How often had Mika used those words in the last few days?

What a nightmare.

Rafe...no, *Raoul*...had been sucked out of her life in an instant and the void had been filled by a crowd of ugly strangers who had no respect for her privacy. They wanted photographs of, and interviews with, the girl who had been the constant companion of a prince who had been hiding from the world.

That dreadful first night—and the whole of the next day—Mika had been too terrified to leave the safety of her locked room. She had never felt so alone and so scared. So utterly devastated.

A broken heart should be the least of her worries. She had undoubtedly lost her job and she couldn't even try to find another one. Not in this town, anyway. Probably not anywhere in Europe. New Zealand would be the best place to hide, but how on earth could she get there? It was half a world away and travel was expensive. She'd spent all her savings on that camera and barely had enough to meet this week's rent.

The camera that Rafe thought she'd sold. Yes...he

would always be *Rafe* in her head. And her heart. The man she'd fallen in love with. Not a fairy-tale prince who couldn't exist in her world.

Did he really believe that she'd sold *him* as well?

That hurt so much that her precarious financial situation seemed to pale in comparison for long stretches of time. Time when, with the spotlight of despair, she could understand why he'd believed that. She could look back on that encounter with James from his point of view and see exactly how the shreds of evidence had come together in a way that made it look as if she'd betrayed him.

And she *had* taken that photograph. Secretly. Thinking that she might need a memento of a very special time in her life.

What a joke… There were a thousand images of Prince Raoul de Poitier on the internet. Pictures of him in his military dress uniform with a red jacket, a row of medals and a sword hanging by his side. Formal pictures that probably hung in gilded frames in his palace. There were less formal ones of him in his flight uniform at the controls of a helicopter and some with him in a suit, performing royal duties, like opening a new museum. And there were way too many of him in immaculate evening dress with a beautiful woman by his side.

Tall, blonde women in designer gowns who clung to his arm and looked up at him, smiling, as if they'd never been so much in love. Like his *fiancée*, Princess Francesca…

His *almost* fiancée, her heart whispered.

As if it made any difference, her mind answered. It

was a done deal. And this Francesca was precisely the sort of woman the world expected this prince to wed.

Besides, none of those pictures was of Rafe. The smoothly shaved man with impeccable hair was nothing like the tousled, bearded stranger she'd met on the Footpath of the Gods that day. And maybe that was something that would give her some comfort one day. None of those beautiful, polished women knew this prince the way she had.

Even if she had been nothing more than a holiday fling, he *had* loved her, she was sure of it.

Not that anyone else would ever know.

Mika had read the articles that had been splashed everywhere in the media frenzy. What a shock it had been to see her name in print. She had been a friend, apparently. A friend who'd reached out to him when he'd needed help, having lost his wallet and other possessions. A friend who'd helped him find employment and shown him what it was like to live in the kind of world a prince never really got to experience.

They must have excellent media consultants on those islands, Mika decided. The spin that this prince's heart was so much with his people that he'd actually wanted to experience the kind of hardship that many people dealt with in their lives had turned him from a spoilt royal looking for escapism into some kind of hero.

A prince of the people who would very soon become their beloved King.

And she was who she'd always been and always would be. An ordinary person. Someone who'd been a *friend*. Nothing more…

But she had been more. And, like the secret they

had shared during that first meal together—that what had made the day so memorable had been that crippling episode of vertigo—there was silent communication to be found in things that she read as well. The prince's personal history was revisited again and again. She saw pictures of the stoic little boy standing beside his grandparents when his parents were being laid to rest after the tragic plane crash that had claimed their lives, and it made her heart ache for him.

They both knew what it was like to grow up without their parents and Mika could actually feel what the glance between them would always have been like— if they'd stayed together—as they acknowledged that bond again and again. At Christmas time, perhaps. Or when they saw a young mother holding the hand of her small child. Maybe he had been luckier than her, in that he'd had loving grandparents to raise him, but how hard would it have been for a boy to grow up without his father as a role model and advisor?

It had been bad enough for her. She'd never met her father—had no idea what he even looked like—and it felt like a part of herself had always been missing. If he had known she existed, would he have come to find her? Looked after her? Given her a safe place to live and loved her, even?

Given her a place to call home?

Mika could understand why Rafe had had to leave as soon as his true identity had been revealed. She could understand how he had been convinced that she'd betrayed him.

What she couldn't understand was how he hadn't realised how wrong he was as soon as he'd had time to think about it. Time to remember exactly what things had been like when they'd been together.

How much she had trusted him.

Loved him...

They had been so, so much more than merely *friends*. And they had been, ever since the moment they'd met. Had she given him her heart, without even realising it, in the instant she'd taken his hand up there on that mountain track? Had he given her at least a part of his, in that same instant? Even when he'd known it was something forbidden?

They'd both denied the physical attraction, hadn't they? They'd been fighting it for very different reasons but the barrier had been huge for them both and it had taken something traumatic to push them past the point of no return.

And Rafe had wanted it to continue as much as she had. She'd joked about him being a politician because he didn't want to give her a straight answer to her questions. He had wanted that time *just for them*...

Because he'd known it had to end the moment she knew the truth.

That was what hurt the most. That he'd taken her heart and soul *knowing* that he was going to destroy her in the near future. How could you do that, if you really loved somebody?

Had he been trying to protect himself from further scandal by dismissing their relationship as no more than friendship?

There was a part of her that refused to suffocate under the weight of betrayal. The part that would always love Rafe. It had a tiny voice but it made itself heard occasionally during the cacophony of heartbreak. It told her that he *had* loved her. So much that he couldn't bring himself to hurt her by telling her the truth. And that dismissing that love in public was the only way he had now to try and protect her.

If that was the case, it was working. Slowly. The number of paparazzi was dwindling as the days passed and her best friend amongst the waitresses—Bianca—had come to knock on her door one evening.

'You can come back to work,' she told Mika.

'Really? Has the crowd gone?'

'There's a new crowd now. People who want to see where a prince was working. Business has never been so good.'

'Marco wouldn't have me back. I didn't even tell him I was taking time off.'

'He knows why. We barely got to serve anyone apart from the journalists for a few days, anyway. And I think Marco likes being so famous. He's still sitting at his table all day, every day, happy to have his photo taken and talk to everyone.'

'I don't want to have my photograph taken. I haven't even been for a swim for days because I'm too scared to go out there. I'm terrified someone's going to be outside my door whenever I go to the bathroom. They shout at me from the street but I'm not going to give any interviews, no matter how much money I get offered.'

'They're offering you money?'

'Huge money. If I told them that we'd been sleeping together, I could probably buy a house.' Mika's eyes filled with tears. 'But I wouldn't do that. I couldn't...'

'You really loved him, didn't you?' Bianca drew her into a hug. 'Oh, hon...'

Mika drew back from the embrace with a sigh. 'You do need money, though. What are you eating?'

'I had some cans of stuff. And coffee. I've almost run out, now, though.'

'So come back to work. Not front of house yet—that's the message I was told to give you.' Bianca's smile was wry. 'Marco probably doesn't want to share the spotlight. But he says you can have Rafe's old job, if you want. We're all having to take turns washing dishes at the moment and nobody's very happy about it.'

There really wasn't a choice to make. Mika was going to be in serious trouble if she didn't start earning a wage but how ironic would that be—to take Rafe's old job?

How much more miserable was it possible to become?

Quite a lot, it seemed.

Sneaking around to get in and back from the restaurant and avoid being seen was horrible. Not being able to go swimming was even worse. The job itself was unpleasant and backbreaking but Mika fronted up to do it day after day. It became automatic and gave her mind far too much time to wander.

To remember things that made her feel so stupid. Like sharing her dream of becoming something as important as a travel writer. Or suggesting to Rafe that they pretended they were living in the villa that was as close to a palace as she'd ever been inside. Things that made her so sad, too. Like the conviction that giving her heart to Rafe would be worth it even if he disappeared because she would always know how perfect life could be.

It didn't help at all now because Mika knew that her life could never, ever be that perfect again.

Her whole body ached.

Her heart was splintered. Nothing could ever put that many broken shards back together again.

Even her belly ached. So much that it made her feel sick sometimes. One day, Bianca brought in a load of plates that had congealed egg and bacon rinds on it and Mika took one look and had to flee to the toilet to throw up.

She was splashing cold water on her face when Bianca slipped into the tiny restroom and closed the door behind her.

She met Mika's gaze in the spotted mirror above the hand basin and her eyes were troubled.

'Are you in trouble, hon?'

'What do you mean?'

'Are you pregnant?'

'*No.*' The thought was so shocking, Mika had to grip the sides of the basin to persuade her legs to keep holding her up.

'Is it possible?'

Was it? Her mind flew back to that silent conversation in the pharmacy that night.

Is it too late?

It was a safe time, I'm sure of it.

But how long ago had that been?

Weeks…

Way *too* long…

'Oh, my God…'

The basin wasn't enough support any more. Mika's shoulder was already against the wall of the tiny room. She leaned against it as she let herself slide to the floor where she could curl up, hug her knees and hide her face by resting it on her arms.

She would have to ask Bianca to go to the pharmacy and buy a test kit for her to avoid attracting the attention of any lurking journalists but Mika already knew what the answer was going to be.

It would be better, in fact, if she went somewhere else to do it herself so that her friend wouldn't be involved. Somewhere a long way from here where nobody would recognise her as being the 'friend' of the prince. She couldn't afford to go back to New Zealand but there were a lot of big cities in Europe that she could hide in. A train ticket wouldn't be expensive and she could carry everything she owned in a backpack, couldn't she? If she sold her laptop, that would not only give her enough money, it would make the backpack lighter to carry.

The thought of being so totally alone was terrifying. The prospect of facing it came with a wave of dizziness that reminded her of the moment she had realised she was in so much trouble on that mountain track.

The day that Rafe had come into her life…

As impossible as it might have seemed, her heart broke a little more.

Had she really thought that working as a dish washer would be the most miserable extra change in her life now?

How wrong had she been?

CHAPTER ELEVEN

PRINCE RAOUL DE POITIER WAS standing in front of his bathroom mirror. A gilt-framed mirror that reflected just how completely the circumstances of his life had returned to normal. How different was this to the shared facilities of that boarding house, with the vastness of the private room, its generous showering and bathing facilities, countless soft, fluffy towels and a selection of skin products any pharmacy would be proud to display?

The aftershave he'd just splashed on his face still stung even though the beard was long gone. How long would it take for his skin to stop feeling oddly raw and exposed?

His heart still felt raw, too.

Unbelievably heavy.

And he didn't like the man he was staring at in the mirror.

His journey of self-discovery had been a disaster. He'd learned something that he wasn't sure he could live with.

That he was a man who could take someone's heart and then crush it for the greater good of others.

Had he really believed—in his heart—that Mika

had sold that picture and betrayed his identity? That she knew she'd fallen in love with a prince?

Of course she hadn't. She had fallen in love with the man she believed him to be. An ordinary bloke by the name of Rafe.

He'd let his mind overrule his heart in that instant. Allowed himself to feel betrayed and then angry because that was the easiest escape route as the reprieve of an ordinary life had exploded around him.

He'd left Mika believing that he'd simply used her. That he hadn't really loved her.

And she deserved so much more than that.

But what could he do?

His duty.

As he had been doing ever since he'd been whisked back to *Les Iles Dauphins*, away from the media circus in Positano. The look of shock on the faces of his grandparents when he'd walked into the palace with his long hair and beard, wearing his shorts and the 'I heart Positano' tee shirt had told him just how far past acceptable boundaries he had wandered. The days that followed had been a matter of damage control and, thanks to a quick-thinking team of media experts and the unwavering support of his grandparents, what could have been a complete scandal had been turned around to make him some kind of hero.

A man of the people who, thanks to a courageous action, now knew exactly what it was like to be an ordinary person. He was someone who understood them and whom they could trust to rule them with compassion and wisdom.

But Raoul would never feel like a hero.

He had a million images of Mika imprinted on his

mind and in his heart, but the only one he could hold in his hand was the one taken in that dreadful moment they'd been spotted at *Pane Quotidiano*. She had been wearing that white singlet top that was his favourite, because it showed off her gorgeous brown skin and revealed the tattoo that was a symbol of the sea that meant so much to her.

Dolphin blood…

The voice of the sea…

The way he could dance with her with only the music in their hearts to follow…

The mosaic tiles of his bathroom floor were not un-like the surface they had danced on in that old villa.

The house that Mika had thought a palace.

That she'd wanted to pretend to be living in. With him…

Dear Lord…he'd never known how much it was possible to miss someone.

Or maybe he had and that was why this was so difficult. It took him back to being that scared five-year-old, standing so stoically during the final farewell to his parents.

Doing his duty, even then, because he knew what was expected of him by so many people.

And today, he was about to take his next step into doing what was expected of him. Francesca was due to arrive later. It was time to propose. To make the engagement official. His mother's ring was in a velvet case on his dressing table, waiting for him to slip it into his pocket. There would be a celebratory lunch and many, many photographs to go with the press release. There would also be the first of what would probably be many, many meetings to arrange their wedding—

a train of events that there would be no possibility of stopping once it had begun.

The sensation of a ticking clock had never been so strong. He had to do something before it was too late. Something that would, at least, give Mika the comfort of knowing that he cared.

That he was truly sorry.

One of his personal assistants had his suit ready for him when he left the bathroom suite that adjoined his bedroom.

'Their Royal Highnesses are taking breakfast in their suite,' he was informed. 'They would like you to join them.'

'Of course.' Raoul donned the crisp, white shirt and held out his wrists to have the cufflinks inserted. His favourite ones, which were gold, embossed with the image of a leaping dolphin.

His heart grew even heavier. It was like a very personal punishment that the symbol of his homeland was going to remind him of Mika every day for the rest of his life.

'Pierre?'

'Yes, sir?'

'I have a task for you this morning. I want you to source a camera. A Nikon D4—or something better if there's a new model available.'

'Certainly.'

Pierre was his most trusted assistant. Raoul would have described him almost as a friend, except that he now knew what real friendship felt like.

What true love felt like…

Pierre held out his jacket so that he could slip his

arms inside the silk lining. 'Are you becoming interested in taking up photography?'

'No. It's a gift. I want you to buy a range of lenses to go with it, too. And any other accessories that are recommended. And I want everything in a case. Gift-wrapped.'

'No problem. Would you like me to arrange delivery, as well?'

'Not yet. I need to think about that. It will need discretion.'

Pierre didn't bat an eyelash. 'Just let me know, then, Sir. I'm sure something can be arranged.'

The palace of *Les Iles Dauphins* was on a headland that gave it sweeping views of the Mediterranean and the suite of rooms that was his grandparents' private domain had a terrace with the best view of all because you could see the royal beach—a tiny, private bay that could only be reached via the stone staircase from the palace gardens.

On a beautiful morning like this, the only thing that could disturb the clear blue of the calm water was the way the bay's permanent residents greeted a new day. The joyful leaping of the small pod of dolphins that claimed this well-protected bay as their home base was such a pleasure to watch, it was no wonder that this was the preferred spot for Prince Henri II and his wife, Gisele, to take their breakfast.

There was something about the scene on the terrace that made Raoul pause for a moment before he joined them. His grandparents, as always, were sitting close together on both sides of a corner. At this particular moment, they weren't eating or admiring the view, they were looking at each other. Smiling.

The heavy lump that was Raoul's heart this morning twisted a little in his chest. He loved these people—his family—so much. And he loved that they still loved each other, after so many decades of being together. Remembering that they were both well into their eighties now was a poignant reminder that their time was limited, and as Raoul moved close enough to bestow his customary kiss on the soft skin of his grandmother's cheek he made a silent vow to make the rest of that time as perfect as possible.

They had given him so much.

'Good morning, Mamé... Papé.' The childish names for his grandparents had never been relinquished in private. 'It's a beautiful day, isn't it?'

'Help yourself, darling.' Gisele waved at the covered platters on the serving table behind them. 'I ordered your favourite cheese and mushroom omelette.'

'Can I get you something? More coffee?'

'Some orange juice for Henri, perhaps. He hasn't taken all his pills yet.'

His grandfather made a grumbling sound that suggested he didn't need to be nagged but he winked at Raoul.

'Big day for you, today,' he said. 'What time does the beautiful Francesca arrive?'

'Late this morning.'

'There's a formal luncheon,' Gisele added. 'And photographs this afternoon. It's in your diary, Henri.'

Raoul put the plate with its fluffy omelette and pretty roasted tomatoes in front of him at the table. He picked up his fork but then put it down again. He really wasn't hungry. He sipped his coffee, instead, and watched as his grandmother arranged the morning medication for his grandfather, handing over each pill and watching carefully as it was taken. It was impossible not to notice the tremor in his grandfather's hand and the way Gisele put each tablet into his palm with enough care that it wouldn't be dropped.

'Is there something wrong with the omelette, Raoul?'

'No, Mamé. It's perfect. I'm just not very hungry.'

'But you're losing weight. You haven't been like yourself ever since you got home. I'm worried about you, darling…'

His grandfather reached out to pat her hand. 'The thought of marriage makes any man a little nervous.' He smiled at Raoul. 'Don't worry, lad. It gets better.'

But Gisele looked anxious. 'It is a big step. And so close to your coronation. Is it too soon? We haven't finalised the date. Francesca's grandmother is one of my oldest friends and I'm sure we could arrange for it to be delayed…'

Raoul saw the glance his grandparents exchanged. A delay wasn't something they wanted and he could understand why. These two had been together since before Henri had become the ruling Prince of *Les Iles Dauphins*. He had always had the loving support of his wife by his side.

They wanted the same thing for him, didn't they?

That support was something that came naturally when you loved someone. Mika could have given him that. As he would have given her…

Would delaying his marriage change how he felt?

No. It would make things worse because he'd have

more time to imagine a very different future. With Mika as his princess. Sitting out here, one day in the future, having breakfast and watching dolphins play...

'What's the secret?' The question came unexpectedly. 'For a happy marriage?'

'Respect,' his grandfather said.

'Love,' His grandmother smiled.

'Were you both in love when you married?'

'In *love*?' His grandfather grunted. 'Stuff and nonsense.'

But Gisele's eyes twinkled. 'Oh, yes, we were. You couldn't keep your hands off me, Henri.'

A huff of surprised laughter escaped Raoul. 'Too much information, Mamé.' His laughter faded. 'You chose each other, though, didn't you?'

'What do you mean?'

'Your marriage wasn't arranged.'

'That's true,' Gisele murmured. 'I was his mother's secretary. It was all a bit of a scandal, really.'

'But everybody forgave you, didn't they? Because they knew how much in love you were?'

'Oh... Raoul...' Gisele's words were no more than a sigh.

A coffee cup rattled loudly as Henri tried to put it down on its saucer. 'Are you saying you don't want your marriage to go ahead?'

The coffee had spilled onto the tablecloth. His grandfather was suddenly looking older. Almost grey. Unwell...?

Raoul backed off from whatever he might have been about to say. 'Francesca is beautiful. She's already a princess. She's an ideal choice.'

'But not *your* choice.' His grandmother's faded blue

eyes looked suspiciously bright. 'You're not in love with her...'

'In *love*.' Henri's words were dismissive. 'Stuff and nonsense. It's no more than lust.' The old Prince was rubbing his chest with one hand. He pushed back his chair and got to his feet, leaning on the table as he did so.

'Are you all right, Papé?' Raoul was alarmed. 'You don't have a pain in your chest, do you?'

'I'm fine. I'll see you...*and* Francesca...at luncheon.'

Raoul caught his grandmother's gaze.

'I'll go,' she said quietly. 'I'll call the doctor.' She paused to touch Raoul's head as she passed. 'It'll be all right,' she added. 'Don't worry...'

That Gisele chose to join him in what was supposed to have been a private meeting before lunch was more than a surprise to Raoul. How was he supposed to propose with an audience?

'Is something wrong? Is it Grand-père?'

His grandmother took a seat beside Francesca, opposite him, on a matching small, overstuffed couch.

'He's resting,' she said. 'The doctor thinks it was his angina. He needs to use his spray more often.' She turned to smile at Francesca. 'How are you, my dear? I've just been having such a lovely chat to your grandmother.'

'Oh?' Francesca's smile wavered.

Raoul frowned. This meeting had been going well. He and Francesca had a lot in common and, while things felt a little awkward still, they just needed more time to get to know each other better. He liked her and she seemed to like him.

They hadn't got near discussing the really important business between them but it had been a good start.

'You've done so well in your studies,' Gisele continued. 'I didn't realise how close you were to graduating as a doctor.'.

Francesca bit her lip. 'I've arranged to take leave from my studies. I'm hoping I can finish them one day and, while I know I could never practise as a physician, I hope I can become involved with the health systems in both our countries.'

'It's your passion, isn't it?'

Francesca looked down at her hands. She spoke quietly. 'I've been brought up to understand my position in life and my duty—to both my family and my country. I would never do anything to harm the people I love.'

She raised her head to look at Raoul and he could see a determination that reminded him so much of Mika that he had to smile back. He could respect that.

'But what about Carlos?'

Francesca turned her head with a gasp. 'Oh…my grandmother swore she would never say anything…'

Raoul blinked. 'Who's Carlos?'

Gisele patted Francesca's hand. 'Another passion, I think.'

Francesca's eyes filled with tears as she looked back at Raoul 'I'm sorry,' she whispered. 'I would never have said anything. And it's over now. It had to be…'

Raoul's smile was gentle. 'I understand. Believe me…'

'Of course he does,' Gisele said. 'Now, I'm going to leave you two to have a talk. Just bear one thing in mind. Anything is possible.' She was smiling as she got to her feet. 'Just look at what Raoul managed to do in his time away. And how well it was handled. Everybody understands true love.'

The silence in the room grew louder as he and Francesca sat there, both more than a little stunned.

'What did she mean?' Francesca asked finally.

'I think she knows more than I realised,' Raoul admitted. 'I... I met someone while I was away.'

'You're in love with her?'

Raoul swallowed. And then nodded. He cleared his throat. 'And you're in love with...with Carlos?'

The glow in her eyes was more than enough to confirm it.

'But you were going to go ahead and do your duty and marry *me*?'

It was Francesca's turn to nod.

He had been going to do the same thing but this changed everything, didn't it?

If there was one thing that Raoul had learned from his escape from his real life, it was that he was, at heart, a good man. Someone who could love, nurture and protect. A man who could trust his instincts about what was right and wrong.

And this was wrong. Was that the message his grandmother had been trying to leave him with? That it was possible to follow his instincts? That anything could be managed and forgiven in the name of true love?

'We both have a position in life that carries a huge responsibility,' he said slowly. 'A duty to do the best for all those that we are responsible for.'

'Yes.' Francesca's head was bowed. 'I'm only

twenty-five,' she whispered. 'But I feel like a parent. One with many thousands of children.'

'Have you flown anywhere recently?'

'What?' Her head jerked up. 'Of course... I flew here. What's that got to do with anything?'

'I don't mean on a private jet. I meant on an ordinary commercial flight.'

'Oh, yes. I've done that.'

'Did you watch the safety briefing?'

Francesca's eyes were wide and puzzled.

'They tell you what to do if an oxygen mask appears,' Raoul continued. 'They tell you that you should put your own on before you help others.' He took a deep breath. 'We have a duty to many people, Francesca, but we also have a duty to ourselves. To make sure that we are in the best position to do our best for others.'

'You mean...?' Her words died but he could see the birth of hope in her eyes.

'I mean that you should be with the person you love,' Raoul said softly. 'And so should I...'

The private helicopter with its royal insignia touched down in Positano late that afternoon. Carrying the heavy, beautifully wrapped parcel, Raoul and his bodyguards made their way as discreetly as possible to the *Pane Quotidiano*.

Marco was sitting at his usual table on the pavement. His jaw dropped when he saw the group approaching.

'I've come to see Mika,' Raoul told him. 'I...have something for her.'

'She's...ah...she's not here.'

Others had noticed his arrival. Bianca came outside.

'She's gone,' she told Raoul.

'Where?'

'I don't know.' Bianca shook her head. 'She just vanished. Days ago. I went to her room when she didn't show up one day but it's empty. She's gone…' She touched Raoul's arm. 'You have to find her,' she said quietly. 'It's important.'

CHAPTER TWELVE

IT WAS A fairy-tale palace. With tall stone walls and turrets and spires that were becoming a dramatic silhouette as the blinding sunshine of the day began to fade.

With her dark sunglasses, a big, floppy hat on her head and the backpack over her shoulders, Mika knew she passed as any ordinary tourist who'd come to these remote islands.

Someone who even advertised her love for the creatures this land was named for by wearing a tiny, silver replica around her neck.

She had walked up a big hill from the marina where her ferry had docked and she hadn't needed a map to find her destination. She might have sold her laptop but it had been easy to find an internet café, in the village where she'd been lying low for the last week or so. She'd done her research as thoroughly as she always did and the route to the de Poitier Palace was imprinted on her mind.

So was another email she had received. One that had given her confidence to face a new future. The *National Geographic* not only wanted to buy both her articles, they wanted more...

She could do this.

She could support not only herself but the baby she was going to bring into the world.

What she couldn't do was repeat the mistakes of the past.

Her baby was not going to grow up with no idea of who its father was. Not knowing a land where so many generations of his family had come from. He—or she—was never going to feel abandoned. Or unwanted.

This baby was going to be loved. And cared for and protected.

And that was what had finally given Mika the courage to make this journey.

Her father had never known she existed, so he'd never had the chance to fill even a tiny part of the gap that had been left in her life.

In a way, Mika was doing this for herself—to put right a past wrong. She was doing it for her baby, too, of course. And she was doing it for Rafe. He had the right to know that he was going to be a father. And, because she had no intention of hiding the truth from her child as it grew old enough to understand, the royal family deserved the courtesy of a warning.

It would cause a scandal one day, but maybe, with enough time to prepare for it, something could be arranged to protect the small, illegitimate prince or princess who was going to be born.

Mika had no idea how that might be done.

Now that she was here, she had no idea of what to do next. How did one go about asking to speak to a prince? She was just an ordinary tourist, standing here outside the palace, gazing through the enormous, wrought-iron gates. A rather wilted tourist. It had been such a hot day and a long walk up a decidedly steep hill.

The sound of an approaching helicopter made her look up. The sound grew louder and louder as the helicopter circled and came lower, finally disappearing on the other side of the palace where, presumably, there was a heliport.

Was Rafe at the controls?

Mika's heart skipped a beat and then sped up.

If she stood here long enough, would a guard of some kind come and ask her what she wanted? There had to be people watching. Security cameras at the very least.

And, if someone did come, would they simply laugh at her request or was it possible they could pass on a message of some kind?

It wasn't possible.

Raoul had barely caught a glimpse of the figure standing outside the palace gates as his helicopter had come in to land but he had known instantly who it was.

Had he seen her with his heart instead of his eyes?

He barely registered what the voice in his headphones was telling him.

'She hasn't used her passport.' His head of security had been busy on the flight home. 'Not at an airport, anyway. So she can't have gone back to New Zealand.'

'No.' Raoul closed his eyes as the aircraft touched down gently. He could still see the shape of that small figure standing there outside his home. 'I don't think she has. Don't worry about it any more, Phillipe. I can handle it now.'

Mika had come to find *him*…

Hope was filling the dark space he had entered after finding that she'd disappeared from the café in Positano.

He ducked his head to stride beneath the slowing rotors of the helicopter. He waved off his bodyguards as he avoided the nearest palace entrance. He knew there would be many eyes watching him as he ran through the gardens, only slowing as he finally reached the front of the palace, but he didn't care.

Would Mika still be there?

The turrets and spires weren't the only silhouette against the fading light. Indecision had kept Mika immobile but it seemed that her plan might be working. A guard was coming around the corner of the palace. Not someone in a military uniform that she might have expected but a tall man in a dark suit. He looked like a bodyguard. A member of some special forces, perhaps, who'd been dispatched to find out what she thought she was doing, standing here and staring for so long.

Except…there was something about the way this man was moving. And well before he got to her—when he'd only just reached a long, rectangular pond with its blaze of flowering water lilies and the fountain that was a whole pod of leaping dolphins—the massive gates in front of Mika magically began to swing open.

Inviting her in…

But she couldn't move.

Not until the figure got even closer. Until she could see the expression on Rafe's face. Until he'd taken off his sunglasses and she could see the expression in his eyes…

Even then, she couldn't move.

This was like nothing she could have prepared herself for.

Rafe didn't even know she was pregnant.

But he wanted *her*.

As much as she wanted *him*…

This was perfect.

If he'd had a magic wand to wave, this was the one place he would have chosen to bring Mika.

A place that could provide the things that she loved most in the world.

The sea.

And dolphins.

He'd done no more than take her hand as the palace gates swung shut behind them because he knew how many people were watching.

'Come with me,' was all he said.

There was no one here on the private royal beach. Oh, it was quite possible his grandmother could see them, but if she was watching she would be smiling.

Crying, perhaps. The way she had when she'd taken him aside after Francesca had gone earlier today.

'*You reminded me this morning of what it was like,*' she'd said. '*When Henri and I were so much in love. If this is where your heart is, Raoul, you have to follow it. You have my blessing. You'll have the blessing of your grandfather, too, when I explain. And your people…*'

Mika's backpack lay abandoned on the sand. He might have guessed she would be wearing that white bikini as her underwear. His own suit was discarded alongside the backpack. He had nothing more than his silk boxer shorts to swim in, but it didn't matter. The light was fading fast anyway and the rosy glow of the sunset made the shapes of the dolphins swimming around them dark and mysterious.

As dark as Mika's eyes as he finally pulled her into

his arms and kissed her. They way he'd been dreaming of kissing her every night they'd been apart.

'I was so afraid I wouldn't be able to find you,' he whispered, his lips still brushing hers. 'I thought I would be missing you every minute of every day for the rest of my life.'

'I'm here.' Mika was smiling against his lips. 'I had to come. There's something I have to tell you…'

That she forgave him for the accusation he'd made? That she still loved him?

A note in her voice told Raoul that it was time they talked properly. This time in the water had taken them back enough to re-establish their connection. To wash away the pain of their time apart. It wasn't the place really to talk, though.

He led her from the shallows onto the sun-warmed sand. The air around them was still warm, too, but he picked up the jacket of his suit and draped it around Mika's shoulders. And then he sat beside her and took her hand again.

'There's something I need to tell you, too.'

It felt like he was still out of his depth in the sea, looking into her eyes. As if he could drown…

'I love you, Mika. And I'm sorry.'

'For thinking I'd sold that picture? It doesn't matter.'

'I'm sorry for more than that.'

Mika ducked her head and nodded. 'I understand. I know you couldn't tell me who you were. It would have ruined everything, wouldn't it? We'd never have…' A soft sound escaped her lips. An incredulous sort of huff as she left her sentence unfinished. And then she looked up. 'You saved me, you know? Three times…'

'Three?'

'Up on the track. From those men. And…and from maybe spending the rest of my life too scared to ever trust someone. Of never finding someone to be with like that. Of never…becoming a mother…'

It took a long, long moment for the implication of those words to sink in.

When it did, it took another long moment for Raoul to find his voice.

'You're not…?'

Just a single nod and his world changed for ever.

'I'm sorry. I really did think it was a safe time. I must have got my dates mixed up…'

'And that's why you came here today? To tell me?'

Another nod. 'I want this baby to always feel wanted. Loved. Even if we could never be together, I want it to know who its father is.'

Like Mika never had. Raoul's heart felt so full it was in danger of bursting.

'He—or she—will always feel loved,' he said softly. The wonder of it was really sinking in now. He was going to be a *father*? 'Will always *be* loved,' he added. 'So will you…'

It was a long time before they could speak again but it made no difference because the touch of their lips and bodies would always be a conversation in itself.

How had he ever thought he could live without this woman in his life? By his side?

'This is going to cause trouble, isn't it?'

'No.' Raoul pressed another gentle kiss to Mika's lips. 'It will be a cause for great celebration. My grandmother is going to be so happy. She wants nothing more than to see me settled and happy. To be married and raising a family.'

'But…what about your fiancée?'

'We were never officially engaged. And Francesca will be just as happy as we are. She's going to be with the person *she* loves. We will maintain a friendship and work together to strengthen both our countries.'

'But…'

'But what?' Raoul swallowed a sudden fear. 'Are you worried that this isn't the place that you've been searching for? That you couldn't be happy living here?'

'I've only seen a tiny part but I already know this is the most beautiful place on earth.' Mika was smiling as she looked out at the small bay, as if she could still see the beautiful creatures who had shared their swim. She turned back to Raoul. 'And you know what?'

'What?'

'I've discovered something. A place isn't a *place*.' She touched Raoul's cheek softly. 'Or it is, but it doesn't actually matter *where* it is. That place only exists because it's beside a person. You told me that, but I wasn't really listening.' Her voice sounded like it was choked with tears. 'My place in the world is beside you, Rafe. Wherever you are, if I'm beside you, I'm *home*. But…'

Raoul was blinking back tears too. Because he couldn't have put it better himself.

'But…?'

Mika shook her head. 'I can't marry you.'

Maybe the air wasn't as warm as he'd thought. The sudden chill went right to Raoul's bones.

'Why not?'

'Are you kidding? Me? A…a *princess*? It's impossible.'

'You've forgotten something else I told you, haven't you?'

'What?'

'That you can be anything at all that you really want to be. It's one of the things I adore so much about you, my love. Your courage. And your determination. You could be a princess. *If* that's what you want.'

'If it means being with you for the rest of my life, why wouldn't I want it?'

'I was afraid you would never want to be part of my world. That's another thing I love about you. That wildness. Your freedom. Your…dolphin blood. There are constraints with being royal and it might be like putting you in a cage. A gilded cage, but the walls are still there.'

'You'd be inside those walls, too.' Mika's smile was so tender, Raoul could feel his breath catch. 'It's still the place I'd always want to be. But fairy-tales don't really happen. I don't have a fairy godmother out there to wave her wand, put me in a pretty dress and let me dance away with my prince…'

'Oh, but you have.' Any fears evaporated as Raoul kissed her again. 'You just haven't met my grandmother yet…'

EPILOGUE

HER ROYAL HIGHNESS, Princess Gisele, adjusted the folds of her dress as she settled onto the ornate, red velvet chair with its gilded arms and headrest.

Being in this prime position at the front of *Les Iles Dauphins'* historic cathedral meant that she could take in the full majesty of the wonderful old, stone building—the ornate archways and pillars, the glowing wood of the rows of pews and the statues of her country's most significant figures whose mortal remains had been laid to rest in the raised vaults. The stained-glass windows were renowned as well and right now the intricate panes of glass were glowing as they were touched by the day's fading sunshine.

It could be—and often had been—a sombre place to sit but not today.

Today there were garlands of snowy white flowers on every pew and around the base of every statue. There was joyful music thundering from the enormous pipes of the organ and the harmony of a choir to add to its tone. And there was a sea of colour wherever Gisele's gaze roamed. So many beautiful dresses in shades of pink, blue and mauve. So many wonderful hats on the women in the pews that gave way to tiaras and crowns towards the front of the congregation. Nobody had refused the invitation to attend this function so it was a 'who's who' of European royalty.

Only one seat was empty and that was the one right beside Gisele.

Henri's chair.

With a sigh, Gisele shifted her gaze once more and caught that of her beloved grandson. He looked every inch the Prince he was in his military uniform with its red sash and gold epaulettes. His medals shone and the silver scabbard of his sword had been polished to within an inch of its life.

Their gazes held for a long moment. This was such a happy occasion but there was sadness, too. Loved ones who couldn't be here had to be acknowledged.

The music was softer now, so it was possible to hear the faint roar coming from outside the cathedral walls. The sound of thousands of voices in a collective cheer. Gisele could imagine the scene as vividly as if she were standing out there on the top of that huge sweep of wide steps.

The ornate, gold dolphin coach that was only brought out on the most momentous of occasions— pulled by the immaculately groomed white horses of the royal stables—would have just come to a halt at the bottom of the steps.

Another man, in a uniform even more impressive than Raoul's, would alight from the open coach and would be holding out his hand to help the bride climb down.

How wonderful was it that Mika had asked Henri to be the man to escort her down the aisle today?

And what a blessing he was still well enough to do

this. He seemed to have taken on a whole new lease of life, in fact, with such joy to look forward to.

He hadn't really needed Gisele to remind him of what it had been like to be young and in love. Or of how much strength that love had given them both over the decades and how it had got them through some very difficult times.

Mika had won Henri's heart so quickly.

Had won everybody's hearts.

What could have been a dreadful scandal had miraculously become the love story of the century. Raoul was now firmly ensconced as 'the People's Prince' and he had clearly found a princess worthy of ruling by his side. Not only could everybody rejoice on the occasion of a royal wedding, they still had the coronation to look forward to and—even better—the anticipation of the birth of a new prince or princess in the near future. The first member of the next generation of the de Poitier family.

So much happiness.

Gisele had a lace-edged handkerchief clutched in her hand and she had a feeling she would need to use it very soon. She could feel tears of joy gathering as the music paused and then swelled into the triumphant opening bars of Wagner's *Bridal Chorus*. She rose to her feet, as did everybody else in the cathedral.

It was beginning.

The tears started as soon as she saw her beloved husband by the side of this exquisite young bride. They continued as her heart caught at the sight of all the children following the pair. It had been Mika's idea—to go to the orphanage and choose everyone who wanted to be a flower girl or a page boy. The girls wore long white dresses and had colourful garlands of flowers on their heads and the boys looked adorable in sailor suits.

Mika looked beyond adorable. She had approached this intimidating occasion with the same kind of good-humoured determination that she was applying to every aspect of royal life she'd been learning in the last few months. The design of her dress was simple and didn't accentuate her growing bump. Mika had asked for a 'swirly' dress that would look pretty when she danced with her new husband later and the dressmakers had been delighted to oblige. With an empire line, it fell in soft folds, the beaded bodice having a sweetheart neckline.

Gisele had offered a diamond necklace to match the tiara that was holding her veil in place but Mika had been right in choosing something else.

Her own necklace of that tiny, silver dolphin charm.

The priests leading the procession up the aisle reached their positions at the front of the cathedral now and there was nothing to obstruct the lines of vision as Raoul and Mika got closer to each other.

Henri left Mika by Raoul's side and came to sit beside Gisele. Would the television cameras pick up the way their hands touched and then held? It wasn't exactly protocol on a formal occasion but Gisele needed the touch. Her heart was so full it almost hurt.

Squeezing his fingers, she watched as Raoul lifted his bride's veil back and revealed her face. And then, for a heartbeat, and then another, the bride and groom seemed to be lost in each other's eyes.

And those smiles…

Gisele had to let go of Henri's hand, then. She needed her handkerchief too much.

So much joy was simply too contagious...

* * * * *

LET'S TALK
Romance

For exclusive extracts, competitions
and special offers, find us online:

f facebook.com/millsandboon

⊙ @millsandboonuk

𝕏 @millsandboon

Or get in touch on 0844 844 1351*

For all the latest titles coming soon, visit
millsandboon.co.uk/nextmonth

Want even more
ROMANCE?

Join our bookclub today!

'Mills & Boon books, the perfect way to escape for an hour or so.'

Miss W. Dyer

'Excellent service, promptly delivered and very good subscription choices.'

Miss A. Pearson

'You get fantastic special offers and the chance to get books before they hit the shops'

Mrs V. Hall

Visit millsandbook.co.uk/Bookclub
and save on brand new books.

MILLS & BOON